PRAISE FOR *WESTSIDE*

"[In] W. M. Akers's superb debut, *Westside* . . . his research is excellent . . . his prose sharply crystalline."

—*The New York Times Book Review*

"Akers' debut novel is an addictively readable fusion of mystery, dark fantasy, alternate history, and existential horror. . . . It's like a literary shot of Prohibition-era rotgut moonshine—bracing, quite possibly hallucination-inducing, and unlike anything you've ever experienced before. . . . The illegitimate love child of Algernon Blackwood and Raymond Chandler."

—*Kirkus Reviews* (starred review)

"Full of action and colorful characters, this genre mash-up is expertly done and will be enjoyed by fans of mysteries and fantasy alike."

—*Booklist* (starred review)

"*The Alienist* meets *The City & the City* in this brilliant debut that mixes fantasy and mystery. Gilda Carr's 'tiny mysteries' pack a giant punch."

—David Morrell, *New York Times* bestselling author of *Murder as a Fine Art*

"A fascinating, delightfully twisty mystery. *Westside* crosses prohibition-era New York with the dark strangeness of *Neverwhere*. Fierce young detective Gilda Carr makes you believe that small mysteries hold the answers to everything."

—Erika Swyler, bestselling author of *The Book of Speculation* and *Light from Other Stars*

WESTSIDE

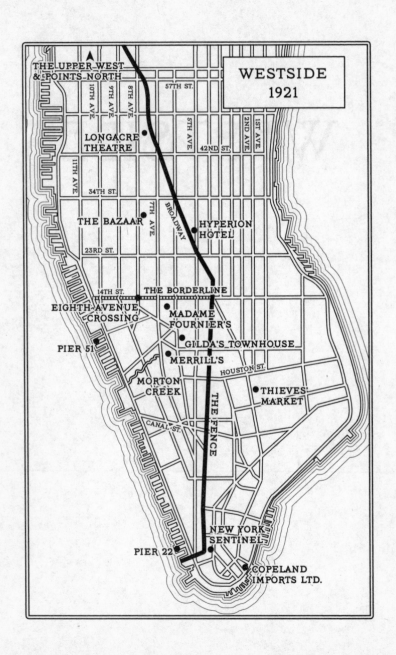

WESTSIDE
1921

THE UPPER WEST
& POINTS NORTH

57TH ST.

10TH AVE.
9TH AVE.
8TH AVE.
5TH AVE.
2ND AVE.
1ST AVE.

LONGACRE
THEATRE

42ND ST.

11TH AVE.

34TH ST.

7TH AVE.
BROADWAY

THE BAZAAR

HYPERION
HOTEL

23RD ST.

14TH ST.   THE BORDERLINE

EIGHTH AVENUE   MADAME
CROSSING   FOURNIER'S

GILDA'S TOWNHOUSE

PIER 51

MERRILL'S

MORTON
CREEK   HOUSTON ST.

THIEVES'
MARKET

THE FENCE

CANAL ST.

NEW YORK
SENTINEL

PIER 22

COPELAND
IMPORTS LTD.

WESTSIDE

A NOVEL

W. M. AKERS

HARPER Voyager
An Imprint of HarperCollins*Publishers*

HarperCollins books may be purchased for educational, business, or sales promotional use. For information, please email the Special Markets Department at SPsales@harpercollins.com.

A hardcover edition of this book was published in 2019 by Harper Voyager, an imprint of HarperCollins Publishers.

FIRST HARPER VOYAGER PAPERBACK EDITION PUBLISHED 2020.

Designed by Paula Russell Szafranski
Map by James Sinclair
Burst from The New York Times © 2019 The New York Times Company. All rights reserved. Used under license.

Library of Congress Cataloging-in-Publication Data has been applied for.

ISBN 978-0-06-285402-5

20 21 22 23 24   BRR   10 9 8 7 6 5 4 3 2 1

For Yvonne

and Dr. Baby

WESTSIDE

ONE

I stole a glove.

It dangled off a table in a decrepit leather shop in Thieves' Market on the Eastside of Manhattan in sweltering late September 1921, and it was in my bag before I even knew it had been in my hand.

It was white leather, paper thin and butter soft, with irises along the knuckles and a strange brand embossed at the wrist that showed a stamp smashing into a puddle of ink. In that vile shop, where canvas walls kept out sunlight but trapped heat, the glove was a splash of ivory in the darkness. It was surrounded by wallets, boots, belts, caps, jackets, aprons, strops, and straps—all stained, stolen, and badly made. The glove was too fine for that dusty stall, and so the shopkeeper was watching when I took it away.

"Girl!" he barked. I did not turn my head, for that is not my name.

He shoved aside a rack of loafers and strode toward me, bowlegged, sweating, a triangle of moles sprouting hairs just to the left of his mouth. He blocked my exit, and the smell of him made the sausage I'd called lunch lurch in my stomach.

"Think I didn't see it?" he said. "This is my place. I see everything."

"That's no great accomplishment," I shrugged. "It's such a small place."

He bristled. "You give it back, or it's trouble."

He wrapped his meaty fingers around a short leather club. My neck brushed against the canvas walls. There was nowhere else to go. I put on my sweetest society girl smile.

"I really don't know what you mean," I said, "but trouble is something I strive to avoid at all costs."

"So hand it here."

I dug into my long, amorphous sack of a purse, and he smiled a horrid smile. He rolled the club between his hands. "Right, right. Nice and slow, and there'll be no trouble at all."

He was right—it was no trouble for me.

My little knife flicked open quick as a stinging wasp. I jabbed it toward the shopkeeper's ample belly. His balance failed him, and he crashed into a table of leather scraps. I turned away, slashed a hole in the canvas, and leapt through it like an acrobat through a ring of fire.

The leather shop was just one of a jumble of tents erected in the middle of the street, where sagging tables offered chipped glassware, stained collars, limp hats, out-of-date calendars, and purposeless hunks of metal. Most of it had been parted from the original owners, just as I was liberating this glove now. The crowd moved steadily, because no one was buying. They browsed to forget that they had nowhere better to go. From somewhere uncertain came the stink of gutted fish. From behind me came the shopkeeper's shout.

"She's a thief! The little bitch is a thief!"

Never mind that half the patrons in the market were thieves, either by vocation or necessity. Never mind that the entire operation was a clearinghouse for items stolen up and down the Eastside. These creatures protected their own. Two other shopkeepers heeded the leather man's call, and the chase, I regret to say, began in earnest.

A greasy hand reached for my wrist. I twisted away, slamming into the rock-hard gut of a man who sold lace. He leered at me, almost licking his lips, and I slipped under his arm before he closed it around my neck, and ran. They came after me, shoving shoppers and upending pushcarts and threatening unspeakable acts of violence against my person. These men had grown fat selling stolen goods, but I take one glove—not even a pair, but a single glove—and they threaten to remove my skin, tan it, and wear me as a coat.

They were bloodthirsty and determined, those three shop-keepers, but I am small and passably nimble, and have spent my life running from bullies. I leapt over a family sleeping on the sidewalk, darted through a beer hall emptying after the lunchtime rush, and slipped through the alley toward Bleecker. When I was a child, these alleys were empty, but since the city was sliced in half, whole families have crowded into them, packed into ragged tents or hud-dling under the awnings of all-night oyster houses. The sun was blotted out by the makeshift shelters on the top floors of the tene-ments, where flimsy structures of two or three—sometimes even four—stories held apartments built of stolen timber and bedsheets that hung limp in the tepid September breeze.

I ran down the narrow strip of pavement, dodging outstretched limbs and sleeping children. The shopkeepers burst out of the beer hall and called after me. My mouth burned with the taste of metal. For that matter, my legs burned too.

I kept running.

The stink of fish faded as I stepped onto Broadway, crowded and gleaming and smelling of money and judgment, and the fence blocked my path. Even in the punishing glare of the sun, it was a dark thing—thirty feet of wrought iron topped by sharpened spikes, stretching up the middle of the avenue, dividing the healthy Eastside from the deserted west. In the middle was a little door guarded by a little man whose uniform buttons sparkled in the light. I danced through the sludgy traffic and slammed against the iron.

"Open the gate," I said, flashing my license.

A half-witted smile spread across chapped lips. "Just what busi-ness has a nice young lady like you got on the Westside?" he said.

"Personal, and urgent."

"I guess you're from out of town. I can't let you through this door without a chaperone, and even then, I would advise against it. Things over there are, well, peculiar."

"I live on the Westside, I work on the Westside, and I have a Class C permit, which allows—"

"Crossing the fence any time during normal business hours."

"So let me through!"

He draped his jaundiced fingers across my shoulder and tried to look concerned. The leather man stepped off the sidewalk and waded into traffic, howling for blood.

"You know, miss, you step through that door, the city cannot guarantee your safety."

"Remove your hand from my shoulder or I will bite the knuckles to the bone."

"Oh, miss," he said, as disappointed as if his favorite terrier had just turned rabid. "Very well. Proceed at your own risk."

The shopkeeper and his friends fought two or three ill-defined lanes of automobiles, pushcarts, and horse carts, screaming for the gateman to stop. He was too preoccupied with the mechanism of the gate to pay them any mind. The squat iron door eased open. The leather man leapt, and his fingers brushed my shoulder as I threw myself through the gate.

Damp moss broke my fall. Broadway was muffled by the sound of falling water. A silver cataract cascaded down the crumbling facade of an abandoned tenement, pouring over broken windows, splashing onto the moss-blanketed street, and rushing into the gutter. I have scaled that unsteady building, and seen the source of that waterfall, which bubbles straight from the peeling black tar roof. It is an impossible wonder. Such things are common here.

When I stopped shaking, I twirled to face the men who had chased me, who now stood before the gate, too timid to cross into the Westside. I waved the glove at them. It was a childish gesture—how could I resist?

The leather man took the gateman by the collar and screamed in his face.

"Retrieve her!"

"Sir. If you would be so kind as to let me go."

"She's a thief."

"I'm sorry to hear that. But my authority stops at the fence. Go after her. Cut her. Gut her. It doesn't matter to me. But I'll tell you what I told her: step through this gate, and you take your life in your hands."

My pursuers shifted back and forth, rubbing the sweat from their necks, each waiting for the other to take the first step.

"Sirs," said the gateman, a touch disappointed, "if you'll not be crossing, it's against regulations to leave the gate ajar."

The leather man was beaten. The gate swung closed, and the locks slammed into place. The rancid odor of September in Manhattan faded, replaced by the crisp, almost metallic Westside air. I dug my fingers into my hair and loosed the shaggy chignon that I generously call a hairstyle. Knotted curls fell across the peaked black shoulders of my jacket, which dangled around my slim black dress. I breathed deep. I was home.

I soaked my handkerchief in the clean, unlikely water, and squeezed it onto my neck with a happy shiver. I sat on the sidewalk, feet resting on the quiet half of Broadway, and inspected the stolen glove. It was precisely what I had been looking for, but something was wrong.

From deep in my bag, past notepads and soiled napkins and the remains of more than one sandwich, I pulled a second glove. Cream, with the same irises and the same rubber stamp, but made of weightless leather and held together by imperceptible stitches. Beside it, the stolen glove was hackwork. The leather was coarse, the stitching ragged, the brand a vague blob. It looked as ugly as if I'd made it myself. I flipped the gloves over. Both were for the left hand. They were not mates. They were twins, one made by an artist, the other by a clod, and the one I'd taken from Thieves' Market had not belonged to my client after all.

Another wasted day.

Life on the Westside has always been peculiar. When the first Dutch settlers came to the island, the Lenape warned them against crossing the old deer trail that would become Broadway. The island's western half was strange, they said. Dangerous. As white men are wont to do, the Dutch ignored them, and found the district fought every attempt at civilization. A 1628 letter from colony director Peter Minuit boasts of crops that grew taller and faster than could be dreamed, but complains of tools rusting and muskets refusing to fire.

"Our homes shift on their foundations," he wrote. "Our wood comes loose from its joints, and my dreams are plagued by visions of pestilence, stigmata, and the armies of hell."

The smart settlers returned to the east. The feckless, greedy, criminal, and mad stayed on, and through sheer Protestant stubbornness beat the Westside into submission. Their houses steadied, their tools stayed pristine, and their crops returned to human scale.

For two centuries and more, the Westside was hardly distinguishable from the east. Perhaps it produced more than its share of suicides, murderers, and artists. Yes, its saloons were death traps. And certainly its brothels were hell on earth. But to the genteel city across the stem, this was no more than charming eccentricity—a badge of honor for refined New York, that the city could thrive in spite of the long, strange scar that marred the west side of its face. So it went for decades. Around century's end, however, the Westside began to change.

As if a sequel to Minuit's letters all those years ago, the plants grew faster. The sidewalks cracked. Modern appliances seized up or caught fire. Guns rusted away to nothing, light bulbs burst in their sockets, and zippers became so unreliable that all but the bravest men entrusted their dignity to the button fly. Streets shifted in the night, and buildings sank beneath the earth. Water sprang up as if from nowhere, and strange new animals crawled forth from the sewers to the bafflement of scientists and the delight of the district's children. The changes happened slowly enough that New York pretended they were not happening at all—you can always trust a New

Yorker to ignore another man's plight—even when people began to disappear.

The vanishings started slowly. A man set out for a growler of beer and never came back. A young lover glanced over his shoulder for a parting look at his sweetheart and saw that she was gone. The story was always the same: someone alone in the dark, alone where she should not be, turned a dangerous corner and was never seen again. Such cases were not taken seriously by the police or the public—until the drip became a flood.

I know the figures by heart:

174 vanished in 1903—hardly more than normal.

In 1905, nearly 300.

In 1907, 419.

In 1909, 912.

At first, the vanishings were written off as an unfortunate off-shoot of a nationwide spike in crime. The mayor's office blamed bad gin, bad water, bad hygiene, and the simple savagery of the Westside gangs. The press blamed immigrants, the poor, white slavers, and suicide. The religious blamed the devil; the superstitious blamed the night itself. There were rumors of monstrous creatures that crept out of the subway tunnels, of an army of corpses that lived in the sewers, of a cadre of killers that roamed the dark. But by all civilized people, the barbaric Westsiders were blamed for destroying their own, for making their once-charming neighborhood an uninhabitable hell.

No matter the actual reason—and I wouldn't be surprised if it was all of these things, or none at all—the Westside was alone. No one listened when we called for help. No one listened until children began to die.

In 1914, over three thousand citizens vanished from the Westside, vanished from alleys and streets, from apartments and houses, from schools and churches and restaurants and parks. Nearly one-third were younger than eighteen. I was twenty-one then, practically a child myself, and I lost many friends. Seven years later, I remember their faces. I have forgotten their names.

All those who could afford it fled across the stem. The Eastside sagged beneath an added million. The Westside, vacant and dark, became more dangerous, and rumors began that its sickness was spreading. Vanishings were reported on the Eastside: first a few dozen, then more than a hundred, and finally, overnight, the city acted.

The fence went up without debate, without warning, without ceremony. The Westside went to sleep and awoke behind quarantine. Thirteen miles of fence sprung up down the middle of Broadway, a tourniquet on a limb that had already lost too much blood. At first it was wood, but wood was soon replaced by iron, steel, and barbed wire. As far as New York was concerned, the Westside no longer existed—and neither did the fifty or sixty thousand too brave or mad or desperate to flee, who stayed behind the fence, intent on living their lives.

After the fence went up, the vanishings slowed, and Europe gave us a war that could kill tens of thousands, not in a decade, but in an hour. The world forgot the Westside, but the Westside hasn't gone anywhere. It is fat on the bottom and skinny on top, bending with Broadway all the way to the island's top, where it is only a few blocks wide. It breeds New York's finest painters, killers, poets, and thieves, and I am proud to be among their number. In what other city do the trees outclass the skyscrapers? Where else do rivers flow where streets used to be? And who would not love a city without guns or automobiles or coal-belching machinery? It is a strange place, insistently wild, and I love it. It reminds me of my father. It reminds me of me.

And if you ask us, if you ask me, what happened, what claimed all those innocent lives? I will tell you that when tragedy strikes, only fools or cowards expect a simple explanation. I know better than to ask questions that don't have answers, because those kinds of questions drive men mad.

And the Westside has enough madness as it is.

A few days earlier, I stared out the window of a shabby Turtle Bay apartment house, a cramped two bedroom whose saving grace was a window that offered a fragment of the East River. I watched the traffic on a river burdened with far too much shipping. A navy ship bore down on a tug that did not look nimble enough to get out of the way. Just before impact, the rattle of bone china on saucers drew me back into the room. Edith Copeland emerged from the kitchen, in a severe white dress grown sallow from too many washings, gripping an overflowing tray of tea and cakes. She slammed it down on the coffee table. Tea sloshed from the cups, and she glanced at me with a practiced look of silent apology.

"Quite an assortment," I said, picking my way through madeleines and lemon squares to find my teacup.

"We rarely receive visitors."

"This is not a social call. Don't pretend we are friends."

"But everyone likes cakes . . ."

"Why are you so nervous, Mrs. Copeland?"

"I've never hired a private investigator before."

"Everyone has to start sometime."

"And your advertisement, it said G. Carr. If I'd known you were a girl . . ."

"I'm twenty-seven, with more than a decade's experience. Hardly a girl. And if you had known I was a woman, you wouldn't have hired me, which is why I prefer to withhold that fact as long as is convenient. I'm sure you understand."

"I'm just not certain that someone so young will be right for this . . . this task."

She leaned forward, elbows on her knees, and straightened a pile of ladies' magazines. She was wistful and silent and slightly infuriating. I began, I am afraid to say, to grow impatient.

"It touches on the Westside?" I pushed.

"I can't imagine that—"

"I expect it will. The city gives us few mysteries that do not. The matter concerns your husband?"

"How did you know?" she asked, looking around, as if someone else would hear.

"The way you're shaking, it wasn't hard to guess. Do you suspect him of murder?"

"Heavens, I—"

"Arson? Burglary? Embezzlement? Treason? Adultery? Rape?"

"My husband is a good man!"

"How nice for him. Is it a dangerous assignment?"

"No."

"Marvelous. I do not take dangerous assignments. I solve tiny mysteries."

"Tiny mysteries?"

"The smaller the better." I bit into a lemon square. "These cakes, Mrs. Copeland, are excellent."

"But what do you mean, tiny mysteries?"

"I answer little questions. Those impossible puzzles that burrow into our brains like splinters and keep us awake at night. I solve the mysteries that spoil marriages, ruin friendships, and curdle joy. A murder is a dull thing. It simply ends a life. Tiny mysteries destroy us."

"I see."

"You don't," I said, waving her concern away. "That's fine." I reached into my bag, and removed a packet of sweets. "Caramel?"

"That's all right."

"But *everyone* likes caramels." If she was stung by this gentle mockery, she did not let on.

Her fingers strained to extract a caramel from the sticky mass. She placed it in her mouth, wary. A flicker of half-suppressed pleasure lit up her face as the caramel melted across her tongue.

"Do you know how it smells on the Westside?" I said, changing the subject quick enough to dizzy her.

"I certainly do not."

"It smells of vegetation, thick and matted. Of rotting libraries and damp wood, dead animals and human waste, wildflowers, fresh rain, and the river. It smells of decay, but also of fantastic life, and it is intoxicating. Last spring, however, the six people with whom I share Washington Square began to complain of a new odor. A burnt smell, not unlike a rubber fire, blowing up from the south. No matter where we looked, its source could not be found."

"It must have been quite a stench."

"The mystery ate at the corners of our minds. I went block to block, searching every alley and breaking into every abandoned house."

"I thought you did not take dangerous assignments."

"I am well known on the Westside, particularly below the Borderline. I have no enemies."

"But with everything they say about the Westside . . ."

"It does not frighten me. It is my home."

"Did you trace the odor?"

"I searched for two weeks—pro bono, mind—until my feet ached and my hands were raw from ripping away rotten wood. Finally, in the basement of a defunct hardware store on West Broadway, I found the answer."

"Was it a dead body?" she said, eyes wide, and popped another caramel into her mouth.

"Tinier."

"A broken sewer main?"

"The sewers of the Westside haven't functioned for years."

"Then what was it?"

"You're eating it." She grimaced. "He's the finest confectioner in the city. Supplies all the nicest hotels, from the Plaza to the Hyperion. A tiny old Italian man who has been making sweets on the Westside since before the fence, since before I was born."

"And the stench?"

"The unfortunate result of a new recipe, since discarded, for almond brittle." I dropped another caramel onto my tongue. It melted like ice. It was a good story, even if nearly none of it was true.

"May I have another?"

"Take as many as you want, and tell me what troubles you."

"It's a very small thing."

"Splendid."

"Only, it isn't, really."

"That's my point—they never really are."

She nodded absently and rose, light as helium, and went to her bedroom. I took out my notebook and the squat little fountain pen I use for interviews. She returned with a single ivory glove, which she placed beside the rapidly dwindling bag of sweets. One left hand.

"Beautiful, isn't it?" she said. "Feather light. Perfect for summer. Of course, there used to be two. I was shopping at Aylesmere's, the department store, last weekend. I'd just left, and I wanted to get my compact from my purse."

"And then?"

"I set my packages on the ground, tugged the glove from my right hand, and set it beside me."

"On what?"

"I don't know, a wall or—no, it was a postbox."

"You're certain?"

"Does it matter?"

"I have no idea."

"Well," she said, not quite hiding her irritation. "It was. I checked my makeup and put the compact back. When I reached for the glove, it was gone. It's outrageous, isn't it? To steal a single glove. There are people in this city who are . . . who are animals."

"And what does it have to do with your husband?"

"The gloves were a gift. For my birthday, in July. He gives me so few presents, and these were so beautiful. If he learned I'd lost it, I don't know . . . I don't know what he'd think."

"Is your husband a jealous man?"

"When given cause."

"And would he consider this cause? Would he assume you had left the glove in some other man's bed?"

"That is a disgusting question. Galen is . . . Galen is a wonderful man."

She then told me about a wonderful man who spent most of his daughter's life at sea. Who burst into the house at odd hours, rum on his breath and brine in his clothes and roaring laughter in his chest, and gave his wife and daughter unwanted, crushing hugs. Who was three times mistakenly reported dead and never considered the fright this caused his family. Who humiliated his employees, ignored his daughter, and treated the wife he once doted on with the affection one might give a dishrag. Who built a modest shipping fortune but refused to relinquish control until the business withered to nothing. Whose family begged him to spend more time at home, but who preferred to go on doing wonderful things in a wonderful way and not giving a thought to how it might hurt those who loved him.

Fathers. Aren't they marvelous?

For the last year, their daughter, Juliette, had run the shipping firm. Business was good. Galen had no friends, no hobbies. When he wasn't taking long walks, he was in his office, staring at the river, chewing plug after plug of tobacco, spitting until the floor around the spittoon was stained black. At night he read, drinking rum until drowsiness overtook him, and he fell asleep in the chair.

Wonderful.

It was an ordinary picture of a man in decline. Mrs. Copeland had resigned herself to watching him slip away, a little piece every day, and though that thought terrified her, it was the sort of numb terror that is dangerously easy to ignore. But then he gave her the gloves, and that day, his eyes shone for the first time in years.

"I'd hoped it was a new beginning," she said. "I worry I've spoiled it."

"Do you know where he bought them?"

"No. And there's no way to ask without encouraging suspicion."

"Never mind that. I'll find your glove, and if that proves impossible, I'll find a replacement."

At that, she smiled, and it was like a beam of light sweeping across a field on a gray day. I reached for another lemon square, but we had eaten the plate bare. Even the bag of caramels was empty. This explained the pain in my stomach. I hauled myself up, trying not to show the effort, and was reaching for the doorknob when the door swung open and nearly caught me in the face. On the other side was a slender woman, just past thirty, with gently curled hair, a crooked smile, and eyes the color of silt.

"What are you doing in my house?" she said.

"I'm Gilda Carr. I'm here on business."

"What sort?"

"Personal, and urgent. You must be Juliette Copeland."

She stared me up and down like I was a gown she was looking for a reason not to buy. Once she was fully unsatisfied with my appearance, she took a step closer, and I caught a whiff of the waterfront—one of those stenches that never scrubs out.

"Whatever nonsense my mother has engaged you in," she said, "I will be inspecting your invoices with a microscope. You will not swindle that woman."

"I wouldn't dream of it."

"You were leaving?"

"Yes."

"Then go." She stood aside. The breeze from the slamming door was strong enough to ruffle my hair. I chuckled and spun around in the hallway, happy to have a case, to have money coming, and to be working for Edith Copeland, who had no idea that I had signed on for this silly business because I knew how cold a house can be when it's haunted by a man who has chosen to let himself die.

There were eight rats, and the fat one was fastest. He pulled ahead at the first turn and never gave back the lead. A handful of racing enthusiasts loomed over the gaudily painted wooden track, old men and young boys who groaned as the fat rat skittered across the finish line. Only one clapped—a twenty-four-year-old wearing a frayed tuxedo jacket and a cavalry saber, whose giddiness was childlike, but whose eyes were ancient and gray.

"Mose, you fat, beautiful bastard," he said, loud enough to echo from the rooftops of the empty tenements. "Mose, you beauty. Mose, you demon. Mose, my beloved—you've done it again!"

He cradled the victorious rat against his cheek, swept the losers' bets into his change purse, and twisted his pockmarked cheeks into a devilish grin. He had oak-brown skin and coarse black hair, cropped tight at the sides but wild on top, like the plume of a distant volcano. His harsh Westside accent was softened by notes of Tennessee, inherited from a family that vanished long before we met. When he felt like smiling—which was often—he was undoubtedly the Lower West's handsomest overgrown child.

"Eight minutes till the fifth race," he cried. "Mose the champion takes on all comers. Witness the greatest racing sensation of the age: the Westside comet, the runaway rat. Get your bets down now, get your bets down now."

No one took him up on the offer. The crowd melted away, and Cherub Stevens was left alone beneath the hanging vines of Thompson Street. He gave his rat a tender kiss and set him back on the track, and I remembered why I had once loved this man. Trouble melted at the sight of him, and for a moment, I was just a woman greeting an ex-lover on a late summer day.

"We are too good for this world, Mose," he said. He saw me watching from the sidewalk and blushed terribly as he tried to remember how to look hard. "Gilda Carr. Come to place a bet?"

I stepped into the street and walked the length of the track, bending to inspect the huddled vermin. Away from the pack was a stringy creature, whose scabby skin showed through patchy fur.

"And who is this thoroughbred?" I said.

"Called Gimlet," said Cherub. "Strictly filler. Hasn't a chance."

On a chalkboard leaning against a rusted streetlight, one of Cherub's pubescent lieutenants scribbled the latest odds. Gimlet was running at an irresistible twenty-five to one. I placed a nickel on the lip of the racetrack.

"I hate to take a destitute detective's money," said Cherub.

"I don't believe that for a moment," I said, and turned north. Cherub followed, saber clacking on the cobblestones. He waved to the boys in the windows of Cleo's Pet Shop, which his gang had adopted, along with every animal in there, the day the fence went up. They called themselves the One-Eyed Cats. Their territory stretched all the way from Washington Square East to Washington Square West, and though they were kind to their pets, they were devils in a brawl—or so Cherub always told me.

He had been a One-Eyed Cat since the city was whole. The

gang's elders taught him to read, to lie, to steal, to fight. They had also, and for this I thanked them, taught him that seducing women is far more amusing if you treat them as people, and not territory to conquer. The older boys dispersed when the fence went up, but Cherub hung on to became chief by default. He was ten years older than the oldest boys in his gang, for whom he was father, gang leader, and babysitter all at once. He said they kept him young.

"Headed home?" he said. "The sun is low."

"Thought I'd stop by Lamb's."

"I'll escort you."

"I'm sure you will."

Once I had told this man truths that surprised myself. But since the day I broke his heart by Morton Creek, we could only trade banter—sweet, flirtatious, and hollow.

We turned onto the southern edge of Washington Square. Oaks, sycamores, and elms, their trunks as broad as a subway car, towered over the blackened wreckage of the ruined arch. They rose two, three hundred feet into the sky, their leaves forming a canopy thick enough to block out the sun. On the park's western edge, surrounded by the rubble of the genteel mansions of my mother's generation, my town house stood alone. A breeze whispered through the hanging vines. Three deep breaths, and an afternoon wasted on the Eastside washed away.

A hatchet sailed past my head. It thumped into the nearest tree and, too dull to bite into the wood, clattered to the ground. A slender ten-year-old with a mangled hand leapt out from behind a barricade and scurried to retrieve the little ax. Cherub grabbed him by the collar and threw him to the ground.

"Roach," he snarled.

"Sir," said the boy, hiding his bad hand behind his back, as if to spare his chief the sight of it.

"What did I tell you about throwing axes at ladies' heads?"

"'Don't throw axes at ladies' heads,' sir."

"And what the hell do I find you doing, when you're meant to be guarding the park?"

I helped Roach up by his bad hand and brushed the dirt off his shoulders.

"Apologies, Miss Carr," he said.

"It's all right," I said. "Hardly the worst reception I've gotten today."

"Can't let him off that easy," said Cherub. "Boys're meant to be an army. Instead they just act like, like . . ."

"Like a bunch of boys."

It was a clever answer. It also didn't please Cherub at all. He clapped, and Roach ran back to the barricade, ax pressed to his chest like a treasured toy.

"It's bad enough for the children to play soldier," I said. "I don't see why you have to encourage them."

"It's not play, Gilda. We've got enemies on all sides. Any gang in the Lower West would bleed for a chance to run the square, and then there's the bastards north of the Borderline, and . . . and would you stop giggling at me!"

"Never. How's trade?"

"Sour. But no matter how sour it gets, Rotgut must be paid."

"Any news?"

"Always," he said and launched into a torrent of half-remembered anecdotes, filthy jokes, bloody legend, and bawdy song. Cherub was obsessed with the minutiae of gangland feuding—rumors that the Bleecker Street Stranglers had overtaken Sheridan Square, that the Sparrows and the Cut-Eyes were at peace, that Horace the Bloodletter had been blackjacked to death and buried beneath the footlights of the Cherry Lane Theater. Normally it made me chuckle, but the sun was sinking, and I didn't have the time. From deep in my bag, I pulled out a package of wax butcher paper.

"Oh," he said, "you marvelous woman."

Cherub unwrapped the sandwich, which had been squashed flat in the afternoon's excitement, and stuffed as much as he could into his mouth. He chewed, spraying flecks of meat across the sidewalk, and closed his eyes in thought.

Two years prior, when I was just cobbling together my practice,

Cherub told me a story from his childhood, when his uncle, a notorious safecracker enjoying a brief interlude between incarcerations, took him to the Eastside for roast beef. The meat was rose pink and sliced thin enough to melt on his tongue. He couldn't remember where they'd had it, but he'd spent most of his life dreaming of that sandwich, and when I needed a case so badly that I couldn't sleep and couldn't eat, he hired me to find it for him. It was supposed to be a simple task, a peace offering to show he did not resent me for refusing his offer of marriage, but no sandwich matched that of his memory, and so the matter could never rest. When I finally cracked it, Cherub would owe me a fortune, but today he shook his head.

"Not the one you were looking for?" I said.

"Do you really believe this is the finest roast beef the Eastside has to offer?"

"It may have been, three or four hours ago."

"Try again, Gilda Carr."

I swung open the door to Judson Memorial Church, the Italianate behemoth that squatted at the foot of the square. Cherub bowed low, scraping his saber on the sidewalk. I chuckled, not because he was being particularly funny, but because he never quit trying to make me laugh.

And that meant more to me than I thought it would.

"Let me know how Gimlet fares," I said.

"He'll lose. They always lose."

"There's a reason he's my favorite."

The door slammed behind me, and I was alone in the church, where a few lonely candles cast faint light on an ungainly mural honoring the martyrs of the Westside. When the painting was finished, the church gave a little party, and an old woman climbed the pulpit to make an unasked-for speech. She raved about the vanished, who she believed had been taken—each and every one of them—by evil angels who swept through the dark like the devil's own press gang. I drained my drink and left the party, unwilling to listen to anyone who sounded so like my father.

When my eyes adjusted to the gloom, I felt my way along the

wall until I found a small wooden door that opened onto a long, steep, poorly lit stairwell.

There are no evil angels in the darkness, I reminded myself. Only madmen think otherwise. I drew in a deep breath, and climbed.

At the top of the stairs, I found a ladder. As I climbed it, cold sweat bathed my palms. In the faint light of a single lantern, the shadows danced. I was nearly at the top when a silhouette moved across the wall. I whipped my head toward it. The shadow was mine.

The trapdoor at the top of the ladder jerked open. My stomach lurched. My hands slipped. I was about to scream when two hands reached down, grabbed me by the wrists, and dragged me into the heat of the late afternoon.

TWO

"Stow those gloves," said Bex Red, "or I will toss them over the side."

To underline the threat, she tipped the last of our three dozen clams down her throat and hurled the shell over her shoulder. It tumbled a hundred feet through the air and shattered on West Fourth Street. We sat on milk crates in the church campanile, which a quietly surly defrocked priest had converted into a make-shift oyster house shaded by the canopy of Washington Square. On the Eastside, it would be called a speakeasy, but there was little law on this side of the fence, and certainly no Prohibition agents, so we drank as freely as we pleased. Behind the rough-cut wooden bar, Father Lamb applied a greasy rag to an equally greasy cup. In the far corner, a middle-aged drunk snored softly, hands resting on his belly as if in prayer. A breeze blew through the arches of the tower, and the sinking sun tinted the sky gold.

"Goddamn it, Bex," said Father Lamb. "Don't toss those clam-shells. They could hurt someone."

"It's nothing but One-Eyed Cats down there. If they're tough as they say, a clamshell won't hurt."

"Those are kids." He spat, and the matter was closed.

"Drink?" said Bex.

I nodded, and she poured from our bottle, which was labeled "rye" but could have just as easily passed for prussic acid. It was the drink that kept the Lower West humming, the toxic brew of Andrea Barbarossa, sometimes known as Rotgut, moonshine queen of New York City. A desperate drunk once offered me a fistful of cash to find Rotgut's hidden headquarters, that he might tap one of her stills, but I am not a suicidal woman, and I refused.

Since the fence was raised in 1914, two monarchs ruled the Westside. The fat section beneath Fourteenth Street was held by Barbarossa, whose laughter flowed like bootleg gin. North of the Borderline, in the skinny stretch between Broadway and the water, the rest of the Westside—miles and miles of it—was controlled by Glen-Richard Van Alen, despot, pyromaniac, recluse. While Barbarossa won loyalty with cheap liquor and punished betrayal with a cut throat, Van Alen styled himself a man of peace and offered his territory as a haven to those respectable people barred from the Eastside and too genteel to live downtown. Above Fourteenth Street was a bourgeois utopia, lit by Van Alen's candles. Fearful people believed it was safer there.

I preferred the cheap liquor.

I waved my hand, and Lamb brought more clams—briny, sweet, and cold as ice. I ate slowly, but Bex raced. She is a woman of many qualities. She is the finest painter on the Westside of course, with an eye that puts the old masters to shame. She has a mane as thick as brambles and arms so hairy they are almost apelike. Of the fifty or sixty thousand who call the Westside home, she is one of the few I am never sorry to see.

"So you got nowhere at Thieves' Market," she said, rubbing the stolen glove between her fingers. "What next?"

"Second Avenue in Yorktown, a few blocks of Chrystie Street on either side of Delancey. After that, Long Island City. If I can find the shop where Copeland bought it, I'll replace the right hand. It shouldn't take more than a few days' work."

"Gilda, I swear, you are too good for these pathetic little mysteries."

"*Tiny* mysteries."

"Fine. Tiny mysteries. Good lord. For two years I've put up with your tiny mysteries. Who left the cap off the ink bottle? The case of the missing corkscrew. The puzzle of the unaccountable stain. What I would give for a nice, honest murder."

"Murders are not worth the trouble."

"Why not just follow the captain?"

"Do you think it's likely he'll pay his leather dealer a visit in the next few days?"

"No. But it's not those gloves you care about. A bitter old man, forsaking his family and drinking himself to death? Where have I heard this story before?"

"Bex, no."

"Don't you want to know what's eating him alive? Follow him. Find out. It could be fun."

"That mystery is bigger than I can handle."

"You underestimate yourself, darling. You're quicker than you think."

She raised the bottle to her lips, and was about to drink when, just to see how quick I was, I snatched it from her hand. I took a long pull and slapped it on the table. The sound drew the attention of the sleeping drunk, who ran his tongue over his teeth and eyed the half inch of liquor remaining in the bottle.

"How 'bout a bite?" he said, massaging the tarnished gold shield mounted on his hip.

"Go back to your nightmares, Thorne," said Bex.

"Please, Gilda? For an old friend of your father's."

"Don't you dare speak his name," I said. Thorne didn't answer. He just looked at me, thirsty to the point of dying. I poured him a drink and pressed it into his hand. "Swill in good health."

He retreated to his spot in the corner to nurse his ersatz rye.

"That man is a disgrace to the NYPD," said Bex. "And I didn't think the department could get any more disgraced."

The bottle made a final circuit. We were just feeling the warmth when a rock crashed through the branches and smashed the bottle out of my hand. Ten stories below, I saw the tiny shape of a massive woman, Hellida Krag, rearing back to hurl another stone. I waved for her to stop. She shook her fist and yelled. The words were lost in the wind, but I knew what they meant.

"The sun is setting," said Bex Red. "Gilda has to go home."

"**You should know** better than to stay out so close to sundown," said Hellida. "Your father always warned against the Westside night."

"My father was not to be trusted."

"Hmph. And I don't like you wasting your time with those artistic types. Swilling cheap whiskey in the tower of a church. You disgrace your family."

"What family?"

"You disgrace *me*." She poured a cup of sludgy Swedish coffee, cradling her silver coffeepot like it was a newborn child. "Drink up."

"It's boiling hot."

"Yes."

The coffee scalded my tongue. I tried not to wince. Hellida grunted, pleased to see me in a little pain. Hellida Krag was hired by my mother years ago, and outliving both my parents has given her a blistering arrogance. I can't fire her. Originally my nanny, she's now my tenant, living rent-free in a basement apartment—an imposition I accept because it's easier to keep her close than kick her out. Once a teenage discus champion, she's only a few years past fifty. Whenever she's irritated with me, she'll twirl a dinner plate in her left hand and I have no doubt she could place it right between my eyes. The Westside night may not frighten me, but Hellida clings to her superstitions like a drowning man to a shard of driftwood. For her sake—and for her sake alone, I assure you—I had not stepped outside after dark for two years.

"Did you accomplish anything with your day, or have you been drinking since breakfast?"

"I worked. All day."

"Did you learn anything interesting?"

I lay the two gloves on the table. She groaned.

"Yes?" I said.

"Two left hands. That's a grave omen."

"You see omens everywhere."

"Because omens *are* everywhere."

"If I can't find out where he bought the glove," I said, bypassing her metaphysical statement, "I might have to follow him."

"Why?"

"His wife says he's been acting strange."

"This woman hired you to find a glove, not stalk her husband. Don't make this bigger than it is."

"Of course not, but if the case demands it . . ."

She rinsed my cup, dried it, and put it away. Her basement rooms were as tightly organized as an ocean liner stateroom, and every surface held a glowing candle. Through the narrow windows in the top of the wall, thin clouds glowed pink.

"I mean it, *flicka*. No risk. No danger. If anything happens to you, so help me, I will box your ears until they bleed."

And with that I pushed myself from the table. "I think I've had enough coffee."

"Would you like to play checkers?"

"Not tonight. I'm going over the box scores. Up to the middle of June 1917. The Giants are in a dead heat with—"

Hellida put up her hands, begging me to stop.

"Please. Any torture but baseball."

I opened the door that led upstairs. She followed me up the narrow stairs. We stepped into my kitchen and were hit by the stench of mildew, rotting garbage, and filth too ancient to contemplate.

"I don't know how it could smell this bad," said Hellida, "when you never cook anything but toast."

"You underestimate me. Just this morning, I fixed a particularly delicious mayonnaise and mustard sandwich."

Past the kitchen was the dining room, still stacked with my father's clothes and books, and the parlor, where I stored the sports sections of five daily papers, stretching back ten years. I passed my evenings going over old seasons, one game at a time, squinting at the tiny print of the box scores until I felt the hard wood of the Polo Grounds' seat on my back and smelled the roasting peanuts in the air. It was a lonely way to pass long, dark nights, but every single girl needs a hobby. If I went slow enough, a single game might last me an hour. I would have to learn to be more stingy—I stopped collecting the papers near the end of 1919, and I had not been to the ballpark since. Why bother, when I had history to keep me warm?

Past the parlor were the stairs, the broad wooden steps where I spent most of my childhood, watching the doorway for my father to come home. Even as I let the rest of the house decay, I kept the stairs dusted and the bannister gleaming. They were stairs to build a life around. Hellida followed me up, hovering like a hummingbird.

We stopped on the second-floor landing, where the hardwood was caked with dust. Across the hall was a door as impenetrable as any bank vault's.

"Have you consulted your father's files about the glove?" she said.

"No."

"We could just cross the hall, open the door, and take a look. Your father had files on everything."

"His mysteries were bigger than mine."

"Even so . . ."

"No."

For a moment, she looked tired—like a woman who has been doing the same job for far too long. She turned downstairs and, finally, left me alone. From my bag, I took Mrs. Copeland's glove. It fit passably. I now saw that I had been looking at the gloves upside down. The brand was not a rubber stamp splashing in ink. It was a clenched fist, dripping blood.

I rested a shaking hand on the office door, but did not step inside. I had spent the week resisting the lure of Galen Copeland's slow decline. That mystery was far less dangerous than the memory of my father.

The office had been the sanctuary of Virgil Carr, once a celebrated NYPD skull-cracker, later a private detective, later only my father, and finally nothing at all. He began life as a Sixth Avenue brawler, chief of a makeshift crew whose name never rose to the pantheon of New York gangs—the Dead Rabbits, the Whyos, the Tub of Blood Bunch, the Plug Uglies, the Roach Guard, the Daybreak Boys, the Baxter Street Dudes—but who ruled their patch of 1870s New York with vengeful sadism. Virgil ran them, and they called him Clubber Carr, in honor of the night he tossed two rival boys through a church window and clubbed them until their blood blotted out the crimson offering of the stained-glass Christ.

He would have been dead by twenty, victim of poisoned liquor or an enemy knife, were it not for dumb chance. As Virgil scaled the scaffolding of a new tenement just south of Abingdon Square, a pigeon landed on his fingers, right on the thick black ring that had broken so many young men's skulls. Afraid it might shit in his eye—for the pigeons of 1876 were no more respectful than those of today—he jerked his hand away and fell fifteen feet to the pavement. He dragged himself to the clubhouse, and directed the treasurer to empty the crate of petty cash, and send for a doctor. The sawbones, a wharf-side drunk who once served as a ship's surgeon, set his leg poorly, and it was two months before Virgil could walk again. While he waited for his bones to knit, his boys stole him books to read, raiding libraries and newsstands for as many dime novels as they could carry. It took less than a week for Virgil to tire of Buffalo Bill.

"This is garbage," muttered Virgil. "Get me something substantial, you illiterate gutter rats."

When his second-in-command protested that the dime novels were the best they could find, Virgil cracked him across the face with the paperback, sending him sprawling across the dirt clubhouse floor. The pudgy toady with the mouthful of dirt was Eddie Thorne, who would one day cadge drinks in Father Lamb's campanile. He apologized to my father, as he always did, and the matter was settled.

That night, Thorne sat across the street from the home of a society surgeon, safely wrapped in the shadows. When the doctor climbed into his cab, opera-bound, Thorne shattered the basement windows and shimmied inside. The broken glass sliced his flanks, but Thorne did not mind the pain, knowing it was nothing compared to what Virgil would do if he came home empty-handed. Thorne left the house with the doctor's entire medical library in tow.

On top of the pile was a dense tome, whose tiny font proclaimed it to be *A New & Detailed Account Of Recent Variations In The Treatment & Pathology Of The Liver*. Virgil struggled to get past the first paragraph. He would not let Thorne see him beaten, not by a book for which he had bled, and so he pushed through. By the end, he knew nothing about the liver, but he had acquired a fuzzy sense that he could be more than a thug and a warped understanding of the scientific method that would guide him to his death.

It took more brains than Virgil had to become a surgeon. It was far easier to become a cop. When his leg was healed, he took his stolen library under his arm and bid his gang goodbye. Puberty had been kind to Virgil, springing him past six feet and giving him muscles enough to batter any hoodlum the Lower West had to offer. That was enough of a résumé for the still-young New York Police Department, which put the sixteen-year-old to work solving the mysteries of the Westside streets. Once again, he could play tyrant, armed now with badge, pistol, and baton instead of his club.

And of course, as he had done all his life, Thorne followed.

Their natural brutality made ordinary police work simple. Even the rumor that they were walking a new beat was enough to make burglary, purse-snatching, pickpocketing, and bar-brawling drop to nothing. Solving petty crime was fun enough, but it was murder they lived for. Give Virgil a killing, a bombing, an assassination, or even a particularly daring heist, and the would-be scientist sprang to life. No cop ever went through so many notepads. While investigating the killing of an alderman found stabbed through the heart in the middle of a stretch of virgin snow, Virgil collected so many sheaves of interviews that he had to requisition a second office to store the overflow. After compiling enough notes to fill one of Carnegie's libraries, he announced that the alderman had been murdered by his brother, a champion archer who fired the knife from a bow, a hundred yards away. As was customary in the golden years of the NYPD, Virgil settled the matter himself, breaking the brother's neck, weighing him down with chains, and leaving the river to take the body away.

Such decisiveness made him a legend on the police force, but it was his earthy wit and scientific pretensions that made Detective Carr a star. Long before the onset of fingerprinting or crime scene photography, Virgil Carr styled himself a scientific detective, and he backed up any arrest with enough pseudointellectual hogwash to fill the front page of the *New York Sentinel*.

"As the gentlemen of the press will happily note," he might say, standing astride a bloodied corpse, "the victim was dispatched with a vigorous uplifting motion of a bluntly sharpened something or other. A preliminary phrenological diagnosis confirms that the culprit is possessed of a distinctly ovoid, even egg-shaped, skull."

And the next morning, to the delight of the boys in the pressroom, a thug would be presented whose hands were bloody and whose skull was undeniably egg-shaped. Never mind that the blood was his own, that his skull had been battered into shape by eight hours under the truncheon. Quick results and a good quote beat accuracy any day.

Avenge enough murdered aldermen, and a policeman's star will rise. He was taken off the beat and put into plainclothes, where he became the pride of the department. The ferocious rage that had made him such an adept street fighter stepped into the background, to emerge only occasionally—when faced with a reluctant interrogation suspect, or in the middle of Thanksgiving dinner. For a decade or two, he was the most renowned detective in New York. In one banner year he caught the mayor's killer, the thief who stole the doors off the Metropolitan Museum, and the labor agitators who blew up the east wing of the Fifth Avenue Hotel. Somewhere in there he married and produced a daughter.

A year or two after the turn of the century, Virgil began to slip.

It was agony to watch, and now the Copeland women were going through the exact same thing.

I lay in bed, staring at the ceiling and thinking about mustard—thick and brown and spicy enough to scour the day's foul taste from my tongue. I slipped downstairs, navigating by touch, and stepped around the piles of junk that decorated my kitchen floor. There was a bit of bread left. I spread it thick with mayonnaise and mustard, and shoved as much as I could into my mouth. It tasted like a corpse. I spat the mouthful across the floor and slapped on the lights. The sauces, opened fresh that morning, had gone rancid—green and black and spotted with mold. I scraped my tongue against my mouth, spitting uncontrollably until the taste began to ebb.

I threw out both jars of sauce. If Hellida found them, she would count their sudden death as yet another omen. She would probably be right.

As I walked up the stairs, my foot snagged on a second-floor nail that had worked its way up out of the wood. I limped up to my room and came back with my heaviest boot. Five minutes of banging would not force the nail back down. I tossed the boot aside and took my bloody foot to bed.

Galen Copeland cut through a crowded sidewalk like an icebreaker through a frozen sea, and I followed in his wake. His suit was snow white, his beard was steel wool, and he pushed his way through the Eastside chin-first.

For three days now, I'd been following him. It was not hard, it was not thrilling, and—as I'm sure Hellida would have been surprised to learn—it was not dangerous in the least. Every afternoon at 2:40, he marched from his waterfront offices to the Battery and took the elevator to the top of the old merchant's building, where a leather-choked bar served ale to old sailors with nothing to do but watch river traffic and sigh. Ladies were not allowed in the club, but I argued that point with the doorman long enough to watch Copeland settle into his perch. He sank deep into a leather chair, with a glassy look on his face like he never wanted to rise again.

So he was depressed, and his wife had no idea why. It wasn't my problem. And yet I kept my vigil, because half a week dragging myself up and down the leather shops of the Eastside had yielded no information about the glove or the brand of the bloody fist. I watched him walk to his club, and I watched him leave a few hours later, flush with drink but still unable to smile.

His routine was tepid and so predictable that on the fourth day I didn't bother tailing him from his office, but instead waited for him on the stem, where the sluggish crowd spilled off the sidewalks, and even Galen Copeland was forced to walk slow. I leaned on a hot granite wall, sweat sluicing down my back, staring over the fence at the broken spire of Trinity Church. I expected Copeland to turn south, toward the Battery. Instead, he went north, and life became interesting again.

He crossed into the Westside at the Chambers Street gate.

Quite interesting, indeed.

By the time I passed through, he was three blocks ahead of me, nearly at the river. I slunk down a block of brownstones that had sunk halfway below the street. What had been third-floor windows now opened directly onto the sidewalk. I passed bedrooms and libraries and servants' quarters: some overflowing with vegetation, others as immaculate as an embalmed corpse. In what was once a little girl's bedroom, a few tramps slept on decaying dresses. The moss muffled my footsteps, and I stayed in the shadows.

At the river, Copeland turned north. The Westside docks were empty, the wharves abandoned, the piers rotted through. The sun was hot enough to strip paint, and the river made no noise. A few blocks north was a half-sunken trawler that had gone unclaimed since a winter storm shredded it on the pilings of Pier 22. Through the gash in its hull, I saw a motor yacht tied up on the pier's far side. I moved closer.

The sun shone blindingly off the yacht's white deck. Everything at the docks that could rust had rusted long ago, but from fifty yards, I could tell this ship was spotless. Its engine roared, and the little ship pulled out into the river with Copeland behind the wheel. From the shore, it looked as though he might be having fun.

The ship sailed north, alone on the river, and disappeared around a bend after it passed the Borderline. I had nothing to do but wait. I settled onto the pier, gathering my black skirt around me, and basked like a lizard on a rock. The situation demanded vigilance.

Within seconds, I was fast asleep.

I was awoken by a boot prodding my chin. I craned my neck, yawning more deeply than a genteel lady should. Above me, blocking the sun, was the stern face of Galen Copeland.

"Oh," he grunted. "I thought you were dead."

"Not today."

"This is a private dock," he said, turning back to his yacht, which bobbed ever so slightly higher on the water than it had before. "No derelicts."

The sky had given up any pretense of blueness, opting instead for a bacon grease haze. The dying breeze carried the suffocating stink of garbage. Beneath my dress, an unspeakable amount of sweat collected between my thighs. A detective's life is ever so glamorous.

"You're an Eastsider," I said.

"And how can you tell that?"

"Your ship is clean. So are you. What brings you to our blighted district?"

He finished coiling the rope and tossed it onto the deck. Without turning around, he said, "You're the detective."

"How did you know?" I handed him a card:

G. CARR: TINY MYSTERIES SOLVED

He tossed it aside, reached into his pocket, and whipped open a scrimshaw knife. I began to worry that he wasn't enjoying our conversation.

"Those foolish women I live with. Think I'm so stupid. Think

I'm blind. Well I can still read a ledger, damn them, and I still track my own accounts. I saw the entry yesterday—'Detective, private.' They're using my own money to spy on me! What's worse? That my family betrayed me, or that they were too stupid to hide their treachery?"

"I don't know." I might have come up with something more clever, but the knife looked sharp. Copeland walked toward me, each step as deliberate as a hammer blow, and I backed away until my heels dangled off the end of the pier.

"It's none of it criminal," he said. "It's business. And those stupid women are going to ruin it for all of us."

"Whatever you're doing on the boat, that's not why I'm here."

"Then why?"

I might have asked what I really wanted to know: What drives a father to stray from his family, to lie to those who love him most? But that question was terribly large, and that shaking knife was drawing closer to my dress, and I only had time to ask the question that didn't matter at all.

"Where do you buy your wife gloves?" I said.

"Gloves? What the hell does this have to do with gloves?"

He growled at me and raised the knife. I looked into his eyes.

And then his eyes were gone.

Copeland's head had been replaced by a cloud of red mist, and I could taste the blood.

The body swayed, then crumpled. The explosion echoed off the warehouses. Even then, it took two more shots for me to grasp what was happening—two shots that tore holes in the wood to my left.

A gun. A gun on the *Westside*, and a body at my feet.

I was flooded with fear, but not paralyzed. I tipped backward and gave myself over to the Hudson. As I fell, another bullet roared through the air, passing right where my heart had been a moment before.

A heavy black dress makes a poor bathing costume, particularly when it has spent the day soaking up sweat. It was like trying to swim in a pair of concrete overalls. My boots tangled themselves in my dress, and the current dragged me toward the inky black of the riverbed. My lungs burned, and my teeth ached from holding shut my jaw. A shadow blanketed me as a passing ship blocked the sun, and I felt the luscious chill of the grave.

Open my mouth, and it would be over. I could stop struggling against the dress, against everything. I could leave the sun behind, sink to the bottom, let the mud settle on top of me. I could let the sun stay behind that ship and never see it come out again. It sounds mad, but as my legs grew heavier and my feet went numb, something in me was tempted to give up.

Thankfully, my body was not finished fighting.

I tore at my stomach, trying to rip the bloody dress in half. Had Hellida been responsible for my clothes, her ironclad stitching would have dragged me to my grave. But I have always preferred to mend my dresses myself, and there are few women in New York as lazy with a needle. The seams ripped, the buttons popped, and I flew to the surface like a champagne cork, in a slip as thin as paper.

The current carried me two piers south, and it took effort before I was able to wrap my arms around a shard of soft timber, spending a few grateful minutes enjoying the rank city air. Once the black spots in my vision retreated, I squinted toward Copeland's body. A man stood over it, tattered overalls dangling from his bare shoulder. He prodded the corpse with his foot.

I inched down the piling, as low as I could get. A few ounces of foul water shot up my nose. I coughed, and the man on the docks looked my way. He squinted, and I prepared to swim for my life. Before I did, though, a stout man bounded out of the yacht, a crate over his shoulder. They walked away, and I saw that the box was marked with a symbol that sent a jagged wave of heartburn surging up from my stomach: the brand of the bloody fist.

Then they were gone, and the river felt as cold as the blood racing through my heart. I hauled my sopping body onto the nearest pier. The sun dried what remained of my clothes within minutes, and I began to sweat again. I didn't mind—it meant I was still breathing.

An old, familiar feeling came back to me, a feeling I had arranged my life to avoid. It was more than fear. It was the sensation of being trapped by deadly coincidence, caught in a battle that I had not started, and that I did not want to fight. That is *not* what tiny mysteries are about.

I was breathing almost evenly when the captain's pier exploded. I couldn't will my legs to stand up. I just rolled to my side and watched it burn. As the flames danced above the grimy Hudson, it occurred to me that there was no ship on the river—nothing that could have possibly cast the shadow that chilled my skin and invited me to die.

THREE

Iron shutters covered the windows of the Fourth Precinct, but the door was gone. Two malnourished cops in tattered uniforms lounged on its steps, hands resting where their pistols used to be. One holster was empty; the other held only the pistol's butt. I'd met them before, on afternoons when Lieutenant Thorne drank too much to walk. I had never been impressed.

"The tiny detective," said Lavangetto, a slow-witted patrolman whose head was as hard and pointed as an artillery shell.

"What happened to your door?" I said. The possibilities spiraled across my brain. It could have been stolen, or sold, or damaged in a storm and taken for repairs. It could have—no, Gilda. We don't need another mystery.

"What happened to your dress?" said his partner, a leathery, hollow-cheeked sadist named Koszler. "You're looking like a drowned rat."

"Keep staring, and I'll be the last rat you ever see. I need you to tuck your tail between your legs, scurry up those steps, and return with Lieutenant Thorne."

"You don't give me orders."

"I have a murder to report. A rather remarkable murder."

"Lieutenant Thorne is out, miss," said Lavangetto. "His duties as a community liaison keep him away from the precinct most afternoons."

"You mean he's in one of Barbarossa's flophouses, sleeping off last night's drunk."

"How 'bout cha leave a message?"

"Fine. A man named Galen Copeland was shot to death on the Westside docks."

"Shot? With what? A bow and arrow?"

"With a gun."

"You drunk, lady, or you got sunstroke?" asked Koszler, laughing in an altogether unattractive way.

"Sadly, neither."

"So if we were to desert our post and saunter over to the docks with you, we'd find a man with a bullet in him?"

"I doubt you'll find the bullet. The shot blew . . . there's just no bullet to find."

"But the body—it'll show a gunshot wound?"

"They blew up the body."

"Who did?"

"The men who robbed the yacht."

"There's a yacht now?"

"For god's sake, if you will just follow me to the docks I can show you the wreckage."

"The department didn't put us on the Westside to chaperone crazy girls."

"We guard the door," said Lavangetto. "Or we did. Now we guard the, uh, the hole."

"Then let me speak to someone else."

"There ain't nobody else left in the building."

"But if you'd like to go inside," said Koszler, "we'd be happy to give you a private tour."

I could have punched him in the nose, stepped on his foot, or insulted his manhood, but none of it seemed worth the effort. This wasn't my case anymore. I left them to their laughter and turned toward home. I saw no one on the streets, save for the girl at the rickety bridge over Morton Creek—the icy stream that runs where Morton Street used to be. Normally, it costs a penny to cross the bridge, but she saw that I had no purse and paid me no mind.

Only in the Westside could a woman with blood in her hair stroll down the sidewalk on a weekday afternoon, wearing nothing but a slip and hearing only the chattering of a few far-off birds. There were days when the echoes of my footsteps were the most peaceful noise in the world. Today, they sounded like someone coming up behind me. Fear rose in my throat and stayed there until I got home.

As the front door creaked shut, I tugged off my gloves and struggled to rip my boots from my feet. I hurled my filthy slip down the hallway, to enjoy the cavelike air in stark naked splendor. I would fall asleep on the cool wood floor, and on waking, the affair of the murdered captain would be behind me. I closed my eyes and saw his head explode. Sleep danced out of my grasp as my mind circled a few simple, unanswerable questions. They came not in my voice, but in my father's.

"Why kill a man, then blow him up, Gilda?

"What was in that crate?

"Why the bloody fist?

"Where did the shot come from, Gilda? Who fired it? How the hell did those bastards find a working gun? And honestly, what could have happened to the Fourth Precinct's door?"

My eyes popped open. Somewhere in the kitchen, it occurred to me, there should be whiskey. The fruit flies were thick above the sink, and the counters were cluttered with dirty jars and rotting jam—the results of an ill-fated canning experiment undertaken in a fit of domesticity. Behind a cracked jar of molding apricot preserves, I found a half-full bottle of Barbarossa's imitation rye.

I poured one drink, and another, putting the bottle back when it became clear the whiskey wouldn't stop the questions circling my head. A shooting murder on the Westside. It was a black miracle.

It was also not my concern.

As if trying to will that true, I wrapped myself in a blanket and leaned back onto the parlor floor. A few seconds later, it's midsummer at the Polo Grounds. A holiday doubleheader, already the third inning, and I'm lost in the concourses. The crowd roars, but I can't tell why. I run down a tunnel, the ceiling vibrating from the pounding of feet above my head, and emerge onto the field.

It's silent. The sky is black. The field is white. The players are translucent, ghostly. The seats are filled with silhouettes. The crowd stares, mouths open, their eyes empty sockets that burn with white fire.

"Goddamn it, you stubborn little girl," came the oil-slick voice of Lieutenant Thorne. "Open this door."

I rolled sideways, blanket tangling around my hips, and pressed myself underneath the windowsill. Metal rapped on the glass above my head.

"You're not fooling me. Come on out and talk."

I wrapped the blanket into a makeshift toga and opened the door. At the sight of me, Thorne whipped his head around and pretended to admire my stoop. The flat afternoon breeze carried an emerald hawk in lazy circles around the great oaks of Washington Square. In the empty lots that flanked my house, a pair of snakes twisted their way through the tall grass.

"It's about, uh—it's about that report you gave to my deputies over at the Fourth."

"I'm glad they passed it along."

"Galen Copeland, huh? Shot and then exploded?"

"That's the way I saw it."

"It seems a bit—well, it's tough to believe."

"If you weren't too shy to look, you could see I'm wearing his blood around my neck."

"How 'bout I come inside? I don't like you standing here like this, in full view of everybody."

"And just who is this 'everybody'? The wonderful feature of this neighborhood, my dear detective, is that no one watches anyone else. You would be utterly scandalized if you knew how many summer hours I while away in the park, with nothing between my body and the earth. If you were a brave man, I'd suggest you drop that ragged uniform and join me in enjoying the night air."

"That's not funny, Gilda. Mocking the uniform, it's going too far."

"I was mocking *you*, but never mind. Perhaps it would be better if you just told me what you wanted."

"I came to take your statement."

"You're investigating this crime?"

"It's a murder, isn't it?"

"I wasn't aware the NYPD still cared enough to look into a Westside slaying. For that matter, I was never really convinced you worked for the NYPD. But of course, I will cooperate fully. How may I assist, officer?"

"He was really shot?"

"Yes."

"But that's . . . but that's impossible."

"Indeed. I can't tell you a thing about what sort of gun it was, but it made quite a racket. I suppose the shot came from the roof of one of the warehouses across the street."

"A rifle, then."

"If you say so."

"Listen, Gilda—you gotta make me a promise."

"I have to do nothing of the sort."

"You're a curious girl, I get it. You always have been. I knew you as a kid, remember?"

"You never let me forget."

"Yeah, so Virgil wouldn't . . . I don't want you poking your nose into this."

"I deal in tiny mysteries and nothing more."

"Thank god," he said and breathed in relief. "Lord, guns on the Westside. Don't go telling that to nobody. Something like this would be liable to start a war, and a war—lord. It'd be all the city would need to bulldoze the Westside."

"Or burn it to the ground."

Thorne ran his hand through what remained of his ginger hair. A few strands clung to the passing fingers and bid his scalp goodbye forever.

"A question," I said, needing a distraction from the man falling apart before me. "Simply to satisfy that natural curiosity of mine. Do you have any idea who might have killed the man?"

"Solving murders—it was your father had the knack for it. I just carried his club."

And with that, he walked down my steps into the falling dark, as scared and broken a detective as the NYPD had ever produced.

I shut the door and locked every available lock, then lit a few candles and poured myself enough whiskey to fell a giant. I spent the evening with an old newspaper propped on my knees, but I don't think I turned more than five pages. I stared straight through it, to the shadows on the far side of the room, trying to think of anything but the man I saw die.

"He told me he'd sold the yacht," said Edith Copeland. "He was petulant, my husband, like a chocolate-stained child who stamps his foot and insists he hasn't been sneaking sweets."

Eyes bloodshot, hair smeared across her forehead, she leaned on the iron railing of Battery Park, dropping bread crumbs to the ducks that swirled in the water below. Across the harbor, a boat pulled out from Ellis Island, the passengers a black smudge on the horizon, visible even through the morning haze.

"Have you any idea what he was doing on the Westside?" she said.

"No. You hired me to find a glove."

"And you haven't done a very good job with it, have you?" She snapped her head away. "I suspect he was engaged on some foolish new venture. Trying to recall how it felt to be a merchant, to be young. It's unfair, isn't it? Women are expected to wither without protest, while men get to spend their whole lives pretending they're still twenty-five. You'll understand someday, and soon. I've read that women age quickly on the Westside."

A passing lady nearly clipped my face with her parasol. I ducked, just in time. We were at the foot of Manhattan, where the fence starts, and Broadway empties into the bay.

"He should have died at sea," said Mrs. Copeland. "To be killed in a freak—what did the police call it? A gas-pocket explosion. Ridiculous. And the detective they sent to deliver that rubbish—absolutely pickled with gin."

"It wasn't a gas pocket."

"Of course not. What happened? Did he blow himself up fiddling with the engine? Did he drop a cigar in a bucket of gasoline and set himself on fire?"

"He was murdered."

She dropped the rest of the bread crumbs into the river. As the paper bag sank, the ducks scrambled to get as much as they could, whipping the foul river water into a frenzy. She walked north, left hand dangling on the railing, slapping every iron post as she passed, looking very much like a maiden waiting for her lover to come back from the sea.

I followed her. Not stopping, she said, "You're quite certain?"

"I'd rather not get into the details, but yes. I am."

"And the detective said nothing."

"The police lie like they breathe: compulsively and to the benefit of no one."

We came to the fence. Mrs. Copeland turned sharply on her heel and walked back the other way.

"You will find me the truth," she said.

"I'll do no such thing."

"You forget, Miss Carr, that you are in my employ."

"And you forget you hired me for a very different case."

"Then you're serious, truly serious, about this tiny mysteries nonsense?"

"I'll refer you to another detective."

"That won't wash. You did far too good a job convincing me that when it comes to the Westside, you are the only one I can trust."

"I understand you're upset—"

"You do not understand!"

She shouted loud enough to startle the ducks. I stopped walking. I drew in as much breath as my lungs could hold and let it out slowly.

"You feel helpless," I said. "Like a woman in bed on a cold winter morning who has kicked her blanket off in her sleep. Your eyes are shut, your feet are freezing. No matter how you arrange your limbs, you feel yourself going numb."

"Numb—how did you know?"

"It's how I felt when my father died."

"Did it happen recently?"

"Two years ago."

"Was he murdered?" She sneered, as if eager to show off her recent admittance to the brethren of those whose loved ones have been murdered.

"He disappeared. Went for a walk at twilight and never came back."

"Did the police investigate?"

I was tiring of this. "A Westside disappearance? Has grief made you stupid?"

"Then surely you looked into it on your own. You do call yourself a detective."

Ten months of it. Not sleeping, not eating, not crying, for the sake of answers that never came. A year wasted on misery. A case gone cold.

"Of course not," I said. "I knew better."

"Well, I'm . . . I'm sorry about your father."

"Of course you're not. You're paying for this time—"

"I am?"

"Oh yes. And there's no point wasting your money on ridiculous lies. You care nothing about my father, nor should you. You are wrapped in an all-encompassing self-pity that will consume you for the rest of this year and most of the next. This murder was senseless. All murder is senseless. Who did it, why they did it—these answers will not ease your grief. Don't waste your time. I certainly won't waste mine."

At this, her cheeks grew hot. For the first time that day, she felt something. She wrapped her fist around the iron railing, trying to rip it from the concrete to club me into silence.

"If you won't find my husband's killer," she said, choking on the word, "then you will find my glove."

"You don't really mean that."

"You took the case! Aren't you bound by some kind of detective's code to see it through?"

"Thankfully, no. It would slow things up considerably."

"If you are not bound by honor, then neither am I."

She dug into her purse and slipped out a long, narrow wallet. Inside was a check that I needed more than I could admit.

"It's not very much, is it? But that dress is frayed, Gilda Carr, and you are hungry. I could tear this into strips and feed it to the ducks, or you could do the job I hired you for. Forget the killer. Find my glove."

"Very well," I said. "My investigation will continue. At double my original rate. That will serve as a down payment."

Mrs. Copeland handed me the check, and walked away, her spine as stiff as the iron railing. The ducks looked up at where she had been, hungry for another pittance.

Copeland's company occupied the third floor of an ancient brick building that sagged forward on its foundation, nodding its head toward the Ward Line's Pier 15. Mrs. Copeland had neglected to give me a key. It wasn't a problem. I kicked the door, and its latch ripped through the damp wood like a cleaver through lace. The way she spoke of Copeland Imports Ltd., I had expected a tenth-story office in a sparkling new skyscraper, every surface coated in polished wood and bloodred leather, every chair groaning under a cigar-gobbling plutocrat. This company didn't look fit to ship an envelope. The windows were filmed with salt, letting in a dim silver light that barely showed the puddle of standing water beside the coatrack. The walls rattled with amorous wharf rats. I felt at home.

I pushed open the door to Copeland's private office. The chaos stopped here. On one wall were a thousand tiny cabinets, each labeled according to its purpose. The walls were freshly white-washed, and the window had a clear view of the river, where a tug was passing by. Only a madman could work in such a clean office. I opened cubby after cubby, dropping anything interesting on the floor, then attacked his desk, spilling papers and charts and chewing tobacco across its immaculate surface. Anything that caught my eye, I stuffed into my bag, to be examined later.

Copeland's datebook was filled with jagged handwriting, but on the date he died, there was just one word written: "brass." I tore out that page, stuffed it in my pocket, and dropped to my knees to sift through my mess.

I found a receipt from a corset shop, and a stack of letters wrapped in twine. The corsetry was Madame Marguerite Fournier's, on Twelfth Street, in the heart of the Westside. The letters were signed "Margie," and they were the filthiest I'd ever seen. Margie promised to bathe the captain in lilac oil, to swaddle him in freshly laundered sheets, to coat his body in hot wax, and dig her finger-nails so deep into his back that they would come out the other side. She referenced past assignations, in her parlor and in this of-fice, on his yacht and in her bed. She called him, for reasons I did not wish to contemplate, her "briny Bunyan." I squeezed my eyes shut, trying to erase the image of Copeland's heaving, mirthless body, when a soft cough sounded from the doorway. Juliette Cope-land, in a starched black dress with a high, stiff collar, inspected me with a look hard enough to cut glass.

"You're that detective," she said.

"With insight like that, you could be a detective yourself."

"Why are you polluting my father's office?"

"Your mother, as you may recall, engaged my services."

"My mother is a dear woman, but she is in no state to be making any decisions, particularly financial ones. Leave now, or I'll have you branded a swindler."

"What do you know about your father's murder?"

"His *accident*. That horrible policeman told us it was an accident."

"The police haven't half my wit. Come to the docks and I'll show you what happened—that is, if you're not afraid of the Westside."

"You're searching for his killer?"

"I don't look for killers. They're very dangerous." I dropped Mrs. Copeland's glove on her husband's desk. "I'm looking for its mate. You wouldn't happen to know where he bought it?"

"Of course not."

"Why did your father keep a yacht at the Westside piers?"

"I have no idea. Unlike my mother, I respected Father's right to privacy."

"Can you explain why he was shopping at a corsetry in the Lower West?"

"He was what?"

"If you didn't know about that, then you must not have known about his affair."

"Excuse me?"

I handed her one of Marguerite's letters. She read a few words and crumpled it into a lavender-scented ball.

"So this is how you make your living?" she said. "Prying into the secrets of the dead?"

"I do quite a bit of business in this line—answering the questions that linger when a loved one dies. Nothing melodramatic, like 'Did my daddy love me?' or 'Where did he bury his gold?' but the little things, the important things, the questions that drive you mad. Learn a simple truth about a man who's gone, and you will find a wonderful kind of peace."

"And are you at peace?"

"Why shouldn't I be?"

"You wear black. Who are you mourning? Did your simple truths bring you comfort?"

"No."

"Then don't push your lies on me."

I smiled at her, the way one might smile at a leaping viper. She did her best to smile back.

"Miss Carr—I'm sorry, I assume it's Miss? It's been charming to encounter you here, rooting through my father's private files. I would describe you as a novelty. But while I'm sure there are certain unfortunates on the Westside who enjoy having their grief interrupted by sweat-soaked pests, I am not one of them."

"Then you never met Marguerite Fournier?"

"I have not, and I'm sure I should not want to. Galen Copeland was a mediocre businessman and an indifferent father, but I loved him. My mother, in her own pathetic manner, loved him as well. If he had secrets, they were his own, and they die with him. You are not and were never employed by Copeland Imports. If you cross this threshold again, I shall have you clapped into the Tombs. If you ever take another penny from my mother, I shall scrape those woolly eyebrows from your face."

"Someone seems to have made a mess in here. Would you like me to stay and help clean up?"

"That will be all right."

I nodded and left, hands in my pockets, clutching the rest of Copeland's letters. I wondered if Madame Fournier sold leather gloves.

Just two blocks below the Borderline, West Twelfth Street was a no-man's-land, and that is not a good place to run a business. A strip of blue sky sat uneasily between two rows of narrow, deserted warehouses. Above, it could have been noon, but on the sidewalk it felt like midnight. The temperature dropped twenty degrees when I crossed the fence, a chill as shocking as a summer fever.

Most of the shops on Fournier's block were shuttered, their owners having given up for the day or for a lifetime. A parade of ants as wide as a man marched down the street carrying bits of fabric, plaster, brick, and iron, disappearing into an open sewer grate. From below the street came a grinding, sawing noise. I preferred not to imagine what could produce such a grisly sound. And there, in a hideous brick building on the south side of the street, her display windows fogged by a decade's filth, the corset retailer struggled on.

A forlorn bell announced my entrance, and I was greeted by the spindly figure of Madame Fournier, whose skin was like tissue paper and whose accent was less Riviera than Fulton Fish Market. The little bell had awoken her like a gunshot, stirring a sense of salesmanship that had been rusting for years. She introduced herself— Madame Fournier, but I could call her Marguerite.

The shop was tidy. Towers of corsets in every color and size stretched to the ceiling, immaculately organized but coated in a fine layer of dust. Within moments, I was being spun, measured, fitted, and judged. With every measurement, her unkempt fingernails scraped my exposed skin.

"Such a figure you have, such a figure," she fawned. "How do you like this periwinkle?"

"Perfect."

"This is our finest model—strictly prewar quality. You see the lacing, that's done by hand, of course, and all in front so you can take it off without a servant's help. It's light enough to wear in the summer, but the boning is so strong, it can stand up to anything."

She strapped me into her contraption, wrapped the laces around her fists, and pulled. Stars danced before my eyes, and I knew how it would feel to be stepped on by an elephant. She posed me in front of the mirror. My waist was the size of a nickel, and my breasts appeared to be trying to strangle me.

"Perfect," I wheezed.

"Normally, this sells for a dollar seventy-five, but since the season is changing, it's yours for one thirty-five."

"A bargain."

Her razor-sharp fingernails split open her knot, and the sides of the corset sprang out like a popped balloon. I breathed deeply, feeling my organs rearranging themselves inside my chest.

"Shall I ring it up for you?"

"Do you mind gift wrapping it? We single girls get so few presents. I like to have something to unwrap when I get home."

She curtsied for some reason and reached her arm between two racks of truly terrifying girdles. A shove, and the wall popped open. She swung one of the racks to the side, stooped, and disappeared. I wandered over, rubbing fabric between my fingers and checking price tags until I could see what was behind Fournier's secret door.

It was a storeroom. Two shelves of rough, unfinished wood lined the walls. Between them, busy beneath a bare bulb, Fournier wrapped my prewar quality corset. Beside her was a small crate, not unlike the one taken from Copeland's boat, that bore the bloody fist.

"You were a friend of Galen Copeland," I called. She set down the wrapping paper and picked up her shears.

"Whatever do you mean?"

"'O captain, my captain, how I yearn to smell the salt in your beard once again. How I miss the salty funk of your manhood, the oily suction of your kiss, the roughness of your grip' . . . it goes on like this for quite some time."

"You bitch," she said, dropping the half-baked French accent. "One more word of that—just one more word—and I'll see that you never talk again."

"He's dead, you know."

"How do you mean, *dead*?"

"You know—not alive."

"How . . ."

"On the docks, yesterday afternoon. I saw it happen."

The scissors fell from her hand.

"And just who the hell are you?" she murmured, not looking at me. Not looking at anything at all.

"Gilda Carr. I'm trying to answer a few questions for his wife."

"You tell her about us?"

"She doesn't know a thing."

"How much do you want to keep it quiet? A hundred? Two hundred? Look around. There's not fifty dollars in this whole damned shop."

"This isn't about blackmail."

"Then you just came to rub it in."

Why are people so tedious? First Mrs. Copeland's melodrama, and now this.

I took Madame Fournier's hand in mine. Her skin was cold and dry. She tried to pull away from my touch, but I did not let go. To calm her down, I told a detective's favorite lie.

"You can trust me," I said.

"Yeah?"

"I didn't know Galen well, but I knew him enough to see that he was a truly remarkable man."

"He was a saint."

"You called him, in the letters—I know I shouldn't have read them but they were so beautiful, I simply couldn't help myself—you called him Bunyan. Why?"

"Because he was a giant. When he walked down the street, people got out the way. When he came into a room, you could almost see his head scraping the ceiling. And when he took me in his arms, my god. My god."

"Did you sell him this glove?" I showed her Mrs. Copeland's glove, and her face twisted into an acid sneer.

"What are you thinking bringing that in here? That's his wife's, right?"

"I'm trying to learn where he bought it."

"Not here, I can tell you that. It's cheap. Shoddy. Just what she deserved. The stuff I sell is the best on the Westside."

"It feels quite fine to me."

"You don't know a damn thing. Coming in here, tormenting me, showing me that glove! I've been living and dying for that man since before the war. And now he's gone. Good god. Good god, girl . . . what will I do?"

She began to cry. I looked about for a handkerchief and passed her some scrap of hosiery, which she dragged across her nose. I focused on my notebook.

"Did Copeland have any troubles? Anything eating at him?"

"That wife of his," she hissed. "She's a cancer. She watched him like a prison warden. If he was two minutes late, she'd back him into a corner and give him the third degree. I saw her one time, frail old beast, but she could hit and she could scream. She kept that man in a state of living terror. The afternoons he could slip out and see me—those were the only times he was really happy. He was gonna marry me, you know. Put her right where she belonged, on the curb with all the other garbage, and make me Margie Copeland."

"Did she know?"

"That woman was too stupid to notice the nose on her face. That's why Galen couldn't stand her, the stupidity. He was brilliant. He needed a partner who could match him."

"But if she had found out . . ."

"She'd have killed him, sure as night turns into day. That woman was not too polite for murder."

I didn't want to hear about murder. I didn't want to know about the crate in her storeroom. I wanted to live the rest of my life without the brand of the bloody fist dancing before my eyes, but when I tried to turn away, I felt my father tugging at my sleeve, forbidding me to leave. That damned crate. I would have to ask.

"That crate, in your storeroom. The one marked with the fist. Where did it come from?"

The tears stopped. Fournier slid past me, silent as a ghost, and closed the storeroom door. Her false French accent returned.

"If you're not going to buy anything, miss, I'm afraid I'll have to ask you to leave. This is our busiest time of day."

I looked around the empty room, an eyebrow raised.

"What was he involved in?"

"Get out, young woman, or I shall have to call the police."

"They killed him for one of those crates. They could come after you too."

"On second thought, the police are too slow. Leave now, or I shall be forced to take matters into my own hands."

The police didn't concern me, not on the Westside. But she didn't seem the type for empty threats, so I took her at her word. The shop's bell chimed as I stepped back onto the sidewalk. As I slunk down Twelfth Street, I felt her sallow face watching me through the grime.

FOUR

On maps that still include the Westside, it's called Fourteenth Street, but to the warriors of the Westside, it is the Borderline. Below it: liquor, darkness, and fun, protected by boys playing soldier. Above it: candlelit respectability, policed by the rainbow-uniformed guards of Glen-Richard Van Alen.

I crossed over at Eighth Avenue, where the Jackson Square Gophers held the line. Their chief, whose smeared ocher war paint couldn't hide his acne, glared at me as I passed.

"What business you got in the Upper West?" he said.

"None of yours."

"We got a right to know. We got special dispensation from Barbarossa herself to patrol—"

He was taller than me, but not as heavy. I shoved him hard, square in the chest, and he fell on his back, and the laughter of his lieutenants froze him to the spot. The crossing was open.

Broken glass and twisted metal studded the intersection, thick enough to slow an attack from either side. A crooked path wound through the debris, carrying me into the shadow of the ramshackle wooden platform at the center of the road. Two stories high and nearly as wide as the avenue itself, it held a great cast-iron bra-zier, which at night burned bright enough to illuminate the darkest corners of Fourteenth Street. There was one at every intersection: symbols of Van Alen's promise to beat back the night. Uniformed firekeepers scurried over its catwalks and rope ladders, bringing up the day's wood: fresh-cut timber, unfinished lumber, and smashed furniture looted from houses all over the Upper West. By dawn, Van Alen's fire would reduce it all to ash, to blow away in the morn-ing wind, and fall like gray snow on my sidewalk. A patrol of Van Alen's rainbow guard marched around the fire-stand, toting hunks of charred, nail-studded wood: the signature weapon of the stand-ing army of the Upper West. Passing under the fire-stand, I caught a lungful of sawdust and went into a coughing fit that nearly knocked me down. One of the guardsmen, a slender young man with jagged teeth and an elaborate moustache, took my arm. I took it right back.

"Follow me, ma'am," he said.

"Absolutely not," I said, stifling another racking cough.

"You'll have to follow me."

Eight men with clubs blocked my path north. Behind me, the humiliated, furious chief of the Gophers. To my left, the fire-stand, to my right, a few hundred yards of broken glass. With no real choice, I followed him, and in the pocket of my dress, I gripped my little knife. The guardhouse was a long wooden structure that spilled into the street. It smelled like salted meat. He held the door open for me.

"On no account," I said, "will I be joining you in there."

"Then if you would perhaps wait here? This will only take a moment."

I took a step backward. The guardsmen flanking the door took a step forward, twisting their clubs in their hands. I decided it would be better if I did not move anymore.

My guardsman bounded through the longhouse door. I shifted in my boots, sweating, and wondered if I might sprint back across the Borderline before the guards rallied to stop me. I did not trust myself to make it in time.

The door burst open and my guardsman emerged. He offered me an icy silver cup. A sensible man would have put bourbon in it, but it was filled with clean, pure Westside water.

"Please," he said.

I drained the cup, and thanked him.

"Don't thank me. That comes courtesy of Glen-Richard Van Alen."

"I thought you were going to detain me."

"For what? For coming to visit?"

"For being a stranger."

"This, madam, this is not the Lower West."

He looked hurt. Mumbling something cheerful, I made my escape.

Too many people clogged the streets. Not nearly as many as on the Eastside, but far more than I could stand. They lounged on their stoops, tended their gardens, sold trinkets from pushcarts, and mended clothes in the open air. No one drank beer, no one danced, and no one really laughed.

At the corner of Eighth Avenue and Twentieth Street, an abandoned apartment house paid tribute to the man who made this mawkish society possible: A massive canvas hung from the building's cornice, wrapping around the street corner and dangling five stories to the ground. The banner showed Van Alen, sturdy as a grizzly bear, kneeling low to present a lit candle to a trio of grateful urchins. Behind them stretched the whole of the Upper West, from the Borderline to the heights of Manhattan, lit by Van Alen's fires.

Across the street, a pubescent boy in long-outgrown shorts sneered at the painting from beneath a pitiful moustache. He hopped off the sidewalk, then back up, and then leapt forward and charged at the canvas. I wasn't sure if he was trying to climb it or tear it down, but two guardsmen were on him before he could get a decent handhold. They yanked him off the canvas, sending ripples along its great surface, and threw him into the gutter. Two quick kicks blunted his anger, but the guardsmen weren't finished. One raised his club over his head and was about to bring it down on the boy's skull when I put myself in the way.

"Please don't hurt him!" I cried, as helplessly as I could manage.

"You his mother?"

"He's my baby brother. He's harmless. Please."

"He was trying to deface the artwork."

"He's troubled. He doesn't understand. Please—just let me take him home."

The man with the club reared back to deliver one last kick, but his partner stopped him. They left, muttering something that I believe included the phrase "ungrateful bitch," and I helped the boy onto the curb. I had a strong urge to cuff his ear, but since I wasn't actually his sister, I restricted myself to scowling.

"Are you suicidal?" I asked him. "Or simply a fool?"

"It's lying. The painting. It lies, every day."

I wanted to abandon him right there. This was not simply a sightseeing trip—I had real work to do. But his nose was bloody and his shirt was torn, and he was simply too pathetic to leave.

Besides, a lying painting was a mystery I could not turn down.

"And what lie does it tell?" I said, helping him to his feet.

"That the Upper West is safe."

"Who did you lose?"

"What the hell do you care?"

"I have lost people too."

"Well I've seen 'em disappear."

"What do you mean?"

"C'mere," he said and bolted down the street. What else could I do but follow? He turned down an alleyway, hopped a trashcan, and scurried up the side of the wall to grab the ladder at the bottom of the fire escape. His weight pulled it to the ground, and he began to climb.

It was five flights to the top, and I hadn't gone ten steps before I felt my heart flutter, and my palms begin to sweat. I glanced down through the slats of the fire escape, and regretted it instantly. The ground looked suddenly very far away.

"You climbing," called the boy, already two flights ahead of me, "or you just gonna quiver and sweat?"

Had I not just saved this ungrateful idiot from getting his head bashed in?

I climbed anyway.

By the time I got to the roof, he was already gone. I shaded my eyes against the morning sun, and saw him vaulting the low wall that separated this building from the next. I shook my head, and followed his lead. Across one roof, and then another, and then there was a gap—two or three feet between this brownstone and the one that held the painting. The boy—did he have a name, I wondered— leapt it without thought. I stopped short of jumping and nearly fell.

I should have said goodbye and gone back down to the sidewalk. If he'd yelled at me, if he'd been angry, I probably would have left him. But instead he laughed, and that I couldn't bear. I pulled my skirts up high and executed a dainty little hop from one building to the other—as though death weren't one misstep away.

"It wasn't that far," I said.

"No, it wasn't."

"Now tell me what the hell you've brought me here for."

"Down the stairs." He opened the trapdoor that led down into the building, and he told me his story as we climbed. "I lived in this building my whole life, me and Ma. 3B, right by the fire escape. It was a good building. Even after '14, it was mostly full, and people were friendly. But then, they started dropping off. Knock on Mrs. Richards's door, and it just swings open, and the apartment's bare. Mr. Goodes goes out for midnight Mass, and he never comes back. Ma and me, we laughed it off, and we kept laughing until we're the only people here."

"I'm sorry," I said. It was a story I'd heard before. That didn't make it any easier to take.

The hallway stank of mold, and rotten food, and worse. We went down a flight of stairs, and he swung open the door to the apartment that had been his home. Creeping vines had come in from outside, shattering the window and taking over the parlor. Brown light filtered through the canvas outside, and I sensed the presence of countless bugs and vermin in the walls and under the floors. By the way he ran his hand along the sagging wallpaper, I could tell it had once been a fine home.

"One night Ma asks me, put the kettle on and fix her tea. She loves tea. So I fill the kettle up in that week's barrel of water, courtesy of Glen-Richard Van Alen, and I light the fire, and my match hasn't even gone out when I hear her yell. It's my name—Bruce. She's yelling my name. And she only gets out half of it, just 'Bru—' before she cuts off. I drop the kettle, and I get back in here, and there ain't nothing but the night outside and nobody in that chair. She got taken."

"By who?"

"I told you. By the night."

Taken by the night. Definitely a story I'd heard before.

The last time I saw my father smile, I assumed he was drunk on Boulton's Rye. He was, of course, but it was more than that. He told me he had found the breakthrough he'd been looking for: the grand universal theory that tied every tragedy the Westside had ever suffered into one neat, awful bow. It would have been perfect, had it made any sense.

"The night is hungry," he said, glass loose in his left hand, so tilted that with every word, he spilled a little liquor on the carpet. "The Westside . . . it's killing us, Gilda. Every one of us, breath by breath. It's nothing but the night."

"I'm going to bed," I said. "You are too."

"I have notes, I have to get this down. If I could get this to the mayor—no! To the press. I could heal this city, Gilda. I could save so many lives."

He kept talking.

I had stopped listening years before.

I believed in the magic of the Westside. I had seen flowers bloom and die in an hour; I had heard the songs of birds known nowhere else on earth. That a woman might be stolen by the dark was no more peculiar, and yet, I could not believe Bruce's story, because that would mean admitting that my father might have been right.

It did not matter what I thought. The pain on his face was real.

"After that, they moved me across the street," he said. "Put me in with some other family, had taken in a bunch of kids whose parents were gone. They felt bad for me. Gave me the best bed—right by the window, so every day, minute I wake up, I could see that painting where my life used to be."

"Have you a knife?"

"I'm a boy, ain't I?"

I told him what to do. I returned to the street the way we had come, but he stayed behind. I was half a block away when I heard the unique sound of forty feet of canvas tumbling to the earth. The streets went silent, and guardsmen charged the scene to stop the crowd from trampling Van Alen's great monument to himself. They tried to get into the building, but the fallen painting blocked their way. From the street, there was no sign of anyone on the roof.

"It just fell," said an old woman selling flowers from a basket over her arm.

"Just one of those Westside things," I said and walked on.

I loathe the Upper West, but it has certain luxuries in abundance. It has churches that haven't been converted to saloons, and a few makeshift schools. There are chophouses above the Borderline, and gardens, and of course, there is the bazaar. There is also a library, and that is why I came.

Before it was converted for academic use, the Eighth Avenue free library was a boxing gymnasium, and the tang of sweaty feet clung to every book they had. The shelves were a mess, but the librarians, a stooped old couple with hair as soft and white as fresh cotton, knew the collection by heart.

"I'm looking for books on gloves," I said. "Or leatherworking. Maybe one about corsets too, and general fashion history. But mostly, I need to know about gloves."

They brought me what they had. The books were strange, disreputable academic treatises with half-finished indices and incoherent sourcing. At any reputable library, they would have been pulped, but they were the best the Westside had to offer, and they were far better than what I would find below the Borderline. An optimistic young teacher had tried to open a free library on the Lower West once. The shelves were ransacked within a week, and the would-be librarian was never seen again.

I worked for hours, learning far more than I wanted about man's obsession with covering women's hands. I found nothing useful. I'm not sure I expected anything different. I could have searched for information on Galen Copeland. I could have tried to understand the meaning of the word in his datebook, "brass." But those were bigger mysteries than were safe to contemplate, and I was already feeling rattled by Bruce's story about the disappearance in 3B.

When it was clear the trip had been wasted, I walked home along Fifth Avenue. It was mine, and mine only. North, this canyon of skyscrapers was clean and precise. South of the Borderline, for a few glorious blocks, it was the avenue of my dreams: vines twisting tighter every year, buildings caving into the sidewalk, strange light dancing up a street of broken glass. The air was rank with glorious decay—like the water in the bottom of a vase of rotting sunflowers. I breathed it deep and forgot the wasted afternoon.

The shop windows had been smashed long ago, but you could see the remains of mannequins, whose blank faces had so terrified me as a child. Every Sunday afternoon, my mother and I strolled the avenue, laughing at the latest fashions and pitying the women who flocked here every week to empty their wallets. We imagined their faces when they got home and laid out their purchases on the bed, and found that no amount of silk could ease the creeping terror that spoiled their sleep and curdled their days. My mother was not a silly woman, and she was not a cruel woman, but since she married Virgil Carr she had never had money, and nothing made her laugh like imagining the secret heartaches of the wealthy.

The late-afternoon sun lit up Washington Square like a bonfire. A fallen elm lay in front of the arch, rotting into the matted green carpet. I could have walked around it, but it was more fun to climb over it, and so I did. I spent my childhood playing in this park, but

I never had so much fun as I have since the district emptied out and the forest was left to grow. It was a private garden now, shared between me and those peculiar people who still lived around the square. Only I, and a few brave and hardy children, had the nerve to venture into the square's darkest corners.

So I found it peculiar to find a funny little man waiting on my stoop, asleep underneath a hat so old it had begun to decompose. I was going to prod him with the toe of my boot, but I thought better of it. I scoured the edge of the park for the ugliest tree branch I could find and swatted him across the face instead. He tumbled down my steps and landed on his back, hat in the street. He didn't know whether to look angry or afraid.

"Hell, woman!" He searched for more words, but couldn't find them. "Hell!"

He had the thinnest moustache I'd ever seen, a single strand of hair glued to his lip. He was as bald as a bank president, but despite a whiskey bloat to his face, the skin was taut. He couldn't have been older than twenty-five.

"Why don't you put your hat back on?" I said. "The glint off your forehead is blinding."

"That's no way to talk to the star reporter of the *Sentinel* city room. That's no way to talk to Max Schmittberger."

"I suppose not. Goodbye."

"Wait—wait. Hold on, lady. Hold on. Is this yours?"

He handed me a card, scorched around the edges:

G. CARR: TINY MYSTERIES SOLVED

"Where did you find this?" I said.

"I think you know. Just like I figure you know what exploded there, and who got, uh, exploded."

"You're writing about the explosion at the docks?"

"Trying to. Gish squirms any time you mention the Westside."

"Gish?"

"Mr. Gischler! City room chief. Don't you know nothing?"

"Not if I can help it. Now please stop dancing up and down my steps. You'll wear out the stone."

He stopped, or tried to. His feet tapped as he talked, or he bit his lips, or his fingers played up and down his frayed lapel.

"We only cover the Westside because the publisher grew up in the Upper West, back when it was fine, and he thinks a little token reporting keeps him in touch with the old neighborhood. Never mind that the guy lives in the biggest, plushest, brightest penthouse on the stem. So anyway, Gish hears about this blast, right, and he says, 'Schmittberger! Haul it over to the Westside docks,' and so I haul. Some of the other boys, they don't like coming this way, but I'm Max Schmittberger and I don't scare. And what do I find?"

"I couldn't say."

"Not much. Police swept the place cleaner than the ladies' washroom at the Hyperion Hotel. But there was this card stuck half an inch into the dock. Explosion shot it in there like a bullet."

"Why do you say 'like a bullet'?"

"Did I? Words just fall out of my mouth, you know. I don't really pay attention. It's just an expression. The real question is, G. Carr, who bought it at the docks?"

"The police wouldn't say?"

"I got foisted off on some gin-soaked wreck at the Fourth. Had about as much vim as a worn-out handkerchief. He didn't know a damn thing."

"I can hardly hope to best him."

"Come on. You gotta have something. Ain't you been investigating?"

"I'm pursuing a matter tangentially related to the bombing."

"So it *is* a bombing. A bombing could be page one."

"Pardon me. I misspoke. 'Explosion' is the better word."

"Certainly, miss. Certainly."

His hand rubbed the pocket of his jacket, yearning to reach for the notebook inside.

"Have you a theory?" I asked.

"A thousand. But none fit to print."

"What's your personal favorite?"

"If this is a bombing, then there's only one man in the city could be responsible. Van Alen. There's a reason they call him Firecracker. You remember '14, don't you?"

The month after the fence went up, when it was still flimsy, and the mayor promised it might come down at any moment. A string of bombings up and down the Eastside—banks, theaters, power stations, subway stations, luncheonettes, and the homes of the wealthy. In six weeks, 237 dead, and then the Westside sealed off forever.

"Everybody knows it was Firecracker planted those bombs," said Max. "One last kiss-off to the Eastside before the door shut for good."

"It was never proven."

"But *everybody* knows."

"Surely he's happy with his middle-class kingdom. He has the bazaar, his night-fires, his schools. Why start trouble?"

"Every man that ever had anything wanted a little more."

"That's quite profound for the city room."

"You gonna loop me in on your little investigation, or aren't you?"

"I assure you, Max, I couldn't provide you with an inch of copy. Anything that goes boom is far beyond my purview. If you'll excuse me . . ."

"Surely, miss. Surely." He pocketed my scorched card. "I'm gonna hang on to this. A souvenir. You hear anything about that bombing or explosion or whatever you want to call it, you can find me in the city room."

He tipped his cap and stepped backward, grinning like a mule. It would have been a dapper gesture had his foot found the step. I left him sprawled across the pavement, feeling blindly for his hat and his pride.

If my father made notes on the hunger of the night, they would be in his office with all the others. I could throw myself down the pit that had swallowed him, asking questions of the dark, or I could give myself the gift of a much-needed nap. I was still undecided when I reached for the bannister and my hand found empty air instead. I tumbled sideways, airborne, and crashed into the small table where my father once left his house keys. The bannister, that treacherous bit of wood, had deserted me.

"Goddamn it!" I got myself up, rubbing my various damaged parts. The posts of the bannister were shorn off at the base. Actually, no—not shorn. They were smooth, polished, as though the stairs had simply been built without a handrail. First my condiments, now this. I would have cursed more, or kicked the stairs, or simply stood and marveled at the impossible mysteries of the universe, but something far more interesting than a vanished bannister caught my eye. The frame was cracked, the glass was broken, and the photograph made the bile rise in my throat.

It was a family portrait, taken when I was a fat, disgruntled baby. My father held my mother as tight as he could, and she held me, straining her wrists to keep me from wriggling out of her grasp. She looked like she always looked, like the most beautiful woman in the world. I wore an expression of extreme displeasure, but she clutched me to her chest, holding me tight.

Holding me through gloves nearly identical to Edith Copeland's.

I found the gloves deep in my parents' closet, in a box of her clothes Virgil never got around to giving away. They were muddy brown, unadorned by the flowers that danced across Mrs. Copeland's glove, but the brand was the same. They were as roughly cut as the one I'd taken from Thieves' Market. I could not imagine my mother wearing something so clumsily made.

My mother was Mary Fall, a peculiar creature of New York society. She expended the last of her fortune to buy the town house on Washington Square and spent my youth pretending we still had money, stuffing me into lavish dresses that I would revenge myself against by picking at their barely visible seams during interminable Sunday teas.

I'm told she was delicate, with a bird's laugh and thick brown hair that fell in curls across her shoulders. Her hair I inherited; her delicacy I forewent. How porcelain Mary Fall was courted and wed by the NYPD's brilliant barbarian was one of the most powerful love stories of the nineteenth century. Or so I assume—no one ever bothered to tell it to me.

She died of pneumonia when I was ten—a tiny mystery all its own, summer pneumonia, especially since I recall the house smelling like Christmas the day she died. My father kept vigil outside their bedroom, in the least forgiving chair he could find. I lay at the other end of the hall, outside his office, curled in a tight ball, face pressed against the floor, staring down the endless hallway at Virgil, who waited hours for good news that did not come. In my memory, he does not cry. He never cried. But again, in my memory, it smelled of Christmas, so perhaps I am not to be trusted.

My mother had been a Methodist, of all things. Her family buried her as they buried all their people, but Virgil arranged a separate memorial at a Quaker meetinghouse. I don't know why he chose it, but it was apt. I spent the Methodist funeral squeezed into another of those terribly fine dresses, enduring hours of platitudes about the wonderful place she'd gone now that she had died. At the Quaker service, there were no clichés. It was a long, peaceful silence, broken only occasionally by the words of someone who had known Mary Fall. There was no false comfort, and that suited me. I had lost mother, and comfort felt wrong.

From then, Virgil went weekly to the Quaker meetinghouse. I don't know what he did there; I was never invited. He had been drawn into the contemplation of truly large mysteries, cosmic and earthly, and they would consume the rest of his life. He began to ask the question that no one on the NYPD could bear: What was happening to the people of the Westside?

Even as the department refused to admit that the mounting disappearances were anything to be concerned about, Virgil plotted every vanishing, collecting hundreds of pounds of evidence that added up to nothing. Like all those who trouble themselves with big mysteries, as he failed to find answers, he let his mystery grow larger. The vanishings became a question of corruption at the highest levels of government. Every murder, every suicide, every death was part of the same question.

"This city is a cancer," he bellowed at a particularly unusual press conference in 1910. "And the mayor and his cronies are so many vile, infected cells. The Westside is withering. Corruption has choked the life out of it, and that dead limb will putrefy. You take shelter on the stem. You take shelter in the light. But until the cancer is excised, all our heads are in the noose. Now—are there any questions?"

There were none.

It only takes a few such press conferences to end a career. Virgil was forcibly retired in 1912, and the V. Carr Agency was incorporated a week after his farewell banquet, which he marked with a particularly profane, drunken toast.

When the fence went up, his was the only detective agency remaining on the Westside, and he could have done very well solving the thousand puzzles of our blighted district. Instead, he assaulted the largest mysteries the city had to offer, emptying his bank account and withering his sanity as he barreled toward death.

Mary Fall had been gone nearly twenty years. Hellida and I were perhaps the only people in New York who remembered her name. To me, she was less a person than an idea—beautiful, perfect, funny, and fearless, and stronger than Virgil Carr. I would not let her be tarnished.

I put the gloves back into the box and kicked it hard into the recesses of the closet. My bannister. My mother's gloves. Push against the Westside, the Westside pushes back.

That's okay.

I push harder.

FIVE

I eased the front door shut, counted my breaths, and heard no sound from downstairs. Strange animal sounds came from within the park; screams of joy or pain came from beyond it. A chill spread across my back. I tried to pretend I wasn't afraid.

As my eyes adjusted, familiar sights rose out of the gloom. Shattered benches, broken streetlights, the twisted railing looking taller than it ever had. The moon was slender as a clipped fingernail; the shadows were deep. Night was less inviting than I remembered.

My foot touched pavement. Two more steps, and my knee crashed into the front gate. I cursed, rather louder than I intended, and Hellida's front door opened beneath the stoop.

"Is that a burglar?" she cried.

"It's me."

"Gilda Carr! Are you trying to shatter my nerves? Get back inside. Quick, *flicka*, quick!"

"I have work to do."

"Work can always wait till dawn."

"There's someplace I have to go. I can only get in at night. You really needn't worry."

"I wish that were true."

"Go back to sleep. I'll be back for breakfast."

Hellida was dressed for bed in a worn flannel nightgown, and she clutched a carving knife in her right hand. Graying blond hair fell limply across her shoulders. Her lips were pursed too tightly to scowl.

"Step inside," she said. "I'll have to change."

"I don't want you along for this."

"You want whatever you want, and I'll be right by your side. Shall I bring the knife?"

"I think we'll be fine on our own."

Forty-five minutes later, we were feeling our way through an alleyway just off Twelfth Street, and Hellida was complaining about her coffeepot.

"I've had it twenty-two years, and now I can't lay hands on it. I was fixing coffee this morning, and I turned around to get the paper. When I turned back, it was gone. Perplexing. You didn't take it?"

"No."

"You're certain? You didn't sneak down into my apartment, crouch outside my door, creep across the floor, and snatch the pot while my back was turned?"

"I hope I'd remember if I had."

"Has anything strange been going on in your part of the house?"

"No," I said, lying all too easily.

"Just my coffeepot, then. Just one of those Westside things. I'd thought this sort of nonsense had stopped with your father. Things were always disappearing around him. Cuff links. House keys. Dollar bills. I told him, again and again I told him, ask mad questions, and madness will come home to roost."

The alley ended. My hands searched the wall until they found the corsetry's back entrance. I opened a small leather case. Silver instruments gleamed in the dark.

"I don't like you owning burglar's tools," Hellida said.

"They were a gift from my father the year I turned twelve."

"And did he teach you how to use them?"

"What do you think?"

The latch popped open as gently as a baby opening her eyes.

"We have penetrated Madame Fournier," said Hellida.

"Don't be vulgar. Burglary is a noble art."

We crept through the back room and into the main storeroom, where faint moonlight fought through grimy windows. We kept low and felt our way toward the yellow corsets.

"Just what are we looking for?" said Hellida.

"That damnable crate. I spent all night trying not to wonder what was inside."

"And?"

"I failed."

Hellida picked up a particularly fearsome buttercup girdle, which had enough buckles and straps to restrain an inmate at Bellevue. She pressed it to her torso, considered it for a moment, then cast it aside. Some women have better things to worry about than an eighteen-inch waist.

"Call me simple," she said, "because I know you'll think this is just another stupid Hellida question, but isn't there a chance that the crate is full of corsets?"

"Galen Copeland was not murdered for corsets."

"Who's to say? Fashion is cutthroat. Men have been killed for less."

I reached deep into the rack of yellow corsets. The ones in front scratched my cheek, and dust got in my mouth.

"And besides," she went on, "what business is it of yours how a man chooses to get murdered? Breaking and entering is one thing, but going out after dark is suicidal, Gilda. It reminds me of your father, the year before he left us, when we'd stay up all night drinking cocoa. You'd shake, remember? From the tips of your fingers to the split ends of your hair, and you'd tell me it was only the cold. But you were afraid for him, afraid he might not come back, and I was too. You can't do that to me again."

"I owe it to Mrs. Copeland. I—she hired me."

"Your whole life, you've been happy to quit when something gets hard. So quit now."

"I tried. I couldn't. I promise, I'm as surprised as you."

I withdrew my arm from the depths of the corset rack. I stared at the wall, and I stared at my hand, and I tried not to look at Hellida pleading with me to leave.

"There's a door back there," I said. "I can't reach it. We'll have to move this rack."

"Yes, of course. Whatever you say."

Without waiting for my help, she picked it up and moved it silently across the floor. There, faint but unmistakable, was the seam of the hidden door. I pressed on the wall, and it swung open. Beyond was darkness.

I reached inside the door and found a small lantern hanging on the wall. We lit it, dimmed the light, and stepped inside the storeroom, closing the door behind us to hide the glare from any unlikely passerby.

The light swept across the long, dusty storeroom, and I saw it wasn't just one crate. It was dozens, stacked to the ceiling, going back thirty feet, perhaps more. All with the sigil. All begging me to peek inside.

"You didn't happen to bring a crowbar?" I said.

"Crowbars are for weaklings."

Hellida wrapped her hands around the lid of the nearest crate, braced her feet against the side, and ripped it open. She shoved it across the floor, scattering sawdust into the air, and laughed like I hadn't heard her laugh in years.

"Congratulations, detective," she said. "Corsets. As many as we want, and factory fresh."

"Prewar quality," I said, lifting the corset and holding it to the light. It was periwinkle, the same suffocating model I had tried on. I tossed it aside and it landed, thud, somewhere in the dark.

"Where next?" said Hellida. "We break into the vault at Aylesmere's, maybe, and try on bridal gowns. Or better yet, we go home."

"We should," I said, but instead I picked up the second corset in the box. I ran my hands over it, tracing the stitching, testing the strength of the boning, wondering how much a woman must hate herself to strap herself into one of these every day. When I lowered it back into the box, the light glinted off something in the bottom of the crate.

I yanked out a few more corsets, hurling them over my shoulder, and halfway down the crate, my hands hit glass. I held the bottle to the lantern. The liquid sloshing around in there was crystal clear, and a quick sip, followed by a truly unladylike coughing fit, told me it wasn't water.

"Copeland was moving liquor," I said.

"Now, *flicka*," said Hellida, finally stern. "I close this crate, and we go home."

"I won't stand in your way."

She took the bottle out of my hand and lowered it back into the crate as though it might explode if mishandled. She was right to. I'm always happy to drink bootleg gin, but even I am not stupid enough to ask where it comes from. In Barbarossa's New York, those kinds of questions are generally answered with a cut throat.

Hellida stacked the corsets tidily and replaced the lid of the crate.

"I need a hammer to close it proper," she said, and I was just about to look for one when the shop's front door tinkled open, and my stomach turned to pudding.

"Kill the light!" I hissed. Hellida killed it, and we dropped to the floor.

"Where is it?" snarled a voice from outside. "Now, you skinny tramp, or you're done."

"Takes a lot of nerve to hit a woman," said the unmistakable rasp of Madame Fournier.

"I don't have to hit you. See?"

"You think that scrap iron scares me?"

"It should, sister. It should."

I was wedged between the shelves and the walls. Hellida was

on the other side of the room, her great bulk not quite concealed by the merchandise. The door swung open. Light poured in from the shop's main room. I held what was left of my breath.

Fournier and her tormenter entered. I screwed my eyes shut and dug my fingers into the sawdust. The goon rapped hard on the crate closest to my head.

"Which crates?" he said.

"You're stealing from dangerous people, you know that?"

"The man that looked out for you is dead. You wanna join him? Where's the booze?"

"Any of 'em," croaked Fournier. "Just follow the bloody fist."

"How come this lid is loose?"

"I don't know."

"What the hell kind of operation are you running here?"

Another pause, another awful pause. I couldn't understand how, in that evil silence, no one else could hear the thumping of my heart.

"What do you care?" she said. "It's free liquor."

"You know, woman, that's the first smart thing you've said all night."

A cork popped out of a bottle. I twisted my neck and peered out above the crate. The thug, a squat figure in tattered linen pants with a gap between his teeth as wide as my thumb, tilted the bottle down his throat. In his hand was a stubby pistol, shiny with grease, from which Fournier could not look away. Across the room, the crown of Hellida's blond head peeked up past the crates. I tried to catch her eye, to make some silent plan, but she was looking the other way.

I tried to make myself smaller. I must have made some kind of noise, because in the moment before I disappeared, Madame Fournier looked at me, her defiance tinged with terror. With a word, she could have gotten me killed. Yet she kept silent. I'd told her she could trust me, and this is what it looked like. I tried to smile for her.

The ogre erupted into a hideous belch and smashed the bottle on the floor.

"That's more like it!"

The bottle's jagged neck rolled across the sawdust, coming to rest a few inches from my hand. I took it and gathered my nerve. If I shoved one of the higher crates off the shelf, I hoped, it would distract the ogre, giving me the half second necessary to get to my feet and bury the bottle in his neck. I braced my shoulder against the crate and was about to shove when the blast of the pistol tore through the air. The room vibrated as a body thudded to the floor.

It was like ice water down the neck of my dress. I froze, unable to move, unable to hear. When the screaming in my ears faded away, I heard the thug laughing in the display room. I raised myself onto my knees and saw Hellida across the aisle, holding a finger to her lips. She looked down, and I did too, and I wished I had not. Madame Fournier was crumpled on the floor, looking small, frail, and broken. Blood seeped out from the crack in her head and soaked into the sawdust. All that remained of her face was a single eye, still staring into mine, defiant forever.

I dropped the neck of the shattered bottle and tried to find some way that this was not my fault. I did not get very far.

A bottle sailed in from the display room, a flaming rag dangling from its neck. It crashed into the far wall and bathed the room in fire.

The next few minutes were a dream painted red.

The crates burned quick as kindling, but the heavy bottles kept the liquor from igniting. Hellida and I scrambled up, our lungs filling with toxic smoke. I wrapped my arms around Fournier, intent on dragging her body clear. But I slipped in the sawdust, dropped the dead woman, and had to reach for her again. Hellida yanked me away. I yelled something, or maybe I just screamed. Hellida screamed back.

"Leave her!"

I was still reaching back for Madame Fournier when Hellida dragged me into the showroom. The killer was gone. The fire was everywhere.

Have you ever found yourself in a room of flaming corsets? They burned brilliantly, scarlet, turquoise, lilac, and rose, licked by fire as tenderly as one cat grooming another. It might have been beautiful had I not been blinded by smoke and sickened by murder. I fell to my knees coughing, and Hellida helped me up. I made a feeble move to escape through the back, but she was through with creeping. She hurled me at the front door.

I crashed through onto the sidewalk. I fell to my knees, trying to suck down every ounce of air on the Westside, and heard Hellida land beside me. I had just stopped retching when I looked up and saw we had fallen at the feet of the man with the gun. He pointed it at my head, furrowed brow sweating in the heat of the fire, slippery red lips leering, tongue sliding along the gap between his teeth.

"If I may explain—" I said.

"No witnesses," he growled.

It was then that the shadows began to move.

They surged across the sidewalk, swallowing the light of the flame. They swept over the gunman, blotting him out like black ink spilling across a page, and then they came for me. Ice flowed up my legs, my chest, my heart. My body disappeared. I turned back to see Hellida reaching for me. The cold raced up my face.

I blinked.

When my eyes opened, we were in my dream.

Have you ever seen a photographic negative, where light is dark, and dark is light, and the people look like ghouls? That's where the shadows had taken us. As strongly as I have ever believed anything, I was certain that the inky world I had been thrown into was some kind of hell.

Hellida was frozen—skin, hair, and eyes the same muddy black, lips a corpse's gray. Her fingers brushed my skin, but I couldn't feel her touch. I couldn't feel anything at all. Behind her, the fire danced white, tossing gray sparks into the gray night sky. I spun around and saw the gunman. He was still clutching his pistol, as desperately as any child ever held a blanket to his chest, but he wasn't pointing it at me. He stared down the barrel at the woman in the street.

She was dressed for a night out, in a long black gown whose

tattered train dragged across the sidewalk. Its fabric ran down her arms, stopping just above the wrists—or where her wrists should be. Instead of hands, there were tendrils of thick white smoke—like that which heralds the selection of a pope—and instead of eyes, she had empty sockets lit by white fire.

She raised her arms, and smoke poured from her dress. It clouded around the gunman's legs, and he screamed silently. He pulled the trigger. One, two, three jets of soundless white flame shot from his pistol. The bullets punctured her dress, and smoke poured from the wounds, but she did not slow. The fog twisted up his body and poured into his mouth and blotted out his eyes. The pistol fell to the sidewalk, and I took it in my hand.

She took a step back, and the smoke retreated and again took the shape of something that could have been called hands. Before her kneeled the gunman. I thought he was praying for his life, but then he turned toward me, and I saw white fog where his skin should be and fire in the place of eyes.

Together, they came for me.

I pressed myself against Hellida's frozen chest and drew back the hammer of the pistol. The woman's fingers billowed out to brush my cheek. They felt like burning ice. I pressed the pistol to her quivering, indistinct face. I was about to kill her, or die, when the liquor bottles exploded, belching a ball of white flame up the face of the building. The shadows—and the awful creatures they held—were hurled back by the burning light. But then the flames settled down and the shadows swept forward once more, and the two fiends sprang right back to their feet.

I had a few seconds to look for a way out. I consulted Hellida's ashy face, and her blank eyes reflected the burning sockets of the creatures, advancing again. They were inches away.

I turned the gun around.

I ate a bullet.

I woke in Hellida's arms and felt her tears on my face. The night was dark, the fire was orange, and we were both alive. I could only laugh—isn't that what we're supposed to do when we're alive? She didn't seem to think it was funny.

"The shadows," she said. "I thought they'd taken you too."

"What did you see?"

"The night came alive. The shadows walked. They leapt forward and swallowed that man whole, and then they took you too. And then an explosion, and the fire went higher, and the night was beaten back, and you were here on the sidewalk, but the man was gone. I suppose he got away?"

Hellida had spent most of my life warning me against the dark. I had only laughed. There was no way to tell her what had happened—both because I could not stand the sight of watching her learn she had been right all along, and because I didn't need her worrying when, inevitably, I stepped back into the shadows.

"He must have," I said. "I blacked out. I had . . . I had an unsettling dream."

The smoke was thinner, the flames not as bright. The street was empty, and the shadows danced. I still held the pistol in my hand.

One bullet left.

"I'll need to consult my father's notes," I said once we reached Washington Square.

"Why?"

"I'm reopening the case of Alice Pearl."

"Oh, *flicka*. No."

Alice Pearl. That name. That awful name.

Even now, I know the case by rote.

On May 15, 1903, Alice Pearl made the mistake of walking home alone. It was just after eight P.M. when poor Alice, a secretary to a Times Square theatrical agent, turned off Broadway onto West Forty-Eighth Street. The shows had started, and the sidewalk was empty. An usher, sweeping the lobby of the Longacre Theatre, saw her pass. He later described her as a middle-aged redhead who gathered her scarf around her face to protect herself from the cold.

As far as the police could tell, she never reached the end of the block. Alice Pearl was not seen again, in life or in death, but the usher thought—he wasn't sure, he simply thought—that a few seconds after she passed his lobby, he heard a woman scream.

In this long-forgotten case, Virgil saw the first sign of what would become a Westside signature: a lonely person vanished in the night. He walked endlessly up and down Forty-Eighth Street, plotting angles to and from the Longacre lobby, scouring the sidewalk for some sign of the woman who had disappeared more than a decade before. He interviewed and reinterviewed Alice Pearl's family, her employers, her few friends. He pestered the beat cops of Times Square until he was barred from the precinct, until he had no one to discuss the case with but me. Night after night, he presented his theories. I listened politely, my answer always the same: "People don't just disappear."

How pleasant it was to be such a fool.

Now I would tempt madness and dig into his case files, to find out if his work had ever turned up examples of leaping shadows, of people dragged into the night, of a city where light was dark and demons killed with hands of smoke. That line of inquiry, Hellida would not understand.

So I said, "He knew every bootlegger in the city. If Copeland was moving liquor . . ."

"Then it isn't your concern."

"I have a case—"

"You have *nothing* but me." She pulled me close enough to see the lines of worry cut deep beside her bloodshot eyes. "You won't, Gilda. Please. Tell me you'll let this go."

"I will, of course I will. But first, I must have a look at his files."

The answer broke her heart, and I looked away.

My front door swung open as if it had been pressurized. Inside, the air was heavy. It caught in my throat like a rancid oyster.

"Do you feel that?" I said.

"Is someone here?"

"I certainly hope not. I've had enough someones for the night."

I reached for the baseball bat I keep on hand for nights when I feel like imitating High Pockets Kelly. Hellida lit a candle. We found no one on the first floor, and so we took to the stairs, hugging the wall. I went first, my shadow flickering tall and fearsome in the candlelight. At the sight of the missing bannister, Hellida shook her head and muttered something Swedish. I wasn't sure what she said, but it sounded like disappointment.

To be fair, most of what she said sounded like disappointment.

The first thing I noticed was that the nail that had been sticking out of the second-floor landing had worked its way out of the wood and was lying flat on the floor. The second thing I saw was that my father's office had disappeared.

There was no door. No door frame. No nothing. In its place was a curiously ugly print, a color rendering of Napoleon, dejected after his defeat at Waterloo. The emperor sits in the back of his tent, his maps crumpled, his generals ignoring him to watch the battle. They are still optimistic, but he knows the end has come. He slumps, knees spread apart, stomach hanging forward like raw dough sliding off a counter. I had no idea what the picture meant, but I suspected it meant nothing.

I slammed my fist against the wall. It was as solid as brick.

"This is insane," I said. "This is my goddamned house!"

"Oh, Gilda," said Hellida. "Gilda, I told you."

I hitched up my skirt, raised my leg high, and kicked the wall as hard as I could. I did it again and again, scuffing the paint and cracking my heel and doing nothing to ease the fury and fear and pain that sat on my chest like a boulder. I kicked until the heel of my boot snapped off, then I sank to the floor, too exhausted to cry. Hellida was gone.

At the base of the wall was a strip of bare wood, where I once sat on rainy days and peeled paint. I peeled a little bit more and flicked the chip down the hallway to land, silently, in the dust.

Hellida returned with a bottle of aquavit. She sat me on the landing and poured a stiff drink into a grimy teacup.

"To Marguerite Fournier," I said. "She deserved better than she got."

"*Skål*," she said, and I answered joylessly. The silence was filled by a vision of the single dead eye of Margie Fournier. I took another slug of liquor, and it helped not at all.

"I could have helped her," I said. "It was my intention. If I'd just had another few seconds, she'd still be alive."

"Or you'd be dead, for the sake of a stranger."

"It just happened so fast. Or it happened very slowly, and I was frozen. What am I doing wrong?"

"It's your methods, Gilda. Breaking into corsetries and having guns waved at us by ugly little men. You'll never get anywhere unless you buckle down."

"My father never buckled down a day in his life. You saw that office. You remember how he died. 'Erratic' was too kind a word."

"And you must be better, *flicka*. You must be better. Promise me, you will let this case go."

I couldn't give her the answer she wanted. She went downstairs. She took the cup, but she left the bottle. I took a long pull, stripped off my dress, and lay down on the dusty floor, one eye open, watching the floorboards run together toward the darkened horizon. Sleep escaped me. I relit the candle and carried it downstairs to the parlor to sift through stacks of newspapers.

The newest of them, the least yellowed, were under the windowsill. The one I wanted was right on top. I had spent two years ignoring it, certain I would never be strong enough for what it had to say. But this night I had already passed through death. What harm could an old newspaper do? I held the candle over the newsprint, and twenty-four months fell away.

September 7, 1919, was a Sunday, and the weather report testified that it was a beautiful Sunday indeed. Wilson pressed Congress to uphold his plans for peace and Congress refused. Several thousand coal miners marched across West Virginia, although no one particularly cared why. In New York, the city garbage commissioner introduced a new scheme to handle the overflow produced by the

Westside refugees. A headless body washed up along the Palisades, and three sets of lovers leapt to their deaths from the center of the Manhattan Bridge.

The mayor pledged to double the number of guards along the stem by 1920. Prohibition was debated, though it seemed impossible that it would ever come to pass. The city braced for the first bite of winter. On the Eastside, balls were planned. Plays closed. Wealthy men ate steaks, gave toasts, and were cut down by strokes. On the Westside, three men, seven women, and two children of unspecified gender were reported missing. Just another day in a dying city.

Page twelve. Sports. The Yankees battered the Senators; there was tennis on Long Island; and the Giants split a doubleheader at the Polo Grounds. Here was the thing I had been afraid of—the last box score I ever saved. I squinted at its narrow columns and tried not to stain it with my tears.

First Game. Kelly, 1b. Ab: 4, R: 2, H: 2.

In that little row of crooked type, I saw High Pockets Kelly, back from the war and an idiotic stint in Pittsburgh, hulking over the first base bag. He was my ideal Giant, with a dopey grin and a nose that looked like a squashed strawberry, strong arms, and impossible grace in the field. I watched him closely that day. He played a remarkable game.

It had been an awful summer. The once-promising V. Carr Investigations was collapsing into dust, as Virgil impaled himself on unyielding mysteries. He spent his days lying flat on his couch, counting the cracks in the ceiling and yanking bits of thread out of the carpet. Nights, he was away from the house, wandering the darkness trying to understand the cancer of the Westside. His cheeks were sunken, his beard gray and wild, his gold eyes shot with blood. But on afternoons when I could coax him to the ballpark, he groused with a smile, and the wooden seats were warm from the sun. The cheering fans blotted out the demons that whispered in Virgil's ears. At the Polo Grounds, he was mine.

That September morning, I eased open the door to my father's office and was hit by the stench of newsprint, spilled whiskey, and rotting food. Virgil sat up sharply, trying very hard to pretend he'd been awake.

"Get dressed," I said. "Stuff something down your throat. We're going to the Polo Grounds. Unless you have something better to do?"

"I'm going back over the Alice Pearl scene. There are new angles that demand pursuit."

"Like what?"

"I had a dream last night of Alice, slipping into a storm drain. It may be pertinent. I shall inspect every gutter on Forty-Eighth Street."

"It's a doubleheader. Please."

"Well . . ." He twisted the thick black ring that never left his hand. "If I leave now, I can probably canvass Forty-Eighth and still make first pitch."

"I'll come with you."

"And risk boring yourself to death? You get our seats—on the first-base line, mind—and I'll see you there."

The day was warm and the ballpark was full without being crowded. First pitch came and went, and my father's seat was empty. Between every pitch, I craned my neck, straining my eyes for him. The first game went far too quickly, a blur of clumsy play and unlucky hitting, and Virgil Carr was on the verge of missing an easy Giants victory when, mercifully, our boys botched a ninth inning rundown, and Boston tied things up. A few minutes later, the game came down to Kelly.

"Come on, you bastard," I muttered. "Strike out, you beautiful son of a bitch. We can't win yet, Kelly. I need a few more innings, you son of a bitch, you bastard, you beautiful goddamned fool. Please—wait for Virgil Carr."

He did not hear me. Kelly spun on his heels, nearly falling over backward as he sent the ball sailing four hundred feet into the sun-blasted bleachers of left field. I cheered with the rest of the crowd, but my smile was forced and I stopped shouting long before my throat was sore. My father had missed it all.

Second Game. Kelly, 1b. Ab: 3, R: 1, H: 1.

The second game went just as quickly, and the Giants lost badly. The only entertainment came in the fifth, when a deranged fan whipped a soda bottle at home plate, just missing the Boston catcher. The crowd howled for blood at this offense to good sportsmanship, but I understood how he felt. I only wish I'd thought of it first.

I fled after that, leaving the ballpark to those naive enough to hope for miracles, and rode downtown in a deserted elevated car.

I smelled my father's rancid cologne in the hallway, but his office was empty. In the kitchen, I found Hellida kneading a loaf of bread, pressing into it like she was trying to drive her fists through the table.

"And where," I asked, "is the great detective? Because he certainly isn't at the Polo Grounds."

She just kept kneading. Her eyes were fixed on the chipped white bowl beside the oven, where she kept her rings when she was making bread. In there, along with Hellida's three silver bands, was my father's ring.

"He'll be back for dinner," she said. "I'm sure."

It took two days before we were convinced he was really missing, that it wasn't just a bender or a new avenue of investigation in his ever-expanding, unsolvable case. After a week, everyone but Hellida gave up hope. "The Westside took him," she said, "and it could give him back." I could not accept that consolation. I assumed my father died a drunk's death—that he stumbled in front of a subway car, or slipped and drowned in the river. Perhaps he killed himself. He had every reason to. The *Sentinel*'s report of the doubleheader captured none of that, but I saw my father's disappearance in the box score.

I rapped Virgil's ring on the table and blew the candle out. I fell asleep wondering: Had the shadows taken Virgil Carr—and could I get him back?

SIX

My dreams were terrifying and indistinct. Images of bullets lodged in my heart, two mangled skulls, bleeding hands, and a shadow cast by a ship that couldn't exist. An army of ghouls with fire in their eyes, slouching up a wide white street. I ran slower and slower, until I felt dead breath on my neck, and cold crushed my heart.

I awoke before dawn, tangled in sweaty sheets, shivering and overheated all at once. In the light of day, it was so tempting to dismiss the prior evening as one long fever dream. Forget the death of Virgil Carr. Let the dancing shadows take care of themselves. Buckle down and wonder why Fournier's killer had torched the storehouse. Wonder where that liquor came from and who might have killed to stop it from going any farther. These were big questions—deadly questions—but compared to hungry shadows and people made of white smoke, they were tiny indeed.

It would take a special breakfast to wash that night away.

Had it been a church, Aylesmere's would have been the finest cathedral on the East Coast, but it was management's stated opinion that such glorious architecture was too expensive to waste on God.

Gothic arches, classical columns, and Byzantine gold mingled in a head-spinning collision of styles, combining to remind the little people who passed through the department store's gold gates that no matter how much money they had in their wallets, Mr. Aylesmere had more.

My wallet was empty, but I had not come to shop. I had come to eat. A colossal atrium ran up the middle of the store, from the first floor to the seventh, and Aylesmere's Café was perched at the very top. A breeze drifted up from the departments, weighted with perfume, leather, spices, housewares, and fresh, laundered cotton. Far below me, the marble was inlaid with granite, creating the illusion that the floor was covered with spikes. I stared at them, palms sweating, the breeze parting my hair, and felt an overwhelming urge to jump.

"The illusion is meant to dissuade unfortunates from taking their own life," said Mrs. Copeland, buttering a paper-thin slice of toast.

"Does it work?"

"How can we say? A few jump every year. Without the spikes, it could be more."

"They could raise the railing and stop the suicides entirely."

"But that would spoil Mr. Aylesmere's view."

Breakfast had been my idea. I didn't realize we'd be dining on a cliff face. I turned away from the drop and tried to focus on the platter of fried eggs, smoked bacon, corned beef hash, and brown gravy that I had ordered on Mrs. Copeland's dime. I could not shake the image of my body twisting through the cool department store air and landing on marble or on spikes or in the icy Hudson. I picked at a piece of toast and tried to ask some questions.

I have an eye for black dresses, and Edith's was as fine as they come. It was old-fashioned, almost Victorian, with sleeves that ran nearly to her wrists and a neckline that tickled her throat. It was the perfect costume for the happy widow, but beneath the intricate lace veil, Edith was skeletal. Her hands shook, clattering the knife against the butter dish, and when she finished caking her toast in fat, she took the smallest possible bite before setting it aside. I had no good tidings for her, and she had nothing for me.

To the news that her husband had been smuggling liquor, Edith only shook her head and shrugged. I informed her of her husband's dalliance with Madame Fournier, even quoting some particularly foul selections from their love notes, but her reaction was minimal. Though I held back the incident with the shadows, I detailed Fournier's unfortunate end, laying on the gore thick enough to scandalize the women at the adjoining tables, and Edith only chuckled.

"I suppose their affair can continue in death," she said.

"You knew none of this?"

"Of course not. The man I loved never existed at all. The creature that shared my bed for all those years—he was a demon. A born liar. Why should anything you have to say surprise me?"

"Have you any idea where he might have gotten that bootleg liquor?"

She might have looked amused if her eyes hadn't been so hard. "Do you know what we talked about? What dominated our conversations for the last, oh, six or seven years? The newspaper. He read his sections, and I read mine. He related some amusing anecdote from the business pages, and I laughed politely. I showed him a spread of the latest fall dresses, and he pretended to care."

"He never spoke of the Westside?"

"He never spoke of anything at all." Another morsel of toast. "There's no point in you continuing this."

"I disagree."

"He's dead. What does it matter who killed him?"

"It seemed quite important to you yesterday."

"Yesterday was a long time back."

"So put it aside. What can you tell me about this symbol?" I turned my hands over and showed her my gloves. Every woman in the café wore them—wrist-length or elbow-length, rose or sage, silk or kid leather—and I had not wanted to look out of place. I wore my mother's, brown and ugly, with the hideous bloody fist.

"It was on my gloves."

"Where else?"

"It was . . . this is a bit embarrassing, actually, but Galen had it, as a tattoo."

"Where?"

"His shoulder blade."

"How long had he had it?"

"Since Juliette was a child. He sailed for Jakarta and came home with that awful brand."

"And what did he tell you it meant?"

"It was a symbol of the South Seas. Some horrible pagan non-sense. I don't believe it meant anything at all."

"Then how did it get on my mother's gloves?"

"I don't know, and I don't believe I care."

She drained her coffee and reached for the gleaming silver pot. The last sludgy grounds slid into her china cup. She drank them, and her lips curled into a bitter frown.

"You should eat something," I said.

"So should you."

My breakfast had congealed into a foul, inedible pile. I set my toast atop the mess.

"What would you say," I asked her, "if I told you our city were this toast?"

"It's dry, tasteless, sickening. I wouldn't disagree."

"But beneath our city"—I pierced the toast with my knife. Egg yolk and bacon grease spluttered through the wound, soaking the bread and making my stomach lurch—"there is something else."

"Breakfast?"

"Breakfast is benign. What if I said that beneath our city were shadows and smoke and death?"

"I'd say you should stop talking rot, lest I withhold your next check." She dropped some money on the table, and we walked to the elevators, two women in black, drawing unwanted pity from everyone they passed.

"How is your daughter?" I asked, as the elevator glided down.

"How should I know?"

"Try to find out. This week is bad. What comes next will be worse."

"That doesn't seem possible."

"In a few months, her friends will no longer tolerate her grief. They will expect her to put her black dresses away and be who she was before. Be there for her."

"I shall," she said. I wondered if there was anyone to be there for Mrs. Copeland.

We parted outside the gates, and I was halfway down the block when a flash of lightning shot through my brain. I turned around, shoving through the molasses-thick Eastside crowd until I found Mrs. Copeland waiting at a light. I grabbed her by the wrist and jerked her up against the nearest wall. She was as light as tissue paper.

"Miss Carr!" she rasped.

"You lied to me."

"Release my hand."

"Show me the postbox."

"Have you lost your senses?"

"You set the glove on a postbox, you said, and it was taken."

"Exactly."

"But there's no postbox outside Aylesmere's gates."

"Then I must have left it on a fireplug, or a wall, or a streetlight."

"You said postbox. You were certain. You lied."

"What does it matter?"

"I nearly died for that damned glove," I said, and for the first time, I heard how mad it sounded.

I'd knocked her veil sideways when I slammed her into the wall. Her eyes were bloodshot, her lids as heavy and yellow as candlewax.

I saw how stupid I'd been, and my anger melted into cheap, ordinary shame. I released her.

"Why did you lie?" I said.

"There was no reason to tell you the truth."

"You were with another man."

"Worse. I was out looking for one."

"Where?"

"Could we please discuss this somewhere private?"

"If you want privacy, move to the Westside. Right now, we're on your side of the fence. Tell the truth, and quickly."

"When Galen stopped coming home at night, I began going out."

"To do what?"

"To get drunk. What else was I supposed to do?"

"Where did you manage to find liquor on the Eastside?"

"The waiters at the Hyperion Hotel. Slip them a dollar, and they'll spike your coffee with atrocious whiskey. For a few weeks, it was a lark. Finally, I had a secret of my own, and the hotel was light and beautiful and gay. But the crowds became unbearable. They were all so happy."

"So where did you end up?"

"I read about it in the newspaper. Merrill's. The *Sentinel* called it one of the most wretched dives of the whole Westside. Do you know it?"

"My knowledge of the Westside stops at sundown."

"The thought of venturing somewhere so vile, it terrified me. It made me sick. But when I dressed that night, I shook with excitement. I tried my hardest to look, well, cheap. I took a taxi to the fence and bribed a guard to let me through. He looked at me like I was suicidal. He may have been right."

"That was a stupid risk you took, just to get a drink."

"I thought you didn't fear the Westside."

"I'm learning all the time."

"I couldn't believe how dark it was. It was like a nightmare. Nothing to see, but the sounds . . . the sounds were terrible."

"And still, you marched on into the dark."

"I felt my way forward—it took me an hour just to get from the fence to Sixth Avenue. But I found my way, and they let me in, and I had—oh, Miss Carr, I had the most marvelous time."

"I'm terribly happy for you."

She didn't react to my sarcasm. "It was like I was another woman. Unmarried. Unencumbered. Happy, you know? The liquor was awful and the place stank of human filth, but the music was so loud, I forgot to be afraid. I wanted a man, the way I'd never wanted one before."

"Did you find one?"

"He was Italian. Handsome, in an ugly sort of way, or ugly in a handsome sort of way. You know how Italians are. He had a scar down the side of his face, the left side, and maybe it was the liquor—that awful, wonderful liquor—but I swear it was shaped just like Manhattan. He had the roughest, most wonderful hands."

"What was his name?"

"I don't know. Why would I want to? I hardly spoke to him. I was so drunk. The last thing I recall, we were dancing. I'd never danced like that before. And I kissed him, and it must have been more than I could bear, because the next thing I remember was waking up on the bench across the street from my apartment, with a spike through my brain and one glove gone."

She pressed a token into my hand. A poker chip, with a rabid dog in the center, and "Merrill's" in green letters around the edge.

Slummers. They are a plague on the Lower West, traipsing through our alleys, drinking our liquor, staining our gutters with their blood. I might have screamed at Edith for taking such a stupid risk or pushed her into traffic for risking my life on a lie, but the blood was receding from her eyes, and a smile was sneaking across her lips, and it didn't seem right to knock her back down.

The *Sentinel* linotype machine was as grand and twisted as the devil's pipe organ. At its foot sat a tiny man with an overflowing belly, whose eyes seemed to have grown closer together from the daily effort of staring down minute pieces of type. Those narrow eyes stared through Max Schmittberger, who had worked himself into a frothing rage as loud as the *Sentinel* presses.

"With two *T*'s!" he shouted. "It's Schmittberger with two *T*'s— just the way it sounds! You're a nitwit, you know that? A war criminal! You should be arrested, chained up, tortured, and shot for criminal negligence, for crimes committed against newspaperdom. You should be hung by your toenails, and your sinuses should be stuffed full of hot linotype lead."

"Don't they teach you cub reporters nothing?"

"I am not a cub reporter, you syphilitic buffoon. I have a byline."

"Then you should know that this is a rough and ready operation. An afternoon rag. We work quick, we do not proof. Any word uncommon, or longer than six letters, is in danger of being misspelled. That goes for the governor's name, and it goes for Schnittbergens."

"Schmittberger!"

Max attacked the linotype, an iron beast that had been standing before he was born and would remain long after he was gone. Three swift kicks left the machine undented, but tore the thinning leather on his right shoe. Rage seeped out of him; his shoulders sagged, and he could not meet the linotype man's eye. I took him by the shoulders and guided him out of the room.

"That fink had better be careful when he leaves tonight," he said, almost in tears. "I'll wait in the alley. I'll shatter his skull."

"Of course you will."

He wiped his eyes and saw me for the first time.

"G. Carr. What are you doing here?"

"I need a look at your morgue."

He smoothed what remained of his hair and stood a little taller.

"And just what do I get in return?" he said.

"The name of the dead man. Galen Copeland."

"Never heard of him."

"A modestly successful Eastside merchant."

"And just what was he doing on the Westside docks?"

"I believe," I said, lowering my voice to a melodramatic whisper, "that he was a smuggler. Moving liquor out of the Lower West and taking it upriver to god knows where."

"That's an expert way to get yourself killed. If it was liquor, that means . . ."

"Barbarossa."

"I may be stupid, lady—I may be real stupid—but even I'm not dumb enough to go after Rotgut Barbarossa. Not even for a spot on the front page. Not even for nothing."

"I gave you the information. What you do with it is up to you."

"You really chasing this story?"

"As fast as I can."

"Don't expect me at your funeral," he said, but led me to the stairs.

The *Sentinel* morgue was just below street level. A strip of frosted windows ran the length of the room. Their meager light was swallowed by the cloud of dust that hung in the air, as stagnant as old news. Max made a show of displaying his press pass to the stooped Turk who guarded the entrance, but the old man paid him no mind.

"Your name, miss?" he asked me.

"Gilda Carr."

"If you will be so kind, miss," he said. "Right this way."

He led me to a long, scarred table, withdrew a chair, and brought me all the clippings I asked for: whole lives reduced to wads of newsprint stuffed in faded yellow envelopes. Max lingered until he saw that no one was going to be impressed by him, then disappeared into the stacks. When he was gone, I popped open the first envelope and spread Andrea Barbarossa across the table.

Her file was thin. A 1920 item about gangsters expected to profit from Prohibition mentioned her in passing, as did a 1916 feature about the spread of vice through the walled-off Westside. In each article she was granted precisely one adjective: "ruthless." No further explanation was needed.

The longest article was the oldest. "Rivers of Blood Flow over Tenderloin," screamed the headline, which topped a column of smudged, miniscule type. It told the story of a rough night at Lasko's

Twenty-Seven, an old-style Tenderloin dance hall. There, at the climax of a floor show that could only be described as "infamous," dancer "Starlight Angie Barbossa" leapt from the stage, smashed a bottle, and tore its jagged edges across another woman's cheek. She continued stabbing until the girl's face was stripped to the bone, then stood over the poor, dying creature, fighting off any who tried to help, until her victim heaved a last breath through her ragged, ruined mouth and, mercifully, died. The dead girl was Vivian Pretzker. The motive was unknown.

"She should have known better than to come in here," Angie was quoted. "Not after she done what she done. Not when I was dancing."

Starlight Angie was arrested, but there was no mention of a trial.

In the narrow drawer marked "Co–Cr," I found a single article on Galen Copeland, credited in 1902 for saving a pair of ginger twins from drowning in Spuyten Duyvil Creek, at the mouth of the Harlem River.

"Water up here is too wild for children," said the captain, laughing as loud as a First Avenue fire brigade. "I was just going for a swim!"

I returned Copeland's clipping to his envelope. If I'd felt like wasting time, I would have pulled the file on Alice Pearl and read over the three faded clippings that had been pinned to my father's wall for years—"Vanishes On 48th," "Usher Tells A Tale," and the hopelessly brief "Police Enthusiastic In Search." If I'd felt like making myself sick, I could have pulled the file for Virgil Carr. Instead, I remembered the odd notation in Copeland's datebook. The scrap of paper was still in my pocket: "brass," scrawled out in Copeland's quivering hand.

The old bookkeeper brought me three heavy envelopes on the subject. An hour's reading taught me more than I needed to know about brass piping, brass wiring, brass cookware, brass bands, brass clocks, alpha brasses, beta brasses, gamma brasses, and white brasses. Brass was germicidal, I learned—totally resistant to infection, and that seemed true in a spiritual sense as well. In all those clippings, I saw not one reference to criminal misbehavior. Brass must be the most genteel alloy known to man.

"Are you happy, Hellida?" I said, rubbing my reddening eyes. "I'm buckling down."

I reached for the next envelope. I was struggling through an item on copper mining when Max dropped into the chair beside me and threw his feet onto the table. He inspected a handful of clippings and tossed them aside in disgust.

"Brass," he said. "Brass, brass, brass."

"You're getting the idea."

"You sure it's the metal?"

From his back pocket, he pulled a wrinkled copy of the day's paper. He slapped it onto the table, open to the city page. I scanned headlines—"Blazing Oil Burns Ten Men To Death"; "Banker Shot Dead By Masked Youth"; "Taxicab Kills Boy As Sister Looks On"—until Max tired of waiting and jabbed at a teaser for the society page.

"A party at Aiken's penthouse," I said. "Pictures inside."

"A. P. Aiken."

"I don't know the name."

"You don't know nothing."

He tore the paper open to the society column. There, in the penthouse of the Hyperion Hotel, a withered old man sat before the largest jazz band ever assembled on the stem.

"The man's a certified jazzhead," said Max. "That's why they call him Brass."

"It seems like a stretch."

"Better than whatever you're reading."

He was probably right.

He retrieved Aiken's file, and I paged through it without enthusiasm, learning more than I cared to about the city's foremost fight-promoting, jazz-loving, gin-swilling, white-shoed gangster. I was about to give up when Max pulled the clipping from the back of the stack, an artifact from 1903.

"A. P. Aiken Invests In Shipping Firm," it said—a short little item beneath a grainy photo of Aiken and his new partner, Galen Copeland. Between them stood "an old friend"—a "leading light of the NYPD," whose eyes shone as brightly as the medals on his chest.

"Say, this fellow's name is Carr, same as you," said Max. "Now ain't that a funny thing?"

SEVEN

The Hyperion Hotel may not have been the city's most fashionable, but it was certainly the gaudiest. Clumsy jazz poured out of its grand entrance, loud enough to disturb the sleep of the pigeons in Madison Square. A pack of drunks clogged the front steps, unsure if they were coming or going. Max and I hugged the left side of the steps, easing around the crowd. A man whose gut looked like it was trying to escape his tuxedo tried to climb two steps and instead went down three. He swerved toward me, arm swinging, his cigar nearly scraping the side of my cheek. I plucked it from his fingers, drew a long puff, and blew the smoke back in his face.

"My Monte Cristo!" he cried. "Boys, this damned widow snatched my Monte Cristo!"

"If you can catch it," I said, "it's yours."

I tossed the wet butt into the air. It spun, the glistening chewed end catching the thousands of white bulbs in the Hyperion's block-long sign, and fell through the gentleman's fingers into the gutter. Max ushered me through the Hyperion's famous swinging doors, the drunk screaming epithets all the while.

The lobby was decorated with all the subtlety of the *Titanic* ballroom. Cocktail-sodden couples clung to each other as though the floor were sliding out from under them. Men and women competed to laugh the loudest. In the corner, the four men—game, but untalented—of the jazz combo punished their instruments in an attempt to be heard. Beneath my feet, a carpet the color of spilled red wine seemed to stretch for miles. It was deep enough to swallow a baby.

"Where to?" I asked Max.

"Back there, behind the palm fronds? That's Aiken's private elevator. Takes you straight to the penthouse in fifteen seconds flat."

"You're a regular guest here?"

"Only in my dreams. But I read about the parties every day."

A redcap leaned on the elevator, a cigarette pinched between thumb and forefinger. He took a long, last drag and flicked it onto the carpet. It sank like the *Maine*. He was monstrously fat, with skin the color of raw kielbasa. He looked around, saw nothing worth looking at, and lit another cigarette.

"Just tell 'em your name," said Max, "and we're golden."

"My father's name."

There was a little bit of money in my bag. There was also a loaded gun. I could bribe the elevator operator. I could threaten his life. Or I could do it the hard way.

"Two for the penthouse," I said.

"Let's see the invitation."

"We have none."

He shook his head and dropped the half-smoked cigarette between my feet. It sizzled. A burnt odor tickled my nose. He lit another.

"Perhaps, if you aren't too busy, you could pass a message up to Mr. Aiken. Tell him it's . . ."

"Tell him it's who?"

"The daughter of Virgil Carr."

"I don't like bothering Mr. Aiken, you know. Not while the party's swinging."

"Please," I said, and there was enough hurt in my voice that the young man was moved. Wearing black had its advantages. He put in a call to the penthouse. It rang for a long time before someone upstairs picked up the phone. Through the receiver, the party blared like a packed house at the Garden.

"Virgil Carr!" screamed the redcap. "I said the name is Virgil Carr!"

There was another long pause before the redcap replaced the receiver.

"Well?" said Max, hopeful as a little boy on Christmas morning. The redcap sighed, shook his head at the lowering of standards that threatened to destroy high society as we knew it, and jerked his thumb toward the cage.

The ride was swift. Music echoed down the elevator shaft like far-off guns—intoxicating, dangerous, and impossible to resist. At last, truly hot jazz.

The elevator opened directly into the penthouse—a touch that nearly overwhelmed Max. A couple was leaning on the elevator doors when they opened and fell into the operator's lap. He pushed them back toward the party with a practiced shrug, and I dragged Max across the threshold.

The penthouse appeared only slightly smaller than Grand Central Terminal. A few dozen couches formed the party's main drag, where hundreds of the city's most beautiful drunks shuffled like the exhausted finalists in a dance marathon. Half the couches held coupling couples; the rest were occupied by guests who had given in to the need for sleep. The band was howling at the far end of the room, and there I saw Aiken, sitting close enough to put his head into the trombone. I snatched a highball from a passing waiter and began the long journey.

"The ceiling," said Max.

"What about it?"

"It's not there."

It was, but only barely. The roof was green glass, held up by nearly invisible latticed steel. Surrounding the bubble was a wide terrace, where a few dozen had stepped to catch their breath. The setting sun could not compete with the stem's blazing lights, which were corrupted by the penthouse glass and lent a jaundiced tinge to the faces of Aiken's guests.

"Ain't that just the most gorgeous thing you've ever seen?" said Max.

"All I can see is cigarette burns on the carpet, grime on the windows, and unidentifiable stains on every hundred-dollar dress."

"It must be awful."

"What?"

"Living in that sour head of yours."

"Why don't you go find yourself a story to report?"

"Here?"

"We just passed the water commissioner, three of Broadway's least reputable leading ladies, a pair of known killers, and half the starting lineup for the New York Yankees. Surely even you can find a story."

I left Max to goggle and found Brass Aiken slumped against the bandstand. The man had been pickled by good gin and loud jazz. He was long and bony, with a razor-thin moustache and lime-green eyes. His tuxedo was cut slightly too tight, and it strained as he rocked to the music, tapping his pipe on his knee to keep time. His eyes were shut. He was in rapture. He didn't seem to know he had guests.

I waited until the band finished scorching their way through "Tiger Rag" and tried to grab Aiken's attention. His head spun around and his eyes rested on me dreamily.

"You're the one who knows Clubber," he said.

"I'm his daughter."

"I wonder if you have a name."

"Gilda."

"Gilda Gilda. Gilda Carr."

I took his hand. Like a broken-down circus pony, he didn't object to being led. The door swung shut behind us, and the ringing in my ears began to subside. From the terrace, the penthouse glowed like a firefly's tail. I arranged him on a deck chair and lit a pair of cigarettes.

"Eventually, everyone comes to Brass," he said. "Want tickets to the fights? I know every boxer in town. Or are you interested in box seats to the new production of *Tosca*? I have friends at the opera, the ballet, and half the legitimate theaters along the stem—and almost all the illegitimate ones. It is within my power to fix parking tickets, trade stock tips, acquire rare animals, reroute highways, and set fire to tenements. I help those who ask, but I do not love them, not like I loved Clubber Carr. For him, for his kin, tell me what I can do."

"In 1903, you partnered with a man named Galen Copeland."

"With Galen? Did I? Oh, that's right. I did. His firm had run into some trouble, and he asked me to bail him out. I took a third of the company and sold it back to him a few years later, once he'd found his footing. Not a very interesting story, is it?"

"You saw him the day he died."

"That's not precisely true. We had plans to dine together. The kitchens here produce wonders untold. It was going to be a fine evening, but Galen never arrived."

"Do you know why he wanted to speak with you?"

"He'd telephoned a few days before. He sounded lost. Depressed. A man in that state can do all sorts of inadvisable things, including wallowing in nostalgia with old friends."

"Would you please stop whistling?"

"Was I whistling? I didn't notice."

He had been. Whenever he wasn't talking, he wheezed out a jaunty little refrain that cut through me like the wind in January. He promised to stop, but I wasn't sure he could.

"Is this really what you came to talk about?" he said.

"No. It's not."

A waiter sailed by and I relieved him of two highballs. I offered neither to my new friend. The white lights of Broadway shimmered through the gin like gasoline in gutter water. Past the stem, the darkness of the Lower West stretched out like a carpet. Above the Borderline, Van Alen's night-fires flickered on, one by one.

"You knew my father," I said.

"I loved him like a brother."

"Then what is the meaning of this?"

I bent my wrist toward him, like I was presenting my hand to be kissed, to show the brand on my mother's glove. Brass pressed his hand against his eyes and may have been holding back tears.

"Oh, Clubber," he said, "Clubber, you break my heart."

"What does it mean?"

"Truly? He never told you?"

"I'm beginning to think he never told me anything at all."

"What do you know of your father's wayward youth?"

"He was a street tough."

"A street tough! He was the greatest brawler in the history of the Westside. His arms were like sledgehammers. His eyes were blue ice. Every hood west of the stem lowered their gaze when he passed. Women threw themselves at his feet. He was a legend and a demon, and he gave it up for a shiny little badge."

"I knew he had a gang."

"He had a six-man army, the gang to end all gangs. We were nothing until he came along, until that night he kicked open the door at Pinky's, and the snow swirled in after him, and he screamed he'd cut every throat on Grove Street if he didn't get a drink of gin."

Funny. I had never known Virgil Carr to drink gin.

"He was a vintage Sixth Avenue lunatic. I doubt he was older than fourteen, but he was past six feet, with shoulders as wide as Broadway. He drank like a man, and he fought like a god. That first night, he grabbed us by the necks and hauled us into the street. Said we had a debt of honor to defend, that a clan of misfits from across the street had insulted all those who drank at Pinky's, and they must be destroyed."

"Why? Why risk your neck for a man you just met?"

"Your father had a way of inspiring people."

"I never saw it."

"You never had him standing behind you, club in hand, promising to crush your skull unless you charged. It was very inspirational indeed. Those other boys were doomed from the start. We stained the snow with their blood, and your father danced in the gaslight, and a magnificent legend was born."

Brass grabbed my wrist, tight enough that I couldn't pull away, and traced his fingertip along the brand on my glove.

"This emblem here, he drew it in the snow, and from then on, it was our sigil. 'Forevermore,' he said, because he was always talking like a knight out of some silly book, 'we shall be known from Houston Street to the Borderline. Every moll, every mort, every rabbit, every thug will crumble before the Seven Bloody Fists.'"

He had always seemed a gentle man. I knew, even as a girl I knew, that when he stepped out of the house, he changed into something else, but I had never really seen him as a killer. I traced my finger along the imprint of the leather brand. My father's bloody fist. The music from inside fell away, the lights grew dim, and I saw him fighting, a boy I had never known stepping out of the darkness to break necks and frighten children, running from something I could never understand.

"The Seven Bloody Fists," I said.

"He called us that because we were too broke to buy gloves." Aiken twisted his hands into fists, and the ancient cracks in his knuckles glowed red. "All winter, our hands were the color of a bad drunk's nose."

"Whose hands? Yours and my father's. Who else?"

He was whistling again, that same awful melody. I wanted quite badly to lift him by his suspenders and fling him over the ledge. He looked light enough. I twisted my highball on the glass side table, and the screech got his attention.

"Whose hands?" I said.

"It was quite a lineup. Several of our alumni went on to great things. Others never managed to escape the gutter."

"You and my father." He nodded. "Eddie Thorne?"

"A pathetic little man. Well, not that little."

"Galen Copeland?"

"A strange boy. Always unhappy."

"That's four. Who else?"

"I'm quite proud to say that I once battled side by side with the lord of the Upper West."

"Glen-Richard Van Alen?" I said, swept up again by that dizzy feeling of being caught in a coincidence too awful to ignore. It was a sensation, I'm sorry to say, that I was growing accustomed to.

"We called him Firecracker," said Aiken. "He liked to make things go boom."

"Two more."

"The Fists were a progressive gang. Coeducational, right from the start."

"Don't tell me." He smiled wide. His teeth were white in the front, yellow on the sides, and black at the back of his mouth. Good liquor burned in my stomach, and I felt that familiar, deadly coincidence tugging at the back of my neck. "Andrea Barbarossa."

"She was as tough as your father, and much more lovely."

"One more."

"Can you guess her name?"

"Not . . . it wasn't Mary Fall."

"Of course not. That porcelain goddess never strayed west of Washington Square. Our last member was an unfortunate woman who did not live to see the dawning of this most glorious century."

"Vivian Pretzker."

"Myself and Clubber, Galen and Viv, Barbie and Thorne and sweet, mad Firecracker."

"That's quite a group."

"We had fine times."

He talked, and he whistled, and he talked. Heists and kidnappings, murders and extortion, an endless recollection of impossibly vicious brawls. Through the film of nostalgia—which turned every ragtag street gang into an army, every chipped tooth into a shattered skull—I could see my father as a child. Not posed in a sepia picture or frozen in a memory, but as a gin-swilling boy, chasing every night into the dawn, brawling and screaming and setting fires rather than admit he was afraid of the dark. I saw that boy, tough and scared, and I understood how he would grow into a man, bigger and smarter but no less horrified at the prospect of going into the darkness by himself. Every silent dinner, every night he came home drunk or didn't come home at all, every morning that Hellida found him passed out in the dirt of Washington Square, he was wrestling with that young boy's fears. I understood, but I could not yet forgive him for being gone.

"It was Barbie who spoiled it," Aiken said, after too many drinks, and too many cigarettes, when the fine, sweet music streaming out through the glass had melted into noise. "That awful night at Lasko's."

"What reason could she possibly have for killing Vivian?"

"Now, Gilda, we have passed from friendship into the realm of favor. Explaining that tragedy will force me to reveal some unpleasant truths. Instead I will shake your hand and return inside where it is light and gay and loud. Thank you for the conversation."

To keep him from leaving, I asked the question.

"That tune you're whistling. That awful tune."

"Do you know it?" he snapped.

"No, and neither do you. Every time you run through it, it's a little different. You've no idea how it finishes."

"Or how it begins. But this middle—it's been running 'round my head for as long as I can remember."

"Is it a jazz number?"

"I don't know! It could be a waltz, or a show tune. Maybe a hymn, though god knows when I last heard a hymn. I whistle it for everyone who comes in here. No one can give me the name."

"I can." His face softened, and his eyes watered, like those of a dyspeptic being offered a glass of Bromo. "Before the week is out, I'll have the sheet music on your bandstand. If it's been recorded, the record will be yours."

"That would be a minor miracle."

"Precisely my line of work. Now why did Barbie kill Vivian Pretzker?"

"Oh, you are a kind girl, and here I am, about to break your heart. That night at Lasko's, it was freezing cold, with the snow blowing in through the cracks in the walls, and Barbie was doing her act. Did you ever hear of her act?"

"Only that it was infamous. The details have been lost."

"A shame. It was a unique piece of the Westside's cultural history. For the evening crowd, she sang and danced a little, and my that woman could not sing. But after two, when the slummers went home, she stripped, and it was legendary. She dropped her clothes without ceremony, like she was the only person in the room, and then she called for an oyster."

"Dear god."

"God had nothing to do with it. She'd crack it open with her bare hands and slide the meat onto her forehead, and then she'd start to writhe. She could shake that oyster all the way down to her collarbone, to her waist, down the inside of her leg, and onto the top of her foot."

"And then what?"

"She'd kick it right back up in the air, catch it on her forehead, and start all over again."

"That is vile."

"Maybe. But it was certainly unique. Andrea was halfway through the act when she saw Viv come through the door. As she told me later, she knew her by silhouette. Viv was drunk—Viv was usually drunk—and with Andrea gone berserk, she didn't stand a chance. Andrea jumped about fifteen feet off the stage, landed square on Viv's chest. Snatched the bottle right out her hand, smashed it, and that was that. The band never even slowed down."

"But why?"

"For Clubber. He was the greatest brawler on the Lower West. What else would two girls fight for?"

"Barbarossa loved my father?"

"And he loved her too, like fire loves gasoline, from the age of fourteen until . . ."

"Until when?" I said, so softly that through the noise he may not have heard me at all.

"Until he died, child."

"Virgil Carr loved Mary Fall."

"He may have. But he always loved Barbie more."

"That's not possible."

"Those gloves you're wearing. They were your mother's?"

"A gift, I think, from my father."

"A twisted gift indeed. Before she bottled her first batch of bootleg liquor, Barbie had a very brief, very undistinguished career in a leather shop on Seventh Avenue. The Fists were long finished then, and she sent us these hideous gloves as a token of better days. I'm not sure why she gave Virgil women's gloves, but if he passed them on to your mother, well . . . he must have been laughing at her."

I emptied my drink and slammed the glass down hard enough to crack the table. Brass whistled again, and I wished my father was there to break his spine.

"Where can I find her?"

"I'm not certain that's a wise course of action. What Barbie's become—she makes the girl who killed Viv Pretzker look like a saint."

"Where is she?"

"The best way to find her, as far as I understand, is . . . do you know a speak called Merrill's?"

EIGHT

An hour later, I was lost in the dark. Carla Stone's inexplicably popular New York guidebook, *A City Divided*, spends most of its 128 pages cautioning the reader against venturing into the Westside, where the innocent tourist is certain to be defiled, molested, abused, attacked, subjected to a fate worse than death, or—when euphemisms fail Mrs. Stone—simply raped. If a visitor to the city does find herself caught on a darkened Westside street and is unsure how to find the stem, Mrs. Stone recommends three possible approaches:

1. Creep forward slowly, feet always on the ground, feeling for obstructions.
2. Run as fast as you possibly can, in any direction that seems appropriate, trusting that eventually, you will get somewhere.
3. Scream until help finds you.

Bex Red and I had always laughed at that passage, but alone in the Westside dark for the first time, I was beginning to see the appeal of her third suggestion. I'd left Max at the hotel—he caught my eye just as the elevator doors were closing, shocked that I would leave such a marvelous party—and crossed the fence at Fourteenth Street, where Van Alen's billowing night-fires beat back the shadows as best they could. I followed them to Sixth Avenue and turned left into the dark.

What should have been a ten-minute walk stretched out into a nightmare. The Westside darkness was limitless, and in every pool of shadow I saw the one staring eye of Margie Fournier. The night before, the shadows had lunged for the gunman and then taken me too. Wherever they dragged us, I escaped by death. What would it take for them to move again?

I passed under a tree whose roots had split the sidewalk. Was it my overheated imagination, or were the shadows cast by that thinning moon beginning to quiver? I stopped and held my hand beneath the branches of the bulbous, overgrown tree. In my palm, the shadows pulsed in 4/4 time.

I lit a match. It pushed the shadows back and gave me a moment to breathe. I was in one of the nameless alleys of the Village, where my father had forged his legend. It was a sticky night, but the sweat on my back was cold. A shattered horse cart blocked half the street. It was surrounded by smashed, bird-pecked, rotting fruit. The scene was still, but the shadows were moving, and they seemed to be moving toward me. My match began to die.

Just before the light went out, the shadows charged, swallowing the sidewalk, the horse cart, the street itself. I pulled another match, but my shaking hands dropped the pack. I did not see it hit the ground. A bottomless black obscured the pavement. It rose, and my feet were gone. I fell to my knees, reaching into the dark for anything that might be a match. My arms and legs began to go numb.

I screamed for help, for light, for a friend. Carla Stone herself couldn't have screamed louder. I screamed until my voice broke, and the mounting darkness rose toward my heart. I screamed until I saw the fire.

Torchlight flooded around the corner, beating the shadows back and warming me right down to the tips of my fingers. It was a gang of children, and they were singing a comforting song.

"Benjy's Bloody Stump" is an endless chantey that has amused Westside toughs since before Clubber Carr ever cracked a skull. It was just getting to the good part, when Benjy's stump is severed anew. I ran out of the alley and found three dozen boys armed with spiked table legs, rusted knives, knuckledusters, heavy chains, and jagged lumps of twisted iron. The vanguard waved a torch, asking safe passage from the lords of the block, who waved them on from the roof of the disused pharmacy on the corner. They began to march away. In the flickering torchlight, I saw their standard—a stuffed cat mounted on an oar. The One-Eyed Cats were on the warpath.

"Cherub Stevens," I shouted, almost sobbing with relief. "Show yourself!"

"Gilda Carr!" cried Cherub from the middle of his pack of boy soldiers. He stepped out of the throng, saber drawn, beating back the dark with his smile. Beside him, bobbing and weaving, was Roach, who carried the stuffed feline with undisguised pride. "What are you doing out at night?"

"I'm going to kill Rotgut Barbarossa."

The boys greeted this with howling laughter, but Cherub pulled me aside, dropping the fearless grin of the gang leader in favor of a look of honest concern. It was the same way he looked at Roach when the boy faltered, and normally I would have bristled at it, but tonight it felt like a balm.

"You're joking, ain't you?" he said.

"Probably."

"I don't like you being out in the night."

"Join the chorus. Half the city seems to feel that way. Truly, I'm fine. I just got a bit turned around."

"Please, then, let me walk you home."

God, how I wanted to say yes, to take him by the hand and lead him back to the town house to shut out the city for a night and a day and a few nights more. It would be easy, with his help, to forget the glove, the case, the two dead criminals—but we both knew from experience that no amount of tenderness could wash away the memory of Virgil Carr. So I turned his lifeline down.

"Too much work," I said. "Could you spare a torch?"

"You scared of the dark, bitch?" said one of the Cats, a fat little thing whose face was in danger of being swallowed by acne. Before Cherub could smack him to the ground, I lunged forward and clapped my hands in front of the young wit's face. He leapt back, startled, and the other boys laughed some more. The warriors of the Westside fear nothing—except, perhaps, a grown woman.

"I can spare more than a torch," said Cherub. "Roach—escort the woman wherever she likes."

"But Captain," said Roach, his squeaking voice hardly more than a whisper, "we're on the Borderline tonight."

"We can spare you for an hour. The lady needs your assistance."

"Do you, miss?" he said, with a look so plaintive that I couldn't refuse him.

"I'll be fine with the light," I said. "Let Roach help you guard the line."

Cherub shrugged and handed me his torch. He snapped his fingers, and the gang got back into ragged formation.

"Before you go," I said, "there was a question I wanted to ask you. As a man blessed with a fine, clear tenor, do you happen to know any song that goes like this?"

I whistled Brass Aiken's dreadful melody. It sickened Cherub.

"I never heard that before, and I hope I never do again."

"Damn. Well perhaps you can help lay to rest another tiny mystery."

From my bag I took a soggy, squashed roast beef sandwich, bought at Aylesmere's that morning on Mrs. Copeland's dime. Before I could even ask if that was the one he'd been looking for, he shook his head, nearly as upset by the ruined food as he had been by the awful song. I was about to toss it to the sidewalk when I saw Roach begging for it with his eyes and handed it to him.

He took it with both hands, dropping the gang's standard to the cobblestones.

"Goddamn these boys," said Cherub. "Roach, you oaf, be careful. You'll get mustard on the cat."

He grabbed Roach by the wrist and marched him north, like a schoolteacher dragging a hurt boy off the playground.

"Thanks for the light," I called after him. "And Cherub?"

"What, Miss Carr?"

"Stay out of the shadows."

I meant it, more than I'd ever meant anything, but I don't think he could have heard. He waved his saber, and his warriors struck up another chorus of "Benjy's Bloody Stump." On the rooftops, the local gang doused their lantern and watched their rivals march to glory.

I turned south, feeling safe in the light of the torch, thoroughly embarrassed that after years of good sense and reasonably clean living, I had become afraid of the dark.

Merrill's was long and narrow, with sawdust on the floor and candles on the walls, most of which had burned down to forlorn wax puddles. The air was toxic, and the deafening Dixieland band barely had the talent to hold their instruments. I could have been at home, scanning old box scores or enduring a jigsaw puzzle with Hellida. I could have been asleep. But instead I was leaning on a dented brass rail, trying to catch the eye of a bartender who was either cross-eyed or blind.

"Hey!" I barked. "You mule—slide the bottle down here, and I'll pour a drink myself."

He was resolutely ignoring me when I was rescued by an angel in a fringed purple dress. Bex Red appeared at my elbow, kissed me on the cheek, and snapped her fingers. The bartender came in an instant.

"What's it tonight, ladies?" he said.

"Two glasses of rye," said Bex. She took a long look at me. I suspect I looked tired. "Doubles."

There were only two kinds of bottles behind the bar: brown and clear. Both were marked "Barbarossa's Special Reserve." The bartender pushed two large glasses of brown across the liquor-slick bar and waited for us to pay. Before I handed over the money, I had one more question for him.

"What happens when people lose things?" I said.

"That's a philosophical question. Beyond my ken."

"At the bar, I mean. Don't you have a box or something for lost items?"

"What'd you drop?"

"A white leather glove." I pulled out Mrs. Copeland's glove. "Like this one."

The bartender waddled away and returned with a shoebox. He dropped it on the bar and went back to his work. I dug through the box, finding a red beret, hairpins, garters, a switchblade, seventeen cents in loose change, a pocket New Testament, a sheaf of unread flyers from the Westside Temperance League, and no gloves at all. I pushed it back across the bar and sipped my imitation rye.

"Someone's out past curfew," said Bex.

"So these are the places people go after dark. I'd always imagined it . . . I don't know . . . lovelier."

"It's bright in here, crowded and loud. That's lovely enough."

"And what happens to the people who leave . . . who walk home alone?"

"Most won't. They'll stick till morning. It may not look it, but Merrill's does a respectable breakfast. Are you all right, fair Gilda?"

I wanted to tell her about the shadows, about the gunman, about the dead eye of Madame Fournier. She would have swept me into her arms and told me everything was fine, but I wouldn't have believed a word. I was too far along to start seeking comfort. I had work to do.

"Near enough," I said.

"Have you ever mixed the wrong colors together, and you try to add a bit more of something else to fix it, and you keep mixing and adding and mixing and adding until you're left with the sickliest, most unpleasant gray-green-brown?"

"No."

"Well, that's what your skin looks like. Do you want me to walk you home?"

"I have a date."

"With what lucky gentleman?"

"The back door. I'll see you this week. Tonight, Bex . . . don't leave alone."

"I'm proud to say I never do."

I kissed her on the forehead and set my empty glass on the bar. I pushed through the crowd, past the band, to the double-wide iron door at the far end of the room. There was no knob to turn, no lock to pick. I was looking for another way in when I caught the unmistakable odor of gin and cabbage that clung to the Fourth Precinct like pine tar.

"No customers back there," said Lieutenant Thorne, slumped against the wall in a broken wing-back chair.

"Edward. And I thought this bar was only for people who could afford to pay."

"I drink on the cuff. Privilege of the job."

"And does that job also grant you a key to this most impressive door?"

"Go home, Gilda."

"Not until I've seen Barbarossa. Simply unlock the door, and I shall leave you to your stupor."

"What do you want with her?"

"Galen Copeland was murdered for smuggling liquor. I believe she might be involved. I wanted to give her a chance to plead her case."

"You got any proof?"

"I wouldn't bore you with it. I'm much more tempted to take it across the fence and hand it over to a real cop. Or better yet, a Volstead agent."

"She's a dangerous woman to provoke."

"I'm counting on it. Unlock the door."

Thorne killed his drink. His face twisted up like he wanted to belch, but couldn't. When that discomfort passed, he reached down to the floor and tugged on an overflowing ashtray, and the door popped open.

"Cute," I said. "What happens if someone tries to empty the ashtray?"

"In this dump? They'll declare a national holiday."

The steps were steep, and they stretched far into the dark. I took the first step, and Thorne followed.

"I need no escort," I said.

"If anything happened to you, Gilda . . ."

"Don't pretend you'd cry for me."

"I'm not much of a cop, and I know that, but I don't want to be the one to let Clubber Carr's only kid disappear into the dark."

"What sentiment."

"Besides, it's a long way, and I hate giving directions."

I followed him down, far past the bend in the stairs, until I felt cool air for the first time in months. At the bottom was another door. Thorne's match went out as he opened it. The darkness was complete. I tried to remember to breathe. I followed the shuffle of his footsteps through the door, tripped on something unseen, and fell onto my hands and knees. Beneath my palms was something metal, long, and ice cold. He lit another match, and I saw that I was clutching the third rail.

"Nothing to worry about," he said. "No juice."

"This is the IRT?" My voice was hoarse, scared. Not my own.

"Seventh Avenue Line. Started it, I don't know, ten years back. By the time they finished, you think any one of them drivers wanted to work a tunnel in the Westside?"

"And Barbarossa moved in . . ."

"The day the IRT cleared out."

We moved slowly, staying between the gleaming silver tracks, picking our way over rats, dead and alive. The breeze, at first sewage-sweet, gradually became fuller, rounder, like baking bread.

I was happy to have Thorne in front of me. I did not trust him well enough to have him at my back.

"So just what brings you to this particular patch of paradise?" he said.

"Did he love her?"

"I don't follow."

"My father," I said, and I was surprised by how angry I sounded. "Did he love Barbarossa?"

"Oh."

"Well?"

"Oh lord, Gilda, I guess you could say he did, like an addict loves the needle or a drunk gets warm just looking at the curve of a bottle's neck. I'm sorry, kid. It's not easy, learning something like that."

It was like acid, straight to the face. Every time I stumbled, I felt the rage surge within my chest, rage at a woman I'd never met, who made my father forget my mother and took him away from our home. I was not sure what I would say to her when I met her, and that uncertainty took root and blossomed into something that might have been fear, or might have been hate.

My bag banged against my shin. One squeeze of the trigger—to punish my father, avenge my mother, and see how it felt to have a gun kick in my hand. The law would find no fault with me for gunning down a bootlegger—if the law even came to the Westside to investigate at all—and perhaps it would let Vivian Pretzker's ghost rest a little bit easy. I played the fantasy over in my mind a few dozen times. If she had put this gun in the hands of the man who killed Margie Fournier, the last bullet was meant for her.

The tunnel dipped down, and we came to a wall hammered together from old wood. On the far right, a metal door hung loosely. Thorne was about to knock when I drew the pistol. It was heavier than I remembered. I cracked it across his skull. He crumpled across the rails, and I left him there. It would not be the first time he awoke in a strange place.

I hopped across the tracks to the downtown side. I crawled

underneath the makeshift wall, dragging my belly through the muck, and reminded myself that stains do not show on black.

A lavender subway car occupied the center track. From the far side came soft pink light and strange industrial sounds—liquid boiling and the clank of a wrench on iron. In the dim glow, I could just make out the tile: "Christopher St./Sheridan Sq." A pristine station where the trains would never run.

Still holding the gun, I pressed my back against the subway car and crept around its nose. In the darkness of the tunnel, I saw shapes in the shadows, moving with the rhythm of breath. Surely, I thought, they were not people of smoke. Surely the flickering of the shadows was only my imagination. I put them out of mind and looked for the woman I had come to fight.

Running the length of the uptown platform were two dozen metal tanks, each slightly taller than myself, which bubbled and chirped and dribbled out endless gallons of bootleg alcohol. The stench of spoiled wheat nearly caused me to retch. A shadow flitted back and forth at the far end of the platform, roughly the size and shape of the still it was tending. A hiss of steam, a trickle of liquor, a long gulp—and the station echoed with a formidable burp. Here was Andrea Barbarossa.

I'd expected a bodyguard of ten or fifteen young soldiers, but aside from one man dozing at the door, she was alone. I peered down the sight of the pistol just long enough to remember that I had never fired a gun before, and that if I was going to start it would be good to be close. A bridge ran from her subway car to the platform. I placed my gun on it and climbed up. I'd hoped to sneak across the bridge and down the platform, to bury the gun in her back and see whether or not I could pull the trigger, but the bridge creaked under my weight, and Barbie turned her head.

"Who's that?" she roared, with a voice as wide and powerful as Broadway itself. "Who's that lurking in the dark?"

I held the gun at my hip and crossed into the light, and a smile exploded across her round, red face.

"It's you," she said. "It's finally you."

She stepped toward me. Before I knew what to do with the gun, she swept me into a suffocating embrace. She smelled of spilled liquor, mothballs, fermentation, and damp, like the shack of a fisherman who's given up catching fish. Soft arms crushed me against an even softer chest, as she buried my head in the folds of her infinite, amorphous velvet dress. Finally, she allowed me to breathe.

"And what are you doing with that pistol?" she asked.

"Let's decide together." The words sounded wrong in my ear. I felt every stitch of fabric on my body, every ounce of steel in my hand. Her awful liquor coated my tongue, and I felt like any choice I made would be fatally wrong. I forced out a few more words. "Did you kill Galen Copeland?"

She leaned back on the nearest still, mouth wide, teeth black, laugh loud enough to shatter glass.

"Kill him! Did I kill Galen? You darling girl—why should I kill that ridiculous old sailor?"

"For running liquor in your territory."

"You're not half the snoop your father was," she said, and I wanted to blast the words out of her mouth. "You don't know one-tenth of what goes on in the Lower West. You don't know anything at all."

I did my best to hold the pistol level.

"But he was running liquor?"

"Of course," she said. "What do you think I was paying him for?"

"It was your booze in the storeroom."

"Naturally. No one moves a drop below the Borderline without my permission. Galen and that little yacht of his had been shifting my product for years."

"And Marguerite Fournier?"

"Was just one of dozens of local business owners who have chosen to boost profits by joining my organization. She was a skittish woman, but strong in her way. What happened to her was a tragedy."

"It was gruesome."

"I don't doubt it. Now then—what is our decision? Are you going to kill me, or will you give me back my gun?"

"My gun." Such a little phrase, and yet it sliced through me as neatly as a paper cut. I was searching for a response when the door at the far end of the station slammed open and nearly fell from its hinges. The gatekeeper woke but could not get to his feet before Eddie Thorne stormed in, leapt onto the platform, and marched our way.

"You!" he howled. "You brat!"

"Quiet, Edward," said Barbarossa. "The adults are talking."

"She has a gun."

"Obviously."

"She hit me. She knocked me out. She snuck in here t-t-to—"

"Be quiet this instant, or I'll let every man in the outfit know you were knocked unconscious by a five-foot-tall woman."

"I trusted you," he moaned.

"I'm sorry," I said, and nearly meant it.

"I've known you since you were born. I thought we were, well, I thought we were friends."

"Oh for god's sake," said Barbarossa, "you pathetic scrap heap of a human being. Grab a rag and act useful. Still fourteen needs scrubbing. There's a bottle of raw whiskey in it for you if you make her shine."

Thorne broke, lowered his head, and reached for a rag. While Barbarossa sneered at him, I dropped the pistol back into my bag. I'd come for the sake of my mother's honor, but the way Barbie bullied Eddie Thorne reminded me that my mother had no taste for revenge, even against a woman who stole her husband's heart.

She grinned when she saw my hands were empty. She swept toward her private subway car, and I followed her across the bridge. In the tunnel, the shadows stirred again. I admit, I flinched at the sight. Barbie waved, and they settled, and I realized for the first time that there were at least twenty boys there, waiting in the dark.

The door to the car was heavy blue wood. Across its top, in tall proud letters, was written "Fourth Precinct."

"Did you steal this off the precinct house hinges?" I asked.

"I didn't have to. I asked for it, and they gave it to me. I keep it here to remind those rats who they work for."

She said it just loud enough for Thorne to hear. A tiny mystery solved.

Barbarossa's private car was as cool as a crypt. The seats and straps had been removed and replaced with two long burgundy couches. Scarlet curtains covered the windows, and wood as rich as Costa Rican chocolate ran the length of the floor. There was almost no room for furniture, but that hadn't stopped her from filling the space with as much looted treasure as the Westside had to offer. Stuffed into the corners and piled on the couches, I saw stacked portraits, family silver, Chinese vases, illuminated manuscripts, a six-foot globe, and a carved mahogany chair tall enough to serve as a madman's throne. Somewhere in the back, I saw a four-poster bed.

Barbarossa, walking noiselessly on her peculiarly small feet, glided toward the conductor's compartment, which had been replaced with the most ornate bar I had ever seen. She handed me a frosted glass of rye, so cold that it ran like sludge down my throat.

"Boulton's," I said. I hadn't had it in years.

"The good stuff."

"So the gun is yours."

"It used to be. It was stolen, along with a few dozen of its mates, off the docks by whoever killed poor, sweet, melancholy Galen."

"And the rifle that killed him?"

"That was stolen too, a few days earlier, right out of his office."

"Why do these guns work? Why don't they rust away to nothing? How the hell is any of it possible?"

"I have no idea."

"Where was Copeland getting them?"

"Somewhere upriver, where liquor is scarce and guns are cheap. A military base, perhaps, or just some awful hick town. He didn't tell me, and I didn't ask. He's been selling my booze there for years—just enough to keep that pathetic business of his afloat—but the guns are something new."

"Who stole them?"

"That, my dear, is what I'd like you to find out."

My hand twitched, wanting to pelt the heavy, frosty glass through the surface of that hideous globe.

"In the past days," I said, "I have nearly been exploded, shot, and burned alive. I have been menaced by shadows and forced to try on a corset. My father's home is vanishing, joint by joint. My client is an uncooperative shrew, my only ally a nitwit newspaperman. My clothes are tattered. My feet are tired. You want me to find your guns? Well, I want to know what in the seven hells of Greenwich Village is going on!"

That was when I threw the glass. It punched straight through Greenland and left an oddly Greenland-shaped hole.

"That was a seven-hundred-dollar globe," said Barbarossa, and for a moment I thought she might plant her jewel-studded fist right in my face.

"Not that you paid for it."

"No," she said, forcing out a chuckle. "No I did not."

She arranged herself on a chaise so stuffed with pillows that there was hardly room for her to sit down. She patted the seat for me to join her. I did not. "I loved your father, you know. We all did."

"I don't believe it."

"You don't have to. He and I had a fine stretch. Fifty years. He loved me, Gilda."

"And you expect I shall love you too?"

"You might consider it." She worked her face into something approaching a gentle smile. "Those guns are my property. It's natural I should want them back, isn't it? So why won't you find them for me?"

"I don't mind thieves, because I own nothing worth stealing. I've no quarrel with killers, because my life is worth nothing to me or anyone else. But guns . . . after what I have seen this week, I prefer the Westside with no guns at all."

"The quiet, is that it? You are a daughter of the Lower West, and you love every silent alley, every empty theater, every abandoned promenade. Guns are noisy, greasy, ugly things—nothing to the sweet, sharp beauty of the knife. We were better off without them, yes. You're right. But when Galen said he could bring them to me, that they would work? I'm hemmed in, Gilda. Van Alen to the north, honest cops to the east, the Volstead boys sniffing around every empty bottle. I suffered a moment of weakness. I told him to get the guns."

"I don't believe you've been weak one moment of your life."

"You see right through me. Your father always had that power."

"Mention my father again, and I'm leaving."

"I'll do my best, but he has a way of imposing himself on a conversation. Find the guns, that's all I ask. Take them back from the bastards who stole them, and then do what you will. Toss them in the river. Hand them over to those who are laughably called the proper authorities. Either way, I'll survive, but if those guns remain west of the fence, Madame Fournier will not be the last unfortunate to catch a bullet to the brain."

I parted the curtains and stared out at her long line of stills. I had spent years drinking the toxic filth that bubbled out of them. Even after a mouthful of Boulton's, I could still taste that sewage on my tongue.

The beast made her point well. A responsible detective would do whatever it took to stop further bloodshed. A sensible one—or a cowardly one—would return to hunting down roast beef sandwiches for an ungrateful gang leader. I was about to ask for another drink when I looked at the table and saw Mrs. Copeland's glove.

It had been in plain sight all this time, folded neatly atop an imposing leather-bound dictionary, but I hadn't noticed it through all the junk. Ivory white, immaculately stitched, the irises as delicate as spring, the glove as light as nothing.

"Where did you find this?" I said, and for the first time, she was rattled. Not frightened, not shaken—simply confused.

"That? Barman at Merrill's found it under one of the tables."

"Why did he bring it to you?"

"He thought it was one of mine. The brand on the wrist. The fool didn't know a thing about leatherwork. I was an artist with leather. Whoever made this was an oaf. The stitches are too small, straight, and boring, the leather too thin. It's a dainty glove. It wouldn't last a season. My gloves were made to survive."

"Then you didn't make this for Copeland to give to his wife?"

"No."

"What about this one?" I showed her the awful glove, the one I'd stolen, the troublemaker.

"That," she said with undeserved pride, "is one of mine. Older than you, and in much better shape. I told you, I made them to last."

"You didn't think it peculiar, finding a glove identical to one you sewed in the last century?" I was shouting. I wasn't entirely sure why, but I didn't think I could stop. "With the same pattern, the same color, the same brand?"

"Why would I worry about a silly thing like that?"

"Can I take it?"

"Why should I mind? It's only a glove."

"It could be very valuable to me."

An ounce of leather, and I could extract myself from my obligation to Mrs. Copeland. I could give her what she asked for, and absolutely nothing more. No answers. No peace. But I would be released.

Instead, I poured another drink, and asked the question.

"How did my father die?"

"First you accuse me of killing Galen, and now this?"

"I didn't say you killed him. I asked how he died. You were a . . . part of his life until the very end. Surely you have a theory."

"I always assumed he threw himself into the river or under a train. His mind was diseased."

"That's what I thought too."

"Until . . ."

"Last night. I saw the shadows come alive. I saw . . . something kill the man who shot Fournier. What if they killed my father too?"

"Oh, girl, don't be stupid. That's just superstition."

"It's what I saw."

"Then I'd be worried, because madness is hereditary. What do you remember about the day he died?"

"He was supposed to meet me at the Polo Grounds. Instead, he was on Forty-Eighth Street, going over an old crime scene."

"That's what he told you. That's always what he told you. Going to have another look for Alice Pearl. He was with me, child. Always with me. He came here, about four in the afternoon. He stayed until seven. He drank from this bottle. Clubber Carr's last drink. After he was gone, I could never find an occasion special enough to open it again. When I saw you, I knew it was time."

She handed me the bottle of Boulton's, half full and caked in dust. I swirled the liquor in the bottle, watching it slide down the thick brown glass, smelling it in the air and tasting it on my teeth. There were fingerprints around the neck. They could have been Virgil's. Why not? I opened the bottle and inhaled as deeply as I could. Boulton's Rye. It smelled like my father's smile.

"That night, he talked of a breakthrough," she said. "The empty city, the deadly night, Alice Pearl. He swore he'd unraveled it all, at last."

"How?"

"There's no point shouting. It was madman's talk. The poor man was gutted. When he left, I knew I'd never see him again."

"Then why didn't you stop him?"

"Could anyone ever stop Clubber Carr from doing anything he wanted?"

"But what did he say?"

"I'll tell you, dear, if you think it will help. And if you find my guns."

I was about to answer when screams came from the tunnel, north of Barbarossa's car. For a big woman, she moved like spilled mercury, pushing past me to fling open the door and shout for order. The noise stopped, save for one hurt voice, one moaning, silken, failing tenor.

"Up here," said Barbarossa. "Get him up here!"

Thorne and two of the boys hoisted Cherub onto the bridge,

blood in his eyes, a long, hideous cut down the side of his skull. His left leg dangled strangely, but he held his saber tight. He fell toward me, and I nearly buckled under his weight.

"Cherub, I'm sorry," I murmured, not sure what I was apologizing for, but certain it would never be enough.

Barbarossa dragged us both back into her car and helped me lay him down. She did not seem to mind the blood. She slapped Cherub across the face. He didn't stir. I wanted to help him, and I knew I could not. I wanted to scream, but I had no voice. It was like being trapped behind glass.

"Came in like that," said Thorne, from the doorway. "His boys with him, in worse shape than he was. Tell 'em, kid, tell 'em what you told me."

He stepped aside, and there was Roach. The stuffed cat dangled from his hand, and his face was pale beneath the blood.

"Three of us dead," whispered the boy. "The rest scattered. Dead on Sixth Avenue. Dead in the street."

Cherub moaned. Barbarossa splashed some rye on his face. He revived, and so did I. I pulled his hand to my chest, and there was a flicker of that smile. I should have let him walk me home.

"Gilda," he said. "Don't you know it's dangerous at night?"

"What happened, chieftain?" said Barbarossa.

"An ambush. On our land. Half block south of the Borderline, those bastards in their rainbow silks."

"Van Alen's guardsmen."

"They knocked us down like we was toy soldiers. Never knew bullets could fly so pretty. Like fireworks in the dark."

"They had the *guns*?"

"And whips and chains and everything else. At the first pop of gunpowder, my best boys froze in their boots, our lines were broken, the rout was on."

Cherub coughed, violently enough that his hurt leg slid off the cushion and crashed to the floor. He screamed like an animal caught in a bear trap, and I pulled him as close as I could.

"I was afraid . . . ," I said, honest at last.

"Stop. I don't want to hear anything about Gilda Carr being afraid."

I chuckled, truly embarrassed, and we tried to remember how we talked to each other when we weren't telling the truth.

"I just hate you seeing me looking so stupid," he said.

"This is what happens when children play soldier." I barked at Barbarossa: "Now how about some goddamned bandages?"

She gripped her lush curtain between both hands and ripped a swath long enough for me to wrap around Cherub's ankle, which was either badly sprained or slightly broken. He moaned terribly, and I cinched the bandage tighter, and that, at last, shut him up.

"Put out the call, Thorne," said Barbarossa. "I want every gang in the Lower West behind my banner. At dawn, we stride up Eighth Avenue to break that border down."

"And the One-Eyed Cats," said Cherub, trying to sit up, "will be leading the charge."

"You can hardly walk," I said, pushing him back down.

"Then I'll crawl."

"You're a moron, Cherub Stevens, but I refuse to see you throw yourself away."

"Three boys, Gilda. My boys. Dead for nothing. Blood demands blood."

"How many men ambushed you?"

"A dozen, maybe."

"Then this is no invasion. It's a scouting expedition, or a provocation. Don't give in."

"You heard Cherub," Barbarossa said. "Blood demands blood."

She poured two more glasses of Boulton's and pressed one into my hand. She smiled at me, and the panic in the room dissipated until it felt like we were just two women, alone in a boardroom, haggling over a deal. I drained the glass and savored the burn.

"Rushing into a war is a good way to lose," I said. "Wait two days."

"In two days, they'll have pushed us into the river."

"So fortify. Plan. Don't attack."

"When word gets out about this ambush, my boys will march

north whether I tell them to or not. If I don't organize them, they'll be slaughtered."

"One day, then."

"Why?"

"So I can find your guns."

This she liked quite a bit. She pulled back her shoulders and puffed out her great chest, and I feared she was going to sweep me into another hug.

"You're that desperate to hear what I remember of your father's ravings?"

"I just don't want any more children to die. Twenty-four hours."

"Clubber Carr could do it in twelve."

"You may not have heard, but Clubber Carr is dead. Twenty-four."

"Oh, all right. I'll rally the troops, and you go sleuthing. Bring me word by midnight tomorrow, or don't come at all."

She offered a handshake. I turned away, and kissed Cherub on the forehead, and left before he could tell me I was being a fool. On the uptown platform, Thorne showed me to a door that led to the surface. He rubbed his head where I'd clubbed him and tried not to wince at the pain.

"If you're smart," he said, "you'll stay home tomorrow."

"Thankfully, no one's ever accused me of being smart."

The door slammed shut behind me. I took the steps to the surface two at a time, exited through a grate, and took a deep breath of humid, sticky, unadulterated Westside air. Pink streaked the sky, and bleary drunks spilled out of Merrill's. I was exhausted, from the soles of my feet to the marrow in my bones, but I did not expect I'd be able to sleep.

NINE

I closed my front door, and a hunk of black metal crashed into the wall beside my head. In the kitchen crouched Hellida, panting like she had just won a gold medal. I picked up her missile—her treasured crepe pan, cast iron solid enough to take my head off if she'd had a less accurate arm.

"Where have you been?" she shouted.

"A penthouse, a speakeasy, the tunnels of the IRT."

She lowered her voice to a growl.

"All night I waited for you, in the window by my door, staring out into the dark. I saw your death a thousand times. A cut throat. Slit wrists. Your body burned to a crisp or eaten by the night. I have done this enough in my life. I will not do it for you."

"I didn't ask you to wait up."

"Bullshit. You take the bannister, okay. Your father's office gone—fine, that is your life, not mine. The condiments go sour, I buy new ones. We don't have the money, but I find it, because that is what I do. My coffeepot slips away while my back is turned? I say goodbye. I don't ask questions. I'm not your mother. I'm not even your housekeeper. I'm just Hellida. I'm just here."

She crossed the room and picked up her pan.

"Hellida . . ."

"Don't be sorry. Just get into your kitchen and sit down at that filthy table. I'm making you breakfast, damn it."

She lit the stove, and I emptied my bag across the table. In one corner, I stacked leather gloves: Copeland's, Barbarossa's, and Mary Fall's. That part of my investigation was complete. The gun I put back in the bag. From now on, I would be asking big questions, or none at all.

Hellida added the flour without measuring, whisked the eggs without looking, and didn't need to check to see the pan was ripping hot. She ladled the first serving of batter onto the skillet. It went straight through. The fire hissed out, and the batter flooded across the stove.

"Curse it!" said Hellida.

"What is it?"

"The pan—"

In the center of the pan, there was a perfect hole. The iron had been eaten away as if by acid. I know because she picked it up and showed it to me—only for a moment, because the pan was hot enough to blister her palm. She dropped it and fell to her knees, fist pounding the floor in pain.

I wet a rag and pressed it to her palm. I wouldn't let her pull away.

"Here," I said. "Under the faucet."

"It's fine. I've burned myself worse a thousand times. It's the stupidity of it that stings. And that pan. I've had that pan for seventeen years, damn it. This is no way for it to die. Damn this city. Damn this neighborhood. And damn your business, Gilda, because that is what's causing all this. You'll kill this house. You'll kill us both."

"I didn't—I never meant to make you worry."

"They never do."

"Is your hand all right?"

"Tolerable."

"Then get your hat. I'm buying you breakfast."

I stood her up. She leaned on the table, and she saw my display of gloves, and the pain fell away from her face.

"This is the glove?" she said, clutching the one recovered the night before.

"That's the one."

She wrapped me tight in the finest hug a girl could ever hope to receive.

"Then it's over," she said. "It's over."

Van Alen's bazaar loomed over Seventh Avenue, the only building in the city that could compete with the Westside trees for stature and respectability. It was less than a decade old, but after the fence went up, it aged quickly. Its floors buckled; its columns tilted and were wreathed in vines; its perfect white surfaces became impossible to maintain. Those grand men who built this building, one of the city's greatest wonders, were quick to throw it away. The Eastside abandoned Pennsylvania Station, and so we claimed it as our own.

Two of Van Alen's gaudy, ragged guardsmen stood at the base of every column, and a faded banner stretched across the building's face, promising "Safety and Bargains" in letters thirty feet high. Safety was a lie, and bargains didn't impress us. We had come to eat.

The station had no doors, because the bazaar never closed. The temperature dropped as we crossed the threshold, and we smelled the rich odor of rotting vegetation, sweating people, and stalls of food. A few hundred shopped on either side of the long arcade that led in from Seventh Avenue. Where travelers had once bought socks, flowers, tie pins, dime novels, toothbrushes, and handkerchiefs, a few dozen vendors sold the freshest meat and veg in New York. As much as I loathed the Upper West, I had to be impressed by the bazaar, where the produce was so fine that even Eastsiders were jealous. The trains came in every day and unloaded the food that kept the Westside alive—every morsel courtesy of Glen-Richard Van Alen.

"This is civilization," said Hellida. "This is life."

"You'd rather live in the Upper West?"

"I'd rather live anywhere than that awful old house."

"You love our house."

"No. Just the girl in it. I'm proud of you, you know? It's a silly thing to say about a daughter who isn't yours, but I'm so proud of you for finishing this case."

She reached out to wrap me up in another hug, but I turned away and tried to focus on something manageable.

"Where should we eat?" I said.

"It's been an awful week, really. I've tried not to let on, but my skillet? My coffeepot? And that man, that man with the pistol. I haven't been able to close my eyes without seeing it."

"I know."

"You'll get rid of the gun now, of course. We can do it together—walk over to the river after breakfast and hurl it in. I feel so fine, I could throw it to New Jersey."

She laughed, and I laughed, and I think she believed me. At a lunch counter just inside the arcade, we worked our way through a pitcher of boiling coffee as the chef turned a spit of pork over an open fire. We laughed at old jokes and made nasty comments about the people passing by and did a reasonably convincing imitation of two happy friends.

The fat dripped, hissed, and perfumed the air. The cook sliced a few generous slabs of meat, buried them under a pile of fried potatoes and blackened onions, and dropped the plates before us. We gorged. Fifteen minutes later, we slumped in our chairs.

"They do know how to eat up here," I said.

"So why don't we stay? Sell the house, or board it up, and come to live where people are happy."

"I'm not going to waste what remains of my youth squatting in one of Van Alen's hovels."

"There's no future below the Borderline. Here, they have food. They have the night-fires. They have men."

"I can't leave the house. It's . . . not now. But what if you left without me?"

"Never."

"I'd feel better with you out of the Westside altogether. We could get you a room on the Eastside, just for the week. Just for tonight."

"Why? What happens tonight? You're not going out again."

"I may have to."

"Why? Everything's finished. You found the glove. You bring it to Mrs. Copeland this afternoon, take her money, and walk out the door."

"There may be a few loose ends."

I slid some change across the grease-pooled counter, and the cook pushed most of it back.

"Westside discount," he said. "Residents only. Courtesy Van Alen."

I grunted thanks, and Hellida followed me down the arcade.

"Why did you bring me here?" she said.

"To mourn a crepe pan."

"What else?"

"I have to speak to Van Alen. The overseer should know how to find him."

She stopped walking and lowered herself onto the nearest bench. She covered her eyes with one hand, and for the first time in her life, she looked old.

"You don't care about my crepe pan," she said. "You don't care about Hellida."

"I don't expect you to understand, but there is a war coming."

"Oh really, Gilda."

"I just have to ask the man a few questions."

"And he gives you answers, and you ask more questions. And those take you all over town, and you keep asking questions, and you keep asking, until you're floating facedown in the sewer and . . . never mind."

"Don't you want to know how my father died?"

"I already know how. Look in the mirror, and you'll know too."

"He was a fool. I'm being careful."

"No, *flicka* . . ." She laughed and shook her head. "I could threaten. I could tell you come with me now, or else. But I know how you choose."

She walked away without looking back. I had no words to stop her.

I stepped to the side of the arcade and leaned on one of the grimy, perfect columns, breathing deeply until I was able to forget how I felt. The roast pork sat greasy on my stomach. I rejoined the crowd.

At the end of the arcade, a mammoth staircase swept down into the main waiting room—a bland name that did no justice to what was still the city's grandest space. Fifteen stories above my head, the vaulted ceilings looked as distant as the sky, and the room was as large and glorious and cold as any cave beneath the earth. Ticket windows had been replaced by a fishmonger, cheese shop, and butcher; the dining room and luncheonette overtaken by breakfasting young people who had come to watch the crowd. The main floor was filled with pushcarts selling things the Eastside could never dream of. Over a thousand citizens were working, shopping, and eating on the floor of that great, useless hall, and they did so without fear.

Management worked out of what had once been the women's waiting room, where ladies had come to avoid the leers of traveling salesmen on tall wooden benches that were almost like pews. The benches were gone now, replaced with a few dozen desks, where workers, mostly women, shifted paper, smoked, and yelled. At the room's north end was a frosted door marked "Mrs. Greene." It was locked, but not for long.

With the pick hidden in the palm of my hand, I had the door open in a matter of seconds. I eased it shut and attacked the desk. If I was hoping for a folder marked "Guns, Stolen," I was disappointed. But there was a stack of correspondence signed "G-RVA"—shipping manifests scrawled out in some kind of code. I was halfway through failing to decrypt it when I was interrupted by a woman in a smartly cut sage dress, with graying hair, tortoiseshell spectacles, and dark brown skin.

"Is your name Ida Greene?" she asked.

"Tragically, no."

"Then get the hell out of my office." She snatched the paper out of my hand. It tore only a little. "What do you want with my shipping reports? Are you hijacking melons?"

"I'm hoping to arrange a meeting with Mr. Van Alen. It is, and I cringe at the use of this phrase, a matter of life and death."

"I do not deal with life and death. I sell vegetables, and the ten thirty-four from Elizabeth is running late. That means I have a full contingent of receivers idle on platform three, very large men who carry clubs and chains and other implements too fearful for two ladies to discuss before lunchtime. If you do not leave my sight promptly, they will compel you."

"How do you manage?"

"I believe deeply in the value of fresh food."

"I don't mean the produce. I mean, how do you ignore matters of life and death? How do you find the strength to stick to vegetables?"

"For one thing, I ignore stupid questions."

From her desk drawer, Ida Greene took a silver whistle and emptied her lungs into it. Through the door stepped a hideous beast, with hairy knuckles and a forest of stubble. Across his left cheek ran a puckered scar, roughly the shape of Manhattan.

"Ugly," said Mrs. Greene, "remove this woman."

"Ma'am."

The beast named Ugly slouched across the room and stood awkwardly at my side, waiting to see if I would come quietly.

"I don't want to touch you," he said, with a thin accent that might have been Italian. "But if she says, I gotta."

"A smart woman would leave," said Mrs. Greene.

"Because I'm only half smart, I'll say one more thing. Barbarossa is on the warpath. I can stop her if you get me to Van Alen this afternoon."

"I don't know about war, girl. I just run a train station."

"And I don't bother with this kind of mystery, but for the sake of several hundred lives, I make an exception."

Mrs. Greene did not look up from her work. Ugly smiled weakly. I held up my hands and left peacefully. He followed me, an awkward step and a half behind, out of the office, past pushcarts advertising the last of the Jersey beefsteaks and the first of the winter squash, to the foot of those lovely stairs.

"Did you mean that," he said, "about war?"

"I did."

"You ever see a war?"

"No."

"I fought for Italy, in the mountains. I was—the word, I think, is 'sapper.' You know what this is?"

"Explosives."

"Trench warfare, you know . . . it's not as fun as people say."

He waited there, leaning on the railing, smiling at his little joke, waiting for me to ask a question.

"We have a friend in common, you and I," I said. "Edith Copeland. You danced with her at Merrill's. A wealthy woman, slumming. You kissed. You had the roughest, most wonderful hands."

"Oh no," he said, blushing through his stubble. "It was not that at all. She sort of, you know, she fell on me."

"She fell?"

"She tipped off her stool and knocked the drink out of my hand. She couldn't stop laughing. I took her back to the fence. It was very dark. The whole time, she kept laughing, laughing until her eyes were wet."

"Why?"

"She'd lost a glove."

With one of those gestures permitted only to Italians, he dismissed the follies of womankind with a single flick of the wrist. I couldn't argue. How stupid to fret over a missing glove.

"What were you doing getting drunk in Barbarossa's territory?" I said.

"Mr. Van Alen, you know, hates strong liquor. It makes men weak, he says."

"He's right."

"But sometimes, I say, you have to have a drink."

"You're right too."

"No, I don't think so. Mr. Van Alen knows best. He is a very great man. He, well, he has been good to me."

"Have you seen Mrs. Copeland since?"

"Ah, no. But then, I have not gone back to Merrill's. It is too tense now. More guards on the Borderline. Blood in the air. I know how it smells, before a bomb goes off. That is how the Westside smells today."

My god, he was ugly, with that long scar, those chipped teeth, that zigzag nose. And yet, hard to look away from. His fingers strummed on the railing like it was an upright bass. What song was it, I wondered, that was stuck in his head?

"Does Mrs. Greene work closely with Van Alen?" I asked.

"The bazaar is his great love, and Mrs. Greene is the bazaar."

"Will she see him today?"

"They don't tell me these things. They only say, 'Ugly. Meet me at the Thirty-First Street exit at eleven forty-five, sharp.' So at eleven forty-five sharp, that is where I go."

He ground his cigarette inside the nearest trash can until the flame was long past extinguished, and dropped it onto the trash, and left. Something in the way he walked away gave me a grotesque urge to curtsy.

11:45. That gave me an hour. However would I pass the time?

Across the waiting room, by the iron steps to track three, five old men with accordions and brass instruments wheezed out a jolly tune. I listened for a while, and tipped them well, and finally raised the nerve to subject them to my imitation of Aiken's strange, awful song.

"That's a dreadful number," said the man with the trombone, whose head was two sizes too small for his body. "Proud to say I never heard it before."

"I think I have," said the accordionist, who played with hands twisted by arthritis. "You got the opening right, but the next part's all wrong. And there was a bridge. A very strange bridge. It went, hell . . . how did it go?"

He tried it out a few different ways on his instrument, which fought him at every turn, and finally arrived at something that satisfied. One of the trumpet players recognized it, and they played it together, and for the first time, it sounded familiar. It tugged at the edge of my mind, some faint memory. For just a moment, I could almost remember the words.

"What's it called?" I asked. "What's the song called?"

"That I couldn't tell you," said the accordionist.

"You have to remember."

"It could have been one of those songs that didn't have a name at all."

I whistled the melody back to him, and he corrected me, playing it over and over until I had it down. It was not as awful as Brass had made it sound. In the hands of the accordionist, it was almost a lovely tune.

At precisely 11:45, Ugly stepped onto Thirty-First Street with Ida Greene, who scowled at the sun. Ugly deployed a Japanese parasol to protect her, and they walked west to Eighth Avenue, where a fortune in orchids sprouted from the pavement—rosy and rust-colored, bright yellow and pristine white. The street stank of flowers, as oppressive as a funeral home. I stayed half a block behind.

Mrs. Greene walked uptown, Ugly at her side, her gaze swiveling up and down like a general inspecting her guns. At Forty-Second Street, she climbed the steps of a church called Holy Cross, a freshly washed redbrick pile whose priest, I suspected, was more devoted to God than dear Father Lamb. Outside were a half dozen picnic tables, where men in shabby suits played chess, argued baseball, discoursed on the wonders of the female form, or dozed, head in hand. Mrs. Greene had to fight to get through the crowd. Every man she passed wanted to shake her hand or share a joke, and her easy laugh echoed off the stone saints who kept watch over the front door. Not even two blocks east, the fence was locked tight to protect the theaters of Times Square from the pollution of the Westside. I was certain that no one on the stem could be having quite as much fun as Mrs. Greene and her men.

She went on like that up Eighth Avenue, stopping at churches, flophouses, empty theaters, and disused offices. They housed men without families, children without parents, families with nowhere else to go. Ida Greene oversaw soup kitchens, primary schools, kindergartens, revival meetings, dental clinics, a midwifery, and at least a dozen produce stands that operated as satellites for the bazaar. Every person she spoke to smiled at her. Everywhere she went, she was beloved.

She turned around at Fiftieth Street and walked back the way she came. I threw myself into an abandoned Italian restaurant whose walls were decorated with chipped murals of Rome. I dropped below the windowsill, watching the rats doze beneath the Trevi Fountain, and heard Mrs. Greene and Ugly walking by. Peering through cracked glass, I saw them turn off the avenue. I emerged from the restaurant, wiped sweat from the dark circles underneath my eyes, and saw, to my horror, the sign above my head. West Forty-Eighth, backdrop for the disappearance of Alice Pearl.

I knew every crack in its sidewalks, every dip in its gutters, every rusted fire escape. I had celebrated birthdays on its stoops, ice cream dripping through my fingers as Virgil knelt on the asphalt, dragging his fingertips across the blacktop, seeking answers in the grain. I had not stepped onto Forty-Eighth Street since before his death, his disappearance, his murder. It was time to renew the acquaintance.

In the short block between Eighth Avenue and the stem, there were no businesses, no charity. Here, the street sweepers who kept the Upper West spotless did not bother to peel back the vines. I retraced Alice's steps, starting where she died and walking all the way to the fence. I pressed my cheek against the peeling iron. It was hot, and there was traffic on the other side. I rapped on the gate, but no answer came.

Had the shadows leapt for her? Had they dragged her into the world with the white night sky? Had one of those creatures turned the girl to smoke? I tried to see it happen, but my imagination faltered. In all my father's research, he had never turned up a photo of poor Alice. I did not know her face.

I dragged my knuckles across the asphalt's grain, unsure just what I was looking for. My fingers found nothing, but I smelled something strange. Before me was the Longacre Theatre, whose marquee advertised the last show that ever played there—a melodrama evocatively titled "The House of Bondage." The lobby doors had been stolen, and from the house came a faint, impossible breeze.

The breeze did not carry the Westside's rotting jungle stink. It smelled of hot dogs, hot asphalt, sweating commuters, and gasoline. It came from the other side.

I bypassed the lobby and made for the stage door. It was fireproof steel, but the lock put up no protest as I let myself inside. Before the door swung shut and trapped me with a theater full of shadows, I lit a match and pushed the darkness back. I shut the door and held still. The shadows did not move. Whatever dangers awaited me in the Longacre were strictly of this earth.

I climbed a narrow flight of rusted, swaying steps and found myself in the costume shop, surrounded by racks of gaudy gowns. I eased open the door to the backstage. Light came from the orchestra pit. I heard men—and it sounded like quite a few of them—working, grunting, but not saying a word. Another of Van Alen's charitable projects? What might it be this time—an orphanage? A leper colony? I simply couldn't resist seeing for myself.

I crept into the wings of the great lost theater. The stage was lit by three strings of lanterns that stretched all the way from the lobby. They wound their way through the seats, over the pit, and onto the stage, where a long, ugly gash cut through the peeling boards—a hole in the floor big enough for a man to slither through.

In the swaying lantern light, it looked like a pulsing golden wound. Here was the source of the Eastside breeze.

A bag soared out of the hole and landed at the footlights. A half-naked man followed it, climbing a ladder from the depths beneath the theater. More men followed, dragging their loads into the aisles, where the center block of seats had been ripped away, allowing an open space for the young men and children who opened the bags and sorted what they found inside. They worked in silence. It was quite a haul.

Crouched behind a crimson chaise, I saw oil paintings, china, candelabras, and jewels. There were bags of flour, summer dresses, textbooks, medicine, and enough sporting equipment to start a minor league baseball team. Everything was sorted, labeled, written down, and checked off. Here was the engine that powered Van Alen's charity, that clothed his poor and delivered their babies and fed their children and granted all who bought breakfast at the bazaar a generous Westside discount. It was an empire of theft that made Rotgut Barbarossa's bootlegging operation look positively amateurish, and all of it was overseen by Ida Greene. Trains can come in at all kinds of stations.

She watched from a box on the right side of the mezzanine, Ugly at her side. She smoked a cigarette, lowering the holder after every drag to take a precise sip of water from the glass at her elbow. Something in the orchestra caught her eye. She spoke, and all work stopped, her voice filling the theater despite being hardly louder than a whisper.

"That lamp," she said, and the man holding the lamp froze, sweat dripping down his cheeks and into his gaping mouth. "It's Tiffany. Set it aside. Mr. Van Alen will want it for his collection."

The lamp was placed safely at the foot of the stage, and work went on.

The cramps in my calves were becoming unbearable when the curtain opened in Mrs. Greene's box. Work stopped, and the men looked up in awe at the silhouette of a hunched giant. By the way Mrs. Greene bowed her head, I could only assume we had been graced by the presence of Van Alen himself. He spoke to her for several minutes, much too quiet to hear.

I left my hiding spot, darted behind the scenery at the back of the stage, and crept to the other side. If I could intercept Van Alen, I could warn him. I could stop the war. I could save Cherub, Roach, and hundreds of other lost boys. I might have made it too, but the flies were dark, and the stage was old, and the boards creaked beneath my feet. In an ordinary warehouse, where men talked and laughed while they worked, they would not have heard me, but Van Alen's men were silent, and the creaking board echoed all the way to the back of the theater. It was followed by an agonizing silence, broken by the terrifying whisper of Mrs. Greene.

"Is someone there?" she said.

Heavy footsteps came my way. There was no use hiding, no use fighting. I might have run, but those great beasts came around both sides of the scenery, trapping me against the brick wall at the back of the theater.

"Hello," I said, and one of the men belted me across the face, knocking me to the ground and opening a wound on my cheek that spilled blood into my mouth.

"You bastards," I said, and they did not respond. Their hands were calloused, but their grip was light as they lifted me off the ground.

"Really, gentlemen," I said, "there's no need. Mrs. Greene and I are old friends. She values me more than any Tiffany lamp. Set me down before I shatter."

The man holding my right arm, the man who had found the Tiffany lamp, gave a strangled moan. His head lolled toward me, and his mouth fell open into a smile, and I saw scarred gums where his teeth should be and a tongue cut out at the root.

I pulled as hard as I could, fighting to escape his sallow skin, sunken cheeks, and friendly smile, but his grip was like a vise. Mrs. Greene stepped onto the stage. She snapped her fingers, and the men set me down at the top of the great dark hole, the source of the Eastside breeze. I did my best to meet Mrs. Greene's eye.

"Who are you spying for?" she said. "Barbie? The police?"

I fished out my card case and presented a card with as much ceremony as I could muster.

"And what in the name of God," she said, "are tiny mysteries?"

"You deal in vegetables, not war. I am the same. All of this"—I swept my hand, taking in everything from the gash in the stage to the workers' horrible, mutilated mouths—"all of this is strictly outside my field of interest. I would not report you to Barbarossa, the police, or the *New York Sentinel*. But it is essential that I speak to your boss."

"Essential to you, perhaps, but certainly not to me."

"That depends on whether or not you'd like this operation of yours kept secret. I have friends at the Fourth Precinct who would be quite interested to learn of a tunnel under the fence."

"The Fourth Precinct is a rotted-out shell."

"This would be quite the coup for them. It would mean promotion, escape to the Eastside. I assure you, they would be happy to hear of it."

"Then it's better for us, isn't it, Miss Carr, if you don't leave this building alive."

"Please, Mrs. Greene. One working woman to another. I need only five minutes of his time."

For a moment, she considered it, but that moment did not last long. She snapped her fingers again, and my wrists were back in the vise.

"Chuck her down the pit," she said. "We'll see how she does in the tunnel."

The man with no tongue was not smiling anymore. There was a look of apology in his eyes as he dragged me toward the hole, my feet scrambling on the splintered floorboards, my heels unable to gain purchase. He felt sorry for what he had to do, and I felt sorry too. I gathered up every ounce of mucus that had oozed into my throat over that long, hot morning and spat into his open mouth. He was surprised—who wouldn't be?—and his grip loosened just long enough for me to wrench myself free.

I scrambled across the floorboards and grabbed the first thing I could find. It was, as luck would have it, a hammer, but I was not arrogant enough to think I could fight off a roomful of strapping, disfigured young men all by myself. I turned as I ran and whipped the hammer sidearm across the stage, like a third baseman throwing across the infield. I was aiming for one of the lanterns, hoping it would splash liquid fire across the stage and give me time to escape, but the hammer sailed clear through all three strands of lights, all the way to the far side of the stage, where it slammed into the lever that held the rotten Longacre curtain aloft and sent it crashing down to the stage, shattering the Tiffany lamp, and dooming any hope I had of escaping through the orchestra.

"Ugly," said Ida Greene. "Sever her head."

There was a gleaming silver fire ax strapped to the backstage wall. Ugly tore it loose and, with the smallest of shrugs, walked in my direction. I ran straight at him, and he lifted the ax over his head. I kept running, and the ax whistled through the air, and the hairs on the back of my neck stood up, anticipating the kiss of the blade. I threw myself forward, crashing into his knees just as the ax bit into the wood behind me.

He was on his feet quickly, but I was quicker, charging through the costume shop, knocking dresses down behind me to slow his pursuit. I clattered down the rusted stairs and burst into the heavy afternoon heat. I ran down Forty-Eighth Street, toward the East-side, toward civilization, toward the spot where Alice Pearl began her final lonely walk.

I threw myself against the chipped iron fence. Mrs. Greene and her men spilled out of the Longacre's lobby and ran in my direction. I pounded on the fence, kicked at it, screamed at it, until the little iron grate snicked open.

"The door," I said. "Open the door."

"No access here," said the guard, and the Longacre men came closer.

I jammed my license through the slot.

"I'm on police business," I said. "Deputized by the Fourth Precinct. Ask Lieutenant Edward Thorne. Ask your sergeant. Ask the mayor. But just open the goddamned door."

"Sorry, girlie, I can't help you."

"Open this gate now, you rat-faced incompetent, or I'll drag you through this slot nose-first."

The vanguard of Mrs. Greene's phalanx reached for me. I smelled their breath and felt the heat of their hands, when the gate opened and I fell into the Eastside. The Longacre men did not follow. On the steps of the theater, Ugly stood with his ax over his shoulder and winked as the gate slammed closed.

TEN

"I remember your father," said the detective. "His work was . . . inconsistent."

The Times Square precinct house was as crowded as anywhere else on the Eastside, every surface stained with sweat, the air pregnant with mildew. I shifted in the wobbly wooden chair and steadied my voice as best I could.

"There is a tunnel under the fence at Forty-Eighth Street," I said, "where mutilated men bring all manner of stolen goods to hand over to Van Alen. In a tangentially related but still quite important matter, a shipment of pistols has been stolen, pistols that work beyond the stem, and tonight there will be a war."

"Yes. That sounds like something your father would say."

His name was Shearing. He was blond and packed into his uniform like meat into a sausage casing. He must have been used to handling hysterical women, for he wore a smile that might have been comforting if it had not seemed so rehearsed. He had the glazed look of someone who wants to help everyone but has resigned himself to helping no one at all.

"I can take you to the tunnel," I said. "I can bring your patrolmen to the place where Barbarossa makes her moonshine. I can help you break the Westside."

"And what do you want in return?"

"Protection."

"For yourself?"

"For a friend." Shearing straightened the stacks of paper on his small, rickety desk and snuck a glance at the clock. "Why aren't you writing this down?"

"I've got two million people on this side of the fence. Two million people in eleven square miles. You think the stem is crowded? Walk two blocks east. It's the Battle of the Somme. Every day, we got four or five murders, on top of dozens of rapes, assaults, burglaries, and god knows how many crimes people don't bother to report. You hear what happened on Third Avenue last night? An inferno. Fire department was completely overmatched. They just let it burn. Three city blocks, right down to cinders. At least thirty dead, but they're still pulling out bodies, so that number'll rise. And you want me chasing shadows."

"Westsiders are still citizens. They—"

The desk sergeant tapped my shoulder. On his arm was another woman, with a young body and an ancient face, in need of an audience with Detective Shearing. I gave her the chair and headed south.

"When all else fails," my father said more than once, "return to the scene of the crime."

All else had failed. In ten hours, Barbie's war machine rumbled north, with Cherub Stevens and the One-Eyed Cats on the front line. I had done nothing to save them.

I crossed back into the Lower West and passed my house without going inside. I still didn't know what to tell Hellida, and I could not bear to be tempted by my bed. I was not just hungry for sleep, I lusted after it, as desperately as I had ever lusted after any Westside tough. Trouble was, I needed hours of sleep, and I could not afford a minute.

The charred remains of the pier stank like wet charcoal. One dock south, where the rusted trawler had sunk a few inches deeper into the mud, Copeland's yacht bobbed softly in the river. The deck was blackened on one side, whitewashed on the other, and peeling salt-stained gray in the middle. Wielding a paintbrush like a conductor's baton, Juliette Copeland attempted to reverse the damage. Her hair was pulled back in a sweaty bun, and she had somehow managed to keep from splattering any paint on her starched black dress. The sun was bright, but she did not squint.

"Oh god," she moaned, as tenderly as one might greet an open sore. "You."

"A few days ago," I said, "you didn't know this boat existed. Now you're painting it?"

"The coast guard delivered me a stern telegram, saying that if I didn't take ownership of the yacht, she would be impounded. I'm a Copeland. That means I will never let the government take that which is mine by right. I came aboard this morning, intending to sail her to the East River, and found her infested with rats, her lines a tangle, her deck peeling and scorched. I'll be on my way as soon as she is presentable enough to sail."

"You're not uneasy, working on the Westside?"

"I've never understood the superstitious attitude people have toward the Westside. An empty street is just that—empty. Nothing to harm you. Nothing to fear. Don't you agree?"

"I did, until last night."

She flicked her fingers across her paintbrush and found the bristles had gone stiff. With an irritated little "hmph," she tossed it onto the deck.

"I'd like to talk to you about your father," I said. "Our fathers."

"There's blood on your cheek, Miss Carr."

"I'm not surprised."

She looked away, scanning the horizon to make sure no one respectable could see what she was about to do.

"I may have some peroxide belowdecks. Come aboard and I'll clean that wound."

She lowered the gangway, and I made my way unsteadily across a yard of murky water. She sat me in the cockpit, my back to the wheel, and disappeared below. I felt the first tightness of sunburn creeping up the side of my face.

Juliette returned with a tidy first aid kit. She swabbed my cheek, ignored my whining, and bandaged the cut. Beside the peroxide was a flat pint of brandy. She cracked the seal and offered me a sip.

"I don't drink alone," I said.

"I hardly believe that."

"Even so. A toast, to two dead fathers?"

"Yours too?"

"Mine too."

We drank. The brandy hit her like a kicking mule. When she finished coughing, she came close to a smile.

"They knew each other," I said. "Your father and mine."

"That's not possible."

"Where did Galen grow up?"

"In a tenement on Sixth Avenue, just north of Houston. I don't know much about it. My mother preferred he keep those old stories to himself."

"My dad was born on Bedford Street. Right around the corner."

"What did he do?"

"He was a cop. But before that, he was a thug."

"Papa did not consort with thugs."

"Maybe not when you were watching. I'm learning that our parents got up to all sorts of things when we weren't around. Yours, for instance . . ."

"Yes?"

"He was a smuggler."

"And he was killed for it?"

"You don't seem surprised."

"I wish I were." Another long drink. Another cough. "I keep the company's books. A few months ago I noticed some irregularities. We lost a ship in a storm off Tierra del Fuego. By all rights, the loss should have sunk us, but just after it happened, a few of our regular accounts started paying off a little bit extra—just enough to cover the gap."

"The captain was padding the payments."

"Rather clumsily too. I wonder—did he think I wasn't looking? Or did he not believe I was clever enough to find him out?"

"Maybe he trusted you to keep your mouth shut."

"Or maybe he just didn't care. What was he smuggling?"

"Guns and liquor. What else?"

"Good lord. Good lord!" She laughed, hard and honest. I couldn't help but laugh along.

"What's so funny?"

"My papa, smuggling guns and liquor. This is a man who couldn't look at a painting unless it had boats in it, who thought boiled potatoes were the finest delicacy on earth, who enjoyed listening to marches, for god's sake. He just—he never seemed that interesting!"

"They have a way of surprising us after they're gone."

"If only they'd let us see how interesting they were before, maybe we could have been friends."

"Maybe we could have loved them."

"Instead of spending every night waiting on the steps for them to come through the front door!"

We cackled at that, harder than we should have, harder than we wanted to, until our shoulders were sore and tears burned our cheeks.

"A smuggler," said Juliette, several times, until she wasn't laughing anymore. "If I'd thought about it at the time, I would have put it together, but I had no desire to let such thoughts cross my mind."

"It's always easier not to."

"And now, because I took the easy route, he's gone." She took a long draft. This time, she didn't cough. She peeled a piece of blackened wood and tossed it into the river. It floated for a moment before the current sucked it down. "What was your father's name?"

"Virgil Carr."

"Virgil Carr." She clapped her hands together, and her eyes lit up. "Wait! Just one moment. I remember him! The cop, of course. The cop!"

"You met him?"

"He came to our house once, on Christmas Eve. This must have been ten years ago, or more. He was in his dress uniform. It was terribly stained."

"By that time, his standards had relaxed."

"I could tell, from the liquor on his breath. He wanted to speak to Papa. He was terribly upset. We were in the middle of dinner. I was shocked Papa even answered the door. I could tell they hadn't seen each other in a long time. Virgil couldn't meet his eye, but Papa greeted him without judgment, without rage."

"Was that unusual for him?"

"He loathed drunks and could not abide men who let their emotions get the best of them. I expected him to turn your father out, but he welcomed him inside, fixed him a plate of food, and brought him into his office. Mother and I were stunned."

"Did Virgil talk?"

"He said . . . he said something odd. 'They're all gone.' Said that several times. It was more than a drunk's rambling. There was something about his tone of voice that sliced right through me. He sounded empty."

"He was."

"They talked for fifteen or twenty minutes. When they came out of the office, your father stood straight. They shook hands, and Papa—he looked at him with real warmth. I'd never seen that from him. It made me jealous, even angry. Your father didn't notice, but Papa slipped some money into his pocket as he was walking out the door. It couldn't have been much. Father was never very generous, even at Christmastime."

I remembered that Christmas. It must have been 1910 or '11—when he was doing everything in his power to turn the department against him. He came home late that night, singing carols, a bag of sloppily wrapped presents in his arms. Even then, I'd wondered where he'd gotten the money. A tiny mystery solved, ten years late.

"And there was another time," she said. "He came by the office."

"When?"

"Last summer."

"He was dead last summer."

"Then it must have been the year before. It was summer, though—I remember having the windows open. Your father burst through our door like an artillery shell and demanded Galen Copeland. I explained that an ill-mannered man, especially one dressed as he was, had no business with my father. I was about to throw him out when Papa opened his door and waved Virgil in."

"Did you hear what they talked about?"

"No. But when Virgil left, Papa was the color of this whitewash."

"You don't, by any chance, remember the date?"

"The office was empty, so it must have been a weekend, but that's all I know."

"He died on a Sunday. That could have been the day."

"I heard one word. Your father shouted it, with venom. 'Barbarossa.' Does it mean anything to you?"

She fixed her eyes on me. Even softened by the liquor, her look was hard enough to cut. For no reason I could think of, I decided to lie.

"No," I said. "I don't recognize the name."

She handed me the bottle. I drained what little was left and hurled it into the river.

"Does it get easier," she said, "having him gone?"

"It changes. In a year, there will be days when you don't think of him at all."

"Something to look forward to."

She turned away from me, shielding her eyes against the sun, and I had the terrible sensation that she was going to cry.

"What's your happiest memory of your father?" I asked.

"I don't know that there are any happy ones to choose from. He was so seldom home. When I was a girl, a trip might take him around the world for a year or more. When he returned, he'd stay with us four or five days, then be gone again. It's like he thought he was some kind of old-time whaler, rather than a very minor merchant. There was no reason for him to be gone so much, or for so long, but it was the only way he would live. He didn't love us, I finally decided, or he loved the water more."

"There must have been one good day."

It took some prodding, but she eventually produced a happy memory. A birthday party where Galen surprised her, swept the little girl off her feet and took her sailing all around the harbor, to watch the sunset on the banks of Liberty Island. Or perhaps it was Coney Island. I can't be sure. By that point, the brandy, the sun, and the rocking of the boat had drained every ounce of pain right out of my shoulders, and I was half asleep. She was too. We traded stories like that for a while, daydreaming about good days that hadn't seemed so good at the time, but were now all we had left.

It was nearly dark when I left her. She said she was going to sleep on the boat, and no matter how strongly I warned her against the dark, she only laughed, and I laughed too.

The shadows were long, and I did not hide from them. A last burst of energy caught me as I crossed the railroad tracks, caught hold with enough force that I forgot to be afraid. I had just five hours to stop a war, and I knew I would never make it. Let Barbie and Van Alen bleed each other dry across the Borderline. I'd find some other way to keep Cherub off the front lines. I'd tie him to a telephone pole or drag him back to my house by his belt, throw him into bed, and hold him there until the city burned to the ground and was born anew. I danced through the shadows, taunting them to take me. They didn't have the nerve.

I was crossing Hudson Street when I started to sing—gibberish or some half-remembered nursery rhyme. I was about to strike up the second verse when cold snaked down the back of my arm. I slapped at it. My hand hit nothing. The skin of my arm did not even sting. Ice washed up my legs. In an instant, the flesh was numb. I whipped around. There was nothing there. I tried to shake off the numbness and keep walking, but my legs would not cooperate. I slipped down to one knee. In the corner of my eye, the shadows darted toward me, eating up the sidewalk a few inches at a time. My throat opened in an animal scream.

I felt a hand on my neck, and the day turned black.

I awoke in a coffin. My arms were crossed on my chest, tight enough that I could hardly breathe. I tried to control my breathing, tried to keep from screaming, tried not to scratch my nails bloody tearing through the velvet-lined lid. It did not work. I was in the dark, with a splitting headache and a howling fear that if I wasn't dead yet, I would be soon. I screamed until my voice broke, and then lay quiet.

The coffin swayed slightly, which meant I was not yet buried, but merely on my way. I could not find my purse, and the pistol it contained, but a few minutes' agonized movement brought my hand to my hip, where I kept my pouch of burglar's tools. I inched out the tiny hammer and chisel and went to work on the wood.

I held the chisel over my right eye and pulled the hammer back along my cheek. The chisel tore through the lining and bit into the cheap, unfinished pine.

As I worked, I sweated. I breathed harder, and the air turned foul. I grew weak and wanted desperately to sleep but kept going as the muscles in my forearms burned with strange exertion and the wood dust collected in my eye sockets. I closed my eyes. There was nothing to see, anyway.

My hands sweated, and my grip weakened. After a particularly vigorous hammer blow—I must have drawn it back nearly three inches—the chisel slipped out of my fingers and was lost in the dark. I did not flinch, and I did not panic. I was finished screaming. I rested the hammer on my face and felt along my neck until I found the escaped chisel, and I started again.

I don't know how long it took to break through the wood. Perhaps twenty minutes? It felt like a month. At last, the chisel sank through the top of the box, and a few breaths of night air trickled in. For a few minutes, I rested and tried to hear the world outside.

I heard the high, hard tapping of hooves on pavement and

couldn't help but smile at the thought of a horse-drawn hearse. The villains of the Westside love tradition.

Fragments of conversation slipped in from outside, achingly ordinary chatter about music classes and boxing and when will the damn summer end. It was so wonderfully ordinary. We must have passed onto the Eastside. I heard tinny music, cheap laughter, and two children having a vicious argument about whether the Giants would beat the Yanks in the World Series. The season ends tomorrow, I realized. I should have gone to a game.

At an intersection, a busker tortured a saw into something approaching music. It took a few bars before I realized that he was playing the song that haunted Brass Aiken. I pounded on the side of the coffin.

"What is it called?" I shouted. "What is that damned song called?"

He didn't answer. The hearse pulled away, the music faded into nothing, and it occurred to me that it might be the last song I heard before I died.

Where would I be interred? Some little family plot near Second Avenue? One of the new cities of the dead that sprawled across Queens? Or would I rate a place in one of the grand old vaults of Green-Wood? I wondered how they would mark my grave, and if Hellida would have any way to find it. She would feel cheated if she never got a chance to deliver that final heartbroken reminder that she had been right all along.

I wrapped my fist around the hammer and attacked the hole in the wood. Sawdust filled my mouth, but I did not let the coughing fit slow my arm. Soon the hole was big enough for my fingers, and then my fist. I pushed my arm through the jagged wood. I could not find the latch. The hearse stopped moving. I yanked my arm back inside, tensed my legs, and clutched the hammer. The door opened, and the coffin slid out of the trunk and thudded painfully to the ground.

"My coffin!" cried the driver. "You crazy girl—what have you done to my coffin?"

The lid creaked open, and I saw my captor: the man called Ugly, without his ax. He smiled at me, the guarded grin of a man who has just loosed a starving tiger. I pounced.

It does not take a big hammer to break a kidnapper's nose. He fell backward into the dirt, clutching his face, blood spurting through his fingers. I stepped back, unsteady on cramping legs, and he charged, head down and feet wobbling. I clipped the side of his head, and he staggered off to the right. I shook out my legs, looked to the south, and saw we were certainly not on the Eastside.

We stood on the heights of Upper Manhattan, at the foot of a lighthouse whose double beam swept in a slow circle, throwing light across the river. Below me were two cities: one decked out in gaudy white, the other far more beautiful in muted orange. The happy people I had heard talking outside the hearse were not East-siders stepped out of their crowded tenements to escape the heat, but citizens of the Upper West, who stared down the new moon without fear, shielded by the glow of Van Alen's night-fires, which burned at every intersection from here to the Borderline. The smoke was heavy above Manhattan.

My kidnapper charged again, but not in a straight line. He was disoriented, and he would have missed me by two feet if I hadn't stuck my arm out to stop him. His throat crashed into it, and his legs went out from under him.

"You awful girl," he rasped. "You trying to kill me?"

"I'd be within my rights. If you knew how to swing an ax, I'd have been in real trouble this afternoon."

"Of course I know how to swing an ax. I missed on purpose."

"You lie."

"I let you escape."

"Then why," I said, pressing my foot down on his throat, "did you bring me here?"

"To see Van Alen. The boss. He needs to hear what you have to say. I don't want to see another war."

"I would have accepted an invitation, you know. I thought I'd been buried alive!"

"Mrs. Greene wouldn't have stood for it. If she'd seen you, it would have meant your neck."

I kicked his ribs a few times—just enough to hear him say he was sorry—and then I helped him up. He was blushing again and could not meet my eye.

"What's your right name, Ugly?" I said.

"Furio La Rocca."

"Ugly suits you better. Where's my purse?"

"You don't need it."

"A woman has a right to freshen up after she's been brought back from the dead."

My bag was in the trunk of the hearse, beside the coffin, snuggled up alongside his ax. He handed it over with a look like he wanted to say something but knew better. The weight of the bag told me the gun was still inside.

He opened the door to the lighthouse, and I climbed alone. The steps were iron, steep, and far too numerous. I counted the steps, damning each one, and yearned for a tiny mystery. If I survived this suicidal nonsense, I promised myself, I would find the most insignificant case the Westside had to offer. No politics, no blood, no coffins, no shadows. Somewhere below Fourteenth Street, there must be some little girl who's lost her cat. Her I could save.

Before I summited the staircase, I smelled the fire. It was grease, burning dirty. Van Alen was where I had expected him, leaning on his railing, staring at the lights below. Beneath the thick black hair that covered nearly every inch of his body, his skin was tallow white.

"Shut the door," he said. "You'll let out the light."

That did not seem possible. Candles burned on every surface, and at least two dozen lanterns dangled from the ceiling. In the center of the room, steps led up to the platform that held the great light that grinded ceaselessly against the dark. When its blinding beam passed, I saw the room had a second ceiling—a wavering mat of black smoke.

"Hello, Firecracker."

"Call me Glen-Richard," he said, relighting the candles that had gone out when I opened the door. "No, no. Call me Dick. Something to drink?"

"A glass of rye would be a welcome sight."

"I don't keep liquor here. Takes a sharp eye to keep the flame. But I'll brew you a cup of tea."

Somewhere between candles, I found someplace to sit. Van Alen was old, but he was gigantic. He wore an apron the size of my kitchen table, and in his hands, the cast-iron kettle looked the size of a tennis ball. He moved slowly, not with the trembling agony of an old man, but with the care that comes from a lifetime of being too big for this world. He set a chipped porcelain teacup down in front of me. The tea was green as sulfur and stank like a swamp. I left it alone, wondering if it would eat through the cup.

"My Italian boy said something about a war," he said, in a low, rough whisper.

"Barbarossa feels she has been provoked. She's called every son of the Lower West to her banner."

"You think I hadn't heard?"

"Do you know when she plans to attack? Do you know where?"

"I do not," he said, chuckling. "I do not, at that."

He knelt on the floor and dragged a heavy piece of canvas from under the couch. He kicked, and it unfurled like a carpet, covering the floor. In fanciful watercolors, turquoise and lilac and sage, it illustrated the Borderline, from the river to the fence at Union Square. At each intersection, Van Alen's guardhouses were drawn like medieval forts, glowing with pure white flame.

"It's a mile from fence to river," he said, "and I've got a thousand men to hold it. Tell me where she's coming, and we'll grind her into glass."

"If you don't mind answering some questions first."

"Hmph."

"I assume that means, 'All right, Miss Carr. Whatever you say.'"

"It means you're a pain in my side. Your dad was the same. I give you tea. I talk friendly, more friendly than any daughter of that snake Clubber Carr deserves. I could snap your neck like I was breaking an egg, and the only man on the Westside who'd know about it is a Sardinian immigrant who owes me everything he has in the world. So tell me what you know or spend the night in the river."

I didn't argue. I just pulled out the gun and drew back the hammer. It took both thumbs, and it didn't look graceful, but I got that pistol cocked and leveled at his heart before he could take a step. He laughed at it, the reedy laugh of a man remembering that his bodyguard is far away.

"You recognize it?" I said. "It's one of the guns you stole."

"Guns . . . guns are funny things. You ever shoot one before?"

"No."

"They don't fire as straight as you think."

He knocked the table aside and covered the distance between us in a single stride. The pistol pressed against his chest. It rose and fell with every shuddering breath.

"Your dad would cry, he saw this."

"Then it's luck for both of us that he's dead."

"Put it down, girl. You don't have the stomach to draw blood."

"But I can cut glass." I swung the pistol to my right and trained it on the swinging lighthouse lamp. Van Alen licked his lips. "Let's say, just for argument, that I blast that glass of yours into a million jagged pieces. It would get very dark in here, wouldn't it? And all across the Upper West, your subjects would see your light go out."

"That lamp is worth more than you know."

"Then sit down, Dick, and have a visit."

"Okay, okay, okay. So what is it?"

"Why the candles? Why the night-fires? Why this silly goddamned lamp? Why are you afraid of the dark?"

"Because your father told me to be."

"What did he tell you—and for the sake of that light, be specific—what did he tell you and when?"

"You remember '14?" I nodded. Three thousand missing, the

fence, the bombings. The Westside, cut off like a rotting limb. "The first night the fence went up, Clubber came to me and told me it was the night that killed. Told me to build fires, give out candles, beat back the shadows however you can. My whole life, ever since I was just a dumb kid playing with matches, your daddy was the smartest person I ever knew. I believed him."

I never did.

"I offered to build my night-fires all the way downtown," he said, "but Barbie said no. She'd handle her territory her way. And so we fixed Fourteenth Street as the line—a border without a fence. Just men, weapons, and glass."

"Did the candles save anyone?"

"Could never be sure. I know people here felt safer, though. Past that, who can say?"

"So that was all he ever told you?"

"All he ever told me that made sense. The night he died, he came here drunk, sick, sobbing. Told me about another city."

"A shadow city."

Just saying it out loud was intoxicating, like a teetotaler giving in at last to drink. Possibilities unspooled in my mind. If it were true—if it were even plausible—then the world was as big and strange and dangerous as Virgil Carr always believed, and anything could have killed him. Firecracker continued, shaking his head.

"Yeah. 'We see shadows,' he said, 'but it's a city, a whole city of the dead, come to blot us out. And what if,' and this was the part that really made him quiver, 'what if it's not just that city? What if there are other cities past that one, each one more evil than before?' Pathetic."

"You didn't believe him?"

"How could I, man talking like that? It's the rye whiskey rotted his brain, and I can say that for certain."

"How?"

"Because when he was young, strong, whole? If Clubber really thought there was an army of the dead marching on the Westside, he'd have led the charge to fight them back."

"So you don't think the night killed him? You don't think he was taken by the shadows?"

"I burn the lights to keep people feeling safe. That doesn't mean I really think there's something to fear in the dark."

"Then he killed himself."

"Nah, no chance. Your father was broken, but he was no quitter."

"Then what?" I said, knowing the answer and hating it bitterly.

"Your father was murdered, girl, and that I'm certain of too."

Footsteps on the lighthouse stairs. The door groaned open, but Van Alen and I did not break our gaze. In the corner of my eye, Ida Greene pulled off her gloves and set them folded onto the nearest table.

"You didn't tell me we had guests," she said.

"Shut up, Ida."

"Who killed him?" I said. I would get no answer.

Ida Greene took a switchblade from her purse. She pressed the knife to my back, and Van Alen chuckled. The grease in the air got into my throat, and I felt a horrible temptation to sneeze.

"Just an inch," said Mrs. Greene, "and she'll never ask another question."

"What's the point?" Van Alen swung a heavy sack over his shoulder, a demented, soot-stained Santa Claus. "Come on, Ida. We're late for our rounds."

"You're going nowhere," I said, "until I get my answers."

Van Alen threw the sack at me. My arms reached out for it, and the gun fell out of my hand. Mrs. Greene kicked the pistol across the floor, and Van Alen wrapped his fists around my shoulders.

"Kill me," I said, "and it's an invasion."

"Let her invade. I got guards at every intersection, and I got the fire. It's been a long time since we had a proper war. Be good to douse the sidewalks."

"Tell that to the people whose blood gets spilled."

"It's past ten. I've got deliveries, and if you want answers, you'll carry a sack."

Through the bag, I felt dozens of short, smooth sticks. They might have been dynamite, enough to blow the tip off Upper Manhattan. I tugged open the drawstring and found a hundred or so candles, still wrapped in the paper they'd been shipped in.

"It's a new moon," he growled. "People need 'em. Let's get to work."

"Your iron," said Mrs. Greene, offering me my pistol by the barrel. I took it, and she bent double with laughter.

I threw the bag over my shoulder and fought the hot wave of embarrassment that washed over my back.

ELEVEN

Van Alen's subjects waited on tenement stoops. They were not the derelicts Ida Greene tended to downtown. These were families who had once been called middle class and were now just more hungry people who lacked the skills to survive on their own. Van Alen kept them fed, and they thanked him with wide, desperate eyes. Every bundle of candles was received with a sweaty handshake and nauseating praise. Van Alen let no compliment pass without glancing back to make sure I heard it.

"I'll see you tomorrow night," he said each time, as unsubtle as the worst Broadway ham. He was chummy with his people, but I noticed how careful he was to keep his toes from crossing the threshold of their homes.

We trudged from house to house, Ugly watching the crowd to be sure no one got too close, Ida Greene checking every name against a list to make sure that no one got more than their share. Between buildings, Van Alen answered my questions. He often sounded like he was telling the truth. He had not killed Galen Copeland, he said, and did not seem particularly interested in finding out who did. Nor had he any idea who killed my father, though he had suspicions that he refused to share. He swore up and down that he had not stolen Barbarossa's guns and had no idea who had. If she had ever given him a pair of leather gloves, he had lost them long ago. He had not heard Brass Aiken's song, he did not eat roast beef, and he would never, under any circumstances, send his men across the Borderline.

"That's what makes it a border, you got it?" he said.

"Last night, one of her gangs was ambushed by men in your uniforms, firing pistols."

"My men are guardsmen—they guard. That's it. No booze, no women, and not a step across the Borderline, on penalty of death. They know better."

"They killed three boys."

He stopped walking. In the middle of the street, two families huddled around a crackling bonfire, which filled the street with fragrant smoke. They were burning herbs. Rosemary, I thought, and sage. Van Alen dragged a paw across his forehead, glistening sweaty in the dancing orange light.

"Boys?" he said. "Honest to goodness boys?"

"All under fifteen."

"The stupidity of it. The incompetence. Barbie—that coward. What a goddamned shame."

He looked around for something to break, but everything on the block worth breaking had been shattered long ago.

"Tonight, more boys will die," I said.

"I tell you, my men will turn them back with nothing more than a bump on the head."

"I don't think so. The Lower West is out for blood. They'll get it, unless I find the guns."

"And I tell you, we didn't take them!"

"How can you be sure?"

"What the hell do you mean by that?"

"I know about your little operation at the Longacre. You must have gangs of thieves roaming all over the Eastside, taking whatever they can find."

"We steal what we want, and my fences sell it right back to them. Keeps the fires burning and serves the posh bastards right."

"I think one of your raiding parties got overambitious. They raided a shipment on the Westside docks and ended up with something impossible. I think they've gone rogue. I think Mrs. Greene knows and isn't telling."

Mrs. Greene clutched her notebook like a barber wielding a straight razor. She wanted, not for the first time that day, to take off my head. Ugly took the smallest possible step, to put himself between us, in case sweet Ida charged. Instead, she spoke, sweetly and serenely, as she took Van Alen's hand.

"I regret terribly, Miss Carr, that you think I am capable of such unpleasant things."

"You tried to cut off my head."

"You were spying. You broke my lamp. You mustn't blame me for protecting my business."

"You said you ran a railroad station and nothing more."

"And for telling that simple white lie, you would accuse me of betraying my employer, of bringing guns into the Upper West, of killing three young boys?"

"It's a damned serious accusation," said Van Alen.

"I think a woman who cuts out her workers' tongues would be capable of anything," I said.

"Cuts out her workers'—oh my lord!" said Mrs. Greene, chuckling. "Oh, Dick, Dick. She has no idea!"

"Please, then," I said. "Won't you enlighten me?"

"They came that way!" said Van Alen. "I got 'em from the boys' home on Fifty-Fifth, near the river, which closed down when the fence went up. Ida found them, and she came to me, and said, 'Hey, boss, something awful was going on here. We got three dozen boys had their tongue cut out by the bastards running this place. They got nowhere to go.'"

"That's vile," I said.

"You were here in '14. You remember. There was a lot worse than that."

"There was."

"So I took them in, gave them work. They wanted to stick together—they told me, with this sign language they've worked out—and Ida takes good care of 'em."

"But that isn't the best part," said Mrs. Greene.

"It ain't. The guy who done it? The cretin run that boys' school? He thought he was safe over on the Eastside, but we found him, and we let him have it. You know what Ugly here did to him?"

"Cut out his tongue?"

"No. Hell, that would have been good. Ugly just beat him till the marrow leaked out through his nose, threw him in the river. Shit. I like your way better, but you can't have it all."

"So you see," said Mrs. Greene, "at worst we are thieves, and we steal for a righteous cause. We do not stoop to violence unless provoked."

She took that step toward me.

"I still think you lie," I said.

"And that simply breaks my heart. Now, Dick—"

"I know, I know. The schedule," he said, and we turned the corner and I felt the heat of the biggest fire I'd ever seen. It stretched three stories high, throwing sparks a mile into the sky, lighting up Haven Avenue as bright as the surface of the sun. Guards ringed the base, clubs at their side, protecting the flame. A hundred or more people stood on the sidewalk, not minding how the heat scorched their skin, occasionally venturing forward to toss an offering onto the blaze.

"What are they burning?" I said.

"Whatever they like."

There was laughter at every corner—the honest, unstoppable wave of ordinary human mirth. Young boys played stickball, and couples danced in the firelight—not the miserable shuffling of the Hyperion Hotel, but a sweeping waltz, sloppy with life. Old men played the accordion, and others kept time on bass or bucket or anything else they had at hand. A grand piano blocked the sidewalk and thundered out ragtime. Hellida was right. She would be very happy here.

"Come on," he said. "One more stop."

As the fire disappeared behind us, Ugly got close, carrying a torch to keep his lord bathed in light.

"If you didn't take the guns," I said, "your thieves may know who did."

"That is your problem, not mine." Van Alen took the last four candles out of my bag and dropped them into the pocket of his apron. He opened the front door of the building, whose windows were broken and whose air was stale. This time, he crossed the threshold, taking Ugly's torch and bounding into the darkness before I could think of a way to make him answer me.

"No one follows," said Mrs. Greene. "Never."

"Is that so?" I said and pushed past her. Ugly's hand snapped out to stop me, but he was still too slow.

I took the stairs two at a time and found Van Alen at the top, standing in front of an apartment door, eyes closed, hands rubbing his temples like a man unsure if he should cry or scream. I watched him for what seemed like a long time before he noticed I was there. His gruff mask went up again, but it did not fit as well as it had before.

"How 'bout you get the hell out of here?" he said. I shook my head. "Just like your daddy. Stubborn as a goddamned statue."

"Who lives here?"

"My parents been here since 1910, ever since they put enough away to get out of the Village."

"The lord of the Upper West keeps his parents in a burnt-out tenement?"

"A thousand times I offered to find them someplace better, but no. That's not what they want. At least, it's not what my mother wants. My daddy, he's far gone. The man doesn't know . . . he doesn't know where he is half the time. All I can do is make sure they've got plenty of candles."

The door was locked. He knocked, and it opened slowly. Van Alen's mother was only a few inches taller than me, but she was as solid as a brick wall. She welcomed her son with a wordless hug and cast a suspicious eye at me.

"Gilda," I said. "Gilda Carr."

"Clubber's daughter," said Van Alen.

"Clubber," murmured the old woman, and a smile flickered across her face. "Then you'll need to have something to eat."

The apartment was small, with one room serving as kitchen, dining room, living room, and everything else. The furniture was ragged but comfortable. A candle stub flickered in a groove cut in the center of the round wood table that dominated the room. Mrs. Van Alen lit the new candle off the old, setting it on the table with holy precision. The spark of flame caught the eye of Firecracker's father, who sat in the corner, staring out the window at the fire in the distance. His head snapped toward the match, then lolled back to the view.

"Fresh vegetables," said Mrs. Van Alen, placing a bowl of soup in front of me. "All from Dick's bazaar. You shop there?"

"Whenever I have the time."

"You can't do none better, not on Westside or East. Now you eat. I got something in the bedroom you'll be dying to see."

A few sips of soup, and the last remnants of my hour in the coffin washed off me. It was hot and strong. Van Alen drained his bowl before his mother returned. He dragged his sleeve across his mouth and swallowed a belch.

"Clubber Carr was a hard-nosed son of a bitch," said Mrs. Van Alen. She set a long, flat scrapbook on the table and opened to the first page—a photograph of my father having a medal pinned on his chest by Commissioner Roosevelt. "Even as a boy, I knew he was tough as steel. He made a good cop. Most Westside boys grew up without much respect for law and order."

She shot a look at her son. He blushed, and I slipped back into the past. The *Sentinel* morgue had nothing on Mrs. Van Alen. Every great case, every front-page spread was carefully pressed, preserved, and treasured. A diamond robbery on First Avenue. A bludgeoning in an Eastside high-rise. A fraud at the Chrystie Street bank. A woman killed on East Broadway when her father, irritated that she had violated curfew, set his dogs on her. Every case solved by the great Clubber Carr, who always came through in record time and with as many clever quotes as the reporters asked for. How strange to see my father working on the Eastside. How strange to see my father doing well.

There wasn't a page in that book that didn't make me want to cry.

I turned to a full-page spread from 1912, and Mrs. Van Alen tried to take the book away.

"Don't read that page," she said. "I hate that page."

Naturally, I read on.

It was an account of my father's last press conference, the final embarrassment in his career with the NYPD. Asked about the recent spate of disappearances in the Westside, Virgil launched into a tirade against the mayor, the chief of police, and anyone else whose name he could recall. He was clearly drunk, wrote the unnamed reporter, his uniform stained and his badge missing. My father's ravings were incoherent, and according to the newspaper, not worth recording. Instead, they gave the article over to a long quote attacking the deranged detective, a quote from a respected voice inside the department who declared that the time had come to put Virgil Carr out to pasture.

The source's name was Lieutenant Edward Thorne.

"He stuck that knife in hard, did Thorne," said Van Alen.

"I never thought he had the spine."

"Even a spineless man can only take so much. Eventually, he'll lash out, try to prove to himself that he's tough."

"And then what?"

"Usually, they go back to being spineless. Spend every night curled up in the bottle, telling themselves the story of the time they stood up to the bigger man."

"That's the Thorne I know and love."

"Your daddy had a good run there, till he went off the rails. Last time I saw him, he was crowing about how he'd made a breakthrough in some case, some insignificant little thing, must have been almost as old as you."

"Was it Alice Pearl?"

"Now how'd you know that?"

"Fathers are so predictable."

"He said he'd cracked it, and it was all tied up with . . . how did he put it? With what had poisoned the Westside. That was the word he used. 'Poison.'"

"Did he say what killed her?"

"He said quite a bit. Man was as drunk as a jockey. Didn't make a lick of sense."

"Did *any* of it stick with you?"

"Blamed Copeland for it. Can you explain that? Galen Copeland, of all the insignificant creatures New York has ever produced. It was gibberish. And Barbarossa too—a thought that made your dad nearly well up with tears. He loved that woman something fierce."

"I don't want to hear it."

I dug deeper into Mrs. Van Alen's scrapbook and found something even more upsetting than the image of Andrea Barbarossa with my father in her arms.

"I hear you," he muttered. "The way they were together—vile. And him a married man."

"Shut up."

"Watch how you talk to me, girl."

"You goddamned illiterate, I'm trying to read."

I took the candle and held it up to the page, close enough that wax dripped on the newsprint. A class photo. NYPD cadets, 1878, faces hard and buttons shining. My father in the back, ramrod stiff. Thorne beside him, as always, his face not yet fattened by drink. And up in front, a man with thick lips and a half-inch gap between his two front teeth.

"Who is that?" I asked.

"It's a cop, isn't it?"

"Do you know him?"

"Barstow. Victor, Val, something like that. A real pig, he is. A sadist. In the old days, the Tenderloin girls would start running when he came up the block. You didn't want him with his hands on you. He'd beat a girl raw, then start to cry, clutch her hair to his face, and beg for forgiveness. Only bastard I ever met sad enough to look up to Eddie Thorne. You know him?"

"As a matter of fact, I watched him die."

"I hope he died badly."

"In a puff of smoke. What time is it?"

"Just gone eleven."

"Then get me downtown."

"When you finish your soup," said Mrs. Van Alen.

"I can stop this war. I know who stole Barbarossa's guns."

"And who was it, then?" said Van Alen.

"The people in the city who need guns more than anyone else. The cowardly, the corrupt, the frightened. It was the cops who took them, Eddie Thorne, Barstow—the whole Fourth Precinct. They stole the guns, they blamed it on you, and now they're trying to start a war."

Van Alen's gut brushed the table as he stood up, and the whole room rattled. He ripped the napkin off his collar and dropped it on the floor.

"You're not skipping dinner," said his mother.

"Business, Ma."

"Some business, giving out candles. How much can he really make? I mean, I ask you," she said to me.

I couldn't answer her. I was already out the door and charging down yet another darkened stairwell. I'd gotten to the first landing before I felt Van Alen's hands around my waist, lifting me over his shoulder. He took the stairs three at a time, each step a thunderclap that threatened to bring the building down. At the front door, he set me down as gently as a young girl picking a flower.

"Never lay your hands on me again," I said.

"Apologies," he said, unapologetic. "Now where are they crossing the line?"

"Eighth Avenue."

"Ida, send runners to Ninth, Seventh, Sixth, and Fifth. Tell them to send every man. At Eighth, we make a stand."

"You shouldn't trust her," said Mrs. Greene.

"Why not? Didn't you hear—her father and I are old friends. Now run!"

She ran, and I snapped for Ugly.

"Get the hearse," I said. "We've a rendezvous downtown."

"Like hell," said Van Alen. "We're taking my coach."

It was a hulking thing, made of gleaming wood, butter-soft leather, and metal as slick as the pistol in my bag. The horses—four of them, all white and all muscle—pawed like bulls ready to charge. While Ugly took refuge in the cab, Van Alen hoisted me onto the driver's box. He gathered the reins in his left hand and raised his whip high.

"This might be fun," he said, and I had no doubt he was wrong.

He snapped his wrist, and we exploded onto the avenue like sudden thunder. I pushed my feet against the baseboard and braced my back against the cab, my hands scratching the wood for someplace to hang on.

"Drive easy, boss," cried Ugly from below. "I'm trying to sharpen your knives."

The horses churned downtown, relentless as a runaway train, and Van Alen kept them on course with constant, nearly imperceptible twitchings of his left hand. He swung the whip precisely, even gently, a conductor guiding a temperamental orchestra to the performance of its life.

"Every boy under Barbarossa's banner will be stewed," he said. "They're not gonna march on the Borderline—they'll stagger. We'll turn 'em away without a fight."

"I'd still rather it not come to that."

"Oh, what I would give to have your father back among the living, just for one moonless night. There was no man on the Westside quicker to snap a neck or crack a skull. Clubber understood. A night like tonight, a bloody pitch-dark night, was always one to savor."

"You called him a snake."

"Did I, then? I stand by it. But remember this: on a night this dark, it's the snakes that get out alive."

We came to Broadway and hung a hard right, running south between the fence and the sidewalk, then broke down Eighth Avenue at the monstrous wall that cut around Columbus Circle.

Twenty minutes till my deadline, we hit traffic. Sixteenth Street was filled with guardsmen, and when they saw Van Alen's coach they stopped us dead. They crowded around us, hammering the sides, chanting until he dropped the reins, wiped the sweat from his eyes, and raised a fist for the crowd.

"I'll get out here," I said. "I could never stand watching boys play soldier."

"Before you go—you wanna know who killed your daddy? The night he disappeared, after he was finished raving to me, he went to see another old friend."

"Who?" I said.

"That crooked son of a bitch that's too rich for his own good. Calls himself Brass."

I might have thanked him, but there was no time. I leapt down and went looking for a war. The crowd parted easily for me—they had no interest in something as trivial as a woman—and I worked my way toward Fourteenth. It wasn't hard to find. Like a spoiled child, the great iron brazier was fed constantly, by a team of soot-covered boys whose hair had been scorched down to nothing. They shoveled more fuel on when I passed, and the flame belched just a few feet higher, fouling the air with an unnameable stench. I kept far to the side. I was starting to prefer it in the shadows.

I crossed the street, the light from the fire glinting on the glass just enough to show me the safest way through. I checked my watch. The deadline had passed.

Three blocks past the Borderline, I heard children singing. First "Benjy's Bloody Stump," then "The Night Mae Traynor Died." And then I saw the banners. The Sparrows, the Gophers, the Swamp Angels, the Claw-Boys, the West Fourth Particulars, and the Dead Barrow Toughs numbered close to a thousand, and there were a few hundred more under flags I couldn't identify. I scanned the crowd until I saw Roach, the ten-year-old standard bearer, waving the dead feline.

"Go home," I said. "Please, Roach. Go home."

"The chief says to fight," he said. "And we fight. Ain't it glorious?"

"Turn back now, or I'll break that oar over your head."

It was, I thought, a persuasive threat, but the boy marched on.

I grabbed Cherub by his kerchief. He staggered and smiled as sweetly as ever. His saber was unsheathed, and his eyes were glassy with gin. The bandage on his left ankle was loose and grimy, but Cherub had swallowed enough clear liquor to quiet the limp. When I saw him, I found I had failed to shake the feeling that had descended on me in Barbie's subway tunnel: I could not bear for him to die.

"Turn back," I said. "They're waiting for you."

"That just means more of them to kill," he said, to great approval from the pack.

I screwed the kerchief tight against his throat. He slumped on my shoulder, his breath as hot as moonshine.

"Let me walk you home," I said.

"These boys need their chief." I wasn't sure who he was trying to convince—me, or himself. The boys were too young, too deeply Westside, for such subtlety. All they did was cheer.

"It's insanity. You've already lost three. Don't throw these others away."

"I have to, Gilda," he said, low enough that only I could hear how sick he felt. "These boys are going no matter what I do. Only Barbie can turn them back."

"Where is she?"

"Like a true leader, she's bringing up the rear."

He tipped his head, and raised his sword, and spun on his heel without saying goodbye. I shoved my way through the army, exposing my arms to sweat, war paint, spilled liquor, and the awful bristle of pubescent moustaches, and found Barbarossa, flush with liquor, surrounded by her honor guard, all the way at the back.

"Gilda, Gilda, Gilda!" she cried. "The daughter I never had. Come to watch the festivities?"

"Call it off."

"You're too late. Can't you hear them singing? You'd have an easier time calling off a typhoon."

"It's not Van Alen who stole your guns. It's Thorne."

"That can't be."

"Where is he?"

"He got too drunk at the war council. We left him slumped in his chair."

"Find him. String him up if you have to. The man killed Galen Copeland. He lied to your face. He pushed you into this war. Stop it now, or you're giving him just what he wants."

"You're wrong."

"Is it true you loved my father?"

"Like no one could ever know."

"Thorne was the one who betrayed him. Now he's done the same to you."

"Eddie Thorne barely has the ingenuity to button his own pants."

"I can find him for you. You can stop this fight."

"I gave you till midnight, didn't I? It's fifteen minutes gone. This army does not turn back."

"Then at least choose somewhere else to cross. Van Alen's expecting you. He's put every guardsman he has right at Eighth Avenue."

"You sold us out, did you?"

"I was trying to save a few lives."

"And why? For what purpose?"

"They are children!"

"What death could you offer these boys better than a fight on the Borderline? You're as stupid as your . . . never mind." A tremor went through her, and her skin went pale. From her belt she pulled a dented flask. A long pull put the color back into her cheeks. She tossed the flask to me. From her left boot she drew a long, curved knife. "Drink, dear, and enjoy the show. This will be the best brawl the Westside's seen in ages. If I see your daddy tonight, I'll give him both our love."

I stopped, and she kept walking. I tore off the top of the flask and dumped her liquor down my throat. It was good whiskey, as smooth as fire can get, and I drank it like water.

As they reached the Borderline, Barbarossa's boys stopped singing and let out a ragged cheer. They were children playing dress-up, but they would bleed like men. At Barbarossa's word, they charged across the broken glass, throwing rocks and swinging chains, and the guardsmen laid them flat with their clubs. Some of the guardsmen held back, unable to strike a child, and they were rewarded with knives in the gut. Van Alen's guards were well drilled and well equipped, but the Lower West had the numbers, and the suicidal enthusiasm of youth. It would be a close fight.

I closed my eyes and heard metal on metal, metal on skin, and bodies falling on glass. The fire-watchers beneath Van Alen's brazier tossed flaming coals at the charging boys, perfuming the air with singed flesh. A guardsman made the mistake of chasing two Swamp Angels into the darkness. They turned on him and buried knives in his neck. He mumbled a half-coherent snatch of the Lord's Prayer and died in the street.

When her first attack was repulsed, Barbarossa roared for another charge, and from the top of his coach, Van Alen roared right back. The boys held their weapons above their heads and plunged back into the fray. As he'd promised, Cherub Stevens led the pack. I tried to tell myself that this wasn't my fault, that they were dying for something better than a missing leather glove. I couldn't make myself believe.

First from the east, then from the south, the cry of sirens echoed off the buildings. The battle became more frantic, as the armies of the Upper and Lower West fought to finish their business before the police arrived to spoil the fun. But I soon saw it wasn't paddy wagons that were screaming toward the intersection. It was fire trucks—vintage models, drawn by horses far less majestic than Van Alen's and dragged out of storage for a purpose I could not understand.

One stopped behind me, nearly close enough to touch. The men leapt off the sides, unspooled the hoses, and struggled to work the pumps. The way they fumbled with their equipment showed that these were not the brave men of Engine Company Eighteen. They wore the tattered blue of the Fourth Precinct. Every one had a pistol in his belt, and a few had rifles too. Thorne rode on top of the contraption, rifle slung over his shoulder like he was leading a hunt. I'd never seen him standing so tall.

They got the hoses working and trained them on Van Alen's fire. Steam hissed over the battleground, a sickening gray cloud that swallowed the armies of both sides even as black descended. The guards on the platform struggled against the water, throwing what fuel they had left on the dying blaze, but in less than a minute, the fight was lost. The fire died, and night surged up the avenue.

As the water swallowed the last embers, I saw Barbarossa in silhouette, one of Van Alen's guardsmen kneeling at her feet. She clutched his hair in her fist, pressed that curved knife to his throat, and pulled until she hit spine. She wrenched his head back like it was on a hinge and sawed against the bone, and the darkness was total.

I ran. I had no choice. I pushed past the cops and ran north to find Cherub Stevens, because I did not have the strength to let another friend die. I called his name, but my voice was lost amid the sizzling of the dead fire and the whimpering of a thousand frightened children.

Thorne's men opened fire. What happened next, I saw in the light of their muzzle flashes—jets of flame that beat the night back just long enough to show a little scene of hell. A bullet burst through the throat of a blue-eyed boy and sailed on into the crowd. Flash. Another clipped a guardsman on the arm and caught a second in the eye. Flash. Two boys dropped their weapons and were cut down as they raised their hands in surrender. Flash. I did not know what gangs they fought for. Their standards were gone; their uniforms were stained with blood. They were just children now.

It was like a flipbook. With each flash, I saw a little more. A guard's left leg raised, then his right, then his left, then he was dead. With each burst of light, the crowd grew closer to panic, until Lower and Upper forgot their division and united in a desire to get away from the men with the guns. But there was nowhere for them to go. No matter how bright the rifle fire, the light could not penetrate the shadows of the Borderline. There was a wall of darkness about to crash down.

A little hand grabbed me by the wrist and pulled me into the crowd. It was Roach, still clutching the standard of the One-Eyed Cats. At the edge of the massacre, we found Cherub Stevens, waving his saber, trying to rally his men.

"One-Eyed Cats!" he shouted, his voice broken, his ankle twisted, a horrible bloody gash running down his chest. "To me!"

"I found her," said Roach, and Cherub smiled that marvelous smile, and the shadows swallowed us whole. The icy black knocked the wind from my chest and forced my eyes shut, and for a long moment there was nothing I could do but try to catch my breath. When I opened my eyes, light was dark, dark was light, and the battle had gone silent.

Cherub's mouth hung open. He might have been screaming, or he might simply have been in shock at the impossible scene. Behind him, stretching down the white pavement of Fourteenth Street, an army marched beneath the bone-gray sky. Clothes tattered, skin liquid smoke, eyes flickering white fire. There were hundreds of them, those ghouls, those creatures of the shadows: newsies and cops, priests and streetwalkers, gangsters and debutantes and every other specimen of humanity the city had to offer. They held their arms open to embrace the routed soldiers. They swallowed them in white smoke and turned the boys to their side. Inch by inch, they grew closer. I would not let them have us.

I seized Cherub by the wrist, held tight to Roach's hand, and dragged them away from the dark. Shoving through the retreating mob was like swimming against the Hudson current. It took all the strength I had to keep from being picked up and carried along by the wave. I fought to take one step, then another, and another, but no matter how hard I worked, it seemed we had not gotten anywhere, and death was closing in.

If there had only been some noise, I thought. If I could have heard them at my back, instead of just knowing they were there. If I just could have screamed, to release the pressure that had been building on my chest for the last minute, day, week, then I might have been light enough to flee.

Somehow, at last, we reached the base of Van Alen's great brazier. We pressed our backs against it, and for a moment we could breathe. I looked back the way we'd come, at the soldiers disappearing into the impenetrable white night, at the thousands of dead and vanished who had come to take their revenge on the fighting boys of the Westside. How many of those white-eyed people had I met, or spoken to, or even just seen? How many of my neighbors marched in that regiment of ghouls? A question that large could never be answered, but the fact that I was asking it meant that I was still alive, that even in this hellish underworld, a girl could find a few seconds to think, that she could take control.

Thorne and his men stood at the edge of the intersection in their ragged line, picking off the stragglers and the boys too frozen to run, their weapons belching white fire. I pointed that way. Cherub shook his head, that old look that said, "Gilda, this is madness, but I know we'll be doing it anyway," and my god—I may have smiled.

Roach bolted, and we followed, the syrupy paralysis we had felt before forgotten. There were not more than a few dozen men left standing between us and the ghouls, men who had fallen to their knees in supplication or despair, waiting to be taken and destroyed. We did not have time to wait.

Rifle fire cut down a man kneeling in front of us. He tried to stand, to run, but he was too weak to move. I leapt over his body, but the boys were as useless as ever. The dying man grabbed Roach by the ankle, and Cherub stumbled trying to get him free.

"Get up!" I screamed, but no one heard. The ghouls were nearly on us. Cherub kicked the dying man in the face and took Roach by the hand, but the smoke was on him first. Three of them—two old men and a boy no older than Roach himself—their eyes flickering, their twisted tendrils snaking up Roach's legs, pulled hard, but Cherub would not let go. It was a desperate tug-of-war, and I ended it. I grabbed Cherub tight around the waist, and I yanked hard, and I forced him to let Roach go.

Their hands—or what should have been their hands—snaked up Roach's body, flooding his gaping mouth and scraping out his eyes. As he died, or came as close to death as this world would let him, he looked more frightened and more sad than any boy should ever be.

Cherub, broken, let me lead him. I dragged him across the blood-wet asphalt and lined us up in front of the policemen and their guns. They could not see us. They were back in the real world and had the luxury of blindness to the horrors that lay in the dark.

They pressed their rifles against their shoulders and leveled the barrels at our chests. They peered down the sights. They pulled the triggers.

We died, and we came home.

The police were, understandably, surprised. From what they had seen, we had appeared out of the night. If they had fired again, they could have killed us, but they had other things on their mind. Behind us, where the battle had been, where a thousand had vanished, there was a wall of darkness. Inside that darkness lay living death. I knew it, and Thorne, curiously, knew it too.

"The light!" he cried, and two of his men put torches to a pile of gasoline-soaked firewood on the back of one of their wagons. Flames exploded, and the shadows were beaten back. We shoved through the line of cops. If they'd cared, they could have stopped us, but there was liquor on their breath and blood in the air. They had done enough for the night.

We walked home through simple, ordinary darkness, far more inviting than the horror that lay behind. The smell of death faded, to be covered up by the hot, sweet, Westside night.

"Why don't these shadows jump?" he said. "Why don't they swallow us? Why don't they take us . . . there?"

"I think . . . I think the hungry shadows are drawn by blood."

"Like sharks."

"Kill one man, and you attract a few of those ghouls. Kill a hundred . . ."

"And you get an army. How did you get us out?"

"It's like a dream—die in it, and you wake up."

"Is there any way to get . . . if someone was left behind there . . ."

"How should I know? This was my father's sort of mystery. Not mine."

It was a nasty thing to say, and I tried to mean it, but as the words hung in the air, all I could see was the look on Roach's face when I left him to die. He hadn't looked angry. He'd looked surprised—unable to understand how badly Miss Carr and the chief had let him down.

After that, Cherub was silent. From Eighth Avenue to Bleecker to Charles Street. Across Seventh, right at Waverly, past Sixth Avenue, and then just a block back to Washington Square. By the time we got back to the park, the night was melting into gray. His jaw was clenched, and tears had worn tracks in the matted soot and blood that stained his face.

"What will you do?" I said.

"I'm going to kill Edward Thorne."

"It won't fix anything."

"I don't care."

"They'll shoot you down before you get within fifty feet of him."

"That would suit me fine."

"Do nothing. For a day or two. Go back to the pet shop. Eat. Sleep. Rest. I'll fix it."

"Gilda, damn you—I thought I was supposed to be the childish one. The world is ruined. The Westside is broken, and nothing will fix that. Nothing will ever be good again."

I wanted something clever to say, something to make him smile in spite of himself. Nothing came to mind. We stepped off the sidewalk into the mossy street, and the quiet was broken by screams, faint and piercing. They came from the far side of the park, and they came in Swedish.

I ran, and Cherub stumbled after me. The night's horrors were not through with us yet.

The top floor of the house had blown away like smoke. Below, where the vines were thickest, my home was putting up a fight it could not win. Hairline cracks shot from the foundation up through the brick. The stone shattered, but the windows could not be broken. I knew that immediately, because Hellida was on the first floor, banging on the glass with my father's favorite reading chair, and no one in New York was stronger than Hellida when she was angry.

The gate was latched and would not open for me. I hopped over it, and Cherub called after me, but the breeze had turned into a tornado, and I couldn't make out the words.

I tried to jerk open my front door. The knob, white hot, burned my hands.

"Where's your goddamned sword?" I screamed at Cherub, my words lost in the wind.

Something thudded against the window—Hellida's crepe pan. She retrieved it, ran deep into the parlor, spun, and let it go, hard enough that it should have shattered the glass and sailed all the way across the park. But the window would not yield.

The second floor followed the third into the shadows. All that remained was the dust-covered wood. The vines flopped across the second story—my father's office, and the room where my mother left this world—and squeezed. The cracks in the brownstone opened wider, and from them poured inky black light.

The thudding stopped, and above the wind I heard Hellida scream my name.

She ran her finger across the window. The house began to split. As the room melted around her, she did not wince and did not cry. She simply disappeared.

A final gust blew me down the steps, which were gone by the

time I opened my eyes. Cherub and I stood in an empty lot, over-grown with a decade's moss and vines, just glowing pink in the light of dawn.

I clawed at the dirt, looking for some sign of my home, scream-ing through my blackened fingers until my voice choked down to nothing, and Cherub pulled me away. Even the foundation was gone.

TWELVE

It was a putrid Sunday at Ebbets Field, and the Giants were down by three. I hated the Dodgers, I hated their fans, and I hated Ebbets Field—a cramped, meaningless little ballpark that struck me as Brooklyn personified: stunted, scrawny, ugly, and rude. I shifted in the hard wooden seat and tried to understand why I was there.

I wasn't entirely sure how I got to Brooklyn. As the sun rose on my vanished home, I lay on my back in the dirt until the cold seeped through my clothes and I had to stand or go numb. I forced Cherub to go back to his pet shop and wandered west until I reached Bedford Street, where Bex Red lived in the narrowest home in New York, a three-story scarlet town house that was barely wide enough to hold its own front door. I knocked only once before the door opened, and she swept me into her arms, in a dressing gown sticky with plaster and lime.

"I heard the shots," she said. "I saw the fires. Come inside. I'll feed you some whiskey."

Past the door was a stack of accordions. Eight feet wide and forty long, Bex's first floor stored watering cans, cracked mirrors, wilted plants, typewriters, rosaries, vases, taxidermy, cellos, inaccurate globes, and poorly made pots. They were artifacts rescued from the homes of the vanished, kept by Bex in tribute until the constraints of the space forced her to make room for more.

"You don't want an accordion, do you?"

I couldn't say a word. I followed her through the stacks of neatly organized refuse to the second floor, where she thrust a glass of rye into my hand.

"It's not Boulton's," she said. "Apologies."

I raised the glass in a feeble toast and tried to take a sip. It slipped through my hand and cracked on the floor. I sank into the puddle of cheap whiskey, folded into myself, and sobbed. Bex, praise her, asked no questions. She helped me onto the couch, arranged me on a pile of pillows, and swaddled me in a wool blanket. I was asleep before she blew out the light.

I awoke looking at Washington Square. The sun was shining and the park was crowded, more crowded than I had seen it in years, with the moss gone, the trees stunted, the fountain full, and the arch gleaming. And on a bench just inside the western gate, a young woman in a tangerine dress sat with her mother, a delicate woman whose hair was just beginning to go white.

"It's sublime," I said, rising from the couch and leaning close to the canvas, which stretched from ceiling to floor.

"It is a bit, isn't it? I'd forgotten it ever looked like this, full of life and smiling children, but a few weeks ago I saw it in a dream. Amazing the lies we tell ourselves in sleep."

"And my mother and I were there?"

"Laughing like schoolgirls. Of all the strange things my cobwebbed old mind has dreamed up, few are more fantastic than Gilda Carr in a tangerine dress."

"You never met Mary."

"But I've seen pictures and things at your house. Did I do her justice?"

"I don't know. I think so. She loved reading in the park."

"She was much younger than that when she died?"

"She never had time to go gray."

"Darling, darling Gilda. There's no reason to cry."

But there was, and I told her all about it: the massacre, the shadows, the ghouls and their city of death. I told her about my house, blown away like smoke, and Hellida trapped inside behind glass that would not yield. I don't think she believed any of it, but she was kind enough not to tell me I was mad. How useful it is, to be friends with artists.

"Hellida was the only family I had left," I said once I had gotten the tears under control. "And that house was the only thing I owned. I've nothing now."

"You have friends. Anyway, you've got me, whether you want me or not. I feel guilty, you know, pushing you toward grander mysteries."

"It turned out I hardly needed the push."

"Still, this house is yours as long as you need it."

"It's hardly wide enough for one woman, much less two."

"We'll find space. Tiny girl like you can fit anywhere."

I suppose she fed me, and she must have slipped some money into my purse. At some point she started painting, because Bex can't go more than a few hours without holding a brush in her hand. I slipped out the front door and crossed the stem at Broadway. I don't think I knew where I was walking, but I believe I entered the BRT at Canal Street. Twenty minutes later I passed through Ebbets' ridiculous marble rotunda and took a seat along the first-base line.

I didn't cheer when the Giants tied the game in the fifth. I didn't flinch when Brooklyn took the lead right back. The game mattered to no one in the ballpark, and it mattered least to me, but every few pitches I glanced over my shoulder. I really expected to see him there—craning his neck in search of me, ready to wave his program when I caught his eye.

In the seventh, or perhaps the eighth, one of the Giants' backups made a nice catch in right field. I tried to muster some applause. It didn't come. I stared up at the featherweight blue sky.

"I can't stand it either," said a man to my right, "when the season closes out."

"Giants still have a chance."

"Sure about that, miss? Look around."

I followed his advice. The seats were empty. Crumpled garbage whipped around the infield. Ushers moved down the rows with brooms, sweeping up cigarette butts and abandoned scorecards. The game had been finished for an hour.

"What's that you been whistling?" he said.

"Awful, isn't it? I heard it two days ago, and I can't shake it."

"'We'll skin your back, make your bones crack, and burn your face with lye,'" he sang, in a voice bottomless and smooth.

"Pardon me?"

"There's more to the words, but I don't know it."

"But tell me, please tell me, that you remember the name."

"As far as I know, it doesn't have one. They used to sing it in the saloons on Sixth Avenue, back when the Westside was just a curiosity and not a mass grave."

"You lived there?"

"I drank there. For a few years, it was the same thing. And while it would be charming to reminisce about my wasted years, the ushers are looming."

"We have to go, don't we?"

"I'd stay all winter, if I could," said the man. He took off his hat and ran his hand through a few strands of thin gray hair. "Let's get before they kick us out."

I followed him up to the concourse. At the top of the aisle, I glanced back for a last look at the patchy brown grass. It wasn't my ballpark, but it was better than nothing.

I said goodbye to the old man outside the main gate.

"Lucky, aren't you?" he said. "Giants fan. Series starts Wednesday, don't it? Season's not over yet."

The train inched over the Manhattan Bridge. The walls of the tent city that crowded the riverfront flapped in the late-afternoon breeze. Beneath my seat, I found a crumpled copy of the afternoon *Sentinel*. Max got his front-page byline, attached to a rancid portrait of the pride of the NYPD: the valiant Lieutenant Edward Thorne. His statement was strictly official, the kind of concrete verbiage that Thorne could have never wrapped his lips around even while sober. It gave no details of the massacre, describing it simply as "a joint action of the police and the fire department," but assured readers that the "unsavory element" of "that blighted district" had at last been "routed, turned back like the tide."

"The day will dawn soon," it claimed Thorne said, "dearest reader of the *Sentinel*, when gentility returns to Eighth Avenue, and ordinary folk reclaim their homes, and the fence comes tumbling down. This I promise."

The next time I saw Max, I would have to ask if Thorne snored during the interview. He must have woken up toward the end, because at the bottom of the long, narrow column, there were a few words that had the sour taste of the Westside.

"Tell that uptown ——, that great bully calls himself Firecracker, you tell him this was only the start. An opening act. Soon we cross the Borderline, and we do it in force, and the whole Westside is gonna know how heavy the law can come down."

Finally, the train picked up speed. The sun dipped behind the towers of lower Manhattan, and the air whistling through the windows turned cold. I crumpled the paper and tossed it out the window. It fell through the tracks, down to the crowded river. The train dove past the tenements of the Lower East, and in a few flashing seconds I saw whole lives lived on the roofs of those buildings.

At the top of one of the wood-and-paper shacks, a hundred feet above East Broadway, a girl who could have been eight or could have been a malnourished thirteen looked to see that she was not being watched, then reached under her shirt for a sticky bun the size of her head. She ate it like she had never tasted anything so sweet, and never would again. By the time the tunnel swallowed the train, the sticky bun was gone. I touched my cheeks. I was not crying.

"You gotta get this looked at."

"Pardon me?"

"It's incumbent on you, as a resident of the area west of Broadway, to ensure that your paperwork is up to date and in accordance with all city ordinances, rules, regulations, and decrees."

"This license is valid until December."

"Every license issued by the city, for transit of peoples back and forth across the Broadway dividing area, has been called up for review."

Where the fence slashed across Houston Street, there was a gate as grand as any in the city. A cast-iron relief exhibited scenes of Westside landmarks for people who would never gaze upon them again. Below a depiction of the pristine Washington Square Arch stood a pert little man with deep wrinkles around his eyes and tufts of hair bristling out of his ears. His hands shook violently as he pointed to the scrap of paper pasted to the door, whose font was too small to read, that bore the signature of Lieutenant Edward Thorne.

"How long will this license be valid?"

"It ain't." He crushed my precious little paper into a ball and licked his lips in a truly obscene way. "Cross over if you want to, but they'll never let you back."

I pushed past him, shoving hard enough to knock the wind from his gut, and the door slammed shut behind me. I did not smell the familiar Westside damp. The air was all wrong. From the north, I saw the smoke. Something was burning on Washington Square.

I was not ready to return to the park. The thought of stepping onto that moss-covered pavement, looking at the arch, and seeing the sun set through the gap where my house used to be—it was simply not possible. But my feet disagreed. I charged up Mercer, turned at Fourth Street, and saw the church on fire.

Flames licked up Judson Memorial's high yellow tower, and smoke poured from the campanile that Father Lamb called a bar. The wind blew the fire toward me, and the smoke carried the tragic stench of spilled liquor. Broken glass and shattered barrels littered the sidewalk. The remains of Barbarossa's liquor trickled into

the gutter as Koszler and Lavangetto, the worst scoundrels of the
Fourth Precinct, practiced their club work on Father Lamb.

"Kneel, old man," muttered Koszler, spitting the words through
the gaps in his teeth. "Kneel, goddamn it, kneel or we'll break you.
Kneel and we'll leave you be."

Lamb did his best to stand, whispering some foul obscenity just
loud enough to be heard. Koszler swung his club on a long, smooth
uppercut that connected squarely with Lamb's chin and knocked
him sprawling across the shattered glass.

"Pick him up," said Koszler, and Lavangetto shook off his dazed
expression long enough to hoist Lamb under the armpits. "Now
make him kneel."

Lavangetto did his best to contort Lamb's dead weight into a
kneeling position. The liquor-soaked glass cut deep into his knees,
and Koszler choked out a laugh.

At my feet, half a broken bottle lay caught in the gutter. I
wrapped my fingers around it, held it at my hip, and ran. My feet
left the ground a yard before I reached Koszler, which meant the
bottle sank into his back just a moment before my weight sent him
sprawling across the glass. Blood flowed like someone had turned
on a faucet, and the park echoed with his screams.

Lavangetto dropped Lamb and scrambled for his pistol. By
the time he leveled it to fire, I had vaulted over the toppled oak,
dropped softly onto the moss, and picked up a stray cobblestone.
I crept farther into the park and looked for a tree to climb.

The one I picked was just past the fountain. When Washington
Square had been a potter's field, this was the hanging tree. Now it
was two hundred feet tall, as stout and wide as a subway car turned
on end. I had been climbing it since I was a girl, and I knew every
twist of its branches. I gripped the vines and scaled it quickly, high
enough to see the edge of the park, where Lavangetto had just made
it over the oak and onto the moss. I twisted the vines into a harness,
held the cobblestone against my chest, and dangled.

As a child, I used this tree to escape children who saw reading
as a sign of weakness. I would climb high enough for the wind to

diffuse their taunts and read in peace, straddling a branch with my back against the oak, only occasionally distracted by the beauty of the city laid out beneath my feet.

In those days, I wanted to be alone forever. Now, I hoped to be found. I had never climbed so high before. I've no fondness for heights—not because I fear falling, but because I worry that I might be seized by a mad impulse and jump. Today, at least, that fear was gone. I waited ten minutes or more, eyes locked on the dirt below my feet. Lavangetto did not appear. A thicket of leaves rattled on the far side of the park.

"Moron!" I shouted. A few minutes later, he appeared beneath my feet, out of breath and out of ideas. I held the cobblestone over his head, drew in my breath, and let my missile go. It fell, straight, silent, and heavy, and landed just wide of my mark. The cop knelt, raised his gun, and fired three shots without bothering to aim.

The bullets thudded into the wood a few branches below my perch. My palms went slick. The cop tucked his gun into his pants, wrapped his arms around the lowest branch, and started to climb. My legs locked in place. I took a deep breath, and the muscles loosened. I glanced down, and Lavangetto was a few branches closer. He stopped, drew his pistol, and pointed it at me.

I swung to the next branch just as he fired. The shot crashed through the canopy of red and yellow, inches behind my back. I did not look down again. I swung around to the far side of the tree and crashed down as fast as I could. I was halfway to the ground when he intercepted me. He glared up, gun held loosely in his left hand.

"You stabbed Emil," he yelled. "You cockeyed lunatic. You stabbed him in the back."

"He was going to kill that priest."

"The man was selling bootleg liquor. Or haven't you heard that's against the law? We just wanted to talk to him, break up his stock, shut down his place. It was his choice to fight back."

"Disrespecting a thug cop is no reason to die."

"And who are you to care?" I didn't have an answer for that. I don't think he really wanted one anyway. He held the pistol tighter and pointed it my way. "Now come on out of this tree, so I can take you over to the precinct without you getting hurt."

"It's my tree. I was here first."

"Girl, don't make me pull this trigger."

"Go ahead. I don't think you can hit anything that moves."

That made him laugh. It wasn't a nice laugh, and it wasn't a pretty laugh, but it was a useful one. When he laughed, he blinked. He didn't see my hands let go of the branch, or my feet, sailing through the crackling autumn leaves, directly at his head. A grunt thudded out of him when I made contact. We fell together, the branches knocking us sideways, scratching our faces, slowing us just enough that when we landed, we did not die. The ground knocked out my breath. By the noises he made, he was alive, but not much more than that.

I took his pistol, which looked the same as the one I had been dragging around, and opened the chamber after a few seconds of fiddling. I dropped both bullets into my pocket, hurled the gun toward the fountain, and strolled out of the park.

Lamb leaned against the side of his burning church, picking glass out of his knees. His clothes were streaked with blood, and soot covered his face, but his teeth shone yellow when he smiled.

"I'd have thought you'd have taken care of that one quicker," he said, "the way you knocked this boy down."

Koszler squirmed along the sidewalk like a roach on its back—legs pumping air and bloody fingers searching uselessly for a hand-hold. Horrible heaves escaped his mouth when he saw me coming his way.

"Do you want him to die?" asked Lamb.

"No."

"Then let's shred that uniform and bandage him as best we can."

At first, Koszler writhed away from our touch, but Lamb and I were strong enough to hold him down. Where it wasn't hot with blood, his skin was getting cold. Lamb ripped the uniform into strips, yanked out the biggest shards of glass, and tried to blot the wound.

"Now don't you wish you'd left me some liquor?" Lamb asked the patient. He gripped the pistol by the barrel and rapped it on Koszler's head. "I'd like to crack that rotten egg you call a skull."

"Die, old man," spluttered Koszler. "Remember who made you kneel."

Lamb stroked the pistol along Koszler's face, drew it back, and brought it down hard, smashing it on the sidewalk until the butt splintered and the mechanism broke into a dozen pieces.

"You're lucky I'm still half priest," he said and tossed the remains of the pistol into the storm drain.

"Can you walk?" I asked Lamb.

"A bit."

"Then get him on his feet. He's due back at the Fourth Precinct."

A long time ago, I promised my father that no Carr would ever again enter a precinct house. That day, with Emil Koszler's blood seeping down the sleeves of my dress, I broke my pledge. The Fourth was an antiseptic green pit. Dim light crept in through boarded windows. Overturned filing cabinets and smashed wood desks littered the floor, and vile script covered every wall.

Three empty barrels of Barbarossa's finest lay broken at the bottom of the stairwell, and the cops still felt the whiskey's effects. They slumped in corners, across sagging benches, their uniforms stained with vomit and blood—some of it theirs, and some, no doubt, belonging to the men and children whom they had slaughtered. They moaned, and Koszler moaned back, and the sleeping cops told him to shut up.

"Some friends," I said, and Koszler mumbled something hateful. Lamb and I wrapped his arms tight around our shoulders and hefted him up the stairs.

I'd spent a lot of time here as a child, coming after school to play hide-and-seek beneath the desks of the detectives. I knew my way around. My father's old office was on the second floor, and I did not doubt Thorne had taken it for himself. We were dragging Koszler down the hallway when the office door opened and out stepped the immaculate figure of Ida Greene. Ugly stood behind her, ax on his shoulder, the faintest smile on his lips.

"A half-dead cop," said Mrs. Greene. "What a lovely sight. Miss Carr, you continue to surprise."

"Why are you here?"

"Dick—Mr. Van Alen—was quite upset at last night's unpleasantness. He does not want that kind of horror to befoul the Upper West. We came to offer truce."

"I'm surprised he made it out alive."

"It took three guards to drag him back from the battle. He wanted to die with his men."

"I'm sure. Another chapter for the schoolbooks of the Upper West: the Battle of Eighth Avenue and Van Alen's heroic retreat. What about Barbie?"

"Dead, thank god. Gunned down by her own bought cops. It's a lesson, Gilda, to invest in quality."

"What did Thorne say to your offer of peace?"

"Nothing at all."

"The bastard's drunk," said Ugly. "Could hardly open his eyes."

"A man like that has no hope against the honest citizens of the Upper West," said Mrs. Greene. She said it gracefully, even beautifully, but there was fear in her eyes. "No matter how many guns he brings to bear."

"I hope you're right."

"I always am. When you tire of life in the dark, Gilda, come across the Borderline, and we will find you a home."

We stepped aside, and they walked away. The door to Thorne's office was open. We dropped Koszler on the floor. Thorne didn't stir.

"This is more time than I like to spend in a precinct house," said Lamb. I felt the same way.

"I can handle the situation from here."

"That I do not doubt. Goodbye, Gilda. If you get the chance, stab a few more cops for me."

He did not bother stepping over the puddle of Koszler's blood on his way out the door. His feet tracked red all the way down the hall.

I dug my fingers into Thorne's greasy curls, yanked him back, and smashed his face into his desk. That woke him up. He batted my arm away, leaned back in his chair, and reached for the nearest glass. It might have been water, and it might have been gin. Thorne swallowed it without a grimace and got to his feet. His dress uniform strained against his belly, and sweat flowed down the gullies of his jowls like a trickle of water cutting through rock. He dragged his tongue, red and swollen, across his lips.

"What the hell," he said, "have you done to my man?"

"He was like that when I found him."

"Bullshit. I'll lock you up for this. I'll shred your license. You've always been a spoiled brat, kid. Today you learn that you can't just do whatever you want. The law has come back to the Westside, and you're gonna heel."

"Quite inspiring. It'll look fine in the *Sentinel*. But arrest me, take my license, and no one will tell you where his partner is. If you think Koszler's hurting, you should see Lavangetto. I doubt he'll survive the afternoon."

"You think I'd desert my post in the middle of a war?"

"I think that, as wretched as you are, you do not want that man to die."

"Goddamn you, bitch. Fine."

Thorne banged on his desk until two of his men slouched in. Thorne gave them some instructions, and they dragged Koszler away.

"And his partner?" said Thorne.

"I'll tell you when we get outside."

He sighed and let his gut sag out, and I saw the shattered man I had known for so long. In the corner of the room, tossed aside like a stained undershirt, I found the rifle. I slung it over my shoulder and led him outside.

I kicked open the flimsy warehouse door. Thorne followed, stepping lightly, like he didn't trust the floor to hold his weight. He was right not to. The floorboards were half rotten, springy like floors should not be. The stairs were half iron and half rust. Through the shattered windows of the stairwell, the sun sank over the river. The stench of waterfront was in the air.

"So your boys killed Barbarossa," I said.

"I fired the shot myself. Right between the eyes I got her. Burned her body like we burned the others. It was better than she deserved."

"Barbie was an awful woman, but she was better than you."

"I'm a cop. I brought down a notorious criminal. Don't that make me some kind of hero?"

From the sickly pride in his voice, I could tell he was smirking, but also earnest—somewhere in his pickled mind he thought he'd done something noble. I was tempted to turn around and kick him in the face, kick him hard enough to send him tumbling down to the first floor bloodied and broken. I saw it vividly in my imagination, and the ease of it terrified me. I kept climbing. Barbarossa was not worth defending.

"And what about my father?"

"I loved that man. I never had a dad, you know? Clubber was . . . he was it. And I've always tried to look out for you. I sort of owed it to him."

"You were his Brutus."

"His who?"

"When the knife went in his back, you were the one twisting it. And when he was finished, I don't recall any visits to the house. I don't recall any notes of sympathy. I don't recall, Edward Thorne, that you did anything at all."

"And what the hell do you know about it?" he said, banging his fist on the flaking whitewashed wall. He did not look as big as he wanted. "When Clubber Carr spent his whole career breaking me down. His whole damned life. Kicking me in the side. Calling me names. Put a few drinks in him, and all he'd have to do is look at me to fall down in a heap of laughter. Ever since we was kids, wasn't a day passed that he didn't . . . Jesus. All I ever wanted . . . And he never gave a damn."

"Of course he didn't. My father had no time for human trash. Stop sniveling. Take a drink, if that's what you need."

He took a long pull from a nickel-plated flask. It quieted him. We continued up.

The door opened onto the roof, where the soft black tar was streaked with silver. Its west side sloped upward, and the lip overlooked the docks. I walked to the edge. Most of the dock where Copeland died had been washed away by the river. What remained was blackened and twisted. No sign of the yacht. Juliette had taken it home.

"Are you going to tell me what the hell we're doing here?" he said.

I took the rifle off my shoulder and held it by the strap. The wood was not warped. The barrel was not rusted. The Westside had not touched it at all. I didn't know how it was possible, but I felt an awful urge to find out.

"Where did they come from, these magic, terrible guns?" I said.

"You know full well we stole 'em from Copeland," he said, looking frightfully impressed with himself. "Right from under Barbie's nose."

"But where did she get them?"

"You think she told me that? You think she told me anything? That fat old cow thought I was stupid. Look what it got her."

"And Copeland?"

"Same thing."

"A bullet, courtesy Lieutenant Edward Thorne."

"Right between the eyes."

"That would be quite a shot, then, since the bullet hit Copeland in the back of the head."

"You don't know what you're talking about."

"When I close my eyes, it's all I see."

I tossed him the rifle. He caught it gracelessly.

"You really trust me with a gun," he said, "after what you saw me do last night?"

"I didn't see you hit anyone."

"I'm a crack shot, Gilda."

"So prove it. Just hit the dock, Thorne. We're not that far away. Just put a bullet through the dock."

He wrapped his quivering fingers around the stock.

"Perhaps it would be easier if you lay prone," I said.

"Yeah. Yeah, of course." He lowered himself clumsily to his belly. "Can I have a drink first?"

"As much as you require."

He drank deep. It steadied his fingers, but it didn't matter. When he fired the rifle, it bucked hard enough to bruise his shoulder. The bullet slapped harmlessly into the Hudson.

"Damn it!" he said.

"You didn't shoot Barbie last night, did you?"

"I shot at her! Maybe mine wasn't the bullet that killed her, but what the hell difference does it make?"

"She could still be alive."

"I tell you, I watched her body burn!"

"And Copeland. There's no way you could have shot him from here. So who did?"

"I . . . I have no idea."

Disgusting man. Just being near him made me want to wash my hands.

"You're too stupid to plan all this mayhem," I said. "You worked with someone else. Someone who knew when Copeland was going to dock, who knew what was in his hold, who knew the best way to turn Barbie and Van Alen against each other. Who was it?"

He dropped the rifle and clutched the flask close. I picked up the rifle and ejected the clip. It was empty.

"Your boys burned through a lot of ammunition last night."

"Don't worry about it. We're bringing more in."

"From *where*? Without Copeland, how?"

"Keep asking questions, Gilda Carr. Your daddy was the same way. Questions, questions, questions, writing every little detail down on his notepad. It never got him a thing. I know how to bend. That's the difference between your daddy and me. I know how to bend. He just broke."

"Who killed him?"

"Who cares?"

I squeezed the rifle until my hands turned white. I held it like a club, high over my head, and Thorne covered his eyes as I brought it down on the roof. I swung it until the stock snapped, and I tossed both halves over the edge.

"Who's running this insanity?" I said.

"I am! Sure, you think I'm a coward. You think I'm a worthless waste of a badge. But back at that precinct, at Centre Street, at the mayor's office? I'm a hero. I'm the man who saved the Westside. As soon as our next load of guns comes in, I'll break Van Alen too. I'll march the Fourth Precinct across the Borderline, all the way to the goddamned Harlem River, and we'll have a bullet for any citizen fool enough to get in our way. Every man who ever laughed at me will be dead. If that's not winning, what is?"

He laughed and covered his mouth with his hand. He did not stop laughing, even when I took the pistol from my bag. My finger rested lightly on the trigger. The barrel pressed against his head.

"Kill me, Gilda! Shoot me dead, right here. You been itching to do it all day, so why not? Come on. Shoot me, shoot me in the face, and choke on my blood. Do it, girl. Do it, you goddamned coward. Your father killed as easy as he breathed. Why can't you?"

I smacked him across the face with the barrel of the pistol. He laughed at that, laughed a mouthful of blood. When I walked off the roof, he was laughing still.

THIRTEEN

There was no one on the Borderline. No guards on either side. No bodies. No blood. Even the great fire-stand was gone. Either the cops or the shadows had picked the scene clean, and I didn't trust the Fourth Precinct to be so thorough.

I crossed into the Upper West, not sure what I would find. For the first few blocks, I saw no one, but gradually, life emerged. People chatted on their stoops. Children played hesitantly in the streets. The gates of the bazaar stood open, but its great hall was deserted. It was an ordinary day in a city under siege, where life goes on, but no one can be sure how long that will last.

I found what I was looking for on Fortieth Street: a dusty old shop whose display cases were two stories high and filled to bursting with music of every kind. Thousands of rolls of sheet music nestled into small cubbyholes, and the air was heavy with dust. It was like some lost library of the ancient world, and the shopkeeper was just as much an artifact. Tall, grinning, and skeletally thin, he looked like death, and he was happy to see me.

"Where are your phonograph records?" I said.

"Don't sell 'em. Ain't a working phonograph on the Westside. No demand."

"All you have is sheet music?"

"Instruments too, in the back. You looking for something particular?"

"It's an old song."

"All I got is old."

"'We'll skin your back, make your bones crack, and burn your face with lye,'" I sang, as best I could.

"That's not how it goes."

"You know it?"

"I know every song the Westside ever sang. That one I don't like."

"What's it called?"

"'The Bloody Fist Dirge.' Awful number. Just awful. But the lyrics—they go a little different. Let me find it," he said, and he climbed slowly up his ladder, to the top of the western wall, and he flitted his fingers from sheet to sheet until he found the one that would save Brass Aiken from the music in his head—and give me a chance to inspect the man Van Alen claimed had killed my father.

I tapped my foot on Forty-Eighth Street. I knew where I had to go, but the thought didn't thrill me. At the end of the block was the fence, and a gate I had passed through once before. Now, I had no license, and no way out. But there was an alternate route.

"All right, Alice," I said. "Perhaps I'll see you soon."

The doors to the Longacre swung open. No noise came from inside. But then, when your workers have been relieved of their tongues, noise is never a problem. As I crept across the faded rose lobby carpet, I wondered if I believed Van Alen's story about discovering those mutilated workers at a crooked boys' home. I eased open the orchestra door, saw the theater was deserted, and decided he had probably lied.

The aisle sloped down to the orchestra pit, where the walls had been removed to allow easier passage of stolen goods. From there, a steep ramp led up to the gash in the Longacre stage. The string of lanterns dangled overhead, extinguished. I lit a match and climbed down into the dark.

When my feet touched dirt I felt a pang of terror. It wasn't a fear of dying, or the shadows, or the tunnel. It was the realization that I had become so terribly alone. Where was Hellida? Where was Virgil Carr? Where, for the love of the god whom I had never trusted, was Mary Fall? If I died in this tunnel, who would even care? I would care, I decided, and that would have to do.

"Shut up," I said, "and start walking."

The tunnel was low, rough-hewn, and cold. It stretched on for longer than seemed possible, but I had plenty of matches, and the shadows did not stir. At the end was a ladder, and a trapdoor that opened into an alleyway just east of Times Square. The air was rancid, and I was alive.

The daytime elevator operator at the Hyperion Hotel had a neck as white and soft as mashed potatoes. He was so surprised to feel my hand around his throat that he did not flinch when I threw him out of his car. He fell into the plush red carpet, moaning in embarrassment, and turned over only when he heard the elevator grate close behind him.

"My car!" he shouted to no one in particular. "That little nut snatched my car!"

I'd never operated an elevator before. It was not as easy as it looked, but it still wasn't hard. I plunged the lever forward and shot into the darkness, past twenty-some floors, until I reached the penthouse. The elevator was harder to stop than it was to start. It crashed into the roof of the shaft with a sickening crunch, then sagged on its gears, a few inches above the lip of the penthouse floor. I opened the grate and hopped into Brass Aiken's apartment, where the party was definitely over.

It was barely night, but every light was blazing. The stench of spilled liquor was sickening. The long couches were flipped on their sides. Wind whistled in through a broken pane of glass, joining the faint click of a phonograph needle to make an eerie melody.

"Would you flip that record?" Aiken called. A pile of cushions filled the bandstand, and he perched on the top of the heap, back pressed into the corner, surveying the room. A half dozen lamps leaned on the bottom of the stage, pointing bright enough at his face to obliterate all shadows. His skin was ghostly. His head pressed into the heels of his hands, and his fingers dragged long yellow fingernails across his cheeks.

"Hiding from the shadows?" I said. "What gave you that idea?"

"Clubber. Clubber always knew best."

"You saw him, didn't you, the day he died?"

"We had dinner. Sole bonne femme. The sauce was good, but the fish was overcooked, a little dry."

"I don't really care about the fish."

"Barbie's dead," he said. "Rated half an inch in the afternoon paper. Van Alen will join her soon. Galen, Viv—dear lord, your father. That's five. Only Eddie and I will still be kicking. Look at me. Do I look strong enough to be the last to die?"

"How about a song?"

Aiken's face relaxed into a smile. I approached slowly. Beneath one of the couches I spotted a not-quite-empty bottle of the whiskey he had been so proud of two nights before. I walked with it out in front of me, a peace offering that he took eagerly into his hands.

"Now tell me," I said, "that you know how to play that piano."

"A bit. Yes, a bit. I mean, I can't play songs, precisely, but I'm quite expert at getting it to make noise."

"That won't be enough."

"Ah, well. Maybe you can play?"

Two years of lessons, begun the week my mother died. Some demon relative convinced my father it was a good idea—a way to take the poor girl's mind off her troubles. I'd never taken to the instrument, and I remembered almost nothing. I sat on the stool and arranged my music in front of me. The soft rustling of the pages sounded, as it always has, like recent death. I played the dirge.

"Do you recognize it?" I said.

"I might, if it sounded at all like music. Try playing . . . better."

I did what I could, picking it out, note by note, with fingers stiff and fearful. Finally, something like a melody emerged.

"That's the song!" cried Aiken. "That hateful, awful, ugly, wonderful song! Do you have the words?"

"They're written right here."

"Then sing with me, you beautiful little woman. Sing!"

We sang. It wasn't pretty, but it wasn't meant to be. The song was a warning to those who would cross the Seven Bloody Fists. Its verses named the vanquished enemies of that greatest of Westside gangs, heaping scorn on every boy whose skull was ever broken by Clubber, Eddie, Galen, Barbie, Viv, Brass, or Dick. The song spoke of the Fists like they were titans littering Sixth Avenue with the bones of their enemies, leaving scorched earth and grieving mothers in their wake. It was a gruesome song, and it made Brass smile.

The music salesman was right—the lyrics I'd heard were not quite right. It went, and Brass sang with gusto:

"'We'll skin your back, make your bones crack, and scrub your wounds with lye. There's a blacked-out pier in the river, oh, where old sailors go to die.'"

When we finished, I closed the sheet music and inspected the cover—a lithograph of seven towering demons stomping the life out of some poor urchin. The text credited music and lyrics to "J. W. Howe," who had written it for a forgotten Bowery spectacle of 1910 called *Devils of the West Side*. I set the music aside, hoping Brass wouldn't ask me to play it a second time, and heard him choke back a sob.

He lit a cigarette. His lips were so wet, they soaked straight through the paper.

"Something in this city has it out for us," he said. "I see it in the corners, no matter how loud the music gets, no matter how bright I turn up the lights. It's just a flicker. They dart in from the balcony, the elevator shaft. You have to be quick to escape them, and I get a hair slower every day. Do you see the shadows move?"

"I have."

"That's lucky, then. If you see them, you can get out of the way. Or maybe it's not so lucky—maybe if you see them, that means they're coming for you, no matter what."

"What else did my father tell you?"

"He said he'd put it all together. I didn't think he had. What he talked about . . . . it didn't make sense. He told me all about this, this . . ."

"Shadow city."

"A city of the dead, right here, all around us, sharing our streets and our buildings and our bedrooms, and never crossing paths. He said it had been here forever, that maybe it was what made the Westside so odd, but that the two cities never touched until 1903."

"The vanishing of Alice Pearl."

"That's the name. He said he had it all sorted out."

"How?"

"It came down to the date. She disappeared when?"

"May 15, 1903," I said—a date I knew like my own birthday.

"Galen made his first run upriver two days earlier, with my money and his bankroll. That, your father said, that is what killed Alice Pearl. Because he wasn't just going upriver—he was sailing into that shadow city and coming back with goods that couldn't be gotten anywhere else. Those trips opened up some kind of tear between the two cities, and poison—that was his word, 'poison'—flooded forth."

"I've seen the shadow city. There's nothing there but death. Nothing to sell or trade. There's no easy way to get there and no safe way out. What was Galen doing there? How was he traveling back and forth?"

"That's what he came to ask me. And I told him, 'Clubber, if you want to fix a fight or court an heiress, I'm your man. I know every crook and blue blood on the stem. But I haven't set foot in the Westside in years. Its mysteries are beyond me.' I tried to let him down easy. I thought he was drunk. I mean—what the hell kind of sense does it make? Some woman disappears in Times Square.

Things like that happen. I'm sure there was another woman who'd disappeared the week before, the month before, and no one had any clue where she'd gone. It's not like they saw her taken by shadows. But your father was stuck on it."

"There must have been a reason."

"He'd lost his goddamned mind. That's your reason. He thought it was my fault, mine and Galen's. What the hell could I have had to do with it? I just gave an old friend a little money to expand his business, and now it's my fault some woman nobody heard of died? How is that fair?"

Brass seemed to want me to absolve him, but it was not within my power.

"They're bringing in more guns," I said. "A bigger shipment, Thorne said, big enough to wipe the Upper West off the map. Do you know where Copeland might have hidden a boat big enough for all that?"

"I don't. That's what I get for losing touch with old friends. But anyway, what do you care? You know what's coming. Why not run?"

"Last night, I heard those boys dying in the dark. I saw the *things* that killed them. The way they screamed . . . that doesn't need to happen again." I put on another record, took the bottle from Aiken's clammy hand, and drained the last of it into my throat. "After you—who did he go to next?"

"Barbie. He wanted her to shut down their operation. Silly bastard. He told me, 'She loves me, Brass. Always has. I'm not worth a damn but she loves me anyway. And when I tell her what's been going on, she'll quit, or I'll tell the world.'"

"She should have laughed. She should have dared him to tell the papers, to make a fool of himself one more time."

"But it wasn't a joke to her. It was real, wasn't it? The whole silly thing."

"And they killed him to protect it. Copeland or Barbarossa. My god."

I'd thought such a revelation might mean relief from the acid that had churned in my stomach the last few days, but it only stoked the flame. Solve a tiny mystery and forget it forever. But as I felt the wind whistle through the windows of that broken hotel room, I understood that finding the answer to this question might require me to take action in a way I could not abide.

Aiken inspected the bottle and was disappointed to see it was empty. He tossed it over his shoulder, breaking another pane of glass.

"The management is going to have my head. If the shadows don't get me, the concierge will."

"Before they throw you out, would you mind putting in a room service order?"

"Anything for the girl who got that song out of my head. What are you hungry for?"

"Does the kitchen do a roast beef sandwich?"

"Absolutely not."

"Then never mind."

"They don't do a sandwich because their roast beef is a gift from heaven. Bloodred and tender as spring. Far too fine to waste on bread. A little horseradish is all you need."

"Then make it roast beef with horseradish."

"That's it?" he said and tossed a menu into my lap. I opened the green felt cover, scanned my eyes down the endless columns of tiny font, and realized how hungry I was.

"A mountain of dinner rolls. Prime rib, roast chicken, a crate of roasted vegetables in a vat of brown butter, and a platter of sole bonne femme."

I didn't see how much Aiken paid the waiter, but it was enough to keep the elevator operator from calling the police and to let me walk out of the hotel pushing a room service cart piled high with silver trays. I left him perched on his cushions, bathed in foul light, flinching every time he thought he saw a shadow move. I didn't think he needed to be afraid. Just as a drunk may topple out a window and bounce off the sidewalk unharmed, Aiken was too flexible to be broken by the Westside. After all, nothing stains Brass.

The guard at the fence goggled at the food, but let me cross over when I handed him a wad of Aiken's cash. I was home again, and I wasn't sure I would ever leave.

There were night-fires burning on the streets of the Upper West, but they were feeble. The sidewalks were empty, and Van Alen's guards looked scared. I pushed my cart, its trays rattling with every bump, across Fourteenth Street and into the familiar darkness of the Lower West. The shadows—for the street was mostly shadows—began to creep closer. I felt the cold tugging at my ankles, and I ran.

The street turned to cobblestones, and I had to keep a tight grip to stop the cart from toppling over. A dish of scalloped potatoes clattered off, dousing my shoes in béchamel. The acrid smell of rosemary cut through the frost that wrapped itself around my head. I breathed deep and begged my legs to keep running.

They faltered when I got to Thompson Street. I slipped to one knee, grabbed the room service cart, and dragged myself up. Behind me, the city had been replaced by a black as deep as velvet. A horn sounded behind me—the roar of one of the city buses that had never run on the Westside. The horn sounded again, and my legs went numb. I took the lid off the roast beef, gripped it in my cold, sweating palm, and whipped it through the glass door of Cleo's Pet Shop, which the One-Eyed Cats had once called home. A fine throw. Hellida would have been proud.

A candle flickered on inside. I sank to the cobblestones, tasted their filth on my lips, and wished I was eating roast beef instead. My body deserted me. The horn sounded again. My heart thudded, impossibly slowly, and I heard my father whispering in my ear.

"Gilda?"

I looked up—leaned my neck back and found I still had a neck, opened my eyes and found I still had eyes. Cherub stood on the sidewalk, looming above me like the Colossus over Rhodes, his face and clothes crisp with dried blood. He reached down a hand, and his palm touched mine, and the cold fell away like a nightgown.

"Room service," I said and found the strength to stand. I turned around. The street was dark, but not impossibly, and there were no buses for miles.

We hauled the cart into the shop, past a wall of hungry mutts, and at the first taste of meat, Cherub laughed so hard that the saber slipped from under his hand, and he fell backward onto the mattress he kept in the middle of the floor. It was honest, loving laughter, and it warmed me as much as the roast beef soothed him.

"This is it!" he shouted through a mouthful of sauced beef. "This is the sandwich I've been dreaming of."

"And it wasn't a sandwich at all." I socked him on the shoulder. The bastard.

"I should have expected it. I should have known that in a city that seeps like a pus boil, Gilda Carr could still work miracles. Oh dear god, is it fine."

"As good as you remember?"

"No memory tastes this good. Have a mouthful."

I did, and it was as Aiken promised: a taste of heaven. Cherub put a bit of roast beef on his finger and called softly for Mose. The rat scurried out from under the counter, sniffed the meat, and ate it in one bite.

For a while we talked about nothing that mattered, and I tried to keep him laughing as long as I could. We talked about food, about the first fistful of candy he stole when he was a child, about the abominable pancakes I used to force my father to eat every Sunday.

"Six or seven years back," he said, "when the fence was new, me and the lads snuck over and scaled the walls of Aylesmere's. Got into the air vents, shimmied down to where the restaurant is, and cracked the seals on the iceboxes. One was full of strawberries, the other whipped cream. I ate myself silly, Gilda, and as my eyes started to cross, there crossed my mind the purest thought I ever had."

"Do share."

"When I'm grown, I thought, every day of my life I'll eat all the whipped cream I want." I flicked a spoonful of trifle at him. It missed badly, landing in the cage of a grateful hound. "I suppose I'm grown now. I've lost enough friends to qualify."

After that, I couldn't make him laugh very hard anymore.

When the food was cold, and our plates bore nothing but un-identifiable smears of sauce and starch, I told him the little I'd learned, and what would happen when Thorne's next boat came in.

"Van Alen's people are marshmallow soft," said Cherub. "Scared of the dark. Thorne will crush them."

I disagreed. "I've seen them. What they have up there, they'll fight for it."

"And die by the thousand."

There was a long silence, and Cherub's hand crept across the mattress to rest on mine, and I found myself whistling to banish the thought of kissing him.

"That awful song!" said Cherub.

"'The Bloody Fist Dirge.'"

"Lovely title."

"I learned the lyrics too. They're some of the worst . . . say, Cherub. Did you ever hear of a blacked-out pier?"

"Is this some kind of riddle?"

"A blacked-out pier in the river where old sailors go to die."

"Let it go, Gilda. We've lost enough."

"One that had been painted black, maybe? Or taken off the maps?"

"I'm no Daybreak Boy, Gilda. The river was never my turf."

"Then where do old sailors die?"

"In my experience? Any dive that sells nickel gin."

I paced the length of the dog cages, trailing my hand from wet nose to wet nose. A skinny little greyhound looked up, head cocked like he was waiting for an answer. I closed my eyes and searched the waterfront, block by block, looking for black piers, but every one was brown, gray, or gone. I saw burnt-out warehouses, empty markets, abandoned saloons, and seamans' churches that had been given over entirely to the creeping vines. I saw the pier where Copeland died, and shook my head, and continued uptown. I was nearly at the Borderline when I saw a sagging brick building that had once been almost beautiful.

"There's a boardinghouse on Jane Street," I said, "right by the water. Before the fence went up, it was a convalescent home for old sailors."

"I don't like that gleam in your eye."

"The song mentions it for a reason."

"The song doesn't mean a goddamned thing! It's just a bit of fluff, a tall tale of the deadly old Westside, meant to spook tourists into thinking they'd seen a slice of real New York. The moron who wrote it probably never stepped west of the stem in all his life."

"It has to mean something."

"No, girl. It doesn't. Nothing we've done meant anything at all."

I stood, wiped the crumbs off my dress, and offered him my hand.

"On your feet," I said.

"There are cops on every corner, and far worse creeping around in the dark."

"Please, Cherub. I'm going for a walk. Won't you join me?"

"Well . . . If it means we don't have to wash the dishes."

We scraped the remains of our dinner into the dogs' cages and set out into the night. Cherub leaned heavily on his saber and did not refuse my arm. His skin was hot, and the shadows stayed in their place. We worked our way up to Jane Street and down toward the river. At Greenwich we saw a patrol from the Fourth Precinct, their torchlight throwing long shadows down the avenue. The cops did not speak and did not sing. At the front of the pack, a sergeant led bloodhounds.

We stepped into a doorway. Cherub's breath smelled of horse-radish. I hoped the hounds could not smell it. Their sniffing drew closer, and his body tensed—either from fear, or because he was about to kiss me. In either case, it would have to wait. I turned my back to him and watched the dogs straining toward us. Cherub put his hand on my shoulder.

"Blasted dogs," said the sergeant, tugging on their leashes. "Don't know what's got them fussing. Eat better than I do."

A final yank made the dogs forget horseradish. The patrol continued north.

"Let's wait here," Cherub said, running his hand along the small of my back in a not-unpleasant way. "Just another minute."

"Keep walking."

The Sailor's Home was all the way at the river, a squat brick pile whose turret overlooked the inky black strip that was the Hudson. The riverside wall had collapsed into rubble, and the rooms were exposed as neatly as an open dollhouse. We climbed across bricks and broken glass, and over the jagged lip of the building. We lit a match. Ruined furniture filled the lobby, and a weather-beaten mural of a shipwreck dominated the wall.

"When those poor bastards who made it off the *Titanic* came in," Cherub said, "they tried to house them here. First-class toffs wouldn't have it. Refused to step off the dock until they booked them at the Hyperion."

"I remember."

"How many of the steerage passengers did the shadows take that night?"

"Nineteen."

"Lord. You're going to make us climb to the top, aren't you?"

I took his hand, and we found the stairs. They were on the western edge of the building, where the wall had collapsed, which left them completely open to the night. I kept a grip on what remained of the railing and tried to ignore the wind tugging at my skirt.

At the third-floor landing, Cherub stopped to light a new match. I made the mistake of looking down. My mind flooded with images of myself tumbling through the air, handing my body over to death. Two steps to the left would do it. I pressed myself against the wall, holding tight to what remained of the bannister, palms sweaty and throat dry.

"Oh god," I murmured. Cherub didn't say a word. He took a

firm grip on my left arm and marched me up the stairs. Even if I'd wanted to jump, he wouldn't have let me. By the time we got to the top, I was breathing again.

There was nothing to see from the turret. The windows were blown out, and in the furious wind I felt the first bite of winter. The moon was faint. Across the river, New Jersey twinkled stupidly. I sat on a broken marble bench and tried to remember why we'd come. He sat down, close enough for me to feel the stubble on his cheek.

"I shouldn't be here, you know?" he said. "My poor boys. We used to dream of such a brawl. Lower West against the Upper, fists and chains and knives and clubs. Crossing the Borderline and coming home garlanded in the blood of Van Alen's guards. The Borderline. Christ. It's just Fourteenth Street."

"You dying wouldn't have changed a thing."

"I should have died five years ago, before I ever got in their ears, before I ever filled their heads with songs of glory, legends of the Westside. I led them on that last stupid charge. I wrapped their heads in shadow. I put the bullets in their skulls."

"Do you want me to tell you that if you hadn't done it, somebody else would have? Do you want me to tell you that everyone must die sometime, and they were lucky to die for something they believed in?"

"Thirty-two boys, dead by my hand. Even Roach."

He looked empty. I felt the same way. A week of agony and exhaustion bore down on my shoulders, threatening to crush me unless I could find some way to cast it off for a second or two. Too much had happened that I could not help, but there was one thing I wanted that I knew I could have.

"That's the Westside," I said.

"And I'm sick of it."

"I am too."

I brushed my hand against his cheek and kissed him as deeply as I could. It didn't help anything, but it didn't hurt either. He pressed me to his chest and dug his fingers into my hair, and I remembered how good it felt to have him in my arms. Unfortunately, eventually I had to breathe. I stopped and leaned back, and he gave me a kind of smile, and I had to look away. He pulled me in again, and I stopped him.

"Wait—where's the river?" I said.

"Another riddle?"

"No, look. Where did it go?"

"It's just dark. You can never see the river in the dark."

"You beautiful moron—look! You can see it uptown, ever so faintly, you can see it downtown, but right in front of this building, it's absolute black."

"A blacked-out pier."

"Give me something I can set on fire."

With great reluctance, he handed over his handkerchief. I dangled it over a match, letting it twist in the wind until it caught fire, then dropped it over the edge. It tumbled, end over end, burning more and more, until it landed on the sidewalk and cast a faint orange light over the side of the ruined building.

"Do you see it?" he said.

"I do."

"And you're not afraid?"

"I'm not even surprised."

As the handkerchief burned, the darkness on the river slipped back, and a silhouette took shape—the outline of a tramp steamer that filled in as the handkerchief burned. It was like watching a caricaturist sketch a boat. First just the outline, then every detail, from the scarred hull to the single light that burned on the bridge.

"That wasn't there before," I said.

"Isn't it fine that even at our advanced ages, the Westside continues to surprise?"

We tore down the stairs. The ship had not vanished when we got to the sidewalk.

"Get uptown," I said. "Find Ugly La Rocca or Ida Greene. If they're quick they can burn Thorne's ship down to the river before he sails."

"And just what will you be doing, while I'm running all over the Westside?"

"I'm going to search this boat. Go. If you're waiting for a kiss goodbye, you'll be waiting forever."

"So you think." He kissed his hand and blew the kiss in my direction. I tried not to let him see me smile. Cherub hobbled off, and I climbed the gangway. There was a lump in my throat the size of a plum. I turned away from the light in the pilothouse, eased open the first door I found, and slipped belowdecks.

The hold was packed with Barbie's liquor, enough to keep New York drunk for a week. How many guns would these casks buy, and where? Just before the stern, I found an unlocked door that led to a cramped, tightly organized little room. On the metal desk beside the bunk was a photo of Juliette and Edith Copeland. Beside it was a leather-bound notebook. Inside were long strings of numbers written in Galen Copeland's hand. It was a code or naval coordinates—or he was simply practicing his arithmetic. I was trying to puzzle it out when I heard shouting up above. The ship gave a lurch, the engines groaned into life, and we pulled into the Hudson River.

FOURTEEN

I locked the cabin door as quietly as I could and pressed my back against the wall. I checked my bag. One gun. Three bullets. It would take at least four men to make me leave.

Footsteps in the hallway. Two sailors, maybe more. They stopped, uncomfortably close to my beating heart. The doorknob rattled. A fist banged twice against the door.

"What's got you angry?" asked a guttural Irish voice.

"This door, why's it locked?"

"Who cares?"

"I care, okay? Isn't that enough?"

"That's the captain's cabin."

"The captain's dead."

I stood on Copeland's bunk, bracing myself against the bulkhead, pistol in hand. The knowledge crept over me that I wasn't entirely sure how to use a gun.

"You hear what happened to that poor bastard Koszler? Him and his partner, beat half to death by some silly little girl."

"They're gonna live, aren't they?"

"You say that like it makes it all okay."

"Well it does, don't it?"

"You ever get stabbed in the kidney or knocked out of a tree? So you're going to live. Great. Agony is agony."

I pushed the hammer back with the heel of my palm. My hand was sweaty. The hammer slipped.

"Help me break it down," said the Irishman.

"I am absolutely not doing that."

The hammer fell. The gun would have fired had my hand not gotten in the way. My mouth opened in a silent scream. I yanked my hand away, leaving a chunk of skin behind.

"Shift your feet, moron, and let's get back to work."

There was a long silence, then a few more uncreative curses. The footsteps shuffled away. I hurled the uncooperative pistol on the stained yellow mattress. After a few minutes' squeezing my injured hand, I was nearly able to breathe.

We sailed twenty minutes before the engines cut out. I tried to imagine how far that might have carried us from the city and realized I had no idea if we'd gone upriver or downriver, or how far a ship could travel in that amount of time. I was ruing my ignorance of maritime mathematics when something massive rocked the ship, and the sound of scraping metal cut through my spine. The engines stayed quiet. The shadows began to move.

They crept down the walls and raced across the floor like flooding water. I leapt onto the captain's bed, pressing my back to the wall. They surged up the legs, then the mattress, and then my feet. I went numb. I fell to my knees. The shadows were at my throat.

The lights went out. The darkness was black, and then it was blinding white, and there was no sound at all.

I reached for something to hold on to, for some wall to press against, but I felt nothing, saw nothing. My breath was coming far too fast, and had I been able to feel my pulse, I'm sure it would have been racing. I tried to control my breathing, to remember that no matter what evil place I had stumbled into, I was still in a locked room. I got my breath under control, closed my eyes, and waited.

The lights flared on, glowing black, and I saw the cabin in reverse. I grabbed the gun. As I gripped it, something strange happened. My fear was gone. Like all sinners must, I was becoming accustomed to hell. Instead of terror, I felt something far more dangerous: curiosity.

I unlocked the cabin door.

The hall was empty; the lights were bright. There were no shadows, no ghouls. I stepped lightly, knowing no one could hear my footsteps, and kept the revolver pressed to my temple in case I needed to make a quick escape back to reality.

I peered around the corner into the hold and saw the sailors—the cops—huddled on the floor, heads bowed and hands over their eyes. I watched them for some time. They were paralyzed by fear.

Past them, iron steps led up to the deck. I sprinted past them, making no noise. They could have seen me; they could have caught me, but these men who were brave enough to gun down children were too scared to open their eyes in the dark.

I was almost giddy as I charged up the steps. I needed only a few moments on deck to see where we had sailed, to find the location of Copeland's gate, to learn the secret my father died for. Quite an accomplishment, I thought, for a woman working on so little sleep. But before I reached the door, I saw the figure huddled atop the steps. Her dress was white, just like mine, but by the way she pressed her clenched fists over her eyes, I could see she was not as comfortable in the world of shadows.

Juliette Copeland—you are far from home.

Her eyes snapped open. Dark tears stained her cheeks. "Help," she said silently, and I smiled as best I could. I gestured for her to wait, and she shook with fear, pressing her back to the bulkhead like a drowning rat.

I tried the bulkhead door. Locked, and far beyond the capacity of my little pick. Answers would have to wait.

I offered Juliette my hand and led her back to my cabin, closing the door as the engines awoke. The lights went out again, and we were alone in the brilliant white. She leaned on my shoulder. I held her in my arms, and we closed our eyes, and I did not feel so afraid.

Like turning off an electric lamp, the white flashed to black, and the lights came back on, and the world was sane again.

"What," she said, her voice near cracking, "what hell was *that*?"

"Passage. Safe passage through a city of death."

"And it's brought us where?"

"I look forward to finding out. What are you doing here?"

"I couldn't stop thinking about what you said about fathers and their secrets. I went back to the office and took a hard look at Papa's datebook."

"What did you find?"

"There were six Sundays this year, six days when there was no work to be done at the office, but Papa didn't come home."

"That sounds quite typical of our fathers."

"That's what I thought. But I glanced at those pages, and on each one was written 'Pier 51.' Jane Street. I found the ship, I snuck aboard—"

"You found the ship? You mean you saw it when you walked up?"

"No. Not at first. The pier was empty, like a great black gap, but when I turned my head I saw something flickering out of the corner of my eye. I walked toward it—I thought I was going to walk straight into the river—and just before I fell off the pier, my hand found metal, and the ship took shape before my eyes. It was . . . peculiar."

"Do you have any idea where we've gone?"

"I was rather too preoccupied with hiding. The men who run this ship are frightful. The state of their uniforms is disgraceful, and the stench! It's absurd."

We sailed another forty-five minutes before the engines stopped for good. The hallways filled with chatter, but no one tried the door. I gripped my gun, ready for nothing, and nothing came. After an hour, the ship had gone quiet. I slipped open the lock, and we stepped into the hallway.

The hold was empty, the liquor gone. We crept back to the hold, and up the steps, where the bulkhead door swung free. The deck was bare. The dock was lit by a streetlight. Above our heads was the

Manhattan Bridge. We hadn't sailed upriver to some mysterious Hudson hamlet. We had just gone 'round the island to dock on the Eastside. Dizzying, that. I must have wobbled, because Juliette took my hand to steady me.

On the dock, the cops of the Fourth Precinct loaded the cargo onto an open-backed truck while a team of stevedores watched, flicking cigarettes with the calculated laziness common to dock-workers everywhere. There were ships on either side of us, their lights dark. At the end of the pier, the street was empty, save for a long, sleek limousine.

"How are we going to get past them?" hissed Juliette.

"Just wait."

When the last crate was loaded, one of the idle men waved his arm, and the car drove down, lights bouncing as it passed over each slat of wood. It stopped beside the truck, and the back window rolled down.

"Something missing, isn't it?" asked one of the cops, a man I did not recognize. "We bring liquor. You bring guns. The guns ain't here."

I could not make out the response from the car, but it did not placate the cop, who responded with a particularly vile curse. This was a mistake.

The car door swung open and connected with the cop's skull. He tumbled backward, head hitting the pier with an awful thump. From the car stepped Glen-Richard Van Alen, dressed for the op-era, and ready to brawl.

Van Alen took the cop by the throat and slammed his bloody scalp into the hood of the roadster. He groaned, the cry of a dying animal.

"Good lord," said Juliette.

The other cops just watched as Van Alen dragged his victim across the dock as easily as a boy stealing his sister's rag doll. He dangled the man in the space between ship and pier. The ship edged closer, pressing against his legs.

"I could drop him," he said. "I could let the ship snap these twigs he calls legs. Or you scrawny, tattered pieces of filth could take my word for it when I tell you the guns'll be here tomorrow, noon."

No one argued. Van Alen dropped the man on the dock and used the ragged police uniform to wipe the blood from his gleaming leather shoes. Only when the door closed and the car backed down the pier, followed by the truck, did Thorne's men move to help their friend.

"Now," I said.

"Now?" said Juliette.

I slunk down the gangway, Juliette behind me, and prayed that when I stepped on the dock, it would not creak.

For the first time all week, something went my way. The dock was silent, and Juliette and I snuck into the darkness across the pier.

"Lunatic," said one of the cops—the Irishman I'd heard before. "Bastard deserves to be shot down like a dog."

"And how you gonna do it without any bullets?" said another, who had torn his shirt to make a bandage for the injured man.

"Let's get this poor son of a bitch back on the boat. Christ, I hate it here."

"Seconded."

It took a while for them to move him, long enough that by the time Juliette and I reached the street, Van Alen and his truck were gone.

"This is mad," said Juliette.

"Thoroughly."

"Would you be offended if I left you here? I've had quite enough sneaking about for the day, and I believe I'd be more comfortable at home."

"I feel the same way. Before you go"—I handed her the journal I had found in her father's cabin—"do you recognize it?"

"These are shipping coordinates."

"Could you make sense of them?"

"I've spent a lifetime trying not to meddle in my father's affairs. But for you, I will do my best."

"Thank you."

She took a few steps uptown, then turned back, and called, "Are you all right, Miss Carr? You don't look well."

"You're absolutely right," I said and headed west.

It had been a tortuous day. I had walked the breadth of Manhattan more times than a polite girl should. I was hungry, thirsty, exhausted, and injured. I might have been frightened if I weren't so tired. I dreaded what would happen to my city tomorrow, a viscous feeling that pulsed through my veins and weighed down my feet, but did not keep me from longing for sleep. I would bribe the guards, or threaten them, or sneak past them into the Westside. I would walk back to Bex's. I would sink into her couch. I would sleep until I had a better idea.

I tried not to think about where Van Alen was getting guns, or why he, a teetotaler, was swapping them for liquor. I tried not to count the blocks I would have to walk to reach Bex's narrow town house. Instead, I put my mind to work remembering the intricate series of misplays that had cost the Giants that afternoon, but I found I couldn't remember anything but how hard my seat was and how unimpressed I had been with the blue of the Brooklyn sky.

Even late at night, the streets of the Eastside are usually crowded. This close to the river, I expected the sidewalks to be carpeted with the city's most destitute, but aside from the odd dozing vagrant, the sidewalks were bare. October was in the air, and it had driven them indoors. Where, I didn't care.

"Firecracker. That louse."

The voice was my father's, and it came from over my shoulder. I turned, saw no one, and realized he was speaking only in my head.

"You expected better?" I muttered.

"He was always a bully, but he was never smart enough to be a liar. It doesn't make any sense."

"You taught me to never trust anything that made sense."

"Hmph. Then what are you going to do about it?"

"I don't know."

"You've got a long walk to figure it out."

"Who can I go to? Who would care? Barbie is dead. Cherub is crippled. La Rocca can't be trusted. Brass Aiken is a mess. I can't go to the police. I can't go to the mayor. They would love to see Thorne wipe out the Upper West."

"Maybe he's not after the Upper West. Maybe the guns are a kind of peace deal—Van Alen paying Thorne to get him off his back."

"Arming your enemy is a strange way to make peace."

"Maybe they were never enemies in the first place. Could this all have been some kind of scheme—a plan to get rid of Barbie?"

"Don't call her Barbie."

"I'm your father, and I'll call her what I want."

"You are *not* my father. You're my imagination, and I'd prefer not to imagine you and her doing *that*."

"Your mother has been gone a long time, child. Andrea had her charms."

"Bring up my mother again and I'll bash my head out on the sidewalk."

That shut him up, but not for long.

"You could blow up the ship."

"They'd find another way to get the guns across. Through Van Alen's tunnels, maybe."

"Wait until the guns are aboard."

"And then what? What do I know about explosives? I can't even fire a pistol. In fact, I'm quite proud of the fact that I can't fire a pistol. It's a barbaric habit. And suddenly you're instructing me to start blowing up boats. Ridiculous."

"It would save a lot of lives."

"Where would I get the explosives? The only man I know who's confident about that sort of thing is the man who's selling the guns!"

I was so intent on silencing the voice in my head that I did not realize I'd crossed into Washington Square. The arch was gleaming, the trees were stunted, and the creeping vines were gone. The park was cleaner than it had been since I was a girl, and the shadows were perfectly still. I was passing under the arch when it occurred to me that no fence had blocked me when I'd crossed Broadway, and no guard had demanded my license. Thorne had done it. I didn't know how, but he'd done it—broken Barbarossa and reunited the Westside with the East in a single night. It simply wasn't possible, but I didn't care, because on the far side of the park, in the light of a burning streetlight, I saw a three-story town house with a high stone stoop. My home had returned to me.

I raced up the steps, scraping my key along the railing as I had done my entire life, and let myself in. The house was dark and tidier than my house had any right to be.

"Damn it, Hellida," I called. "Who gave you permission to clean?"

I walked to the kitchen, which smelled of soap and the fading odor of roasted potatoes. My piles of newspapers, my closetful of garbage, my counter of rotting jam had all been thrown away. I would reprimand her in the morning. For now, I wanted nothing but a cup of tea and fifteen or twenty hours of sleep. I put the kettle on and saw by the clock that it was five or six hours later than it should have been. Where does the time go, I was wondering, when I heard the voice behind me.

"Gilda. My Gilda."

It wasn't Hellida speaking.

It was my father.

Not in my head, but in my kitchen.

Virgil Carr. Doddering, beautiful, mad. Alive.

When he saw me, he began to cry. I didn't know what to do, so I made us tea and watched him sob.

He was older. His whiskers were still thick, and his eyes were deep-set glittering gold, but the sideburns were white and the lines around his eyes cut close to the bone. His skin was clear—not the rusty red I remembered—and his clothes were clean. He trembled as he reached for his teacup, from age or shock I could not tell. The tea was scalding. I let it scald, drank it quickly, and poured another cup.

"Calm yourself," I told us both.

"Speak softly. Your mother is sleeping."

"My mother?" The phrase made my head swim, my stomach rock. One rebirth was a miracle. Two was more than I could bear. "I've died, haven't I?"

"Of course."

"That boat sank and I sank with it and I'm dying right now, and you are the last thing I'll see."

"What boat?"

"I came here on Eddie Thorne's steamer. From Jane Street to the Manhattan Bridge—a one-hour cruise."

"No, dearest. The milk truck."

"What are you talking about?"

"If you don't remember . . . good. That's good. Then you'll have forgotten the pain. Utter madness—took the turn onto Waverly far too quickly and jumped the curb. Skidded fifteen feet down the sidewalk before it stopped. It landed on you. Cracked your spine in three places, the coroner told me. He said you wouldn't have felt anything, but I've told that lie to too many fathers to fall for it myself. If you really don't remember . . . sweet god, Gilda. You've grown so beautiful."

He hugged me from clear across the table—just reached over and plucked me out of my seat and wrapped me into his arms. All the old smells were there—pipe smoke and hair cream and talcum powder and sweat—but his grip was not as tight as it had been. Through the patchwork bathrobe, which should have been eased into retirement around 1900, his arms were thin.

"When was it I died?" I asked.

"1914. But here you are. A woman. Does that mean—have you come to stay?"

"Do people vanish on the Westside?"

"People vanish on the Westside, the same as they do anywhere else."

"By the thousand?"

"What does it matter?"

"Has the Westside been hollowed out? Have the good people of the city barricaded themselves along the stem, to guzzle champagne while the Westside chokes on vice and bad liquor and fear? Has half of New York died?"

"No," he laughed, that same barking laugh I used to mock as a child. "It's just a city out there, full of ordinary people, who drink their fair share of bootleg liquor but otherwise keep to themselves. The city thrives. Why do you look so panicked, dear?"

"I have not come home. I was never dead. I came here on a ship . . . from my city to here . . . and it is wrong."

"We're together again, Gilda my Gilda. What could be wrong?"

From above I heard a shuffling, one of those night noises that make up the backdrop of life in a particular house, the sort your ear is trained to ignore. My father—or rather, Virgil, since this man was certainly not my father—did not even look up, but I flinched at the sound. I had not heard it in decades, and it sent a shock of terror coursing down my spine.

"We have to go," I said.

"It's all right. You know Mary—once she's up, she's up. When she sees you, Gilda, she'll do backflips."

"She won't see me. She can't."

"Whatever's the matter, the three of us can sort it out."

"We must flee, Virgil, with all available speed. Dress quietly, and . . . do they have guns in this city?"

"We have our share."

"Bring yours."

"You talk like your life is at stake." I nodded, and his smile died. He rose to his full height—still impressive, despite the skinny calves that protruded from his robe—and opened the door to the basement. "Do you want something else to wear?"

"What's wrong with this dress?" I said and suddenly felt quite thirteen.

"There's blood on it. We still have a few of yours, the finer ones. Mary couldn't give them all away."

"I'll wear anything black."

"Black? You haven't worn black a day in your life." A door creaked open on the second floor, and Virgil looked terribly sad. "I really can't tell her?"

"Not unless you want me gone forever."

Footsteps on the stairs. I bolted for the basement steps and closed the door behind me. Through the thin wood I heard my mother, and it was more than I could bear.

"Can't sleep?" she said. "You were talking to yourself again."

"I was talking to Gilda."

"You shouldn't."

"I can't help it. I never could."

"I know, Virge."

"I'll be up in a minute."

"Did you make me tea?"

"I did, but really. You should try to get back to sleep."

She went back up the stairs. I went down.

The basement apartment was just that—a basement, overflowing and dank. The wallpaper that Hellida applied so precisely hung in strips. A family of mice had taken up residence in the nook where she made coffee.

In the corner of the room were boxes marked "Gilda." I opened one and found a composition essay I'd written in eighth grade, on the merits of giving women the vote. My handwriting was like a seizure, awful then and awful now. The Gilda Carr who lived in this house shared my curious spellings of the words "suffrage" and "inevitability." I thought of her, dragged beneath the milk truck. I could smell the milk, and I could feel my spine snap. I closed the box.

Virgil's eyes avoided the boxes when he came through the room. He handed over a flimsy orange dress.

"Will it fit?" he said.

"It should."

"You don't remember it? We bought it just a few weeks before . . . you'd been eyeing it on the mannequin for weeks. Talking our ears off every night at dinner about how smart you would look in that first grown-up dress. You clutched the box to your chest like it was the greatest treasure in the world. You really don't recall?"

"It wasn't me, Virgil."

"I doubt I was buying dresses for any other girls."

"You bought it for Gilda, and my name is Gilda, but I'm not her, any more than you're my father."

"That's impossible."

"Precisely. I'll explain as we walk. Your daughter . . . she isn't coming back."

Sickness crept into his face, and he braced himself on the tilting boxes in the corner. For the first time, he looked as heartbroken as I remembered. I wasn't sure how to console him or if I even wanted to. Instead of trying, I sent him outside and put on the dress. It fit well enough—if anything, it was loose—but the bright orange kept leaping at the corner of my eye and tricking me into thinking I had caught fire. This city's Gilda would have grown into a garish adult. Bex Red would have loved her.

We walked, and I did my best to explain what had brought me here. I told him of the Westside and the shadow city and Galen Copeland's death and the war between Van Alen and Barbarossa. Every name was familiar to him, and every one made him shudder.

"But I haven't seen Galen in years," he kept saying, as though that could protect a man from dying.

"The Galen you know is probably fine. In any case, he's immaterial. It's the Copeland from my city—the dark New York—that was helping Barbarossa trade liquor for guns, and who got killed for it."

"Barbie killed him?"

"I don't think so. Eddie Thorne claims he did it, but he lies."

"Now that's enough. Edward Thorne is one of the most decorated detectives in the department."

"He's a liquor-addled waste of a uniform who saw a chance for power and took it. He has a partner. I'm here to find him."

We walked up Fifth Avenue, because New Yorkers who wander away from Washington Square always walk up Fifth Avenue. The shop windows were unbroken, and the clothes were lit from below with more light than I had seen on the Lower West in years. The sky was melting from black to gray. Garbage men, milkmen, and paperboys walked the avenue, fat and happy and utterly without fear.

"What about your parents?" Virgil asked me. "Are they like Mary and me?"

I could have told the truth. It would have given me a chance to hear consolation from the man whose voice I treasured above all others. It could have smoothed the shrapnel lodged in my heart, the jagged metal I had spent two years ignoring. But this man was not my father, even if he talked like a self-educated street kid, even if his knuckles were as cracked as an old boxer's, even if he smelled like the finest father in the world.

"Identical," I said.

"And are they happy?"

"I would like to think so, but it's so hard to be sure."

"Your mother, is she a strong woman?"

"Like Manhattan schist."

"That's right. That's how I remember her. My Mary, she isn't like that anymore. Not since we lost Gilda, she—it was better, you were right not to see her. And why would you want to, if you have the same woman back at home?"

We crossed onto Broadway, which was hardly crowded. The crowds moved over it freely, unaware that they were crossing the fault line that divided the city, that separated the lucky many from the desperate few.

"My father has this theory," I said, "that our city was doomed the day Galen made his first trip upriver, his first trip through this . . . this hell that exists between your city and mine. Those trips poisoned my New York and caused thousands to die."

"It's mad."

I had a thought. "You ever play with a length of cheesecloth?"

"Mary would rap my knuckles if I meddled with her pantry."

"Pull it, and it stretches. Keep pulling, and every little hole starts to rip. That's what Galen's done to us. He found a hole in the river and used it to make a fortune. Every shipment he pushed through, the other holes stretched and stretched until they tore. Those tears look like shadows, and they swallow people whole. They drag them into this city of shadows, and once they're there . . ."

"Why didn't Galen and Andrea stop?"

"They were making money."

"But if people were dying . . ."

"A disappearance isn't a death. There's no body. No culpability. Every time someone vanished, the people left behind got a little more frightened and needed Barbarossa's liquor that much worse. Of course they wouldn't stop."

He didn't ask any more questions after that, which surprised me. My father would have been peppering me with demands for theories, for data. Whatever I gave him, he would have spun it into a dozen webs of possibility—none of which would have had any relationship to the truth. Those mad webs had comforted him ever since my mother died. This Virgil had never lost his Mary Fall. Even when he watched his Gilda dragged beneath a milk truck, he still had Mary by his side—no longer schist, but still beautiful enough to support her Virgil as I could not support mine.

"Van Alen," he said finally, a few blocks past Union Square. "Hmph."

"Let me guess. In this city, he's a kindly old toymaker who gives out free chocolates at Christmastime."

"He's a savage thug."

"I'm glad to hear it. I was beginning to fear my city had a monopoly on evil men."

"Glen-Richard . . . he kills like other men pick food from their teeth. Since the Volstead Act came in, he's flooded the city with toxic homemade liquor, and we don't even know where he is. We locked down every bridge, every tunnel, every river, every airfield. We raided warehouses, factories, apartment buildings, boxing gyms, gentleman's clubs, nickelodeon houses, Broadway theaters, and anywhere else big enough to hold a still. Even in my wildest theories, I could not have guessed at anything like this."

"No sane man could. That's where you and my father differ. Why do you say 'we raided'?"

"It's my investigation, isn't it? I wouldn't be much of a cop if I let the uniformed men have all the fun of breaking down doors."

Now I was the one too stunned to ask questions. Virgil Carr, king of the NYPD, had never fallen from his throne.

We walked back toward Washington Square, and the detective's curiosity flared. He asked plenty of questions now—not about the case that had brought me here, but about Virgil and Mary Fall. He wanted to know everything, from where they had spent their last vacation to the precise shade of my mother's eyes. I improvised as best I could, hiding the truth not because I didn't trust him, but because I had long ago tired of the look—a flickering of pity, embarrassment, and disgust—that people give when they learn your parents are dead.

We were two blocks from the park when he told me I was lying.

"And just how would you know that?" I said.

"Two years ago, I got a call from a friend who works the river. A couple of kids in Italian Harlem were playing on what passes for a beach up there, and they found what they thought was a cabbage floating in the water. Only it was a cabbage with gray hair, thick sideburns, and a three-inch chunk of spinal column hanging from the neck. When my friend heard my voice, he could hardly talk. 'I was so worried, Virgil,' he said. 'I thought it was you.' That must have been your father's head."

A vanishing isn't a death. It's just a question, left forever unanswered, that hangs in the air like mustard gas: "When are you coming home?"

Two years later, I had my response, and it came in my father's voice: "Never, never, never."

Suddenly, I was sitting on a bench. I didn't remember how I got there, or when Virgil pressed his handkerchief into my hands. It took a long moment before I was able to speak.

"It was September 7, 1919, that he disappeared," I said. "There was a . . . my god, there was an item in the *Sentinel* the next day. I read it, and it didn't even register."

"What did it say?"

"A headless body washed up along the Palisades. No rings on the dead man's fingers. They cut off his head. It didn't even rate a byline."

"Dear god."

"When they called you about . . . about the head, how did you respond?"

"I went uptown to take a look at it. Explained that it wasn't me, it wasn't my twin brother or a long-lost uncle or anybody else in my family. Tried to tell him that it didn't even look like me—that the teeth were worse, and the man had a boozehound's nose—and finally, he let it go."

"What did they do with it?"

"The head was buried in a potter's field in New Jersey. It's an ugly thing, to come face-to-face with, well, your own dead face. I still have nightmares. Mary doesn't know. And . . . oh god. What about your Mary?"

"She died when I was a child. Summer pneumonia. I should have told you from the start."

"Oh lord, Gilda, don't apologize. I don't blame you for lying. With all the mad things you've seen—finding my own head bobbing in the Harlem River was the most horrifying thing that ever happened to me. From what you've told me, in your town that's just an ordinary day. I'm the sorry one, girl. I know what it's like to lose someone."

There was another long silence, and the distance between us was almost painful. I was trying to decide what to say, when he gave me a hug, and I melted into an eight-year-old girl. He held me for at least a minute, and it still wasn't long enough.

"I think I know how to find Van Alen," I said.

"Fine, fine. First, I'm going to run inside and grab a few rolls or something for you to eat. You sit down on this bench—right here. It's a good one. I'll be right back, and you, you just enjoy the park."

He had been gone a minute or two when the door to his house—

not mine, never mine—opened again, and down the steps, shading her eyes against the rising sun, came Mary Fall. From where Virgil had put me, I could see her, but she couldn't see me. I'm certain she had grown old, that her hair was gray, her hands twisted with arthritis. I'm sure her dress was faded, and maybe she didn't smile as she walked into the park and sat down on her favorite bench. But she dragged her left hand through the flowers as she walked, and she had a light in her eyes that I recognized—the giddy look of a little girl who is taking her favorite book to the park to read for the thousandth time.

I could have watched her for hours, but eventually Virgil came down the steps. He kissed Mary on the cheek and walked away—just kissed her and said goodbye, as though it wasn't the most precious thing in the world. He worked his way around the park, doubling back so that she wouldn't see him, but she was buried in her book, holding it close to her eyes, fingers curled around the top of the pages, the way she had read to me when I was a girl, when I knew how to read but pretended I couldn't, because I was afraid she would stop.

"We should go," he said. I nodded but didn't stand, and he didn't make me. Finally, I rose to my feet and turned away. As we left the park, I cast one more look over my shoulder. Mary stopped reading and rested the book in her lap. She ran her hand through her hair, looked up at the sky, and sighed, eyes closed—a moment of torment or exhaustion or peace. From where we were, I could not tell.

Virgil slipped his hand into mine, and squeezed. I did not pull away.

FIFTEEN

I found Juliette in Turtle Bay, waiting across from the apartment that was not really hers. She stared as I approached, not waving and not smiling, like I was long overdue.

"I said I was going home for the night," she said. "It isn't my home."

"No, it's not. I suppose I should introduce—"

"Virgil Carr. We've met before—on Christmas, a long time ago."

"You're Galen Copeland's girl."

"Not quite."

"How did you work it out?" I asked.

"I took my time walking home. By the time I got here, it was dawn, and Papa—my dead papa—was leaving for work, walking alongside a woman who looked rather a lot like me."

"Are you all right?"

"My nerves are singing. To see him like that, so full of life. It was simply . . ."

"I know."

"Have you any idea how to get us home?"

"I've almost got that figured out," I lied. In that moment, I didn't care about escaping this terribly pleasant city. I just wanted to stop the bleeding. "Until then, you can't spend the whole day sitting on this stoop."

"Truly, I am fine."

"You deserve a few hours' sleep. Virgil, what would Mary say if Juliette appeared at the house and said you had sent her?"

"She wouldn't say a thing," said Virgil. "She would fix you breakfast, draw you a bath, and have you tucked into a warm bed before you had a chance to thank her."

"That sounds," said Juliette, "like heaven."

We gave her directions, and Virgil handed her his spare key. She would enjoy a taste of heaven, while we rode north to hell.

We were far enough uptown that the city was quiet, and the sky seemed bigger than was sane. The tenement on 172nd Street was in better shape than when I had seen it last. The stoop was stained, but not filthy. The windows were grimy, but unbroken. A brick propped open the front door. I followed Virgil up the stairs.

The apartment on the top floor was locked. I didn't bother knocking. I opened my burglar's kit and went to work. Virgil stopped me with a rough, heavy hand.

"My daughter is no housebreaker," he said.

"I'm not your daughter."

He reached for his skeleton key. Before he could get it, I opened the door. Virgil tried not to look impressed.

"How are you sure it's this apartment?"

"I see one rather persuasive clue."

In the corner of the immaculate room, a bundle of bones sat wrapped in a rocking chair, staring out the window at the early morning sky.

"Mr. Van Alen," said Virgil, sweeping his hat off his head. "I haven't seen him since I was a boy."

"He was bigger then?"

"Like an oak. A drunk, savage oak."

Virgil knelt in front of Van Alen's father and failed to catch his eye. I leaned by the window, pistol at my side, and waited for the lady of the house to come home.

"For god's sake, Gilda, put that gun away."

"You don't think we'll need it?"

"I've known these people since I was a child."

"And now you've come to arrest their son."

"Put it away, or I'll have you wait in the street."

"You can't tell me where to go." I tried to say it like I was an adult, not a brat pitching a tantrum. It didn't quite work. Virgil stared me down, and the gun went back in the bag.

When the door opened, Mrs. Van Alen withheld her surprise. She set a bag of groceries on the table and hung her hat by the door. Without turning, she said, "Clubber Carr, you beast, what are you doing in my home?"

"We're looking for your son," I said.

"He hasn't lived here for years."

"He doesn't visit?"

"Why should he? A grown man cannot be expected to pay such respect to his parents. Especially a great businessman like my son."

"Please, Mrs. Van Alen," said Virgil. "We don't want to hurt him. We just want to talk."

"Every few weeks, the police come to our door. They barge in. They scuff the floors and upset the furniture. They always come asking the same question—where is Firecracker? And they never believe me when I tell them that I don't know. If I knew, he wouldn't be safe. If I knew, I wouldn't be safe. Now get out, before I call the *Sentinel* and let them know that the police are so incompetent, they've resorted to housebreaking."

The click of the pistol echoed through the room like distant thunder. It attracted their attention. I nuzzled the barrel through the carefully combed remains of Mr. Van Alen's hair. Mrs. Van Alen leaned on the stove. Her hand crept toward a knife.

"No, Mrs. Van Alen," I said. "Don't bother. This is the end of the conversation." She let the knife go. "Perhaps you don't know where your son lays his evil head. Perhaps he does not call as often as you'd like. But you must have some way of contacting him, in case of catastrophe—such as two detectives breaking into your home and threatening your husband's life."

"I don't know what you're talking about."

I pushed the muzzle into the old man's head.

"Fine—there's a grocer on the corner. The owner is one of my son's . . . he calls them lieutenants. He can get him a message."

"Go now."

"It will take him an hour to get here."

"I can hold this gun all day."

"You are a devil."

I nodded. She left. I watched out the window and saw her walk to the grocery, looking not quite as proud as she had a few minutes before. I looked back, and Virgil stared with sad eyes.

"You can put that gun down."

"I suppose you're right."

"You handle it pretty easily for a girl who hates pistols."

"I've grown accustomed to it."

"When we bring Glen-Richard in, your case is finished?"

"Nearly."

"I don't think you should go back to the other side."

"Virgil."

"It's no joke, Gilda. It sounds like . . . the way you've described that place, it sounds like hell on earth. It's made you hard, harder than you need to be. A girl your age shouldn't do work like this. She shouldn't be so easy with a lockpick, with a gun."

"You should see me with a broken bottle."

"That's not funny."

"No, it's not. And it doesn't change the fact that the Westside is my home."

"People leave home. You told me . . . you said your house is gone. Your Hellida is gone. Your Mary. Why go back there?"

"Because I don't belong here."

"You could. Your mother—Mary and I. We'd like nothing more than to have you stay. It would . . . to let you go back, if we can even find a way to get you back, it would be like turning our backs on a miracle. If—"

The door opened. Mrs. Van Alen was home. I picked the gun up and pressed it against her husband's head.

"You sent the message?" I said.

"I told him there were rats in the apartment, that he should come stomp 'em out. He'll understand."

My palm sweated, and my arm grew tired. She fidgeted at her table, trying to read the newspaper, interrupting herself every few seconds to glare at the demon who had invaded her home. Finally, the silence defeated her. She stomped to the stove, grabbed the kettle, and filled it with water.

"I trust you can drink tea and hold a gun at the same time?" she said.

"Thank you."

"I hope it burns straight through your throat. You raise this girl, Clubber? You raise her to behave like this?"

"I didn't."

"You should both be ashamed."

The tea was the same noxious green that Firecracker had served me, just two nights before, in the top of his lighthouse. It didn't smell any more appealing in this city than it had in mine. I set it on the bookshelf and watched the clock crawl around.

We felt Van Alen coming up the stairs before we heard him. The entire tenement shook, and Mrs. Van Alen closed her eyes in gratitude.

"My son well tear you limb from limb," she said. "You will not live to see another day."

The shaking stopped. From the hallway came heavy breathing, like a bull about to charge. The knob turned slowly, and the door crawled open. Glen-Richard Van Alen filled the doorway, a few hundred pounds of rage poured into a straining suit. When he saw Virgil at the table, his face broke into something that might be considered a smile.

"You ugly old son of a bitch," he said. "The hell are you doing uptown?"

"Step inside," I said. "Shut the door."

Van Alen pulled a flask from his coat, emptied Virgil's teacup, and poured him a drink. From across the room, which felt quite a bit smaller with Van Alen inside, I recognized the gasoline punch of Barbarossa's special reserve.

"Drink, pixie?" he said, waving the flask at me. "I suppose not."

"We've questions for you, Dick," said Virgil.

"And who's the insect? A cousin or something? Gods above, Clubber, she looks just like your Mary, or that girl of yours went under the truck a few years back."

"Don't bother trying to intimidate us, Mr. Van Alen," I said. "I have seen the stills that brewed this horrible stuff. I have been fitted for a corset in Barbarossa's secret storehouse. I know that Galen Copeland has been bringing you liquor from our city. I watched him die. But before he was blown to pieces on a Westside dock, Copeland made you rich, he made Barbarossa rich, and he kept a little bit for himself. So if I tell you that I know all of this, you will not lie when I ask you if you know where your liquor comes from."

"A little town I hear they call New York City."

"Yes, but a very different New York. A broken city, split down the middle and haunted by shadows that creep a little farther every time a shipment crosses the divide."

"I should have known you were from the other side. That city breeds 'em crazy."

"You did not cross over to kill Galen Copeland?"

"I'm no killer. I never crossed over at all."

He laid his hands face up on the table, as if to show me that they were not stained by blood. They were large, but soft, their manicured fingernails unmarked by the Westside Van Alen's ceaseless toil.

"Those are not a killer's hands," I said, "but they have counted money made from the blood of lesser men."

"She may or may not be your daughter," he said to Virgil, "but if that little bitch keeps mouthing off, I'll snap every bone in her hand."

"Please, Mr. Van Alen. I'm the one with the pistol."

"It'll take more than one bullet to bring me down."

"But it would ruin your mother's rug." He laughed. His mother didn't. "You're buying liquor with guns?"

"I am."

"I thought guns didn't work on your Westside," said Virgil.

"Those crafted where I come from rust to pieces," I said. "But these are otherworldly and work just fine, apparently. Where do you get the weapons?"

"Bribe a guard at Governor's Island," said Van Alen. "Artillery isn't quite so scarce in my city as it is in yours. But liquor is harder to get. Or it was. Now, I got crate after crate of bootleg hooch coming in, and the police can't trace it, because the world it came from doesn't even exist. As far as I'm concerned, it's been a happy partnership for all concerned."

"But yesterday, you failed to make your delivery."

"You saw that, did you?" He stretched his arms out, and the joints in his elbows cracked like snapping branches.

"Your supply run short?"

"Only a hiccough. Guns are on their way. I don't welch, you got that?"

"Who's your buyer?"

"That sniveling detective you got over there. Thorne. A real laugh, seeing a cop so desperate to touch a gun."

"Who else?"

"It'd been Copeland. I liked dealing with him. We'd been doing it, lord, a long time."

"How long?"

"Close on twenty years."

"1903?"

"Could be. First time he came over, I didn't believe a word he was saying. Thought it was just old Galen, on a bender. But then he took me downtown, made me stand across the street and watch the real Copeland on his way into his offices, and that was when I knew we had something."

"What did he bring you?"

"At first? Whatever he could steal. But every trip he made, things in your city and things in mine, they got a little more different, until what was easy to get in one place was scarce as hell in the others."

"Like liquor."

"That, eventually. But other things too. Like 1914—we had a blight knock out the whole apple crop upstate, and Galen made a fortune bringing over boat after boat, stacked to the waterline with Acey Macs, Cameos, and Ginger Golds."

"That was the year my Westside went to hell. Three thousand one hundred and thirteen disappeared. For apples."

"For *money*. Galen knew what he was about. I was sorry to hear he got finished off."

"And who are you dealing with now?"

"You may as well put down that pistol, girl. Your arm is shaking."

I parted his father's hair with my gun. The barrel traced a bumpy course along the moles and liver spots above his ear. I tried my best to grin like a sadist.

"Goddamn it," said Mrs. Van Alen and slapped her hand on the table.

"Why don't you take a walk," said Van Alen. The old woman didn't move. She was nearly as big as her son, and twice as angry.

"I'm taking you down to Centre Street," said Virgil.

"On what charges, precisely?"

"Smuggling. Bootlegging. Bashing a man's head in with a car door—I'm sure there's a charge in there somewhere."

"And this scrawny, crazy-eyed mouse is your only witness. Tell me, kid, what do you say when the court asks your address? 'Well, I come from New York, but not *this* New York. I'm kind of a traveler, come from another world. I'm a goddamned magician!'"

He seemed to think that was very funny. I was not convinced.

"Gilda's got a message for you," said Virgil. "You're gonna listen, quiet and respectful, or I will make you regret it."

"I've been bigger than you since we were six years old."

"But you haven't been fast enough to land a punch since we were ten."

Van Alen stood, or tried. Before he was halfway up, Virgil reached over the table and slapped him across the cheek. The big man sat back, stunned, one cheek red from the blow, the other from embarrassment. I explained our position.

"Those guns are not going back to my city," I said. "The town I come from is an ugly place, but I love it and I care for its people, and I am sick of watching them die."

"I'm not afraid of any woman."

"Then fear the cops."

"When half of Centre Street is on my payroll?"

"Not the city cops," said Virgil. "The Volstead boys. They've been hungry for you for a year now. It wouldn't take more than a phone call for them to come down hard."

"But you've got no proof!"

"When has that ever mattered? I could get an eviction notice on this door this afternoon," said Virgil. "I could put your parents on the street. I could have them deported."

That last word he said with great relish, stretching out the three syllables like he was savoring the last bites of a meal. By the time the sentence ended, Van Alen was broken.

"Okay," he said. "Okay. I got other ways of making money. This whiskey tastes rancid, anyway. I'll give back the liquor and keep my guns."

"And you're coming downtown."

"Fine. If that's what you need to feel like you're still a real cop, do it. I'll answer whatever questions you've got."

I lowered the gun. My muscles burned. Across the room, Van Alen's mother twitched with rage. Van Alen stood, his head brushing the decrepit chandelier that dangled unevenly above the table. He leaned over and gave his mother a hug.

"Turn around," said Virgil, "and I'll cuff you."

As he turned, his mother smiled at me, a bitter little smile. The knife on the counter was gone.

Van Alen spun on his heels, and Virgil screamed my name. The sun splashed across the knife, blinding me just as the gun went off.

I hadn't felt myself aim the gun. I hadn't felt my finger pull the trigger. It was like it exploded in my hand.

Mrs. Van Alen howled like a gutted pig. Her husband didn't move. Firecracker grew smaller with every breath, a punctured balloon deflating on its way back to earth.

A cockroach crawled down the wall. Van Alen's eyes focused on it. Something came out of his mouth that was not quite a sound. He swayed slightly, then fell onto his mother's table, shattering it into splinters.

He'd said one bullet couldn't stop him. He'd been wrong.

The knife was buried in the floor. The man who looked so much like my father kicked it. The tip snapped off, and it skidded across the rug.

I dropped the gun. I looked away from the body, but I could not escape the odor of death in the air. I do not remember how I felt, my first victim at my feet. It would be some time before I felt anything at all.

"Goddamn, Gilda," said Virgil.

I was looking for the words to apologize when Mrs. Van Alen reached for the broken knife. She charged at me like water from a burst dam. If the knife still had its tip, she would have buried it in my heart. Instead, she contented herself with cutting a long, deep groove down the side of my face.

More than anything, the sensation was surprising. It lanced through me with electric speed, so intense that I had to step away from it, to admire the heat of the blood pouring into my mouth and the blinding force of the pain.

She set the knife against my other cheek, intending to cut a matching scar. The blade was close enough to my nose that I could smell the onions she had cut the night before. My foot slipped, and she fell on top of me, the weight of her enough to push me across her husband's lap, and halfway out the open window.

I kicked. I bled. Neither helped. My finger pulled uselessly at the trigger of the gun that was no longer in my hand.

I didn't blame her for cutting my face, and I wouldn't argue if she pushed me out the window. My spirit had drained out of me as quickly as the blood pouring from Van Alen's blubbery chest, but my body had not given up the fight.

I have never been a brawler. I have always been small. But I had a funny habit of staying alive, and sometimes that's all that mattered. Before she could make her second incision, I let my knees buckle and slid out from under her. The metal windowsill clawed at my dress, and I landed safely on the floor. Mrs. Van Alen would have tumbled out the window if Virgil hadn't grabbed her by her belt, dragged her across the floor, and shoved her into her bedroom.

"Get downstairs," he said, holding the door closed with the full weight of his body. "Find a callbox. Get Centre Street. Get Thorne."

I smeared the blood across my cheek, nodded, and ran. No one in the stairwell looked up as I clattered down the steps. No one on the street was put off by the bloody woman sprinting down the sidewalk. There were callboxes on every corner. The first three were disconnected, and somewhere within me I took faint pleasure from knowing that not everything in this perfect city was shiny and clean.

At the fourth, I got through, and every cop I spoke to responded like he could hear the blood in my voice. They passed me up the chain, grateful to let me be someone else's problem, until I reached the office of Edward Thorne.

"Virgil Carr has a mess that needs tidying," I said.

"Who's this calling?"

"You wouldn't believe me if I told you. Get up to 172nd and get ready to move a body."

"What address?"

"Hell." I looked over my shoulder. The tenement was out of sight. "I don't know. Half a block from Haven, on the north side of the street. For god's sake, it'll be the one with the bloody girl on the stoop."

"I'm not coming until I know who this is."

"Gilda Carr."

"That's impossible."

"Entirely," I said and cut the line.

The sidewalk was crowded with morning traffic, but the commuters parted for me. I dropped onto the stoop and dragged my face across my shoulder to scrape off the blood. The pain exploded like a fireball. I might have cried, but I didn't want to salt the wound. I tried to tear the hem off my dress, to press against the cut, but my fingers were too bloody to rip the fabric.

I slumped against the side of the stoop, eyes squeezed shut, until I heard a siren. Thorne bounded out of the car, slim and shaved, his badge sparkling and his gun gleaming on his hip.

"You look good," I said.

"Gilda. I . . . I don't understand."

"You were never meant to. Virgil's on the top floor. Follow the screams."

Thorne's driver crouched beside me as his boss ran up the stairs. He had crooked teeth, soft eyes, and a moustache that would make a walrus jealous. By his uniform, his name was Asbury.

"A nasty cut there," he said.

"It can wait. Thorne will need you upstairs."

"He told me to tend to you, so I'll tend. And he also wanted me to make sure you don't run off. A girl covered in blood, reporting a murder—she's someone we don't want to lose hold of."

He took a wad of bandages from the car, swabbed my face as best he could, and wound the fabric around my cheek.

"He's a good cop, your boss?" I said.

"As good as any I've ever met. That man's afraid of nothing."

He finished his dressing. The bandage squeezed my cheek. It stung, but not unpleasantly.

"You're good with this gauze."

"A week at Amiens will turn any man into a field surgeon."

He looked at his bloody fingers, then at the spotless pants of his uniform.

"Please," I said. "Dry them on my dress."

"I couldn't."

"It's already ruined. Go ahead."

"Thank you."

"Did you ever know a cop named Koszler?"

"First name?"

"Emil. A tall fellow with the Fourth Precinct."

"Of course! Emil. We shared a beat one winter, a few years back. My god, I haven't thought of him in ages. He quit, I heard. Became a priest, of all things."

"He didn't seem cut out for life as a cop."

"Few are."

We sat, silent, until Virgil padded out the door. He looked smaller than he had an hour earlier, and exhausted. He did not look at me.

"Get on the horn and get an ambulance up here," he told Asbury, "then get upstairs. Your boss'll need you. We're taking the car."

Asbury hopped to attention. He was halfway down the block when I realized I never thanked him for the dressing. I called after him, but if he heard, he didn't respond.

"No reason to thank the man," said Virgil. "It's his job."

We climbed into the car. Getting it started flustered Virgil, who cursed under his breath at the machine. He seemed to take its defiance personally.

"Hate these things," he said. "Never could get used to them. Never had any urge to. You can't drive one, can you?"

"No. Can you?"

"Well enough." We lurched into traffic. "Just as good that I do the driving. From here out, I'll handle this whole situation. It was a stupid mistake bringing you up there."

"As I recall, it was I who brought you."

"Girl your age shouldn't be in a room with a man like Van Alen. Shouldn't never have to do . . . what you did."

"No need to thank me. I was doing my job."

Watching his face as he struggled to maneuver the uncooperative machine onto Broadway, I could tell there was a lot he wanted to say to me. There was certainly a lot I wanted to hear. Instead, we said nothing. I sank into the seat and felt the throbbing in my cheek sync up with the humming of the engine.

"You've ruined that dress," he said somewhere past Central Park. "Your mother . . ."

"She isn't my mother."

"All the same, she'd wring my neck."

"That's why I can't stay. You understand that, don't you?"

"We'll discuss it when this is through."

"You seem to think it's your decision."

"Isn't it?"

"Even if you were my father, I wouldn't let you talk to me like that."

"And that's just the problem, isn't it, with this other city of yours. It's warped you. It's made you hard."

"That wasn't entirely the city's doing."

"I suppose not." He gripped the wheel, bit his lip, and performed a less-than-graceful turn toward the East River. "It was . . . my counterpart, his fault as well. I'd like you to stay, girl. Give me a year or two, see if we can't sand down some of those rough edges, make up for the damage the other Virgil done."

"I like my rough edges. I *am* my rough edges."

"And do you like the taste of blood in your mouth? Did you enjoy the way that gun kicked in your hand? If you did, you should be scared, because those edges will get a whole lot rougher, and quick. I can't change it so that you never killed that man. That road has no turnarounds. But I can stop you going any further. Your mother—Mary—and me."

From his pocket he drew my gun. It was certainly my gun now. He placed it between us on the seat. Two bullets left.

"You want it? Take it. But if you pick that pistol up again, this city is closed to you. I've killed more men than I can count, and I see their faces every time I lay my head down to sleep. They look scared, and they beg me for a mercy that I can no longer grant. If you want that for yourself, take the gun. It belongs to you."

I was reaching for it when the car clattered over a vicious pothole, and I slammed my head into the window.

"Are you all right?" said Virgil, reaching out a hand to steady me. I pushed it away.

"I'm fine. I'm fine."

I rubbed my temple and looked outside, and in the shadows of the side street I saw something I should have seen coming.

"Stop the car!" I said.

"No."

I threw open the door and leapt out. It wasn't so daring—we weren't going that fast—but Virgil was surprised, and frankly so was I. I stumbled but caught myself before I fell—caught myself on the handle of the door to the little shop whose display window held purses, wallets, belts, coats, loafers, riding crops, and gloves of all kinds, and whose door was marked with a carving of the bloody fist.

Virgil slammed the car to a stop and hopped onto the curb, flush with outrage. It had always been so easy to make him mad.

"Aren't you coming in?" I said.

"Goddamn it," he answered, slamming his fist on the hood of the car. He did not follow me inside.

The shop was narrow, long, and dark. The smell of leather was nauseating. The woman balanced on a stool behind the counter, not as fat as in my city, and not as happy to see me. She did not look up when I came through the door. Andrea Barbarossa was engrossed in her work—repairing the heel of a black leather boot—and nothing could tear her away.

I ran my finger along the wall, touching everything. No wonder she didn't bother to greet her customers. Work this exquisite spoke for itself.

At the rear of the shop, a round table held a few dozen kid gloves, fanned out in a circle. They ranged from ivory to jet black, and each was decorated with irises and a single bloody fist. I chose the shade that matched Mrs. Copeland's pair—the pair I had reunited only to lose with my house and everything else—and brought them to the counter.

"Just these?" said Barbarossa. I nodded, and she gave me the price. It was more than I'd spent on any item of clothing in my entire life, and it was not unfair.

"I'm purchasing these on behalf of my employer," I said. "Galen Copeland. I believe he has an account."

"Galen, yes. He still owes me for a pair he bought in July."

"He plans to settle all accounts by Christmas."

"It's all right. I trust him. I don't know why, but I'm a sucker for old friends. Do you want them wrapped?"

"Just the box will do."

She slid the box across the counter. I dropped it into my bag and left the shop. Virgil was waiting in the car, red with irritation. The pistol was gone from the seat. He pulled back into traffic.

"Where is my gun?" I said.

"Why that shop?" he said. "Of all the leather merchants in New York, why did you choose that awful shop?"

"They do wonderful work. You know the proprietor?"

"Let's not discuss her."

"My father knew her too. He knew her before Mary Fall, and afterward, and all the years in between."

I cackled. I couldn't help it. Cruel laughter bubbled out of me like acid and stung Virgil Carr.

"What's so goddamned funny?" he said.

"To think—you wanted to sand down my rough edges, and you're as rotten as he was."

"Don't judge him too harshly."

"And why shouldn't I? That woman is vile. My mother was . . . she was everything."

"She was. Is. No man could be equal to that. If your father reached for a woman like Barbie, he must have been very lonely, or very scared. It doesn't excuse anything, but . . ."

"I'll give you one thing. Your Barbie is a lot more beautiful than my father's ever was. Now where is my gun?"

"We're here," he said, and the car slammed to a halt. Thorne's ship was still moored at the pier. There was no sign of anyone from the Fourth Precinct. Virgil stepped out of the car and opened my door.

"The pistol," I said. "Give it back."

"I need to search that ship. Thorne's partner might be inside."

"Fantastic. Are you going to let me out of the car?"

"As a matter of fact, no."

He shut the door and turned the key in the lock. I yanked the handle. It would not budge.

"Open it," I said. "Goddamn it, Virgil, now!"

"You may not be my daughter, but you *will* stay in my city. I'm going to keep you safe."

My father walked the streets of New York like he owned the pavement, and this man was no different. He dropped his keys in his pocket and strolled across the dock like all he saw was his. He bounded up the gangway, glanced up and down the deck, and disappeared into the ship.

I bruised my shoulder slamming it against that door and cracked my one unblemished fingernail attacking the handle. I did not consider shattering the glass until I heard the woman's scream. It came from the street—a sharp cry, quickly silenced, short enough that even the kindest New Yorker could tell themselves that they hadn't heard a thing.

Two people dragged a woman onto the dock, her slender frame as limp as a bag of straw. Her delicate curls, which looked slightly ridiculous on a woman her age, were mussed. Without seeing her face, I could tell it was Juliette Copeland who had been blackjacked and kidnapped. I did not recognize the Fourth Precinct cop who held her left elbow, but I saw the face of the woman who held the right, the woman with the rifle slung over her shoulder and the devil's smirk upon her face.

It was Juliette Copeland too.

She hadn't been a stowaway on that steamer. She had been the *pilot*. Thorne's partner, his sniper, who killed her father for reasons unfathomable and came to this other New York to do the same to a girl who looked very much like herself. And we had given her directions to Mary Fall.

I lay on my back and kicked both feet at the door window. It didn't crack. I clambered into the backseat and searched the floor for a toolbox, a jack, a spare wrench. It was bare.

The Juliette I knew, who mourned Galen Copeland but asked me not to bother investigating his death, hauled her double up the gangway without stopping for breath. She was at the ship's rail when she saw me struggling to escape the car, shook her head, and smiled.

The glove box was locked, but it wasn't as sturdy as the door. One kick, and it flopped open. I was hoping to find a spare pistol— one of the thousands of guns that seemed to litter this city—but I found nothing but handcuffs, maps, a desiccated sandwich, and a few blank notebooks. I tossed the junk aside and struck gold. Behind the notebooks, I found a nightstick.

I wrapped my fist around the club's handle and punched its short end into the glass. A web of fine cracks spread from the point of impact. I punched, again and again, until my muscles screamed and my knuckles were raw and the glass sagged in the frame. One more blow shattered the window. I did not feel the falling glass. I raked the nightstick around the edge, clearing as many shards as I could, and dragged myself into the open. I flipped the nightstick around in my hand and charged toward the ship.

I was halfway across the pier when the ship pulled away from the dock. By the time I reached the edge, the steamer was nosing its way into the river. Even if I'd had the strength to jump, it was too far. I hurled the nightstick after the boat. It clattered off the hull and sank into the East River.

Juliette watched me from the deck until one of her sailors called to her, and she turned away. Two men emerged from the door to the hold, dragging the broken body of Virgil Carr. They dropped him at her feet. If the wind had been blowing toward me, I would have heard her laugh.

SIXTEEN

I ran west, toward Washington Square, toward Mary Fall, but I hadn't gone more than a block when smoke drew me south. I arrived at Copeland Imports Ltd., just as the fire spread to the roof. A crowd stood around the base of that salt-stained, slanted waterfront building, wondering if the fire department would arrive before the building burned to the foundation. At the moment, the fire was winning.

On the sidewalk, a fruit vendor draped a tarp to protect his apples from the soot. To no one in particular, he gave his account of the blaze.

"Window burst, just like that—like *pop*. Glass came down all over, and I saw the fire. Third floor, Copeland's offices. And now it's burning—hoo. I said for years they need to get these buildings up to code, but does anyone listen? No. Couple of people got the girl, Miss Copeland, they got her out no problem."

"What about Copeland?"

"Well, I suppose he's still up there. Lord. The poor man."

From the third floor came an old man's screams. They sent a

ripple of pleasure through the growing crowd. I threw down my bag, yanked open the building door, and bounded up the stairs.

The smoke was black, and it came in billows. By the second-floor landing, I was choking on it. I dropped to my knees and crawled. The sides of the stairwell danced with flame.

"Sweet god," came the cries from Copeland's offices. "Sweet merciful god—Juliette!"

I made the third floor, and the stairwell windows exploded. The white paint boiled on the walls, falling to the ground in bubbling strips. Copeland's cries grew faint, then stopped.

I crawled into the office. He was strapped to a chair, a slumped old man in a spotless white uniform that was just beginning to attract the fire. I crawled in his direction. The walls were a tapestry of flame.

"Wake up, damn you!" I shouted. He did not. Above Copeland's waist, the smoke was impenetrable. If I stood, I wouldn't be able to breathe more than a few seconds. So I did the only thing that made sense. I bit him. Hard.

"The hell?" he murmured. I kept biting, stopping only when blood ran down my chin. He kicked, and I clawed the knots that bound his legs to the chair. My penknife, naturally, had been left in my bag.

"No use," he said. "Out, girl. Run."

"Hush."

"Those are Flemish loops, tied by an old hand. You'll never . . . there's a knife."

"Where?"

"Desk drawer."

"Wait here." I dug my hands into the tangle of knots on the back of the chair and yanked him down. The crash shook the floor, which would not hold for long. He groaned, coughing up something too black to be blood, and breathed a little better.

The fire had started in the office. The wall of immaculate cubbies was an inferno. The burning ink put an acrid tang into the smoke that made my eyes water but helped me fight back the creeping urge to sleep.

I pulled out what remained of the top desk drawer, and the knife rolled toward me—a scrimshaw pocketknife decorated with a portrait of a narwhal. I snatched at it, and the white-hot metal fused, ever so briefly, with the skin of my hand. I couldn't help what happened next. Bellowing the foulest curses of the Westside, I threw the knife across the room, and it landed in the wall of flame.

In the next room, a beam snapped, and half the floor fell away.

"Quick," said Copeland, "or not at all!"

The office had no fire extinguisher, no watercooler, no pitcher of flowers to douse the blaze. But in the far corner of the room was a ceramic spittoon, half full of a sickening mixture of black tobacco scum. I picked it up, using my skirt to protect my already blistering right hand from the heat, and upended it where I hoped the penknife had landed. The fire hissed into a cloud of noxious tobacco steam, and I fought the urge to retch. There would be time for that later. In a pool of simmering spit and tar-stained cigar ends, the knife was there. I grabbed it through the arm of my dress, pried it open with my teeth, and crawled back to Copeland's chair.

He had lost consciousness, which meant he wasn't put off by the great hole in his office floor, the fire crawling across the wood, or the creaking of the flame-scorched beams beneath our feet. The rope was stubborn. The knife was dull. The fire crept closer.

It took a lifetime, but I freed the captain from the chair. I slapped his face and cried his name, but he would not wake. I refused to watch Galen Copeland die a second time. I held the blade of the knife in the nearest patch of fire, and when it glowed a hellish orange I pressed it against the sleeping sailor's forearm. He awoke to the sound of his own flesh burning, a savage scream in his throat.

"Curse me later," I said. "It is time to leave."

We started for the stairs. After two steps, I was sobbing through the smoke. After three, the floor buckled.

"Is there a fire escape?" I said.

"Not one I trust."

"Then we jump."

"Are you mad?"

I didn't answer, and I didn't let go of his hand. I just leapt through the flaming hole in the floor and dragged him with me. Neither of us landed well. Ankles were twisted and knees were bruised. But the air was cleaner here, and the pain in our lungs began to ebb. We were doing fine.

"Miss," said Copeland. "You're on fire."

Before I could process that, or link it to the searing pain in my shoulder and the scent of burning hair, I was swallowed by darkness—darkness that smelled of burnt wool, starch, and cheap soap. Copeland's hands beat out the flames but did not remove the jacket until we got to the stairwell. We took the stairs as quickly as our battered legs allowed and arrived on the street just as the third floor collapsed into the second. At first I thought the crowd was cheering for us, but they were simply rooting on the fire.

The crisp October air flooded my lungs like rain on a dry field. The fruit vendor reached under his tarp and produced a pair of green apples.

"Nice and tart," he said. "Get the smoke out of your mouth."

I didn't think that would ever be possible. My hair was scorched, my hand was throbbing, the bandage on my face had come loose, and my dress was so burnt, you could hardly see the bloodstains.

"We need some oysters," said Copeland, striding toward the docks. I threw my bag over my shoulder and followed. He limped badly. Most of his hair had burned away. His eyes were crimson and viscous slime streamed from his nose.

"They took her—they took her on the river," I said. "My father too. We have to get after them."

"Your father? Who is your father?"

"Virgil Carr."

It shook him. He broke his stride, looked in my eyes, and swept me up in his arms.

"She looked like my daughter," he said, "but she was a devil. She took Juliette. She burned my office to the ground. The same wind that brought that devil to me, it brought you. Gilda Carr. The city has missed you. My angel."

"We have to get to your yacht."

"Oysters. First, oysters."

"Are you insane? We don't have time for—"

"Do you know where they're going?"

"Not yet."

"Then we eat."

Beneath the Brooklyn Bridge, we found Dover Street, an alley scarcely wider than the two of us. Fishermen trudged in from the waterfront, work done, in search of food and liquor. At the end of Dover was a sagging square house whose pink bricks shone in the early afternoon sun. A squat man in a black apron stepped outside and dumped a bucket of gutted fish on the pavement. Three cats scrambled out of the alleyway and began to feast.

"That's Robbins," said Copeland. "He'll take care of us."

The main room was stifling, warmed by a potbelly stove surrounded by mariners fighting to chase off the morning damp. The air was heavy with garlic. Straight-backed chairs ringed wobbly tables, and a dozen fishermen crowded around the small counter, raiding a free lunch of cheese, salami, and paper-thin onions. They parted for Copeland.

"A dozen Mattitucks," said Copeland. "A dozen Cape Cods. A dozen Saddle Rocks. Quick, and with lemon."

"And we got in some of the black clams," said Robbins.

"Thank god. Thank the lord above. Two dozen of those, Gilda, and I swear our luck will turn around."

The oysters came by the bucketful, accompanied by two earthen cups of steamy, sludgy, blessed coffee.

"You hang on to that knife?" said Copeland. I passed it to him, and he noticed my burnt hand for the first time. He dug deep into the icy bucket and pulled up the largest oyster I had ever seen. He pried it open with a single quick motion and pressed it into my hand. The shell was frozen and soothed my aching palm. The meat was the size of a fried egg. I tried not to think of Starlight Angie, naked and wriggling.

"Take it," he said. "One shot, and drink the juice, every bit of it."

He worked like a machine, bad wrist and all, prying the shells open and casting the tops aside, handing half the oysters to me and taking the rest himself. We moved through the first dozen in two or three minutes, and he did not slow down. As he worked, he talked, staring straight past me and into the fire. The oysters were frigid and salty enough to scrub the smoke from my lungs, clear my sinuses, and uncloud my eyes. Between mouthfuls, I explained what I could.

"Somewhere in the river, there's a . . . a gate, a door that runs through the water, that crosses from my city to yours," I said. "In between there is a nightmare. Galen Copeland found it a long time ago and used it to make himself and a few other people very rich. Every time they came through, my city died a little bit more."

"And now that girl, that Juliette, is doing the same thing."

"She killed her father to protect the business."

"How could she do something like that?"

"He'd been hurting her for a long time. In little ways, over and over her whole life. I think, to her, that made it okay."

"It's abhorrent."

"Yes. Did she say anything before she took your daughter?"

"'This is where I belong.' She sounded . . . not mad. Just cold."

"This was her escape route. She's going to make a tidy fortune selling guns to the NYPD, and she doesn't want to spend that wealth in our New York."

"So why take Juliette?"

"She wanted to make sure there was a place for her here. She was going to kill you, to kill Juliette, then come here and take her place, and the business too. But your wife . . . your wife might interfere."

"My wife?"

"Edith would inherit in Juliette's stead."

"She would, had the fever not taken her in 1919." Copeland's oyster spilled juice down the side of his face. He wiped it with the burnt sleeve of his jacket and looked very much like a man who had lost everything. "You crossed over. You didn't see where the ship made the jump?"

"I was in the hold."

"You sailed from where, exactly?"

"Jane Street, on the Westside. Fifteen minutes, maybe twenty, and then the engines cut out, and there was this horrible . . . scrape of metal. That's when we passed through."

"And then?"

"Another forty-five minutes, and we ended up beneath the Manhattan Bridge."

He snapped his fingers. "A chart, Robbins! The harbor. Quick, now."

Robbins shuffled over—not all that quick—a chart rolled up in his hands. He spread it across the table and weighed it down with our mugs.

"Don't spill a drop," he said. "That's a fine chart."

"Any of this look familiar?" said Copeland, running his finger along the waterfront.

"Not from this angle."

"It's no good. You could have gone anywhere from the Jane Street pier."

"How well do you know Virgil Carr?"

"Better than most men."

"Do you speak often?"

"A few times a year, he comes down to the docks for a few glasses of beer, a few hours of reheated stories."

"Did he tell you about the time they found his head?"

"Aye. It was a strange tale, and I looked past it. Thought it was the ale talking. I should have known better. That man was made of iron, but when they found that head . . . it shook him to his core."

"Where did they find it? Did he tell you?"

"Italian Harlem, under the bridge at First Avenue."

On the chart, the Harlem River was a thin silver band that ran along the north end of Manhattan, from the Hudson to the East River, a little stretch of water that divided a great borough from a lowly one. I walked its banks each summer, on mornings before a game at the Polo Grounds. It was wide, flat, gray, and cold.

"Don't think so hard," he said.

"Quiet. I'm close."

"Have a black clam."

"Quiet!"

He pried open the clam and pushed it across the table. I tilted it into my mouth. It slid down my throat like an electric shock. It was small and sweet as penny candy, with a salty bite that made me sit up straight in my seat. Without thinking, I reached for another.

"There was an article in the paper, the day after my father disappeared. A headless body washed up in my city, in Jersey, actually, along the base of the Palisades. His head came here; his body stayed on the other side. They must have killed him smack in the middle of the gate."

"The animals."

I traced my finger along the water that carried my father's body away. Where the Harlem River emptied into the Hudson, right between where they found my father's head and where they found his body, I recognized a name.

"Spuyten Duyvil," I said. "What is it?"

"A creek. Means 'Spouting Devil.' Nasty spot."

"Copeland—my Copeland, that is—he once saved a pair of twins he found swimming in Spuyten Duyvil."

"That's a miracle. That's some of the roughest water in the city. But I was always a good swimmer."

"Take me there," I said. "Take me there now."

I jabbed my finger at the map. Spuyten Duyvil.

Right smack in the middle.

Copeland leaned on the throttle, and his yacht pulled into the East River current. He held the wheel loosely, gnawing his lip and staring dead-eyed upriver. We turned west into the rough waters that separated Manhattan from the Bronx. The island's heights loomed over us as if we were passing into the hall of some great king. The water frothed white, and on either side the rocks loomed large.

"Is this the spot?" I said.

"Spuyten Duyvil, indeed."

"Steer toward the shore."

Copeland did, reluctantly. The boat shook.

"Closer."

"There's safer channels up ahead."

"Closer!"

He wouldn't dare, so I jerked him backward by the collar, and the wheel spun free. He crashed into the deck, smashing his nose on the wood. He rolled over, spilling blood across the little ship. On the shore, the great shadows cast by the island's heights began to move our way. The ship whipped toward the rocks. Copeland tried to get up, but my foot kept him down. The shadows swept over the engine, and we stopped dead.

"Dear god," he said. "Sweet merciful—"

That was all he could get out before they swallowed him, and then they came for me. I didn't cower or struggle. Like twisted Juliette Copeland, I welcomed passage into the dark.

When they sucked me into the shadow world, I found Copeland cowering in the corner of his boat, no more brave than the cops of the Fourth Precinct. I offered him my hand with a mute laugh, guided him to the wheel, and started the engine. We sailed on black water away from the rocks, toward the far side of the gate.

So this was what my Copeland had seen that day, two decades prior, when he leapt into the water to save those drowning children. I understood why it had caught his attention. Across the roiling slate river, flanked by jagged rocks, there was a hole in the world, a shimmering portal offering safe passage through a nightmare, no suicide required. Behind us, I saw the light city, where the sun shone bright on a crowded, peaceful river. Ahead, I saw the Westside night and the empty, cursed Hudson. We sailed on.

There were no ghouls on the river, but they crowded the shore.

They perched on the rocks and dangled from trees, watching with fiery eyes. We were nearly at the western portal when they turned away from us, as if summoned by a dog whistle, and swept inland up the hills. Something was calling them south.

We sailed through Copeland's gate, as smooth a passage as could be wished, and on into the Hudson. The shadow world fell away behind us, and down Manhattan's slender flank, I saw the perfect darkness of the Westside.

"You damned silly woman," said Copeland, face white and fists clenched tight on the wheel. "You stupid, tiny girl!"

"That's enough. We're here."

"Here. Where is *here*? Where was *there*?"

"Between your city and my city, there is a New York of shadows, of smoke, of the dead. Greed tore a hole between them, just wide enough for a clever sailor to pass through."

"But things like that don't just *happen*."

"They don't in your New York. They do in mine. I spent a long time trying not to see them. If you can, I suggest you do the same. Just sail south. Jane Street. Pier 51, as fast as this tub will carry us."

Scowling, he cranked the throttle, and the ship staggered into higher gear. Van Alen's lighthouse was dark, and his feeble night-fires did nothing to illuminate the black expanse of the Hudson. Down below our feet, I wondered, what terrible shadows were swirling there?

Copeland was silent until we reached midtown and he saw the empty docks of the great ocean liners, their piers shattered, their pilings naked stumps jutting up from the Hudson.

"Cunard. White Star. NDL. CGT. I came this way just last week. They were thriving. It's just impossible."

"Naturally. Keep sailing. Your daughter's up ahead."

I didn't have to tell him what to look for. There was only one ship docked on the Westside. The gangway was down, and the cops unloaded cargo onto the dock. I motioned for Copeland to cut the throttle and let the easy drift of the Hudson carry us alongside the ship. We brushed silently against their hull, unseen by all. A tangle of rotten rope dangled off their port side. I tugged it and was reasonably certain it would hold my weight.

"Could you spare any gasoline?" I said.

"What for?"

"If I told, you'd say I was being stupid, and I'd hate for you to talk to me like that. Give it here."

Copeland filled the gas can and screwed the lid tight. I ran a length of rope through its handle, tying it off to make a shoulder strap, and threw it over my shoulder. Quite a smart little purse.

I balanced on the yacht's railing, grabbed hold of the dangling rope, and began to climb. There was no time to be afraid.

"And what shall I do?" he said.

"Nothing. I'll handle it all."

Such confidence. Such bravado. How good I had gotten at disguising the fact that I had absolutely no idea what I was going to do next.

I was halfway up the rope when I heard the music and cursed silently under my breath. "Benjy's Bloody Stump." The song came from the shore, where the ragged remains of the Westside armies marched toward the dock: two dozen warriors, joined together under the banner of Van Alen and the standard of the One-Eyed Cats. Those idiots. Those wonderful fools. They were too honest for an ambush, too stupid to fight dirty, too blind to see the thick, hungry shadows swirling at their backs.

They turned onto the dock and raised clubs, swords, knives, and chains, ready to charge.

"Surrender!" cried Van Alen, his proud, deep voice cutting through the sticky night air. "Or we'll drive you into the river."

I couldn't see what was happening on the other side of the boat, but I knew it wasn't surrender. I heard a voice, a woman's voice, Juliette's voice, make an offer of her own.

"Die," she called, and her men opened fire. I could not see them fire the shots, but I saw a third of Van Alen's men fall dead. The survivors charged. Van Alen, Cherub Stevens, Ugly La Rocca, and Ida Greene led the pack to the foot of the gangway and out of my sight.

While they fought, I watched the wounded they had left behind: seven or eight men and boys moaning on the dock as their blood dripped down into the river. The shadows crept up on them slowly, eating the pier. Moans turned to screams, and then to silence, as the shadows swallowed the wounded whole. The battle continued. No one had noticed but me.

I lowered my head and kept climbing. It would take quite a light to drive those shadows back. My hands were slick, my muscles aching, my lungs burning, but I had seen Cherub's foolish grin as he charged down that dock, saber held high, and I kept his face fixed at the front of my mind until I finished the climb.

I reached the lip of the deck and hauled myself aboard. If Juliette had posted any guards to this side of the ship, they had deserted their stations. I opened the door to the hold and went below. Any noise I made clattering down the metal steps was masked by gunfire and the screams of dying men.

The ship was lit by dim electric lights—another wonder imported from the other New York—and I had no trouble finding my way into the belly of the ship. I turned a corner and paused, not sure where I was going, but certain I had to get there fast. I knew I'd made an error when I felt the hand on my shoulder and the gun nestle against the base of my skull. I smelled bad liquor and knew it was Eddie Thorne.

"I'm not as stupid as your daddy thought," he said.

"You're still not very bright."

He brought the butt of the pistol down against my head. Pain exploded across my skull, yellow and red and blinding. I fell to my knees and fought the urge to vomit. Thorne laughed. It was an unappealing sound.

"You get it?" he barked. "*You get it?* I've got the guns. I've got the liquor. I'm not a joke anymore."

He kicked me in the stomach. Or, rather, he tried to. He was sluggish, like he was underwater, and I was able to roll onto my back before his boot connected. It wasn't much of an advantage—I was still flat on the deck, staring up at the pistol clutched in his sweaty, swollen hand—but it was a comfort, a shred of hope, until he pulled the hammer back. He squatted on top of me, holding me down with one hand, pressing his knees against my arms to keep me from getting away.

"I'm gonna kill you," he said. Normally, I might have responded with something clever, but nothing glittering came to mind.

"Thorne—"

"Shut up," he said. To drive home the point, he pressed the pistol against my lips. He pushed hard, but I would not part them. Let him kill me if he wished, but I would not tolerate humiliation. "Open your bitch mouth!"

I shook my head, and he pulled back to bash me across the face. I turned my head to the side and said, "Afraid I'll talk you out of it?"

"Nobody talks me into nothing," he said, with a drunk's dizzy confidence. "Not anymore."

"Juliette will have you as her puppet."

"I'm not nobody's—"

"But you are." He did not like being interrupted. He bore down with his knees, and the pain screamed nearly as loud as the ache in my head. But he let me keep talking. "Does she listen to you? Does she heed your advice? Does she respect you any more than Barbie ever did?"

"Barbie is dead."

"We both know she's not. She was a demon, and you weren't strong enough to kill her, which means that someday, she'll be back."

"I'll be waiting. I stopped her once, and . . . and . . ."

He trailed off. A great glistening stream of snot hung from his nose. He wiped it on his shoulder. The stain shone in the ship's hazy light.

"I never considered," I said, "how trying these last weeks must have been for you."

"Yeah?"

"All this scheming. What focus it must have required. What industry. What guile."

"It was tough, yeah. Tougher than it looked."

"And now you're in charge."

"That's what I keep saying!"

"And you see a lifetime of hard work stretching out ahead of you. You're a hero of the NYPD, and heroes don't get to soak themselves in bootleg gin. They are sober. They work hard."

"I can do that too."

"But how hungry you must be for a reason to quit."

He scratched his ear with the sight of his revolver and considered my offer for a time. I was right, and we both knew it. But there are some men who hate a woman far more when she's telling the truth. He chuckled, and grabbed me by the cheeks, and forced my mouth open with his hand.

"This ain't even for you," he said. "It's for your dad. God, I wish I'd had the chance to kill him."

He pressed the pistol against my mouth. The taste burned my lips. I tried to kick, to free my legs. He was too heavy. I let the barrel into my mouth and spat out one final, garbled offer.

"Eyel kih huh."

"What?" he said, pulling out the gun.

"I'll kill her," I said.

"Juliette? She'd shoot you down like a rat."

"Barbie," I said, and he set the gun aside. "I'll find her, and I'll kill her. I'm good at finding people—you know I am."

He stood up. With seizing muscles, I scrambled back against the wall and did my best to stand.

"Yeah," he said, "you could find her. But you really think you could kill her?"

"I absolutely do," I said. He believed it, and I believed it too.

"And what should I do?"

"Go back to your bottle. Let the women sort this out."

He shrugged and holstered his pistol, happy to have orders at last. He wandered back toward the hold.

I wanted to sob, but I didn't have time. I ran deeper into the ship, until I saw the glow of the engines. I yanked the gas can off my shoulder and went to work.

Much later, I received a full account of the battle at the docks. I don't doubt that it was highly embellished, as all good Westside yarns must be. I am told it was a glorious affair, that there were heroes on both sides, that every warrior stood tall, that all proved themselves true Westside men. But I had seen the agony with which the first victims died, and I do not believe it could have been glorious at all.

The fight was short. A third of Van Alen's men were killed in the first barrage, and that many fell again before the little band of Westsiders reached the end of the dock. By then, the numbers were even. Van Alen and his rainbow guard lived for a good hand-to-hand scrap, and they acquitted themselves well. They smashed the rifles out of the policemen's hands, cracked their skulls, and knocked their limp bodies into the river. Cherub Stevens, I am told, ran two of them through with his saber—the first time, I believe, it ever tasted blood. Ugly felled a pair with his ax, and Ida Greene, who insisted so indignantly that she ran a train station and nothing more, cut the throat of at least one cop.

Casualties were heavy, but by the time I appeared on the starboard deck, the battle was won. On the dock, the cops lay slaughtered in a heap. Van Alen stood with his foot on the bodies and pointed up the gangway.

"If there's any of you left up there," he shouted, "come down and die."

The object of his challenge sat outside the door to the pilot's house, her rifle clutched in her hands, her back pressed to the railing.

"That's all right," Juliette called back.

"Who the hell is that?" answered Van Alen.

"The last voice you shall ever hear."

She didn't have to surrender. She didn't have to fight. For she saw what I had seen. From where we stood, the land had disappeared. The dock had been eaten away. In its place was a wall of darkness, of swirling shadows whipped into a frenzy by the blood in the air. They vaulted down the dock, and Van Alen's last surviving guardsmen disappeared with choked-off screams.

Ida Greene grabbed Van Alen by the shoulders and dragged

him backward toward the edge of the dock. Ugly and Cherub ran alongside. The shadows ate away the dock, a few inches a second, until there was only a single plank left for the gallant warriors to stand on. There, the shadows stopped, edging back and forth, almost hesitant, and I gnawed on my knuckle, waiting for the surprise that only I knew was coming.

Juliette lacked my patience.

She stood, unslung her rifle, and leaned on the ship's rail. She peered down the sight and squeezed the trigger. Van Alen didn't say a word when he caught the bullet in his back. He sank to one knee and bled from both sides.

Now the shadows pounced.

Now the engines exploded.

A ball of fire tore through the starboard side of the ship, scorching the deck and driving the shadows back. Water rushed through the gash in the hull. The freighter lurched horribly toward the dock, throwing Juliette and myself into the railing. The fire was bright enough to turn night into day and cast off every shadow for ten blocks in either direction. By its light, I saw Van Alen collapsed in a heap on the dock, surrounded by Mrs. Greene, Ugly, and Cherub. By the same light, Juliette saw me.

"I told you, Gilda, this was not your concern," she called, as her ship sank deeper into the water. She leaned against the railing, holding her rifle at her hip. I looked straight at it, and I felt I could see all the way down the darkened barrel and into the hell that lay on the other side. I could not tell if I was ready to die.

"My life would be simpler if I took other people's advice," I said, "but I simply don't have the patience."

"Take one step, and I'll put a bullet through your heart."

Who was this woman? What was she to me? We had met just a handful of times. We had shared a bottle and memories of fathers useless and dead. We did not rank as friends, but even with her rifle trained on my chest, I could not really consider her an enemy. She was not Andrea Barbarossa, who had been a legend of the Westside night since before I was born. She was just a person, twisted by grief and greed into doing things that once she might have called evil. She was convinced that one of us would have to die. I, who had already killed that day, burned to find another way.

"Did you hurt her?" I said.

"Did I hurt who?"

"Mary Fall. The woman in the house on Washington Square. Did you hurt her?"

"Dear god, Gilda—are you really worried about your mommy? I thought we understood each other, that we were too mature to be restrained by the . . . the idiocy of the family bond."

"Did you hurt her?"

"No. I hardly had the time for anything like that, and really, what would be the point? You see me as some sort of bloodthirsty maniac, Gilda, and that wounds me."

Smoke burned my eyes. The ship lurched again, and from the pilot's house stumbled the other Juliette, blindfolded and bound, and the Virgil Carr who was not my father, whose face was bloody, and who could hardly walk. I gripped the railing hard enough that I felt I could rip it free with a single hand.

"Set them free," I said.

"What do you care about their lives, daughter of the bloody Lower West, detective of tiny mysteries?" said Juliette. "Have you come to arrest me? To—oh, what is that dime novel phrase—'to bring me to justice'? That's quite a concern of yours, isn't it? Who killed whom, and why?"

She reached into her pocket and set Galen Copeland's notebook on the railing of the ship. As we listed farther and farther, it slipped closer to falling into the water.

"You would have been quite interested in this relic of my papa's," she said. "It wasn't shipping coordinates, but a journal written in code—a terrible outpouring of guilt and self-pity for every death the Westside ever suffered, from some nitwit named Alice Pearl right down to the formidable Virgil Carr."

"He was right to feel guilty."

"He certainly knew how to tell a story. He scratched out six pages on the night your father died. A moonlight cruise to Spuyten Duyvil—just your father, my papa, and Andrea Barbarossa. Wouldn't you like to know what happened? Wouldn't you like to hear whose name Virgil called as his throat was cut and whose hand held the knife?"

"That's not why I came."

"I'll give you the book, I'll tell you the story, if you just walk away."

"I made your mother a promise."

"My mother is a nitwit, and I am disappointed in you, Miss Carr."

"Why?"

"Because after you've seen the other side, I expected you would understand. There are many worlds. Impossible variations, each more awful than the last. When we know that to be true, how can any human life matter? Kill one Galen Copeland, there is always another around the corner. Kill one Juliette, and another takes her place."

"We are creatures of the Westside. We belong here."

"Then die with it. I'm getting out."

The ship caught against the dock. The force of the impact knocked the journal off the side, but Juliette caught it without letting her rifle slip.

Somewhere, in a New York that wasn't mine, a woman named Mary Fall waited for her husband to come home. She would have finished preparing dinner. By now, she'd be stretched across the sofa in the front parlor, a drink at her elbow and a book in her lap, watching the lights come on in the park, never doubting that at any moment, Virgil Carr would step through the door.

"Let those two walk away," I said. "They do not belong in this city. They should not die for it."

"The other Juliette will die. That is nonnegotiable. I must take her place."

"Then send down Virgil Carr."

"In exchange for what?"

"For me."

That made her smile.

"What would I want with you?"

"Please—surely I've been at least an irritant. Surely I have made things harder for you. Surely you would prefer to see me dead. Don't deny me that."

"You don't want to live?"

"I haven't, for a long time."

"Well, who needs answers?" she said and tossed Copeland's journal into the river. It floated for a moment, as the water soaked its pages, and then it was gone. "Learn a truth about a dead man, and you will find peace. Didn't you tell me that?"

"I can't be sure. I say all sorts of things."

That made her chuckle. She was still smiling as she thrust Virgil forward, and I walked to meet him. Virgil's eye was swollen shut, and his hair was matted with blood. He could hardly walk, but he did his best to stand up straight. He said nothing and did not look my way. For the first time, this man looked as broken and beaten as I remembered the Virgil Carr who was my father. He turned as we passed, angling his shoulder just far enough that I couldn't see his face. My hand brushed against his jacket, and I found something interesting in the pocket.

"Come to me," said Juliette. "I'm sure I can find an inventive way for you to die."

"I'd prefer both of us walk away."

"That's the beautiful thing about firearms, Miss Carr. You never have to compromise."

I had tried. At least, I think I had. Juliette was correct. That night, it could only be light or dark.

I walked up the gangway. I had nearly reached her when I fired the gun. It bucked in my hand, and the bullet might have flown straight had it not been for the long burn across my palm. Instead, it went wide, and the gun fell out of my grip.

Before it hit the ground, I was on my knee reaching for it. If I hadn't moved so quickly—if I hadn't expected to drop it, if I hadn't been so in touch with my natural clumsiness—Juliette's bullet would have pierced my heart. Instead, it passed just over the nape of my neck. I did not breathe. That could wait for later.

One bullet left.

To hell with it. I let the gun alone.

My fingers touched the deck, and I shoved off like a track runner. Before she could fire a second shot, I had my arms around her waist. My momentum carried us to the prow, and over the railing, and down toward the river.

The icy Hudson washed away the smoke and the blood. Juliette's fingers dug into my throat, my eye. I let go of her, drew my arm back, and bashed my elbow into her face. We moved slowly, our blows deadened by the weight of the water. Neither of us could hurt the other, but the river was stronger than us both. My lungs caught fire.

I kicked her as hard as I could, and her grip on my throat loosened. I brought my elbow down on her nose, and her blood dyed the water pink.

The edges of my vision grew dim.

I brought my elbow down again. She stiffened around me, holding as tight as she could.

We sank. The light of the burning ship faded, and down on the river's bottom, the shadows swirled. How many dead sailors were waiting there to drag us down? How many vanished souls?

From the mud of the river, or the hungry shadows, or the panicking depths of my dying brain, I heard a woman's voice. I'd never heard it before, but I recognized it like I would my own.

"My name is Alice," she said. "Help me."

I hit Juliette one more time. She went limp and sank away. It was dark at the bottom of the river, but not so dark that I couldn't see the shadows swirling to greet her. Noise carries beautifully in water, even oily river water, and I heard her choking scream like it was coming from my own mouth. The noise twisted through the shadows, growing sharper, stronger, more painful, until it wasn't

Juliette's voice and it wasn't mine, until it was the final, unfinished scream of Alice Pearl.

I could have stayed down there forever. A few more seconds, and the last bit of air would have burst out of my lungs, out of my mouth, and water would have come rushing in. I could have just opened my lips and followed her to the black river floor. But I had lied—I wasn't ready to die. Not yet. I kicked, and I rose, and I tasted the foul Westside air. The shadows were gone.

SEVENTEEN

Cherub pulled me from the river. I flopped onto the dock, warmed by the burning ship, and spat out the taste of death and the Hudson, not sure where one flavor left off and the other began. The shadows were beaten back, and all was still.

The question of Juliette Copeland was settled. The solution had been vile, but solving tiny mysteries—I reminded myself as I coughed up a wad of river scum—is about finding the truth, whether or not it's what the client wants to hear.

Before I could delve any further into those weighty questions, Cherub yanked me to my feet and wrapped me in a blessedly uncomplicated embrace.

"Would it be too sentimental to say that I'm glad you're alive?" he said.

"Too much by half," I said and pushed his face away before he could draw me into a kiss. He wanted to celebrate. I was not ready yet.

I freed myself from his arms and saw that I was not the only exhausted Westsider to be saved from the river.

Virgil stood over Eddie Thorne's soaked hide, dripping blood onto his face.

"Clubber," Thorne gibbered. "You came back."

"You're a disgrace," said Virgil. "You've always been a disgrace, but what you've done here is monstrous."

"It was for the sake of . . ."

"Of what?"

"Order."

I tore Thorne's shabby gold shield from his chest and dragged its pin across his cheek until his bloodshot eyes snapped open. I threw the badge in the river. Virgil pulled back to punch Thorne. I stopped him.

"The things he's done," said Virgil. "The children. He killed children. I'll kill him, Gilda, I'll be your hangman. I'll keep your hands clean."

"Do it," said Thorne, head hung low like a humiliated dog. "Just end me. Just snap my neck and dump me in the river and let me be forgotten."

"No," I said, and Virgil looked faintly proud. "He's right. He deserves much worse."

"What do you have in mind?"

I reached inside Virgil's jacket and found a pair of gleaming silver handcuffs. I twisted Thorne's wrists behind his back, and the cuffs clicked as loud as any cocking pistol.

"He goes with you," I said. "Take him back through Spuyten Duyvil and lose him in the Tombs."

"On what charges?"

"Whatever you choose. Don't pretend you're above it. You were ready to railroad Van Alen, weren't you? In this city or any other, no cop ever faked evidence quite as well as Virgil Carr."

"And if he pleads innocence?"

"Let him. The first guard who hears his story will clap him off to Bellevue without a second thought, and Lieutenant Thorne, dictator of the Lower West, will live out his reign as a guest of the asylum."

"Gilda, please," said Thorne, with his old thirsty look. "It's not fair."

"Not hardly," I said. I nodded at Virgil, and he kicked Thorne in the jaw, hard enough to send him sprawling into unconsciousness. He would wake in chains.

Juliette was gone, Thorne broken, and the ship was nearly burned down to the waterline. We collected the rifles and pistols left behind by Thorne's routed Fourth Precinct and tossed them into the Hudson one by one, savoring each tiny, peaceful splash. Every gun went to the bottom of the river, to rust down to nothing, as Westside guns should.

Well, nearly every gun.

When we were finished, Virgil ran his hand through his thick gray whiskers and shook his head. He wanted to say something, but we didn't have the time for him to find the words.

"Thank you for passing me the pistol," I said. "Even if I'll never be a crack shot."

"Is that such an awful thing?"

"I'm just glad you're, well, I'm glad that tonight Mary Fall will get to welcome you home."

"I don't have to go alone."

I was about to answer him when, for the second time that day, I heard Juliette Copeland scream. This time, she did so without fear. It was a squeal, really, the way a girl might squeal on coming face-to-face with a newborn kitten. By the light of the burning ship, she saw a woman who looked very much like the mother she had lost two years before.

She ran to wrap her in a hug tight enough to knock the wind out of the poor old woman.

"What's gotten into you, child?" asked Mrs. Copeland. "Set me down. Please!"

But Juliette would not set her down, and when Mrs. Copeland saw Galen at the end of the dock, she understood why—or thought she did, anyway. They all burst into tears, an impossible family brought back from the dead, crying too hard to speak.

I nodded at Ugly La Rocca, who had fetched my client from the Eastside. He bowed low, threw his blood-flecked ax over his shoulder, and walked north into the shadows, which were behaving themselves at last.

Mrs. Copeland swept me up in a dizzying hug of her own and set me down again, laughing harder than I ever thought she could.

"How did you do it, Miss Carr? How did you bring him back from the dead?"

"The simple answer is that I did no such thing."

"And my Juliette, she's changed. She looks happier than she has in years. What did you do to her?"

"Miss Carr has had a trying day," said Galen. "We can tell the story better than she."

"We'll explain everything on the yacht, Mother," said Juliette, putting more love into that last word than I could bear.

"And the gloves," I said. "They're on the boat. Galen can give them to you all over again."

"My gloves? Who cares about gloves at a time like this!"

"A sound point."

"It's a miracle, simply a miracle."

"When they explain it all to you, you won't be as pleased with me."

She was dangerous. She was murderous. But she was your daughter, and I pushed her to her death. How the hell do you explain such a thing? How can you even try? Mrs. Copeland smiled again and hugged me close, and the whole dreadful week crashed down all at once. I felt so very tired.

"It doesn't matter," she said. "You've changed my life. You've saved me."

"I don't know if that's true. Get on the boat and go."

"But we have to celebrate."

"Please. Go."

They boarded the ship, chattering and laughing like a family of tourists embarking on a pleasure cruise. Virgil helped Cherub hoist Van Alen into his coach. Ida Greene walked up to me, wiping the blood away on the hem of her dress.

"How is the big man?" I said.

"It will take more than one bullet to kill Glen-Richard Van Alen."

"I suppose in this city, that's true."

"Now that, Miss Carr, is something I haven't seen before."

"What?"

"For a moment, you almost smiled."

"The Westside needs that man."

"I'm glad you understand that now. You know, Gilda, you are not such a hopeless detective. If you ever need work, or a home, there is a place for you above the Borderline."

I thanked her, and I smiled like I believed her, but I knew she was wrong. She climbed atop Van Alen's coach and drove north. As they disappeared around the bend, Virgil put his hand on my shoulder.

"You should go," I said. "It's really not safe here after dark."

"You're not coming home."

"*This* is my home."

"It's Edith Copeland's home too, but you brought her to leave with those people she's never met."

"I don't know if it was the right thing to do. It might destroy her, but I couldn't help it. That's the coward in me."

"I've seen a lot of you today, and not one ounce is a coward."

"I couldn't stand telling that woman that I'd killed her daughter, that her husband was never coming back. Somebody deserved to be happy."

"But not us."

"You can be. You have Mary Fall."

"I'd like to have you too."

"You saw what I did today. What I did twice."

"Please, Gilda. For your mother."

"I'm not that woman's daughter. I'm not . . . I don't know how to go back."

I wasn't crying, not really, until he took me in his arms. It was what I'd wanted for a very long time, but it didn't take the pain away. It wasn't what I needed anymore.

I broke the embrace and shook my head, and he climbed aboard the yacht. A peal of laughter from Juliette or Edith, I could not be sure, echoed giddily down the gangway, sending a wave of nausea rolling down my chest, a hot wire that shot up from my stomach and into my throat. I turned away, not wanting them to see me be sick.

"Gilda," called Virgil, but I did not turn around. I held my stomach, willing my body to cooperate for just a minute more. "Gilda."

Finally, the engines started, and the yacht pulled away. My nausea subsided. I turned around and saw the lights of the little boat pulling up the river. In the darkness, I couldn't see the man named Virgil Carr. I fell to my knees, slumped on the dock, and whispered something like goodbye.

I shook the gas can on my shoulder. A few ounces of fuel still rattled around in there. I reached into my bag. One bullet left.

The Christopher Street IRT was deserted. The long dark corridor stank of spilled liquor. A trickle of moonshine dripped down the platform, oozing from the bullet holes in the stills like leaking blood.

Barbarossa's car waited on the downtown tracks. Its stolen blue door, of which she had been so proud, had been hacked apart. The windows had been shot away.

"I heard legends of this place," said Cherub Stevens as we crossed the flimsy wooden bridge that led to the car. "Rotgut's great storeroom. Her museum. Her private car. I always imagined grandeur. This is . . . well, it's a bit like a dragon, isn't it?"

"What?"

"They can have all the treasure they want, but they have to live in a cave."

The inside of the car was a wreck. Her treasured globe lay cracked open like an eggshell. Feathers from a slashed mattress blanketed every surface. Defaced statues, torn paintings, every piece of furniture smashed to pieces. Somewhere in the wreckage of broken glass lay my father's last taste of Boulton's Rye.

"What are you looking for?" said Cherub. I didn't answer. I kicked aside the wreckage. I found nothing worth saving.

"How do you feel about a walk in the dark?" I said.

"I'd rather get back on the surface, if it's all the same to you. Dinner, maybe."

"Go ahead," I said. I left the car and hopped from the bridge onto the tracks.

"Where are you going?"

"North."

I took a few steps into the tunnel. The light of my torch quivered. The shadows wrapped around me like a blanket, and I felt my chest growing cold.

"Gilda?" called Cherub. I did not make a sound. Behind me, he landed softly. His torch chased off the shadows. His hand found mine, and I did not push it away. He was trembling, and I could tell by his breathing that he was trying hard to keep his teeth from chattering. "She's dead. Everyone knows it. It was in the *Sentinel*. Thorne told you himself—he burned her body."

"Cops lie."

"How could she have gotten away from that fight?"

"She knew how to move in the dark."

"You saw what happened in that intersection. You and I were the only ones who got out."

"We would have felt it. This city would have heard the echoes if she died."

"You're mad, you know that? Utterly mad."

"Come on. Walk. There's nothing to be afraid of . . . or at least, nothing we can do anything about."

We walked north along the IRT—the third rail shining through tunnels cut but never used. We passed Fourteenth Street, Eighteenth, Twenty-Third. The only noise was an occasional rumbling, sometimes from a faraway train, sometimes from my stomach.

"Do you think they'll really tear down the fence?" said Cherub, somewhere around Thirtieth Street.

"Not anytime soon."

"Imagine, if they opened up the Westside. Trains running in these tunnels. Unarmed children in Washington Square. It might not be so bad."

"Stop. Close your eyes."

"But the dark . . ."

"Just try it." He closed his eyes, and I closed mine. "Don't you feel the cold sweeping over you? The shadows tugging at the sleeves of your jacket? Your fingertips growing numb? Open your eyes, damn it. As long as the shadows are hungry, the Westside will be no place for ordinary people."

"But without the Copelands running back and forth between the two cities, the Westside will heal."

"Maybe. If it does, it will take some time before things are balanced out, and finding balance can be painful."

"You're not the type who thinks things get better, are you?"

"Some situations are simply insane."

We kept walking, feeling our way through the darkness, our feet occasionally brushing the dead third rail. It was strange, being so close to him in the dark. It was the first time in two years that I'd felt at ease walking next to him and saying nothing at all.

Thirty-Fourth Street was barren and pristine. Our torches found only one blemish: on the black iron column that separated the local track from the express, we saw a smeared bloody handprint.

"She came this way," said Cherub, amazed and almost giddy. "She ran north. She got out. She's alive!"

"It looks that way."

"The IRT hits the stem at Times Square."

"It does."

"There's a fence in the tunnel."

"There is."

"Then either she got through, or she's somewhere up ahead."

"Wait here."

"What do you want her for?"

"I want to know if she killed my father. I want to hear her justify it, to try to lie her way out of it, to crack and admit that she cut his throat and severed his head, same as she did to that poor stupid guard I saw her killing the night of the massacre, killed him because it meant she could make a little more money every year. I want to let the pain wash over me, to really feel that he is gone, and then I want to start to forget."

"And what will you do with that?" he said, pointing at the pistol I clutched in my hand.

"I don't know."

"Would you kill her?"

"Twice now I've killed someone who was trying to do the same to me. I don't feel good about that, but I think I can justify it to myself. To avenge my father, to kill for the sake of justice . . . those are ideals much higher than any I've ever claimed for myself. I don't know if I can do it. I'm going to find out."

"If you're not back in five minutes . . ."

"You'll keep waiting."

"Okay."

Torch in one hand, gun in the other, I proceeded north. Far ahead, I saw the pinprick of light at the Times Square station, where the healthy city was sealed off from the Westside. Every minute, a train thundered past on the other side of the wall, loud enough to shake the bones in my chest. Every time, I froze, certain the train was coming my way. It never did.

Between trains, I heard people. They laughed, clear and pure, a laughter I hadn't heard in a long time. From the joy in their voices, they might have been another species from myself. They certainly lived in another city.

The fence was cast iron, three inches thick but slightly open at the top, just enough to let in a bit of light from the stem and show the Westside what we were missing. But at the bottom, it went all the way to the ground.

That's where I found Barbarossa.

There was blood on her chest, and her fingers were rubbed down to the bone from trying to claw her way through the iron. I could tell, from the way the rats gnawed at her ankles, that she'd been dead for days. On her lips was something that could have been a smile.

I took a short, shuddering breath, then threw the pistol back onto the tracks. It clanked, steel against steel, a meaningless sound.

"**Where now, Gilda?**" asked Cherub. "How shall we waste the rest of our night?"

We'd been walking for an hour or two. The streets were empty, perfectly silent, as even our footsteps were muted by the moss. The week was over, and I would not miss it. I looked at Cherub and noticed that somewhere in the night, he'd discarded his sword.

"I'll wake Bex Red and ask her for breakfast," I said.

"I'd rather you come with me."

"Where?"

"You've lost your house. I've lost my gang. Wouldn't it be fine to start somewhere new?"

"I'm not cut out for life in the Upper West."

"There are other cities, you know. We could be anyone. We could be adults."

"That sounds terrifying."

"It sounds like an adventure."

I looked up and saw we had turned onto Washington Square. The park was a jungle, the trees were mammoth, and the arch was as filthy as it was meant to be. Dawn was flaring up in the east, but it was still night on the west side of the park, and the shadows were hideously thick. They swirled around my empty lot, not level on the ground, but sloping upward, staggered, as though they were standing on—

"My stoop," I said. I snatched the torch from Cherub and ran across the park. The dark cloud twisted to meet me. I vaulted over my old fence, and stood on my land, and bellowed at the shadows: "Take me! Take me back to her!"

They did not move my way. I pulled out my penknife and dragged it across my palm. The shadows flickered in my direction. They were sluggish, weak, dying. They would require more encouragement. I squeezed my fist, and blood poured from my hand, down my arm, and into my dirt. Now the shadows swarmed.

"Get back," cried Cherub. He reached for the collar of my dress. I shoved him hard and sent him sprawling.

"Wait," I said, before the shadows took hold. My body went numb, and the world turned dark.

I opened my eyes and saw Cherub frozen on a white sidewalk. He was shouting, but I couldn't hear. I turned, and beneath an ivory sky, I saw my house standing proud. A dozen ghouls crowded the stoop, pounding against my father's great wooden door. When I appeared, they turned to me. They marched down the stoop on flickering, smoky legs, the fire in their eyes dancing in anticipation. I had my key in my pocket. I only had to clear a path. Their smoke reached out to claim me as one of their own.

I held the torch close enough to scorch my chest and plunged into the pack. Cold smoke slithered 'round me, but the dancing light was bright enough to keep the shadow creatures at bay. They parted, and I saw the dazzling fire of their eyes, and the slack dark clay that hung in the shape of their faces. If they could feel anything, I'm sure it was pain.

I dug for the key and prepared to take the steps two at a time. It was an old gesture, smooth with practice, and it would have seen me through the front door in a second or two had it not been for the smallest of the ghouls: a hungry little child who had once been called Roach, who crouched at the foot of the steps, just low enough to catch my foot and send me sprawling.

The torch rolled one way. The key another. Like water rushing into a lock, the creatures swept toward me. Roach came first.

That poor, ruined boy. Had I the power, I would have saved him, or killed him, but that was far beyond me. He reached out, hungry still, the writhing tendrils that had replaced his arms running up my unfeeling legs.

I kicked him in the face, knocking him down the steps, and stretched for the key. It was hopelessly out of reach.

Roach's smoky limbs dug into the stone, and he launched himself at me. I rolled out of the way. He landed as silent and gentle as a cat, and crawled on all fours, mouth dangling open, eyes burning horribly.

I shoved myself backward up the stoop. Something flickered on my thigh. It was my dress, catching fire. I had rolled onto the torch and not even felt its bite. Roach lunged again. I wrapped my fist around the torch and swung it upward, catching him on the chin and scattering him among the herd.

I scrambled up the last few steps and tried the handle. Locked, of course. I banged on the wood and didn't even feel it shake. I leaned on the door, and the shadowy host climbed the steps to greet me. There was nothing between us but the torch, and it was beginning to die.

The ghouls reached the top step. They stretched out their hands.

The door opened behind me, and I stumbled backward—graceful as ever—into Hellida's arms.

Her hair was wild, her eyes were bright. She looked gaunt, hungry, exhausted. She had been waiting for countless hours, waiting for the door to fail, waiting to fight and die. She was not expecting me.

The ghouls followed me inside and closed us in a ring.

I unscrewed the gas can and tossed the lid aside. They unfolded their limbs across the floor, and smoke swept up our legs.

I upended the can, cascading fuel down our hair and across our faces. It should have stung, but this world was like a nightmare—terrifying but painless. We could not feel the gasoline, and we would not feel the fire.

The smoke was almost at our mouths. I dragged the torch across our bodies, as easy as cutting a throat, and we exploded into glittering white fire. The ghouls scattered and I clutched Hellida tight, dying one last time.

We awoke in darkness. I coughed on the taste of burnt fabric and seared flesh, and kicked and struggled and cursed until finally I was free. There was Cherub, standing in the doorway, holding a heavy blanket that normally lived on my sofa, and which was scorched to ruin.

"Many apologies," he said. "I got through the door just in time for the shadows to clear, and for you two to burst in from nowhere, thoroughly on fire. This was the nearest thing I could think of to stanch the flames."

Behind him, the world was right, the sky was blue, and the soft morning sun shone on my house: three stories of vines, dust, quilts, books, papers, cockroaches, filth, awful memories, and ones too pleasant to ever let go. It was there, and Hellida was by my side.

"Gilda Carr," she said, hugging me tight. "You horrible child. I knew you would come back."

Two months later, a letter came with a return address that would baffle any postman: "236 East 48th Street, The Other New York." It was from Edith Copeland, a short note containing thanks I didn't deserve and money I couldn't afford to refuse. I don't know how she got it across the divide, and I'm not going to try to find out. It's a piddling, unimportant question, and I'm trying to leave those behind. The Westside offers endless weirdness, danger, and death. How could any daughter of Virgil Carr refuse?

Bex Red and I met for a drink one night at Father Lamb's, sometime around the beginning of December. The repaired campanile was warmed by a bonfire, courtesy of Glen-Richard Van Alen. From the top of the tower, we watched snow swirl on the park and saw the night-lights burning at every intersection on the Westside, lower and upper. It wasn't as bright as the other side of Broadway, but it was warm, and the shadows were still.

"What are you painting?" I said, between oysters.

"Oh, nothing grand. Nothing epic. I've gone back to watercolors—tiny canvases, small enough to fit in your hand."

I didn't tell her, but most nights, I wish I could do the same thing.

ACKNOWLEDGMENTS

My deepest thanks go out to Sharon Pelletier and David Pomerico, who got Gilda right from the start, to Bethany Johnsrud for pointing me to Sharon, and to the wonderful women of Squeaky Bicycle—Kathryn McConnell and Brandi Varnell—not just for introducing me to Bethany, but for nearly a decade of support, encouragement, and inspiration as I figured out how to be a writer good enough to dream up Gilda Carr.

Beyond those five, there is no one who deserves thanks more than my parents, who are magnificent; my brother, who's not bad either; and my wife, Yvonne, who is supreme. And although they were more hindrance than help, I'd like to say a final word of thanks to Dr. Baby—named Dash the Flash after this book was first dedicated—and Follow-Up Baby, who turned out to be August all along.

Read on for an exclusive sneak peek at

Gilda Carr's next "tiny mystery"

WESTSIDE SAINTS

By W. M. Akers

Out Summer 2020

ONE

On a night of hard frost, in the ruins of a burnt church, I found a body in the snow.

Its hand poked through the powder, gripping a crumbling stone altar. When I touched the wrist, a fistful of white tumbled away, exposing a derby hat and a tuft of thin orange hair spotted with blood.

"Find it?" called the woman I traveled with.

I wiped my hand on my black dress, which had seen much worse than the residue of a corpse, and walked back to her.

"There's nothing here," I said, and left the dead man behind. It was no feat. I'd been walking away from corpses all winter long. This was March 1922, when our bodies refused to stay buried.

Ten days prior, I was spitting off the ledge of Berk's Third Floor. Owned by one of the rare Westsiders as short and uncompromising as myself, Berk's was a shabby saloon on the Westside half of the stem whose eastern walls and roof had, some years back, simply melted away.

The exposure to the elements made it a pleasant summertime beer garden. In the winter it remained popular only with the committed few: those antisocial types who would happily freeze for a peek over the top of the fence and the chance to drink illegal liquor in full view of the Eastside throng. The people on the far side of Broadway were fat, happy, honorable, and safe, but when they cast their sober eyes up at us, all we saw was thirst. We raised our glasses to say that though west of the fence we had no electricity, no heat, and no conveniences, that though there were no guns on our side of the island but countless murders just the same, that though we lived in what they called hell, we had liquor, and some nights that made it okay.

On the other nights, we spit.

It was at least twenty feet from the lip of the saloon to the fence, but that didn't stop us trying to expectorate clear over the barrier to the Eastside. Long nights were passed in drunken argument about the proper angle to launch one's missile, the ideal texture for flight, and the correct place to stand in order to harness the wind. No one had ever seen anyone clear the fence, but every drinker there insisted that once, just once, they had made it.

My mouth was drying and my projectiles were growing feeble when Bex Red appeared at my side, wrapped in every layer of fabric she owned. Born in Florida, but a fixture on the Westside art scene since before the fence was raised, Bex had never embraced the brutality of the New York cold. Sharp blue eyes peeked out through a slit in the scarves that swaddled her head, yet her voice was unmuffled by the cloth.

"Every time I see you, Gilda, you've managed to find a worse bar," she said.

We sat at my table, a few inches from the edge, and I sloshed some gin into a chipped cup. It ran like sludge, and the glass was cold enough to cling to her lips, but she lifted the scarf and drained it. She dug her mittened hand into a coat pocket and pulled out a carefully folded square of thick homemade paper marked up with ninety-nine shades of blue.

"This is every blue I can mix," she said, "and that's every blue there is, from the not-quite-black of deep river water to this washed-out near white that's too fragile even for a robin's egg."

"They all look blue to me."

"You have always lacked an artist's temperament."

"Thank you."

"Any of these look right?" she said with a theatrical sigh. I ran my finger down the page, squinting until my eyes crossed.

"Blue 72, maybe. Or it could be 74."

"This was my whole afternoon, you know. Do I get paid for the time?"

"You get paid when I get paid."

"Are you going to get paid?"

"Probably not." I put the color chart away.

"Well, while we're on the subject of wasted time . . ."

From deep in her coats she drew a worn paper envelope as soft as an old dollar bill. Inside were three portraits: two I would force myself to look at, and one I could not stand to see. The first showed a man with a gut as round and heavy as a pumpkin, shirtless at a table, a forkful of sausage and cabbage poised before wet red lips. The other was of a woman, handsome but joyless, waiting in line at an Eastside bank.

"These are good," I said.

"Better than last week?"

"Last week's were fine."

"But you like these more."

"Perhaps. They are so, so ordinary."

She swirled her cup, scowling at its emptiness. I tilted the bottle in her direction, but she refused.

"It's not healthy, drinking this filth," she said.

"Beats the cold."

She pulled her layers tighter, then leaned across the table and gave me an entirely unworkable hug. I stared as she walked away and wished I knew how to leave by her side. But I had one more appointment to keep.

A party of slummers poured through the door, nearly knocking Bex to the floor, and flung themselves at the bar crying for gin. Berk slid them a couple of bottles, exacting an outrageous price in return, and they occupied the table beside mine, laughing like only Eastsiders can.

"Isn't it the most marvelous pit?" asked their leader, an overgrown boy in a cashmere overcoat whose slick curls stuck out below the brim of his hat. "Berk's a troll, but she has her uses. I've been coming here for ages, you know, and she loves me like a son."

I eyed the leg of his chair, which teetered beside the drop. If I smacked it, there was a strong chance he would fall to his death. Warmed by that happy thought, I returned the drawings to the envelope, taking care not to see the one that remained inside, and poured myself another drink.

I was watching snow swirl across the hardwood floor, savoring the mawkish burn of Berk's red gin, when the bells of Grace Church sang ten o'clock, and Judy Byrd kicked open the stairwell door.

"I come to preach the electric resurrection," she bellowed, and those familiar with her ministry pulled their glasses close to their chests.

A black woman whose tight curls were just smoked with gray, Judy vaulted onto the oak bar without apparent strain and did not turn her head at Berk's perfunctory cry that she get the hell down. She wore a homespun orange dress and a tightly knotted kerchief, and spoke with a heavy Haitian accent that I knew to be an affectation. She clutched an ancient broom whose few remaining bristles stuck out at odd angles, hoisting it over her head like an executioner showing off his ax.

"What business have I, an honest woman, a god-fearing woman, what business have I skulking in the worst gin mills the Westside has to offer?" she asked the room.

"I think Miss Berk would take exception to that," said the cashmere overcoat. He looked around, waiting for the room to acknowledge his barb, but even his friends were watching Judy. She was well into her reverie, which she would follow, as she always did, down twisting paths of mixed metaphor until it led us all to salvation.

"I tell you why I come here, why I drag my frostbitten feet up those unreliable stairs, why I leap upon this bar the same way we all must leap across the valley of death and into the arms of our savior. I do it for love. I love you drunks, the way you slur like the devil's caught your tongue, the way you stumble like he's hobbled your feet, the way your skin blisters and cracks and turns as red as hellfire, as bloody as the gin in your glass. I love you all, no matter how you try to blot out the light God lit inside you, no matter how greedily you suck the intoxicating sweat that runs off the devil's backside. I love you as Christ loves you, and in his name I will sweep you clean."

She snapped her old broom down on the bar, sending a hail of cigarette butts and stained linen to join the snow on the floor. She ran the length, giggling as she swept empty bottles and dirty glasses crashing to their death.

"By god, boys, she's insane!" cackled one of the slummers, drawing Judy's eye for the first time. With three quick steps, she bounded onto their table. They stopped laughing. The man in the cashmere coat spun around and glared at Berk, who watched the whole scene from a stool at the edge of the room, her face like stone.

"So help me," he said, "if you let this Negro clown spill a drop of my liquor—"

He never completed his threat. With a practiced flick of her wrist, Judy flung their glasses into space—all save that of the leader, whose cup she tipped into his lap, staining his cashmere beyond repair.

He grabbed her by the ankle. She pointed her broom handle at his forehead, a matador preparing to deliver the final blow. He snickered, the way you do when your father has money and you understand the whole world has been set up for your benefit. No one else laughed.

"You'll pay for that liquor," he said. "The coat, too."

"You're the one who'll pay," Judy answered, as readily as a comic taking the straight man's line. "The cost is far more than the nickel Miss Berk charges—it's ten million years in a pit of fire, with snakes pricking your pecker until it bursts, over and over again."

"Cut out that noise and buy us another round or I'll throw you into the street."

"God wouldn't let me die."

The man tightened his grip on Judy's leg. I saw no sign that God was preparing to intervene, and so I stepped in. I placed my hand on his soft black glove.

"Let her go," I said.

"What'd I tell you boys," he said to the friends who could no longer meet his eye. "Westside women are hellcats."

"You are outnumbered and badly disliked. This could be an amusing anecdote for your fellows on the Eastside, or it could be a tragedy. Which would you prefer?"

He chuckled. His laugh sounded like slime. In a room without a wall, he was backed into a corner, and I really didn't know if he'd give up or lash out. I believe I was ready for either. His friends made the decision for him, cinching their scarves and slinking for the exit. Seeing that he really was outnumbered—even rich boys must learn some arithmetic—he broke his grip on Judy's ankle and followed them out.

Even through the cold, my face felt hot. I drained my drink, grateful it had survived the sermon. Judy jumped down and wrapped me in a welcome embrace.

"Gilda Carr," she said. "My favorite sinner. God truly takes all forms."

"Are we getting the gospel tonight, Judy, or ain't we?" asked one of the men at the bar.

"Give 'em a show," I said, and she launched back into her sermon, howling of thumb screws and broken bones, eager demons and weak flesh, evil liquor and the healing power of God's infinite grace. And she told about the coming resurrection, when our dead would rise from their graves and walk the Westside streets, when all the wounds we bandaged with liquor would finally be healed. She punctuated every paragraph by sweeping another heap of the mess she'd made over the edge of the vanished wall, where it crashed onto the street to startle the fleeing slummers. I reached behind the bar for an unbroken bottle, dropped a nickel in the bucket and poured myself a fresh one.

Before I could settle in, a hand brushed my elbow. Behind me was a sallow white man in a perfectly tailored suit that would have been the height of fashion thirty years before. His hands were bare, despite the cold, and he held a tidy wad of pamphlets that offered scriptural backing for Judy's unpredictable testimony. He was her brother, Enoch Byrd.

"A tract, Miss Carr?"

"I'm afraid I've read them all."

Enoch was at least a decade older than me, but there was something boyish about him. While his sister spoke in a rambling torrent, he chose his words with care, pausing for seconds at a time as he searched for one that fit. He reminded me of the sort of boy I met too few of as a young girl, who were too tongue-tied and pathetic to ever seem a threat.

I often saw him on cold mornings, pushing a soup cart down snowy streets, waking those who had passed out on the sidewalk, helping them get warm and get home. He ordered them about with the precision of a drill sergeant, an attitude that would have been irritating if it hadn't saved lives. A few years prior, my father had often been one of those woken on Enoch's morning rounds, and I had been deeply fond of this dull, middle-aged man and his rowdy sister ever since.

The business with the blue ink had started in late November, on what must have been our last tolerably warm day, when Enoch found me on my stoop pelting rocks at pigeons and watching night sweep over Washington Square. He was silent until I asked him to sit down, and then he pointed past the bare trees that filled the park to the clean, pale, eastern sky.

"That blue," he said. "You only get it at this hour, when the sun is sinking and the shadows are long and day is just clinging on. It's my favorite color in the world."

"It's good enough."

"I have dreams in that color. Dreams of hell. Not nightmares. I've had them my whole life. My father used to preach about the blue flames of hell, and I've decided I'd like to do a tract in his honor, with three-color printing, that shows damnation as only he could paint it."

He slid a pile of meticulously printed religious blather, each eight pages long and printed in black, white, and a different shade of blue.

"And no matter how many different blues you try, none of them hits the mark?" I said.

"How did you know?"

"I know the look, that special brand of misery that comes from trying to make the real world line up with something perfect in your head."

"And these are the cases, the tiny mysteries, that are your specialty?"

I was wary. This was the type of thing I would usually turn down. It was tiny, sure, but it was also impossible. Enoch had standards—you could tell just by looking at his perfect little tracts—and that was hell in a client. But that fall I needed work, in every way a woman can.

"I'll turn the city upside down until you have the blue you want," I said. "As long as you can tell me what's so special about this shade."

I chucked another rock, missing the bird badly, and he told me a story about a little boy who grew up in the heart of Lower Manhattan, long before a fence divided Eastside from West, the son of a gifted preacher who loved his children, but loved his ministry more.

"Even when we did get Papa to ourselves, we never got to be alone with him," he said. "Except for one afternoon, when he took me to see the carriage parade in Central Park. Afterward, we walked the length of it. I was watching the sun set over the lake, when he told me to turn around and look east instead. He died soon after. My whole life, that blue has stayed in my heart."

Over the next months, whenever I had the pep to get out of bed, I stalked Manhattan up and down, sifting through shops for printers, authors, artists, stamp collectors, pen collectors, calligraphers, weavers, forgers, pornographers, and anyone else with an eye for beautiful things. To the Lower West I brought bits of paper stained with every blue I found, and to all of them Enoch apologized and shook his head.

At last I found an old woman in an underground shop on the Upper West, who promised she could make ink to match any shade in creation, so long as I could provide her with a sample. But of course that was impossible. In all of New York, there was no paint shard, no fabric scrap, no broken pot or torn dust jacket or dead bug that quite matched the flames burning inside Enoch Byrd's head. I didn't mind. The longer he was unsatisfied, the more I would eventually bill him, and the longer I put off finding something else to do with my days.

That night at the saloon, I smoothed Bex's array of blues out on the table and watched him run his finger down the rows of color, wondering how long it would take him to shake his head.

"Your instincts are good," he said. "Blue 72 is close to what I'm after."

"But close is . . ."

"Still a bit wrong. I'm sorry, truly."

"All part of the job."

With a final cackle, I looked in time to see Judy cast the last of the broken glass over the lip of the building. She tucked her broom under her shoulder and sidled up to her brother, eying his purse.

"Any sales?" she said.

"Three dollars' worth," he answered.

"Berk says we owe two twenty-five for the glassware."

"You might avoid the ashtrays, sister. They are expensive."

"You know better than anyone that Christ demands a clean sweep."

Enoch sighed, counted the money, and dropped it in the bucket on the bar. Berk nodded, and Judy saluted with her broom.

"Have you nearly finished that drink, Miss Carr?" asked Enoch.

"Yes," I said, "but I haven't even started on the next one."

"I wonder if you would consider postponing it. You've done such marvelous work looking for my blue ink and I wondered if, well . . . my mother wants a word."

I pulled the dregs of the gin through my teeth and remembered how Enoch would hold my father's hand as he trembled up our town house steps. My glass thudded, empty, onto the bar.

"Anything for the Byrds," I said.

Down on the street, on the frozen, broken pavement of that road some still call Broadway, the heat from Berk's felt far away, and the lights from the Eastside glowed only faintly over the top of the fence. Judy lit a cigarette and took a slow, sacred drag.

"I thought you were without vice," I said.

"I am opposed to the devil's intoxicants," she said, her Haitian lilt discarded in favor of a bracing Westside brogue. "That does not mean I am without sin."

"Mam is waiting," said Enoch.

Mam was a woman in a soiled white cloak leaning on the fence beside the barred Waverly Place gate. She had thin peach lips and, beneath her hood, hair translucent white. She wore a heavy ivory glove on her left hand. Her right she offered to me.

"Helen Byrd," she said.

"Matriarch of the Electric Church," said Enoch. "Widow of its founder, the prophet and martyr Bulrush Byrd. Mam. And this is my sister, Ruth."

Ruth had a pointed chin and flat hair. A heavy scarf covered most of her face. She stared through me blankly, looking so much like her mother that it made me a bit dizzy. With only the flickering light of Berk's faraway fire to guide me, it was hard to tell if Helen looked young for her age, or if Ruth was old for hers.

"I'm not impressed," said Helen after she finished sizing me up.

"I'd be worried if you were. What is it you want?"

"Something has gone missing from our church. My children insist you are the woman to find it. I don't agree, but they don't care."

"If you're waiting for me to defend myself, don't bother. I'm too cold to beg."

She scowled more, somehow, and went on.

"It is the finger of Róisín of Lismore, a saint. Our saint. It is a fixture of our ministry, the centerpiece of our faith, and it was stolen from our church earlier this week. I am told you specialize in finding tiny things."

"It's the little finger," said Judy. I couldn't tell if she was trying to be funny, but I did my best not to laugh. "Left hand. Pickled."

"When was it stolen?" I said.

"After dark on Thursday night," said Helen. "Ruth noticed it missing at dawn."

"No one saw anything?"

"If we had, we would not have come to you."

"Who has access to the church after dark? Just the four of you?"

"The whole city has access to the electric faith."

"What?"

"We leave our doors open to the neighborhood," said Enoch. "That any passing vagrant might take shelter. We have nothing to steal."

"Not anymore, anyway," I said, ignoring Helen's and Ruth's irritation. "You're certain it was stolen? I find that the smaller the finger, the more likely it is to be misplaced."

"Saint Róisín's finger resides in a small glass case," said Helen. "It is never disturbed, even during services. The only key is kept in my office, and that door is always locked, no matter the needs of the city's vagrants."

"The case was smashed?" I said.

"To dust," said Ruth, so low I could hardly hear.

"Nothing else was taken?"

"As my brother said, there really is nothing to steal."

"And why do you need the finger back?"

"What kind of question is that?" said Enoch.

"It's, what, an inch and a half long? Shriveled? Pink? I can find you one to match in any snowbank on this avenue. I assure you, the donor will not mind."

"It wouldn't be Róisín."

"And you really believe that little scrap of flesh you keep in a box is?"

I thought they would be angry. If they were, it didn't show. Enoch blanched; Judy cackled, and Helen became, if this was possible, even more blank. Ruth's stern eyes softened, and she looked on me with pity as she took my hands in hers.

"You have lost quite a lot," she said, stroking my hands, searching my face.

"So has everyone. That's an easy thing to guess."

"You've lost a parent. Both parents?"

"What does that have to do with your stolen digit?"

"You have no family, few friends. You have seen too much bloodshed, too much pain. This winter has been hard for all of us, but harder for you. You try to carry the city on your back, and it has bent you double."

I tried to keep her from seeing that she wasn't wrong. I don't think I succeeded.

"Róisín is the patron saint of suffering. Her death was more horrible than you could imagine, and she bore it with a smile. Our family has lost much, too, and our parishioners have lost even more. Decades of suffering, and she has always been there. Without her to point the way, our family, our church, will be lost."

"Our city, too," said Enoch. "Without our church, the whole city is in jeopardy."

I had never been inside the building they called a church, but I had seen it. A onetime Italian banquet hall on Carmine Street, its old sign shone through the poorly painted marquee that invited the world to "Join the Electric Church." I had always wondered why they chose it. In a district overrun with abandoned churches, some in serviceable condition, they preferred a dump.

I looked at the four of them, their clothes and bearing as ridiculous as their faith. They were pathetic, but they were kind. In a city and a winter that fought so hard to crush those who believed in anything but greed and death, they pressed on. Delusional, certainly—Enoch couldn't really believe the whole city was counting on them—but their intentions were pure. If they thought the finger would help them continue with that mission . . .

"I'd be honored," I said.

"I still don't like her," said Helen.

"And I don't like you, but that doesn't mean we can't have a bit of fun."

Helen gave me the kind of look you normally expect from a Gorgon. Judy pulled her mother back and whispered, "She's the only one."

"Fine," said Helen. "Fine."

"A ringing endorsement," I said. "I can't wait to get started."

"Thank you, Miss Carr," said Enoch. "And while you're working for Mam, of course, you can let the blue ink go."

I appreciated that. I'm sure Bex would feel it was far more healthy to chase just one impossibility at a time.

I could have gone back upstairs for another drink, but instead I let them walk me home, as they had done so often for my father, to the town house that stood alone on an empty block on the western edge of Washington Square.

I stepped from the frozen street into my frozen parlor, lit a fire, and tried to drive the frost from my chest. I drew a fat album from a high shelf and laid it on the floor before the dancing flame. Inside were dozens of Bex's drawings of the old man and the young woman, drawings of them walking and eating and bathing and living lives too ordinary to be believed. He was the Glen-Richard Van Alen who lived in another New York, far gentler than our own. She was Juliette Copeland. Him I'd shot in the chest. Her I'd drowned. These drawings, which I'd started commissioning from Bex when I realized my guilt would not fade with autumn, were glimpses into the sorts of quiet days my victims would never enjoy.

I pasted the new pair onto blank pages. There was one more drawing inside Bex's envelope that I could not bear to see. I left it inside and fell asleep by the fire, hoping that if the finger of Saint Róisín couldn't save the city, it could at least save me.

The next morning I breakfasted in the Upper West, on a sliver-thin side street nestled between Fifth Avenue and the fence, where the smell of old money still hung in the air. In a double-wide town house painted a chipped, fading blue, I was greeted by a woman with tight white curls whose skin was as wrinkled and clear as cellophane. This was my grandmother: the distinguished Anacostia Fall.

"Did you bring it?" she said, as she welcomed me in from the cold.

"Is there sausage?"

"The way you can gorge without doing the decent thing and be-coming monstrously fat—it simply baffles."

"I assure you—when out of your sight, I eat as delicately as a bird."

She honked out a laugh. I followed her across the polished par-quet, beneath a dripping, wax-encrusted chandelier, past a heavenly staircase that twisted to the floors above. Candles flickered over pho-tos of relatives long dead, posed as stiff as corpses but smiling, as the Falls usually did, like hoodlums. The final picture showed Ana, severely corseted, flanked by her children: a boy with hair as matted as beaver fur and a smirking young woman named Mary Fall.

In a dining room decorated with haunting landscapes of upstate New York, we sat at the corner of a table that could seat twenty-four paunchy men. Ana rang a bell, and a segment of wall shot open to reveal two steaming dishes of fatty sausage, buttered toast, and egg pudding. She carried the plates herself, hands shaking just enough to keep it interesting. The first bite warmed me down to my callouses, and I did not stop until I was numb with grease. I dried my fingers on the tablecloth.

Now it was time to pay the check.

I slid Bex Red's envelope across the table. Ana flipped it open and eased out the picture. She stared at it for a long time, then slumped back and sighed.

"Can I see it?" I said.

"You don't usually like to look."

"The dreams have gotten worse."

She handed it to me. Bex's effortless lines showed a middle-aged woman sitting at her kitchen table, a tomato sandwich in one hand and a neatly folded newspaper in the other. The table was my table. The woman was my mother.

Mary Fall died of pneumonia the summer of my tenth year. I'd thought that pain forgotten until last year, when I killed for the first time and she began to appear in my sleep. The dreams were violent enough to wake me, strange enough that I couldn't shake them, and when they became unbearable I began visiting the only woman in New York who might understand.

I'd hardly known Ana when my parents were alive, but she welcomed me without question and fed me well. When I told her how I was torturing myself with drawings of my victims living the lives I'd cut short, she asked if Bex could do the same for the daughter she'd lost decades before. We rarely spoke of Mary—we rarely spoke at all—but when we did, it was like opening a steam valve that eased the pressure and let me breathe again.

"She looks happy," I said.

"She doesn't. She looks normal. That's enough."

I gave it back to her.

"You didn't approve when she married my father, did you?" I said.

"Why would you ask me such an inane question?"

"I've always wondered how they met."

"Your father was a brute, and after she met him, Mary was never my daughter again. I never bothered to ask how it began."

I followed her down the long hallway, keeping my eyes on the photo of Mary for as long as I could. At the end of the immaculate passage, one of the doors was open an inch. Behind it I saw a heap of broken furniture, rotted books, ruined artwork, tarnished silver, cracked glass, and other refuse far past the point of identification. Ana shut the door, and I pretended I hadn't seen.

She insisted on helping me put on my coat. As I slid my left arm home, I asked, "Was she as good as I remember?"

"Better," said Ana. "There never walked a purer soul."

She called her carriage, an electric green behemoth drawn by a black horse speckled white with snow, and I glided home. As we crossed the Borderline, the tranquility of the Upper West fell away, and I steeled myself for work.